LOST

AND DON'T MISS THESE EXCITING TIME PASSAGES ROMANCES NOW AVAILABLE FROM JOVE!

REMEMBER LOVE
BY SUSAN PLUNKETT

A bolt of lightning transports the soul of a scientist to 1866— and into the body of a beautiful Alaskan woman. But her new life comes with a price: a maddeningly arrogant—and seductive—husband . . .

A DANCE THROUGH TIME
BY LYNN KURLAND

A romance writer falls asleep in Gramercy Park, and wakes up in fourteenth century Scotland—in the arms of the man of her dreams . . .

THIS TIME TOGETHER
BY SUSAN LESLIE LIEPITZ

An entertainment lawyer dreams of a simpler life—and finds herself in an 1890s cabin, with a handsome mountain man . .

Titles in the Time Passages series

_L_OST
_Y_ESTERDAY

Jenny Lykins

JOVE BOOKS, NEW YORK

LOST YESTERDAY

A Jove Book / published by arrangement with
the author

PRINTING HISTORY
Jove edition / February 1997

The Putnam Berkley World Wide Web site address is
http://www.berkley.com/berkley

ISBN: 0-515-12013-8

A JOVE BOOK®
Jove Books are published by The Berkley Publishing Group,
200 Madison Avenue, New York, New York 10016.
JOVE and the "J" design are trademarks
belonging to Jove Publications, Inc.

PRINTED IN THE UNITED STATES OF AMERICA

10 9 8 7 6 5 4 3 2 1

My sincere thanks to:

- My parents, Dale and Eunice Massie, just because.
- My wonderful kids, Price and Marisa, for their support.
- My sister, Linda Hay, and my brother, Bob Massie, for the pep talks.
- My critique partners, Donna Freeman and Loretta Taylor, for *everything*.
- River City Romance Writers, for making me believe I could do it.
- Jan Walker and Molly Prim, who already know why.

Special appreciation to:

- David Garner for inviting me in and allowing me to base Tranquille on his beautiful home, Marlsgate.
- The Father, to Whom I owe everything.

To Richie,
The standard for all my heroes.
My best friend, my hero, my husband.

LOST YESTERDAY

Chapter 1

THE GHOST LEANED against a massive white column on the upper veranda, his gaze surveying the ever-changing shimmers of light on the Mississippi River, as if searching for something only he could see.

Marin Alexander hadn't thought she believed in ghosts. But now her breath caught in her throat and all thoughts of Pierce Hall's tourists flew from her mind. This was no straggling visitor dallying to watch the fiery sunset, but a translucent figure of a man. The setting sun filtered through his body, casting no shadow on the weathered boards at his feet.

Snowy white shirt, black waistcoat, and snug black trousers accentuated the image of lean, sinewy power. A faint outline of the banister was visible through his muscular frame. Marin swallowed hard, caught by a mysterious force far greater than any physical power. Icy chills danced over her rigid spine.

The ghost turned and looked directly at her. Fading sunlight shone through a pair of sky-blue eyes.

Marin felt no threat; in fact, her initial fear melted away. But just as she began to question this odd sense of comfort, the ghost shook his head, then vanished.

Oh, heavens! Now she'd seen everything! Or had she, really? She'd been under a lot of stress with the new job. And the looming anniversary of Ryan's death weighed heavily on her mind. But no, she knew what she'd seen. She glanced around for other witnesses to corroborate her story, but she was the last one to leave Pierce Hall, and she knew it. As director of Memphis's oldest antebellum town house, she always made the final rounds to check the locks and activate the security system.

Not that security helped against the netherworld.

A sense of exhilaration almost equal to her shock swept through her. She'd finally seen one of the ghosts!

Three separate spirits had been sighted at Pierce Hall, but this one didn't fit any of their descriptions. Visitors and docents alike had described a small child, an ancient black woman, and a young man in his early twenties. From their dress, they all seemed to be from different eras. Her ghost was in his mid-thirties. He was definitely not the inexperienced youth sighted by others.

Marin scanned the now unobstructed view of the river. Her first instinct was to go investigate the haunted area, but common sense forced her back toward the brightly lit interior. After all, she was there alone, and no one would be returning before nine in the morning.

Once inside the house, panic finally kicked in—with a vengeance. How ridiculous to have imagined she wouldn't feel fear after seeing a ghost. She rushed through the house, checking windows and doors; then, with a misguided sense of relief, she switched on the alarm system on her way out.

Leave it to her to see a ghost with no other witnesses around. And a new ghost, at that.

Her car was a welcome and calming sanctuary. She slammed the door and hit the electric lock. Grabbing the rearview mirror and studying her face, she was relieved when the cool gray eyes that stared back appeared lucid and not glazed. Though her normally tanned skin looked pale, her cheeks had the glow of health about them. No, she could definitely rule out hallucination. Maybe.

As she floored the red Mustang the short distance to her condo on the Memphis bluffs, the warm air from the open windows tossed her sun-streaked hair and cleared her head.

Who was the ghost? The waning orange sun behind him had made his features somewhat indistinct. Except his eyes. His eyes had been the exact same shade as the summer sky. Blurred though his visage had been, Marin knew she would be able to pick him out of a picture if she found one. There would be no mistaking that face—blurry or not.

She shivered in the humid July air as she pulled into a parking space and cut the engine. Strange how he'd seemed almost irreverent when he turned to look at her. Only moments before, while he'd faced the river, he'd emanated an overwhelming sadness.

Get a grip, Alexander. You probably hallucinated from the heat.

Marin shook off her woolgathering and collected an armful of purse, briefcase, keys, and assorted junk. She bumped the car door shut with her hip and juggled everything into a manageable pile. Between her armload and her shaking knees, she wondered if she would make it to her apartment.

"Marin! Howya doin', neighbor?" Bill Lindsey fell in beside her, his arms as laden as hers. He quick-stepped to the door and grabbed the handle before she could reach it. Holding the door with his foot, he shoved a sheaf of papers under his chin and rearranged his load while he waited for her to pass through. A lock of thick blond hair fell into his eyes.

"Thanks, Bill. Next time it's my turn."

"Say, Marin! I've got a couple of T-bones in the fridge. Want to come over and burn 'em with me?"

A nice-looking guy with a great personality, Bill had been pursuing her for weeks. But since Ryan's death, Marin had sworn off relationships of any kind.

"Sorry, but I've got a whole briefcase full of work, and I'm expecting a couple of phone calls." The fortuitous ring of the phone jangled from within her apartment when they stepped off the elevator.

"That may be one of the calls, now. See ya, Bill."

She fumbled for the key while the phone gave another insistent ring.

"Well, if you get hungry later on, give me a call."

She shoved open the door with a distracted nod and scooped up the cordless phone in the middle of the third ring.

"What! Hello!"

"Marin, what's up? Did you just get in?"

"Yeah, I just walked in the door, Jenna. What do you need?"

"Is this bad timing? You sound preoccupied."

Marin massaged the tension out of the back of her neck. "No. I just had to run for the phone."

"Good. Well, listen. There's a party downtown tonight. Feel like getting a little wild?"

Marin had no desire to be part of the social meat market tonight, or any night for that matter. She might accidently meet someone she liked.

"Thanks, but I've got a lot of paperwork to finish. My review for the first three months as director is next Friday, and I really want to have all the squares filled."

Jenna breathed a loud, dramatic sigh.

"Okay, party pooper. Be that way. If you change your mind before nine o'clock, though, give me a call."

"Sure."

"Marin?"

"Yeah?"

"You can't live the rest of your life in a vacuum."

"Yeah, I can. Have fun."

Marin switched off the phone, purposely shoving the conversation from her mind. She stepped onto her balcony, her favorite place to meditate and relax at the end of the day. Lucky enough to have a condo fronting the river, she'd long ago decided the sunsets were the best part of the view. This one proved breathtaking, with shades of pink and orange and red all watercolored against a flawless blue canvas—the exact color of the ghost's eyes.

A chill snaked up her spine, generating another shiver. Had she really seen a ghost? Of course she had! She wasn't in the habit of seeing things that weren't there.

She sifted her hair through her fingers, loosening the knots caused by the wind, letting the strands fall to her shoulders one by one while she concentrated on the events of the day. She'd just have to wait until tomorrow to investigate this bizarre experience. At least one of the docents who had been "visited" would be on duty then. And she already knew where the pictures were, so she could start her search for his identity.

She turned her gaze back to the river—the same view so recently studied by . . . a man with sky-blue eyes, who'd lived his life long before she'd been born.

Letters, diaries, and old photographs littered Marin's desk a full hour before either one of the docents was due to show up.

It had been hours before she'd dropped off into an exhausted sleep the night before. And then she'd slept only fitfully, waking with a start every few minutes after dreaming a pair of translucent blue eyes watched her. She'd finally given up any pretense of rest and decided to come in to work early.

When she arrived at the mansion, the first thing she'd done was check the upper veranda. With great trepidation and a pair of very shaky knees she turned off the security system and crept through the house as if she could sneak right past a ghost. Her legs had threatened to give out when she forced herself onto the veranda. She'd been both relieved and disappointed when all that greeted her were a pair of harmless wicker rockers left over from the glory days.

Having left the museum in Little Rock to take this position, her days had been too busy with marketing, advertising, and dealing with the board of directors to have time to satisfy her curiosity about the detailed history of the home and its people. But now she planned to dive into the past life of the house until she found her mystery phantom.

Turning her attention to the littered desktop, she sorted through the treasures like a miser sifting through his gold. She would check the pictures first, and if she was lucky enough to identify the man, then she would check the diaries and letters for any reference to him.

His clothing made it difficult to tell what time period he might have belonged to. The black trousers and boots, the buttoned, double-breasted black waistcoat and collarless white shirt could have been from several decades. Now, with the shock over, Marin could see him in her mind's eye more clearly than she had yesterday. She could even see the sparkle of the sun on a gold watch fob chain that draped from buttonhole to pocket.

The slam of the gift shop door startled her so, she nearly jumped out of her chair. She scrambled to catch the now-fluttering picture she'd been holding.

"Whew! It's going to be another scorcher in beautiful downtown Memphis. It's got to be ninety degrees with ninety percent humidity out there already."

Helen Webber, the docent Marin had been waiting for, fanned herself with a magazine as she dropped her purse into a file cabinet drawer. Her eyes widened when she noticed the abundance of yellowed papers on Marin's desk.

"Hey! What's up? Are we getting ready to open a new exhibit?"

Marin threaded her fingers through her hair, then remembered she'd been trying to break that habit. She flicked the strands behind her shoulder.

"No, I'm doing a little research on my own. Helen, you saw one of the ghosts once, didn't you?"

"Twice," Helen said after taking in a deep breath, "and it was two too many times." She sat in the chair opposite the desk and made herself comfortable while she warmed to her story. "The first time I saw him I was taking a group through. I had just moved them from the green bedroom to the master suite, and I went back to get a little girl who'd lagged behind. She was still standing by the velvet ropes when she pointed to the bed and said, 'Is he sick?' Well, I nearly dropped my teeth. There on the bed lay a young man in buff trousers, white shirt, and riding boots. And his shirt had a big red stain across the chest, right over his heart." Helen slapped her splayed fingers across her own heart.

"I don't mind telling you, I was hard pressed to get that little girl out of there and not scare the living daylights out of her. I turned around before I got completely out the door, and he was gone! I tell you, I almost left here and never came back."

"When did you see him the second time?"

"About two years later. I'd say that was about . . . oh, three years ago now." Helen rubbed her arms. "I'd almost talked myself into believing I hadn't seen anything. Then we had a tornado warning, and we were all scrambling to close up and get home. Without even thinking, I dashed into the green bedroom to turn off the lights, and there he sat in the rocker. The shirt was still bloody, and he was slumped over like he was in pain.

"Well, I couldn't move! My feet felt like they'd been nailed to the floor. I just stood there and shook until he looked up at me."

Marin shook her head, afraid to blink. She wasn't sure she wanted to hear any more.

Helen continued. "He raised his head and saw me standing there, scared to death. Then he struggled to his feet and said, 'Forgive me. I do apologize,' in the thickest accent you ever heard, then he just disappeared! Just vanished! And you know what? I haven't been afraid of seeing him again. I don't want to, mind you, but if I do I don't think I'll be scared."

Marin absorbed this information while she formulated what she should say, but Helen saved her having to confess her experience.

"You saw one, didn't you?" Helen asked.

Had she been that obvious?

"You can tell me. I won't think you're crazy. Shoot, I'd have to think I was crazy, too! Which one did you see?"

Marin took a deep breath, held it, then exhaled with a sigh. Maybe it was best to talk about it.

"I saw a new one."

"You're kidding! Who was it? Was it male or female?"

Marin's heart skipped at the memory.

"Oh, definitely male." No doubt about that. "I'd guess he was around thirty-five or so, dark hair, maybe black, and vivid blue eyes. I don't know who he was. That's why I've got all the pictures out."

"Where'd you see him?"

"On the upper veranda. He was looking out at the river when I went to close up."

"Ohhhh! You were here by yourself! I'm surprised you didn't have a stroke!"

Marin gave a halfhearted laugh. "I didn't have time for a stroke, it happened so fast. But you know, I really didn't feel all that scared until *after* he was gone. I didn't panic until I got into the house."

"And you were back here this morning, alone. You're a braver woman than I am."

"I would say more curious than brave. I'm dying to find out who he is."

The arrival of the first tourists of the day cut off any more speculation. Helen left Marin to her search while she sold a family four tickets and began the tour of the house.

Marin didn't need any incentive to get back to the pictures on her desk. She gently lifted each and every one, searched the faces—with a magnifying glass when needed—then filed it back in its acid-free folder. This procedure went on all morning until a dull ache started right behind her eyes. After her stomach started making noisy reminders, she decided to finish up and break for lunch. She'd seen most of the pictures anyway.

With what she hoped was a premature sense of defeat, she slid the last picture into its file and cleaned off the top of her desk. After Helen and Jean, the other docent, declined her offer to bring them back some lunch, she plodded through the muggy air out to her car.

A fine sheen of sweat had appeared on her skin when she'd stepped out of the air conditioned gift shop, but the black leather interior of the Mustang nearly melted her.

"There should be a law against black leather in the South," she grumbled to herself as she settled a towel over her seat, then used another towel to turn the ignition.

Lunch turned out to be at one of the restaurants on the bluff. She opted to sit outside in the shade. The breeze off the water was really very pleasant. She relaxed with a glass of iced tea and enjoyed the view of the Pyramid, Mud Island, and the Hernando de Soto Bridge.

Lost in thought about what the city would have looked like through the eyes of her ghost, the waiter jarred her back into the twentieth century with a pasta salad and fresh tea.

The salad, fresh, tangy, and al dente, took her mind off the morning's search for a while. Having that little cloud of questions lifted from her thoughts, even if only for a moment, felt good.

The waiter ambled over and laid her check on the table, then placed a strawberry daiquiri on top of it.

"I didn't order that," she said, expecting him to apologize and take it away. Instead he pointed to a man at a corner table.

"He sent it."

A thirtysomething executive in the summer business uniform of white button-down, red tie, and black slacks raised his own glass in salute. Marin turned back to the waiter and handed him the drink, along with enough money to cover her bill.

"Tell him thanks anyway."

She grimaced on her way back to work when a finger of guilt tapped her on the shoulder. She knew, deep down, that the guy was probably a perfectly nice person looking for a way to meet someone. But that old, familiar wall she'd built years ago would come rising out of nowhere and encircle her like a fortress every time someone approached her in friendliness, be they male or female. Sometimes that icy wall made her harsh. It was something she tried not to think about, and she didn't dwell on it now.

Spotty patches of sunlight danced on the lawn as she strolled along the front walk of the home, admiring the mansion's sand-colored stone front, which would turn to muted gold in the rays of a dying sun. A breeze lifted her hair and flung it behind her. She raised her face to the wind to savor the feeling.

Then she stopped dead in her tracks.

Her heart slammed against the wall of her chest. Her breathing turned into shallow wheezes.

He stood on the balcony, his right foot resting on the lower rail of the banister. The river held his attention again.

Marin stood less than thirty feet from the house, with a perfect view of him from below. She stood absolutely still and studied his handsome countenance. His solemn profile wrenched at her heart, but that was nothing compared to the surge of heat that enveloped her when he turned and faced her.

She took an involuntary step backward, then stopped. He put both hands on the rail, leaned his weight against them, and studied her as she studied him. Marin tried to look away but couldn't. She had an uncanny sense that he knew her thoughts when the slightest hint of a smile curved his lips and a crescent-shaped dimple creased his left cheek. Her heart thundered, the blood roared in her ears, and heat that had nothing to do with the July sun crept across her neck.

This wasn't fear. This was pure excitement. And that was something she never allowed herself to feel. She enjoyed the nearly forgotten sensation though; enjoyed and savored the staring match with this gorgeous ghost. What could it hurt? The guy was already dead; it wasn't like he could up and die on her all over again.

And again, she felt her thoughts invaded. His hint of a smile turned into a full-fledged grin; a matching dimple appeared in his other cheek.

Her insides developed a bad case of butterflies as she smiled back at that pair of incredibly blue eyes. He reached out a hand, and she could have sworn that across thirty feet of lawn and two stories of building she felt a warm caress on her cheek.

She jerked herself to attention and tried to scramble her thoughts from him. How very disconcerting to think that someone, even a ghost, could react to her unspoken musings.

He drew himself to attention, too, clicked his heels and tipped an imaginary hat. Then, in the blink of an eye, he dissolved into thin air.

"Oh, this is too weird, Alexander. You're going to need therapy if you start flirting with a spook!" Marin had long held conversations with herself when something needed analyzing. She'd found that sometimes just saying the words out loud brought reason to a strange situation.

This was not one of those times.

She continued hesitantly on to the house. Flirting with him when she was outside in broad daylight was one thing. The possibility of meeting him face-to-face in closed quarters was something else altogether.

The cool sanity of the gift shop seemed safe enough. Helen and Jean sat with their stockinged feet propped on a shared chair, magazines in hands. They mumbled a greeting, barely looking up, when the tinkling bell over the door announced Marin's arrival.

She dumped her purse in the file cabinet under "P," rearranging the other two purses in order to shut the drawer. This simple task proved harder than she would have imagined, since her hands shook so badly she could barely control them.

"Pretty humid out there, huh?" Jean always had a firm grasp on the obvious.

"Yeah," Marin answered distractedly. She decided to keep this latest experience to herself. She dropped into her chair and rolled to her desk.

"This is him! Good grief, this is him!"

The two docents jumped up and crowded behind the desk. Everyone talked at once.

"Which one of you found it? This is great! I can't believe you found it!"

Both docents looked at each other and waited for the other to confess to finding the picture.

"Oh, don't tell me neither one of you guys put this on my desk!"

"I didn't."

"Neither did I."

That wave of heat crashed back across Marin's neck. She looked behind her to see if a pair of mocking blue eyes watched. Though the room was specter-free, she decided maybe she wouldn't investigate too closely where the picture came from.

She looked back at the photograph, and her phantom's image seemed to come alive. Though the photo was black-and-white, she could see the color of his eyes as clearly as she had just minutes ago on the balcony.

"Which one is yours, Marin?"

Obviously, Helen had already filled Jean in on the story. Marin pointed to the most dynamic face in the group of people.

"That's him."

The two women leaned closer to the picture. Jean whistled through her teeth.

"Wow! Does he look that good in real life—I mean in person? You know what I mean."

Marin knew exactly what Jean meant.

"Better."

She and her little group perused the photo and speculated on who the people were. Three men and four women stared back at them from the photograph, most in the classic nineteenth-century pose of solemn features and rigid bodies. The other two men in the photo seemed roughly the same age as Marin's ghost, but neither possessed the looks or charisma that leapt from his likeness. Two of the women appeared very young, probably in their early twenties. Another woman, attractive with dark hair and laughing eyes, stood out from the crowd with an impish smile for the camera. The fourth, perhaps in her fifties, wore an expression that suggested she'd just sucked on a fresh-picked lemon.

The door opening to the gift shop set the bell ringing, drawing their attention back to the present. Helen and Jean left to greet the new group of tourists, but Marin remained focused on the photograph. She turned it over to see if it was labeled.

Bingo!

Her heart fluttered when she saw his name. She *knew* it was his name. Written in spidery black copperplate was: *Hunter Pierce, mother Lucille Pierce, companion and neighbors.*

Well, this didn't tell her who the others were, but Hunter and his mother were unmistakable. She knew Hunter had been one of the mansion's owners, and the lemon-sucker must be Mom.

It was impossible to tell which woman was with which man. The men stood on the top step, the ladies were grouped on the next. No one seemed to be standing with anyone in particular. Three men and four women. Which were the wives and which was the companion? And who was she a companion to? A ridiculous flash of jealousy surged through Marin. Funny, but she didn't want any of the women to be with Hunter.

Hunter.

The name suited him.

She spent the rest of the day buried in letters, diaries, and more pictures. His name appeared in a few of the papers, but only as owner of Pierce Hall or as the purchaser on a bill of lading. She was down to a last handful of letters and a diary. The letters would require such painstaking care, she opted to check the diary first.

The flyleaf stated the owner as Julia Beecham Pierce, and the year as 1935. Marin was about to lay the book aside when something slid from the pages and fluttered to the floor. When she bent to scoop up the wayward paper, she nearly fell out of her chair.

It wasn't a piece of paper at all, but another picture of Hunter. She reverently picked up the photograph and studied the now familiar features.

This was a much younger Hunter—probably in his early twenties. His eyes were just as riveting, but his unsmiling face sported a mustache that curved down over the corners of his mouth. She liked him better clean-shaven. The mustache made him look severe, not to mention it threatened to hide those wonderful dimples.

"That's the last of them, Marin. Jean's already gone for the day, and unless you need help, I'm ready to go, too."

Marin glanced at her watch, surprised at how late it was. She gathered up the mess on her desk and told Helen it was all right to leave.

"Are you sure you don't want me to stay and help you close up? I have plenty of time. I'd hate for you to meet the new haunt again after I leave." Marin's stomach flipped at Helen's teasing, but she waved away the concern.

"Actually, I saw him again after lunch and—"

"You what?"

"Yeah, I was walking from the street and he was on the upstairs veranda."

She related the experience to Helen, not bothering to mention the fact that she'd flirted with him. Helen was speechless over the sightings being so close together.

"Anyway, I think it's safe to leave. Surely I won't see him again today. Besides, I just won't go on the veranda."

Marin finally persuaded Helen to leave when she pointed out how long it would take to put her desk in order.

With all the papers finally refiled, Marin arched her back, her hands low on her hips, then picked up her purse and briefcase and started on her rounds of the house. She tried to walk through with the same sense of purpose and nonchalance she'd had for the past three months.

It was hard.

Lightning flashed in the distance. One, one thousand, two, one thousand, three, one thousand. Thunder rumbled. The storm was three miles away.

When she got to the door that opened to the upper veranda she flipped the lock and turned away. An overwhelming urge swept over her before she took a step. Almost against her will, she found herself unlocking the door, stepping onto the balcony.

Her heart thrummed like a drumroll in her chest as she tiptoed to the east end of the porch. Holding her breath, she inched her head around the corner until she had a clear view all the way to the river.

Nothing.

There was just the porch, with the same lonely rockers and the same ugly plastic owl nailed to the ceiling to scare off the birds. She waited a minute to see if anything would appear, but the air, though thick with moisture, remained clear and hot.

Suddenly she jerked around and looked behind her. Nothing. Hers was the only spirit occupying the veranda this evening.

Her laugh came unheralded—shaky and unnaturally loud in the quiet early evening. This was great. In twenty-four hours she had gone from being a serious, levelheaded person to a wacko creeping around haunted houses.

A clap of thunder boomed so loud and near, the vibration rumbled through her entire body. She jumped and dropped her briefcase, which landed a good two yards away. She no sooner collected herself enough to pick up her briefcase than a bolt of lightning flashed and another thunderclap reverberated.

She broke every speed record she'd set for closing up and getting out of the house. Thunder boomed several more times before she got to the river oak where she'd watched Hunter earlier. She turned and looked back at the balcony. An early dusk from the approaching storm darkened the recesses, but a flash of lightning revealed no presence.

When she turned back toward the car, a scream tore from her throat to join another rumble of thunder.

Hunter stood in front of her, not six feet away. Lightning illuminated the landscape and made him seem almost real.

This time she lost both briefcase and purse. She snatched them off the ground with a huff. Fear, or shock, put words in her mouth without benefit of thought.

"Good Lord, don't do that!" She couldn't believe she'd just yelled at a ghost.

He stared at her, then that impossible dimple appeared.

Another burst of light pierced the slate gray sky. Marin thought she saw the tiniest hint of a cleft in his chin.

He reached up and rubbed the area.

She was wrong about his hair. It wasn't black. It was that rich, dark brown that would come alive with streaks of gold in the summer.

He plowed his fingers through it from temple to crown.

"Stop doing that, Hunter! Geez! Didn't anybody ever tell you it's rude to go wandering around in someone else's mind?" This was really too much. She should be having a panic attack instead of giving lessons in manners!

The second dimple appeared. Hunter gave her a look of pure innocence. She could tell by his expression that he was accustomed to charming women speechless.

The landscape darkened, then lit again. She jumped at the sight of him walking toward her. Weren't ghosts supposed to float or something? Hers walked, making his appearance all the more unnerving.

Her gray eyes never left his hypnotic blue gaze as she teetered backward with each step he took. He showed no sign of stopping, even when he was only inches away.

With sudden uncharacteristic clairvoyance she knew what he intended to do.

He wouldn't dare! She stopped in her tracks to protest, but it was too late. His translucent form melted into hers.

An explosion of sensations chain-reacted throughout her body. Instead of the legendary cold, a permeating heat flash-flooded her essence and coiled to erupt in the very center of her being. Her body trembled in paroxysms of unbearable pleasure so intense her legs threatened to buckle.

The erotic sentience lasted for what seemed like minutes instead of seconds. When it abated enough to allow coherent thought, Marin's knees felt like spaghetti, her skin tingled from head to toe, her heartbeat pounded in her temples.

Suddenly she felt more alone than she'd felt since Ryan's death. She yearned to feel all the things she'd worked so hard to repress. She wanted to feel *alive* with someone.

These were dangerous musings. She reminded herself of the hard-earned wisdom it had taken her a lifetime to learn—get close, get hurt.

Shoving all sensations to the back of her mind, she gathered her wits about her and looked around. Hunter stood back in his original position, looking for all the world as if he were ready to light up a cigarette.

She pulled a deep breath of the ozone-charged air into her lungs and searched her mind for something to say.

That left dimple appeared with a tender smile, and he raised his hand. Though separated by six feet, she felt the warm caress of his palm on her cheek. She closed her eyes to savor the feeling. When she opened them, he was gone.

The heavens picked that moment to open up with a reality-inducing downpour. Marin tucked her purse under her arm and sheltered her head with her briefcase as she ran for the car. Drenched to the skin by the time she got the door unlocked and climbed in, she rubbed the excess water from her hair with one of the towels, then fired up the engine and roared down the street, afraid to even look in the rearview mirror.

What in the world was she going to do now? How could she deal with being the director of an antebellum home, haunted by its mind-reading ghost, not to mention whatever that was that just passed between them on the front lawn. There was absolutely no way she could work in that house if Hunter continued to appear on a daily basis. For Pete's sake, she was attracted to a dead man!

How poetic, she thought with a tinge of bitterness. Everyone I've ever cared about has ended up dead. Now they're just starting out that way.

Thunder rumbled and lightning flashed as she floored the Mustang up Riverside Drive to her condo. Deep in thought about how to deal with the situation, she gasped and swerved at the misty sight of a horse and antique buggy in the middle of the road.

The car had nowhere to go but into the bluffs. Her last thoughts were a jumble of shattering glass, pain on her forehead, something warm and sticky.

Then everything went black.

Chapter 2

COLD RAIN BATTERED down on her with a vengeance. She tried to raise up on her elbows but her hands slid through thick, black mud.

When Marin rolled onto her back, her throbbing head sank into the ooze. She had no idea how long she'd lain there.

She tried to rise one more time but felt as if an elephant sat on her chest. Her energy drained from her in waves. Between thunderclaps she heard a masculine voice cursing, then felt a pair of gentle hands checking her for broken bones.

She tried to lift her head to tell the paramedics where she hurt. Rain and mud and matted hair blinded her when she opened her eyes. After dragging a filthy forearm across her face, she blinked to clear her vision.

She must have hit her head harder than she thought. The paramedic looked just like Hunter! More blinking only brought his features into focus.

"Have a care, Miss Sander. My home is not far. I've already sent a man to fetch Dr. Ritter."

She tried to tell him he'd left off part of her name. And he needed to know which hospitals were covered by her insurance. But he interrupted her, his voice both tender and comfortingly masculine.

"No, no. Do not try to talk or move. I'll carry you."

This was really quite funny. At least it would be if her head didn't hurt so much. Within twenty-four hours she had obsessed over a dead man to the point of seeing him in the flesh now. But she'd have time to worry about that particular reaction when her head stopped throbbing.

A pair of strong, mud-covered arms scooped her up to cradle her comfortingly against him. The heat of his chest radiated through the cold, wet fabric that covered them both.

Where was the stretcher? How very unusual. What if she had a back injury?

She snuggled closer to the warmth his massive chest offered. To heck with the stretcher. Maybe they couldn't get it to her, and he was carrying her to the ambulance. She allowed the blackness to creep closer into her warm little cocoon.

Her eyes flew open again when she felt herself being jostled around. She managed to squint through the rain long enough to see that she had just been settled onto Hunter's lap—atop a horse! This was really too much. Had they drugged her before she came to? Was she having an allergic reaction to whatever they'd given her? She struggled against the tight band of his arms, but he held her tight.

"Shhhh. Shhhh. It's all right," he crooned softly.

The encroaching blackness finally swallowed her completely.

*   *   *

"Am I dead?"

The cadaverous doctor standing over her with ancient medical equipment should be able to answer that for her.

She had to be dead. It was the only rationalization she could come to. She'd regained consciousness before arriving at the house—the mansion—where she worked. The rooms, lit with gas and a few scattered candles against the gloom of the day, were a far cry from the museum atmosphere she knew so well.

And then there was Hunter. Try as she might, she couldn't will away his image from the foot of the bed. His face and nineteenth-century clothing refused to metamorphose into that of a paramedic's. She'd pinched herself several times, and even pinched Hunter, but all he'd done was glare at her in surprise. This was not a dream.

Yes, she had to be dead.

"Why, no, my dear. You are very much alive." The doctor spoke to her in a voice he probably usually saved for children.

"Okay. Then I must be in a coma."

The doctor's indulgent chuckle didn't match his looks. He shook his head.

"My dear, one needs to be unconscious in order to achieve a coma." He picked up a towel and wiped his hands. The white linen came away with bright red smears on it. "No, little lady, you will have a doozy of a headache, but I see no reason to worry. You did, however, crack your head a good one on that rock, so we will need to keep you awake for several hours today in case of concussion."

He turned back to studying her forehead.

"I did a fine job with those stitches, if I do say so myself.

Here, have a look-see. I doubt if there will be much of a scar, if any."

He picked up a shaving mirror and held it for her, but stitches were the least of her worries right now. She glanced at the mirror just to satisfy the doctor.

"Oh, my God!" Marin screamed. She grabbed the mirror, denials ringing in her brain as she looked again, then jumped from the bed and staggered to the cheval glass in the corner.

Gas lamps on the wall threw a dim glow over her features as she stared into the full-length mirror. She started to shake and would have crumpled to her knees if Hunter hadn't caught her. She continued to stare at the reflection in the mirror, shaking her head, fearing for her sanity.

The face that stared back was not hers.

"What in blazes is wrong with the woman, Doc?" Benjamin Hunter Pierce sat behind his desk and tapped a letter opener in maddening repetition. The doctor picked up his brandy and sank back into the wing chair.

"The gal is just in shock, Hunter. To tell you the truth, I am surprised she lived through the incident. She must have one solid constitution, surviving that blow to the head the way she did. Or else she has a guardian angel looking out for her."

A guardian angel indeed. Hunter had a feeling he would be needing his own angel before this was all over with.

What had he gotten himself into? All he'd done was hire a companion for his mother, someone who could keep her company and act as a social secretary for himself. And now look at what he had. An invalid with a concussion and his mother spitting like a cat.

It was his mother's doing that he'd had to go out of the area to find someone for the position. No one living anywhere near Memphis who had ever gotten wind of Lucille Pierce's irascible nature would take on the job. He'd finally had to advertise in other cities.

The letter that drew his attention came from St. Louis. The young lady wrote eloquently in a rather flowery sort of script—so flowery as to be almost indecipherable. But what he could read was intelligent, and she very clearly needed the position. That meant she would probably not be wont to leave, even after meeting his mother.

He'd wired her the money for travel, and now here she was, babbling about being in someone else's body and that the time was wrong. How could the time be wrong? There weren't even any clocks in that room.

He shook his head and looked back at the doctor. He stopped drumming the letter opener and tossed it aside.

"How long will she be like this? Or is it permanent?"

"Oh, no, it's not permanent, though it is hard to say how quickly she will recover completely. I must say, though, it was good fortune you saw the boat dock and went to see what was keeping the carriage you'd sent. She might have bled to death if you'd gotten there later, considering your driver was knocked unconscious, too."

Hunter stood and paced the length of his study. Now, not only did he have his prodigal mother to put up with, but he had an invalid who thought she was inhabiting someone else's body.

God's sense of humor was questionable.

"I have another call to make, but I'll return to check on our little patient first thing in the morning." Dr. Ritter gathered up his paraphernalia and stood.

Hunter walked him to the door and saw him off. After distractedly watching the buggy disappear down the drive, he turned and stared up the length of the staircase, wondering what in the world the woman had been talking about with all that nonsense about being in someone else's body. Just exactly how hard had she hit her head? Maybe she was calmer now that she'd had some time alone.

He started up the sweeping staircase before he heard the purposeful *click click click* of feminine heels on the hardwood floor. A groan rose in his throat.

"Well, I see your new employee has arrived in fine form. She has managed to begin her job as a burden and will no doubt continue to be one until you come to your senses and throw her out."

Lucille Pierce pursed her mouth as if she'd just eaten an unripe persimmon. Hunter stared at the vertical lines etched along his mother's lips and wondered if her mouth had ever seen a soft, smiling day.

"Of course, Mother, you are right. I am sure Miss Sander endeavored to arrive here an invalid, and when it became apparent she was altogether too healthy, she called down the lightning that caused the horses to bolt. I am truly surprised she settled for nothing more than a severe concussion and stitches."

"You will remember I am your mother, young man, and I will not be spoken to in such a manner."

"And you will remember, Mother, that I now own Pierce Hall and it is only because of Father's misplaced love for you that I have allowed you back. Had he not made me promise I would do so, you would be left to fend for yourself."

He ended the conversation, turning and continuing up the stairs. Her huff of anger fell on deaf ears.

The door to the guest bedroom stood open. Mamie, his dear old live-in servant, sat beside the bed, spooning broth into the patient's mouth. Hunter knocked on the doorframe before stepping into the room. Two sets of eyes, one chocolate brown and one golden amber, glanced up at him. Mamie collected the eating utensils and pulled the covers up over the invalid's shoulders.

"I's through here, Mr. Hunter. I be back later to check on her."

Hunter laid a hand on Mamie's arm. He was concerned about Mamie's husband, who'd been driving the carriage. "How is Nathan? Nothing more than a bump on the head, I hope."

"Oh, no, suh. He fine. It take more than a whack on the head to hurt that polecat." The affection in Mamie's voice spoke volumes. "But he worryin' 'bout them horses that bolted. He say he gonna have to train them better."

Mamie left the room with a clattering tray laden with empty dishes. Hunter noticed with amusement that she made sure the door remained completely open when she left.

He turned back to the patient, who stared at him with a certain degree of fear and trepidation.

"Are you feeling better, Miss Sander?"

"Alexander."

"I beg your pardon?"

"My name is Alexander. Marin Alexander."

This was a new twist.

"I stand corrected. From your letters I believed your name to be Mari Alexa Sander. I apologize for misreading your name." And she should apologize for all those unreadable curlicues she embellished her writing with, he thought with irritation.

"What letters?"

He couldn't have heard right.

"I beg your pardon?" he said for the second time.

She looked at him as if he were a very slow-witted child.

"What letters are you talking about? I didn't send you any letters, Hunter."

This was beyond the pale. And how dare she call him by his Christian name? He decided turnabout was fair play.

"Well, Mari—"

"Marin."

"*Marin*. I am referring to the letters of our correspondence concerning the position of companion to my mother and secretary to myself." He took pity on her blank look and gentled his voice. "Don't worry. Dr. Ritter advised that you may find yourself disoriented and confused after that blow to your head. Your memory will clear in time."

Marin didn't appear reassured by his words. Instead, her brow furrowed and she seemed to draw into herself.

"I'll leave you alone to rest, Miss . . . Alexander. Is there anything I can have sent up for you?"

She raised her head and focused her gaze on him.

"What year is it?"

He started to laugh, then realized with surprise that she was serious.

"1876. The tenth day of July, 1876. Do you not remember the centennial celebration? Surely St. Louis joined the rest of the country in its revelry."

She bowed her head quickly and seemed to be absorbing this information. He decided to leave her to her thoughts and stepped through the door.

"Your mother—was that older, dark-haired woman your mother?"

He stifled an overwhelming urge to apologize.

"Yes. You will be her companion when you recover."

He waited for more questions—or a tendering of her resignation—but when none were forthcoming, he proceeded through the door.

Just as he stepped into the hallway he heard his patient mumble to herself, "So she *was* the lemon-sucker."

I'm glad someone finds this amusing, Marin thought with irritation as Hunter's laughter echoed off the walls as he disappeared down the hall.

Here she was in some kind of comatose nightmare, and her ghost was laughing like a lunatic outside her bedroom door.

Well, not actually *her* bedroom. And not actually her ghost.

This version of Hunter Pierce was very much alive. In fact, he exuded vitality and masculinity until it was hard for her to concentrate on her problems.

He'd said the date was July 10, 1876. That was exactly one hundred and twenty years in the past.

Was she in a coma from the car wreck? She remembered shattering the windshield with her head. Did a person dream in a coma? She slapped herself on the cheek. Definite pain. She'd tasted the chicken broth Mamie fed her, and she could smell delicious aromas drifting through the open windows from the kitchen.

Maybe a glance out one of those windows would answer some questions. She slowly elbowed herself upright and swung her legs over the side of the bed. The pounding in her head intensified, but she fought off the pain and steadied herself. Her knees wobbled slightly when she stood. She held on to furniture while she inched her way to a window, taking one shaky step at a time.

A gasp of disbelief caught in her throat at the sight that greeted her. She moved onto the veranda for a better look.

The river snaked along just where it belonged, but that was all that could be said. There was no Hernando de Soto Bridge, no Pyramid, no Riverside Drive, no skyscrapers downtown. Horses pulled a variety of carriages and wagons, and all the people within sight wore clothing straight out of a museum display.

Had they given her some kind of drug that caused her to hallucinate?

"Hey! Don't give me any more of this stuff! It's making me crazy!" She spoke aloud with the hope she would reach someone in the real world.

She gripped the railing to steady herself. Strange, the railing seemed higher now. She looked down at her white-knuckled hands. The golden brown tan was gone, and her fingers appeared smaller boned than before. An unfamiliar ruby ring adorned her left hand.

Dizziness coiled crazily in her mind. All she wanted to do was get back in bed and pull the covers over her head. A reflection appeared before her in a partially closed window, and the dizziness worsened. The reflection moved when she did. It touched its hand to its temple when she did. It shook its head in denial when she did.

She knew beyond a shadow of a doubt that she was looking at her own reflection. And she was looking at the image of the smiling woman in the picture she'd found earlier.

She managed to make it back into her room, then sank onto the cushioned stool in front of the ruffled vanity table. After several tries, she gained the courage to look in the mirror again. When she did, she saw exactly what she feared.

The face looking back at her was not hers. There was no hint of resemblance.

She now saw the world through golden amber eyes. Until today her eyes had been gray. Her shoulder-length, sun-streaked hair now fell to her waist, a rich, dark mahogany, with so much body tiny ringlets sprang free from the long braid and curled about her face and neck. Her olive complexion, which had tanned so nicely, was now a pale, peaches-and-cream porcelain.

She stood and turned to the full-length mirror. Without measuring, she knew she was at least three inches shorter than her usual five feet seven inches. Her hands and feet were much smaller. She bunched the nightgown in her fist behind her and pulled the fabric tight to reveal an unbelievably tiny waist. She grabbed the top of her nightgown and peered down the front. She wouldn't say she was underendowed, but these breasts were definitely not what she was accustomed to.

She watched the stranger's reflection shake her head back and forth. A glazed look clouded her eyes with unanswered questions.

What in the world had happened to her? This didn't feel like a dream, coma, or hallucination. It felt terrifyingly real. Had she died in the crash and her spirit invaded this person's body? Did this girl die at the same moment?

The throbbing in her head began to take its toll. She rubbed her temples with the heels of her hands.

"What are you doing out of bed?"

Marin nearly jumped out of her skin. She spun around, sending the room spinning out of control. A masculine oath exploded, and strong arms caught her when she staggered.

Her ghost's face hovered only inches from hers as he carried her back to bed. The warmth of his breath feathered across her face, but no trace of the charming dimple appeared. In fact, his mouth formed a firm line of disapproval. Though he made no effort to hide his displeasure at the foolhardiness of her getting out of bed, he laid her with gentle care on the covers and called for Mamie.

"Perhaps it would be best, Mamie, if you remain in the room with Miss San . . . Alexander. Then if she needs anything she has only to ask, rather than rise and put her health in jeopardy." He flashed Marin a look of annoyance before turning to leave.

She couldn't let him get away without answering some questions. But what could she possibly ask?

"Hunter!"

He stopped, clenched his fists at his sides, and turned.

"You mentioned my letters."

"Yes. What about them?"

"Could I possibly read them?" He raised one brow at her odd request. "You see, this blow to my head has confused me somewhat, and I thought perhaps my letters might help me to clarify things in my mind."

He stared at her for a moment, then nodded.

"I'll see they are brought to you. Is there anything else?"

"No. Not right now." Unless he wanted to show her the dimples she was beginning to think she'd imagined.

Hunter rummaged through a very orderly desk, needlessly strewing papers about in his quest for those blasted letters. He knew exactly where they were, but it was somehow satisfying to toss things about in his effort to get them.

Things were not at all as they should be. Right now Miss Alexander should be entertaining his bothersome mother and anticipating her duties as his social secretary. She should be endeavoring to smooth out the social chaos of his life—one tiny facet of many that his mother had wreaked havoc upon. Instead she was ensconced in the guest bedroom, gallivanting around in that filmy night thing, looking down the front of it, and he was forced to catch her and carry her to bed when she decided to swoon. She seemed to have that effect on herself every time she looked in a mirror.

She did *not* have that effect on him when he looked at her. After Delia, and living with his mother, seeing the hell a woman puts a man through made him resolve he would never again let a woman affect him so. Absolutely not.

And damn it all, who gave her permission to call him by his given name? The way she said Hunter—as though she liked the way it sounded on her lips. He refused to consider any possibility that he found the sound pleasant to his ears.

Now here he was, saddled with a vexatious mother and an invalid companion who wants to read letters she cannot remember writing. How he longed for those placid days before his mother's return, when he was king of his domain with no one to find fault with his every word. His house was filling with women and he seemed unable to stop it.

He had promised his father on his deathbed to honor his mother if she should ever come home. If not for that promise, he would have turned his back on her as she had turned her back on her family fifteen years ago.

"Did your father not teach you better order than that, Hunter?" His mother's harsh voice broke into his thoughts.

"You can be sure what order was taught me was taught by my father. I had no mother here to instruct me in such matters." He regretted immediately the momentary lapse that allowed his thoughts to be voiced. Damn Miss Alexander. She was already affecting him in a negative manner.

He snatched up the letters and forced a disheveled drawer shut on several protruding papers while his mother glared with pursed lips. He took a deliberate moment to lock his desk, nodded to her sour countenance, then strode from the room. *Let her stare at those little triangles of paper jutting from the drawer.*

"Izzy," he called to a young servant with a feather duster in her hand, "take these letters to Miss Alexander."

Izzy ducked her head and sidled up to Hunter with her hand extended. He laid the letters in her hand with a degree of irritation. The chit always acted as if she were dodging a blow whenever he came into view. She'd lived at Pierce Hall her entire life and had never seen a day of abuse. No one living under his roof would ever be mistreated.

He snatched the letters back from her fingers.

"Never mind. I'll deliver them myself."

Now why had he done that? He had resolved to remove himself from his exasperating guest until she was prepared to take on her secretarial duties. Well, he supposed he should check on her welfare and smooth any ruffled feathers his mother might cause. Inconvenient though she was, he needed her to stay and keep his mother out of his hair.

Twilight had descended upon the city of Memphis when he stepped into her room. His elongated shadow stretched from the doorway and lay across her coverlet, but he refused to acknowledge the sense of intimacy that simple sight evoked. He opened his mouth to comment that he was glad she had decided to remain abed, but his words caught in his throat.

A single candle on the nightstand shed a golden glow

across the patient. Marin lay among a profusion of pillows under the gauzy canopy of the bed. She now wore a night jacket covered with all manner of pleated, lacy decorations, buttoned clear to her chin. Her rich auburn hair, released from its braid, now curled about her and the pillows in luxurious waves. Those exotic amber eyes were closed in sleep, her thick black lashes fanned almost to her cheekbones.

A discomfiting lurch jarred Hunter's heart. But any man would react in a similar manner, should he stumble across an unexpectedly beautiful scene. Nothing more.

Mamie, too, was asleep in the chair. Hunter pulled his watch from his pocket and snapped open the cover. No danger in allowing Marin to sleep. Instead of waking her, he crept to the side of the bed and laid the letters on the nightstand where Marin would see them when she woke. He took that opportunity to enjoy the lovely view—so different from the muddy, bedraggled waif he had pulled from the ditch.

One side of his mouth pulled up in the hint of a grin when she stirred and sighed in her sleep. His grin disappeared when her sigh turned into sleepy words.

"I love you, Ryan."

When Marin woke, the three-quarter moon waxed in the night sky. At first she was disoriented, then the events of the day tumbled over her memory when she realized she still lay in the antique bedroom and not in her contemporary bed.

So. This was either a very long nightmare, or it was time to start considering the possibility that she'd been thrown through some kind of window in time. It seemed unbelievable, but the proof surrounded her.

When delicious aromas preceded Mamie through the open doorway, Marin realized she was famished. Her throat constricted when she remembered her last solid food had been a pasta salad in—what?—one hundred and twenty years in the future?

Oh, God, how could this possibly be?

"I's glad you awake, miss. I not be wanting to wake you, but Emmaletta's cookin' be too good to let cool." Mamie's cheerful voice and sympathetic smile lifted Marin's spirits a bit. She realized if she was going to survive this . . . indescribable experience, she would have to keep up her strength. At least her appetite appeared to be cooperating.

Mamie fluffed the pillows behind Marin, then set the laden bed tray across her lap. Thankfully the servant didn't stay around to help. Marin wolfed the food down in a way she was sure would be frowned upon in this time—if she *was* in this time.

Just as she polished off the roast beef and vegetables and prepared to spear her first bite of pecan pie, she saw the letters on her nightstand.

Her heart fluttered for a moment. Had Hunter brought these to her while she slept? No. He'd probably sent a servant to deliver them.

This was ridiculous. She had to stop this train of thought. It was one thing to let her feelings go when she'd seen him as a ghost—it had been a little harmless fun—but now he was flesh and blood. It was time to harness her emotions again and build that crumbling wall back around her heart. The last thing she needed was to let herself care about someone.

Her thoughts stirred the remnants of her dream. Remnants best left unexplored. Tears sprang to her eyes as the painful memories of Ryan's death washed over her against her will.

The memory of their last time together cut like a knife through her heart. The argument had been her fault.

She took a deep breath and shook the images from her mind. She couldn't live through this and dwell on Ryan at the same time. She'd go crazy if she even tried.

The food held no appeal for her now. She set the tray aside and picked up the packet of letters. It took several attempts to rid her mind of Ryan's precious face. Only the necessity of learning the background of the body she now inhabited forced him from her thoughts.

Marin was accustomed to the often elaborate style of nineteenth century writing, but even she had trouble deciphering the flowery script confronting her. She would be in trouble if there was ever a handwriting comparison—unless she'd inherited the woman's writing style as well as her body. That was a troubling thought. It could open up a whole new can of worms.

With no pen handy, Marin picked up a fairly clean spoon from her plate and held it like a pencil, handle down. She wrote a few words against an imaginary piece of paper. To her relief, signs of the unreadable loops and embellishments curled in the air with the movement of her "pen." At least she wouldn't have to try and forge Mari's handwriting. And she could always modify it enough to make it more readable.

She continued with her deciphering.

Apparently, if she translated correctly, Mari Sander was unmarried because she'd remained at home in St. Louis to care for a widowed mother. When the mother died, she'd been forced to seek employment. She'd been twenty-nine years old when the letters were written.

A sense of light-headedness struck her. Mari Alexa

Sander had turned thirty on June 24, the same day as Marin. The similarity in their names didn't escape her, either.

The hair at the nape of her neck rose with an uncomfortable tingle.

She took several minutes to focus her thoughts back to the letters. When she did, she found little more information. Mari had been gently bred but impoverished by the war and her mother's illness. Her father had died in the war. So had Marin's. Only it had been in a rice paddy in Vietnam, when Marin was just five.

Thank heavens, Mari's personality didn't show any signs of the frivolity of her handwriting. She seemed to be a woman who relied on herself and would not expect a man to provide for her.

The lines of the letters began to blur in the dim light. Exhaustion overtook Marin. When her head bobbed forward and the fluffy pillows beckoned, she sank back to rest her eyes.

Sometime later the rustle of the letters stirred her as they were removed from her hands. The soft cotton sheet settled gently over her shoulders, and a warm hand brushed a lock of hair from her cheek. The quiet rattle of dishes roused her when the tray was lifted from the bed. She opened sleep-misted eyes to thank Mamie for her care.

Mamie was nowhere in sight, but the broad shoulders of her new employer disappeared through her door, the laden bed tray in his hands.

Chapter 3

"YOU CAN'T BE serious."

There was no way Marin was going to agree to put on the mound of clothing before her. She'd already sat for an eternity while Mamie wove, twisted, and braided her hair. And that was only after she'd attached a long hairpiece to the crown of her head. Mamie put down the ladies' drawers and felt Marin's forehead.

"Miss Marin, ain't you ready to get out of your bed? These be your clothes. Why you don't want to put them on?"

"Because it's ridiculous for a woman to wear all that. . . ."

She kept forgetting she was now a woman of the nineteenth century, or at least dreamed she was. And stupid or not, the women held to very strict rules of dress. If she was to ever get out of this room she was going to have to put on those clothes.

"Very well, Mamie. Help me get into these things." After all, how bad could it be?

She soon found out.

The dressing gown came off and a huge, baggy pair of lace-covered cambric drawers went on. Next came a white chemise, also edged in lace. Embroidered silk stockings slid over calves that Marin would swear had never seen the sun.

The corset, as Mamie tugged at the lacings, caused Marin to wheeze and nearly call a halt to the whole proceeding. She decided to suffer through it for the time being, though. Anything to get out of this room and start figuring a way out of this mess.

Once the strings were tied, the corset cover went on. Marin stepped into a muslin petticoat that had tiers of full, thick ruffles down the back, giving it a bustle effect. Then finally the dress. Marin thought she would buckle under the weight of it. She couldn't help but admire its beauty, however.

The gown was made of deep blue grosgrain with lemon-yellow trim. The skirt had three tiers of tiny pleats, and above those the fabric draped across the front and was caught up in a bouffant in the back. Slender sleeves had open cuffs trimmed in yellow, and a large yellow bow adorned the gathered drapery in the back. White lace trimmed the neck and bodice.

Amazing how such unlikely fabrics and colors could be turned into such a beautiful creation.

The shoes went on last, and surprisingly enough, they were very comfortable. Or maybe the rest of the outfit was so confining the shoes just felt normal. She did learn something, though. Next time the shoes would go on before the corset. Once that corset was laced up, there was no bending over. Poor Mamie had to struggle to help her into the delicate kid slippers.

The cheval glass in the corner reflected the full effect. She might have reacted differently if she had seen *herself* in the mirror.

The dress was beautiful; the woman was beautiful. But she didn't know this person. She felt as if she'd been introduced to a stranger, and she kept expecting the woman in the mirror to hold out her hand to shake. Who was this woman whose reflection she was admiring?

Mamie indicated that breakfast was being held for her, since she had insisted on getting out of bed. Marin pulled her gaze from the stranger's reflection and thanked Mamie for her help before rushing toward the dining room. She quickly found that in nineteenth-century clothes, one did not rush. Her legs were so hobbled in all the draping material, she felt like she was doing a bad imitation of a Japanese geisha.

Hunter and his mother sat at opposite ends of a long cherry table. When Marin arrived he stood and seated her, which was more difficult than she had expected. She sat, then stood and shifted a handful of fabric and sat again. She yanked and pulled her skirts, then stood to rearrange the gown. A glimpse of Hunter, who stood waiting to push in the chair, and his raised eyebrow, did nothing to daunt her, but one look at Lucille Pierce's glare inspired her to sit on the lumps of fabric and suffer through. Now was not the time to lock horns with the lemon-sucker.

Once she settled herself and Hunter moved back to his chair, Mrs. Pierce started in.

"Well, I hope we do not have to look forward to going through that ritual every time we dine."

Marin gave her a half smile.

"I'm sorry to have delayed your meal, Mrs. Pierce."

"What in the world are you doing in that gown at this time of day? You should have on a morning gown. And that color is atrocious. It makes your complexion look even more sickly than it is."

Marin looked her in the eye and bestowed her sweetest smile.

"How very kind of you to point that out."

"Mother, please. Do not use up all your charm on Miss Alexander in one sitting. You should dole it out in tiny portions." Lucille glared at her son's dead-serious face. "Besides, the color is lovely. And the custom of changing one's clothing every hour of the day is ludicrous."

Any further tidbits of charm were interrupted by the arrival of the meal.

It seemed there would be no conversation that would enlighten her about these people. In fact, there would be no conversation—period. The moment the food was brought forth her fellow diners ceased talking. She attempted a casual remark about the weather, but it was met with a silencing glare from Mrs. Pierce.

As soon as he finished his last bite, Hunter touched his napkin to his lips and scraped his chair away from the table to stand.

"If you will excuse me, ladies. Miss Alexander, if you feel up to it I would like to see you in my study at eleven o'clock to discuss your duties. Until then you may spend your time resting or getting acquainted with Mother."

She could have sworn he gave her an apologetic look with his last words.

Once he left the room, Marin turned to find Mrs. Pierce's sky-blue eyes shooting daggers at her. At least Hunter came by his eye color honestly. But where his were kind, and would probably sparkle if he ever smiled, his mother's were just plain mean. She decided to give the woman the benefit of the doubt and make one more friendly overture.

"Your eyes are such a lovely color, Mrs. Pierce. The very same as your son's—"

"Don't try to worm yourself into my good graces with your insincere compliments." The woman nearly spat the words at her as she leaned over her plate. "I don't know what my son has told you about me, but I do not need—nor do I want—a companion. You can go to the devil, and you can take my son with you!"

Marin was at a loss for words. She hadn't expected Lucille Pierce to be pleasant—a person didn't acquire such a parsimonious expression by being sweet—but she certainly hadn't expected this enmity.

And bad blood definitely existed between mother and son. At least it explained why Hunter never smiled. If she'd had to live with this dragon-lady all her life, she probably wouldn't find much to smile about, either.

Marin's first instinct was to tell the old bat what she could go do to herself. But common sense prevailed. Until she found out exactly why she was here, or even *if* she was here, she would do well to play by their rules.

Obviously, kindness would get her nowhere with the woman. It seemed time to take off the proverbial gloves. She placed her fork on the plate and delivered an even stare to the woman at the end of the table.

Hard as it was for her, she bit back the vulgar retort that begged to be voiced and racked her brain for something acceptable to say.

"Your son employed me, Mrs. Pierce, he didn't confide in me. I tried to pay you a simple compliment, but apparently you don't get enough compliments to know how to accept one. I'll do my best to refrain from insulting you with kind words again."

Well, that wasn't the diplomatic repartee she'd intended, but it was hard to be pleasant with this torture device strapped around her body, rearranging all her vital organs. Ah, well. Might as well continue as she'd begun.

"As for going to the devil, I'm not going anywhere unless your son tells me to, and even then it won't be to the devil. We can either make life miserable for each other, or we can not. I'll leave that up to you. I will advise you, though, that I'm not accustomed to allowing people to wipe their feet on me, verbally or emotionally, and I don't plan to start now."

Marin rose from the table and swished her skirts from the chair as if she'd been doing it all her life. She raised her chin a notch. The bones of the corset dug into her flesh and she fought for a deep breath, but she'd be damned if she'd let it show.

"You'll excuse me."

She swept out the door in the best imitation of nineteenth century haughtiness she could muster.

Hunter's new employee crashed into his chest when she marched around the dining room door.

His arms shot out to steady her when she bounced off of him, and he wondered why it was so difficult to persuade his fingers to release the rigid, tiny waist. He hadn't had a problem in recent years distancing himself from women. His mother and Delia could be thanked for that.

Any other woman would have been flustered to come into such intimate bodily contact with a man, but Miss Alexander simply raised one winged brow and looked pointedly at his hands on her waist, then back to his face. Those exotic amber eyes held no emotion, just patience, waiting for him to remove his hands.

He took his time about it and managed to subdue the smile that threatened to curve his lips. This one was spirited. He knew that for a fact now.

He'd overheard the entire conversation between his mother and this fiery lady when he returned to the foyer to retrieve the pocket watch he'd left on the entry table. His first reaction had been to intervene when his mother began spouting her usual venom. What a refreshing experience to hear this young woman standing her ground, rendering his mother speechless. He'd been hard-pressed not to explode in applause at the end of Marin's speech. As far as he knew, this was the first time a woman had given as good as she got and managed to walk away without Lucille's razor tongue slicing her to ribbons.

"I apologize for blocking your escape route, Miss Alexander." He bowed and gestured for her to proceed past him.

"On the contrary, Hunter, I believe it is I who am blocking yours."

She took a few steps past him while he fought down the irritation at the use of his given name and the implication that he'd been eavesdropping.

"Marin!"

She stopped and turned her golden gaze on him. Was that a flash of mischief in her eyes?

"Since we have . . . bumped into each other, we might as well have our meeting."

He didn't wait for her response. He turned and headed for his study without looking to see if she followed. He had to admit he was almost surprised when he heard the click of the study door closing behind him.

He waved her into a burgundy leather wing chair and chose to ignore her strange seating ritual. After she finally sank to the edge of the chair with a barely perceptible wheeze, he didn't bother to mince words.

"I believe you now understand the reason I was forced to go far afield to acquire a companion for my mother. Her reputation in Memphis precludes any local ladies wanting the position." He picked up his letter opener and tapped it on a book. "There was one young lady brave enough to accept the position, but she didn't make it past the foyer before my mother had her fleeing in a cloud of dust."

The birth of a grin curled Marin's pink lips, but she blinked several times and sobered her delicate features.

"Your mother has already informed me of her . . . attitude toward having a companion." Her gaze was steady. This was a woman who was not intimidated by people, be they man or woman. "I won't force myself on her, but I will be available to her if she decides to tolerate my presence. However," she said with only the slightest hesitation, "it's not completely clear to me exactly what my job description is in regard to being your social secretary."

Hunter arched a brow in question, and Marin wondered if that had been the wrong thing to ask.

"I thought I made clear in our correspondence what would be expected of you, Miss Alexander." She really was going to have to dig up those letters. Maybe they would be with her luggage. "However, I will expand on my description.

"I do not plan to entertain much. No more than is necessary. On those occasions when I do, I expect you to organize the gathering in its entirety and act as hostess. I don't want to be bothered with the details, and I do not want my mother involved in the organizational plans. She will appear at the functions only if she wishes."

Marin absorbed this information and squelched the overwhelming urge to ask why he and his mother had fallen out.

"In the household you will be second in command. The servants are to take orders from you, and you have the authority to countermand anyone's orders but mine." Marin took that to mean she had seniority over Mom. How interesting.

"Now." The tapping, which had tapered off, picked up cadence. "I find that I need to have a dinner party for six cotton buyers on Friday."

Her heart dropped to the pit of her stomach. She had six days to plan a dinner party, and she didn't even know her way around the house yet, not to mention what foods were available, what she would be expected to wear, what table conversation was appropriate in 1876. . . . Would she even be here on Friday? Hunter must have seen the emotion in her eyes and misread it.

"I'm sorry for such short notice. I planned this only yesterday, and I could hardly tell you while you were bedridden." He leaned back in his chair and slid the letter opener between thumb and forefinger. "I will endeavor to allow more notice in the future."

A lot of good that did her now. Instead of saying exactly what she thought, Marin said, "That's quite all right. This is exactly what you hired me for, is it not?" She managed to slide off the edge of the chair and push herself into a standing position. If she didn't get out of this corset soon she was going to rip it off right in front of him—if she didn't pass out first from the heat. "If you have nothing further, I'll get started."

She was about to make her escape when his voice stopped her.

"As a matter of fact, I think it best I introduce you to the household. I'm sure you are already well known to them, but you will need to meet everyone in order to properly do your job."

Marin stopped the groan rising in her throat as she led the way to the foyer. She just hoped Lucille steered clear of her. The way this corset made her feel, if the woman tried to bait her right now, she might drop-kick the old bat across the drawing room.

Marin's bedroom door hadn't even clicked shut before she nearly dislocated her arms undoing the buttons on the back of her bodice. Calling Mamie to help would take too long.

The boned bodice stuck to her damp skin, and she peeled it away and tossed it on a nearby chaise. She pulled the straps of her chemise to her waist, yanked at the top of the corset, and unhooked the row of tiny fasteners in a frenzy.

"Ahhhh," exploded from her lips in a long sigh of relief.

How in the world would she function in this heat wearing these clothes? She flung open the armoire doors with the hope of finding something acceptable yet comfortable. But, unfortunately, the more she looked through the gowns, the more she decided that "acceptably comfortable" was an oxymoron in this day and age.

Her hands rubbed distractedly at the deep imprints on her bare midriff, then she massaged the tingling flesh back into circulation. Warm, muggy air filled her lungs when she inhaled fully for the first time since dressing.

What she wouldn't give for one of her cool, flowery skirts and loose cotton tees. At least she'd be able to breathe in those. She'd been forced to wear Mari's clothing for only a few hours, but the prospect of wearing them as permanent attire was already a fashion hell that loomed before her.

Her eyes scanned the armoire again. There was no sign of a gown she could tolerate that wouldn't be met with disapproval. But a neatly tied packet of letters sat on the top shelf above the dresses. She reached up to grab the letters and realized it was the first time she'd moved freely since she'd gotten dressed. It was going to be hard to talk herself into hooking up that corset again.

Marin had settled onto the chaise to read the letters when a movement on the far side of the room caught her eye. She looked up and laughed out loud.

Before her in the pier glass sat a refined woman of the 1870's. Her rich auburn hair was impeccably styled, her gown elegantly understated—except for the chemise hanging below her waist and the corset gaping open to create a huge vee of bare flesh, not to mention the discarded bodice on the back of the chaise.

She had a sense of what one of the "soiled doves" might look like. Being involved in the world's oldest profession had at least one good point: You got to wear fewer articles of clothing. Considering that, and if Hunter was the customer, the profession might not be all that bad. Not bad at all.

There she went again, with thoughts of Hunter coming out of the blue. She was really paying now for letting her guard down, even with a ghost. She consciously laid a few more stones on the wall around her heart, filling up the hole that had started to crumble her defenses. It was time to forget emotions and warm, fuzzy feelings, and get back to the business of this mysterious charade she was living.

Hunter's letters shed no new light on the past of Mari Sander. One letter asked for references. One okayed the references and informed her that she was being considered. The third letter informed her that the position was hers, when he expected her, and where to obtain a bank draft for her traveling expenses.

She studied the bold handwriting and no-nonsense wording. He'd said as much as he needed to with the fewest possible words. She knew instinctively that it fit his personality.

A gentle knock at the door brought her out of her musings.

She slapped the open letter against her chest to cover all that bare skin. Now what was she going to do? Here she sat, nearly nude from the waist up, and someone wanted to see her.

The doorknob turned ever so slowly, and the door began to inch open. Marin searched the room for somewhere to hide, but unless she dove under the bed she was going to be caught nearly topless.

The top of a woolly, salt-and-pepper head appeared, and Marin heaved a sigh of relief.

Mamie's wide eyes blinked several times as she took in the sight before her.

Marin, on the other hand, forced herself to sit there nonchalantly, as if she were in the habit of sitting around half-dressed in the middle of the day.

"Mamie, I was just going to ring for you to help me." The servant stopped blinking. "I always like to loosen my corset about this time of day. It helps . . . with the digestion."

Mamie just nodded in silent agreement, like one would nod at a glassy-eyed person with a rifle in his hand. Nevertheless, she inched her way into the room.

Marin stood and shook out her skirts, then tried to pull together the front of her corset to hook it. Just what she was afraid of—the top of the torture chamber gapped a good inch and a half between hook and eye. Nothing short of a sophisticated pulley system would make those two edges meet. The lacings would have to be loosened and the whole agonizing process repeated.

The hooks were being refastened, Mamie busily yanking on the strings, when, between explosive wheezes, Marin broached the subject that had been bothering her.

"How long have Hunter—OOPH—and his mother been at—OOPH—odds with each other?" She was sure this ill will was not the result of a temporary family tiff.

Mamie paused in her exertions, allowing Marin to catch her breath. "Oh, they's been like that ever since Miss Lucille come back."

"Came back? From where? When?"

Mamie shot her an uncertain look and shook her head.

"It not my place to be talking 'bout Mistah Hunter, miss. You best ask him."

"I would, but he doesn't seem all that open where his mother is concerned. He hired me to be her companion, and maybe if I know the history behind their animosity I'll be able to do my job better."

Mamie considered this for a moment while she tied the strings and settled the chemise back into place.

"Well." She picked up the bodice and held it while Marin slipped her arms in. "I guess it ain't no secret. Any somebody on the street could tell you the story if they had a mind to."

Mamie still looked uncertain, so Marin sat on the chaise and patted the seat beside her. She had to take the woman's hand and pull her down, and still Mamie sat as if she were on a bed of nails.

"Well, miss—"

"Call me Marin."

"Miss Marin—"

"No. Not 'Miss.' Just Marin. After all, we both work here."

Mamie smiled a brilliant white smile and ducked her head. She tried the name out on her tongue.

"Marin." It must have felt good, because she continued. "Miss Lucille come back here a couple years ago, and things ain't been good since."

"Where did she come back from? Why did she leave?"

Mamie kept her eyes averted and began making tiny pleats in the skirt of her apron.

"Mistah Hunter, he bring his daddy, Mastah Nathanial, back here not long after the fightin' started in the war. Mastah Nate got hisself all shot up. Lost his arm to gangrene. Well, Mistah Hunter cared for his daddy as long as he could, but he have to get back to the war.

"Mastah Nate, he be in pretty good shape by then, so he tell Hunter to go on back to his company." The center of Mamie's apron began to look like a miniature accordion. "Miss Lucille, she couldn't hardly look at the mastah. She ain't never been one to make over a body too much, but she don't even want to be in the same room with him.

"Finally one day she just packed up and left. Said she can't be a wife to no cripple. That be back in late '61. Mistah Hunter never heard about his mama leavin' until he come home for a visit in '63 and find her gone. Mastah Nate never told him. Even if'n he tried, Mistah Hunter probably didn't get no mail.

"Anyways, the mastah make Hunter promise he take her in if she ever come back. Poor man loved that woman. He be blind to her true nature." Mamie stared at something only she could see, then clucked her tongue. "Lordy, I ain't never seed that boy so hoppin' mad as when he find out about his mama leavin'. Unless it be the day, thirteen years later, when she showed up on that doorstep out front, uppity as you please, like she just been gone for a Sunday visit."

The entire apron now resembled a huge ornamental fan. Marin wanted to calm Mamie's nervous fingers, but she hesitated to break the spell. She spoke in a soft, coaxing voice.

"What happened then?"

Mamie took a deep breath and looked Marin in the eye.

"This house ain't never heard the likes of the row Mistah Hunter had with his mama. He almost throwed her out, but in the end he remembered his promise to his daddy and let her stay. I thought many a time since he be about to toss her out, but somethin' always stop him." Marin had the distinct feeling that Mamie wished fervently Hunter would forget his promise long enough to rid the house of his mother.

"That woman ain't never had a kind word to say to nobody. She weren't here when Mistah Hunter come home from the war. She weren't here for Miss Blake's wedding. And she ain't never seen her grandchildren."

The last statements captured Marin's attention.

"Miss Blake? Who's that?"

"That Mistah Hunter's baby sister. She marry a man from Virginia right after the war, and now she gots two sweet little babies."

Well, this was news. Her research, what little she'd been able to do, hadn't uncovered a sister, and Hunter certainly never mentioned one. But then, he hadn't mentioned much of anything since he'd turned into flesh and blood.

Mamie stood and fidgeted with her skirts. Clearly, she was uncomfortable with all she'd told.

"Luncheon will be on the veranda when you is ready, miss . . . I mean, Marin. The others should be there soon."

Marin wasn't anxious to share space with Lucille again, but Hunter would be a nice consolation prize. Now that she knew his story, she felt more empathy than irritation. Abandonment, death—they both boiled down to a sense of loss and loneliness, no matter what the age.

Hunter had just started on his dessert when he remembered the list. He pulled it from his coat pocket and handed it to Marin, then he broke the unwritten rule of not speaking during a meal.

"These are the guests for the dinner party. As you can see, there will be no wives, but I will expect you to act as hostess."

Lucille snatched the slip from Marin's fingers and scanned the list with pursed lips. He wasn't sure if her expression was due to the names or the fact that he'd spoken.

"Heathen Yankees," she said with a hiss. That answered his question. "Why, they are the scum of—"

Marin deftly retrieved the purloined slip of paper and moved it out of reach.

"Pretty strong words for someone who spent the war years up Nawth." She drew out the last word in a parody of an accent.

Hunter's head snapped around in surprise, and he nailed Marin with his gaze. It seemed his mother had finally met a woman she couldn't cow. The first building block of respect lodged firmly onto its foundation.

"How dare you take that from me and speak to me thus? You presume too much as a guest in this house!"

Marin looked at Lucille as if she were a simpleton. Hunter found himself looking forward to her rebuttal.

"Mrs. Pierce, I'm not a guest. I'm an employee. Hunter handed *me* the list so I could do my job. If he'd wanted you to have it, he would have given it to you.

"As for my comment, I was merely making an observation. After all, you *did* spend the war years in the North. Or were you trying to make the point that you spent time with the scum of the earth? With heathens?"

Lucille narrowed her eyes into slits and glared with hate at her companion. When her deadly stare elicited nothing more than a sweet smile, she threw her napkin onto her plate and stormed into the house.

Hunter didn't bother wondering where Marin got the background history on his mother. Mamie knew everything and had obviously shared her wealth of knowledge. He would have to speak to her about her gossiping.

But all in all, it might prove to be highly entertaining, watching the women in this house—at least until one of them killed the other.

"That was well done!" He tipped his fork in salute to Marin. "I fear you may need to deal with Mother in such a fashion on a somewhat regular basis. Are you up to the challenge?"

Marin waved her hand in dismissal, as if shooing a pesky fly. She stabbed another bite of lemon tart.

"At my last job I used to eat women like her for breakfast." She seemed to freeze when the last word left her lips. He watched her swallow hard before glancing up at him.

How interesting. This was a bit of history he hadn't heard. And what an odd way to phrase it.

"At your last job?" he prompted. He speared a bite of the lemony tart and waited for her answer. She stared at him with a somewhat surprised expression. Only after he raised an eyebrow to indicate he was still waiting for an answer did she attempt to speak.

"Oh . . . *ahem* . . . taking care of Mother, of course." She stopped and looked at him. He nodded for her to continue. "Well, you know how little old ladies can be. Mom's friends would come to visit, then spend all their time either making suggestions for her care or bullying me about it outright. I got adept at speaking my mind."

She ducked her head and finished dissecting the dessert with the concentration of a surgeon.

Why did he have the feeling her account wasn't quite complete?

It seemed every time Marin managed to immerse herself in plans for the dinner party, another business associate, neighbor, or general busybody dropped in to meet the oddity she was thought to be as a—gasp!—female secretary. How she would love to inform them that the tables would turn, and male secretaries would be viewed with equal skepticism someday.

But now her job was to sit across from the latest curiosity-seekers, neighbors who had dropped by after church, and try to keep an irascible Lucille from embarrassing Hunter. Fortunately the lemon-sucker seemed to be having a civil conversation with the ladies.

Joseph and Pearline Franklin lived down the road in the eyesore they called Rosewood, which was actually a Federal-style house that had Italian Renaissance updates stuck to it like ears on a Mr. Potato Head. Lyford and Ardis Hawks lived next to the Franklins in a tasteful Greek Revival that still held all the elegance of the Old South. Marin listened to the conversation about Lyford's new hobby with half an ear while she tried to figure out why the two couples looked so familiar.

"Yes, I must say I have found it entertaining as well as highly enjoyable. In fact, I have it in the carriage. We wanted to capture Reverend Balsamer for posterity. Would you care to see it?"

Marin blinked at the question. What did he want to show her? Had he even mentioned what "it" was? She looked over at Hunter, who also waited for her reply. When she raised her eyebrows in question at him, he rolled his eyes and turned to Lyford.

"We would be most interested in seeing your camera." He slightly exaggerated the last word and darted a glance at Marin. "I have always been fascinated by photography."

"Well, then, why don't we just snap a picture of our little group here. Won't take but a minute."

That was it! That was why these people looked so familiar. They were the two couples in the picture Marin had found that afternoon after seeing Hunter's ghost.

She followed the group, including a scowling Lucille, onto the porch. While Lyford busied himself setting up his shiny new camera and giving Hunter an impromptu lesson in photography, Marin fought dizziness and tried to quell the prickling tingles that popped out all over her shoulders and neck. How strange she felt, to know what this picture would look like before it was ever taken.

Lyford gathered everyone on the steps of the porch and placed the tripod just so. He adjusted the camera to his satisfaction, held up a hand, then yelled, "Everyone look at the camera!"

Marin's stomach did a somersault. Lyford had to be in the picture!

"Wait!"

Lyford straightened, his face indulgent, as he waited for her to explain.

"You should be in the picture, too!" She cast about, looking for a way to make it possible for all of them to be photographed. Ambrose's woolly head passed by a window at that moment, and she hustled to the door to call the old butler outside.

"Could Ambrose open the shutter so you can be in the picture with us?"

Ardis fidgeted on the second step. "Oh, do, Lyford. You are never in the picture!"

Like a little boy unwilling to share his new toy, Lyford struggled with the suggestion. Finally he pursed his lips and said, "Don't see why not." With the camera readied and Ambrose instructed on what to do, Lyford took his place on the top step with Hunter and Joseph.

"All right now, Ambrose, are you ready?"

"Yessuh." Ambrose nodded solemnly, showing no hint of either disdain or impatience.

"Very well. Everyone ready? Right, Ambrose. Press the shutter button!"

Ambrose's expression never changed, but Marin thought the old servant was highly amused over the whole scene.

Every hair on her body stood on end as she watched the picture being taken that she would find on her desk in one hundred and twenty years. If someone had told her then what was in store for her, she would have declared the person insane.

Chapter 4

"OOPH! OOPH! OH, for Pete's sake, Mamie. Stop!" Marin let go of the bedpost and turned to give the servant a knowing smile. "We've gone over this before. You know how I feel about corsets, and though I may have to wear them, I'm not going to try to win any contests for the smallest waist." Mamie just *tsked* and shook her head. "Besides, since I had all my gowns let out, they would just hang on me if the corset was tight."

Marin had ordered the alterations of the gowns days ago. After two days of being trussed up like a lunatic in a straitjacket, she'd announced the end of her corset-wearing days to Mamie. However, just as she'd feared, once she'd gotten into a gown—with no small effort—she'd been forced to admit that a corset was necessary. Gowns of the nineteenth century were designed like a work of art, meant to encase a rigid, uniform canvas. When the intricate bodice molded to her soft body, the fabric buckled and wrinkled until it looked like she'd slept in it.

She had compromised begrudgingly and allowed the corset to be tied on. But it was not to be tightened, and all her gowns were to be let out as much as possible. It was a minor victory, but enough of one to allow her to breathe.

Once Mamie finished grumbling and tying the strings, she helped Marin into a dressing gown and began to work on her hair.

Marin watched the intricate weaving process in her dressing table mirror. After a week, it was still a shock to see someone else's reflection staring back at her, but oddly enough she didn't resent it. She was beginning to feel comfortable in this new body, with the amber eyes and mahogany hair. Even her smaller stature didn't bother her. She'd come to realize, in the few spare moments she'd had time to dwell on it, that she felt right at home in this time period. The corsets could go to the devil, but the twentieth-century conveniences just hadn't been missed.

This was a side of herself she never expected to see, and her comfort with the whole situation bothered her more than the situation itself. Why was she not freaking out? Could this be one of those dreams where everything bizarre seems totally normal?

She'd nearly driven herself crazy the first few days trying to figure out what had happened to her. But when the excruciating headaches started she decided to just try and live with the situation. After all, until she knew how she'd zapped herself back to 1876, she was helpless to return to her own time. She sure wasn't ready to go out and drive a carriage over the bluffs to see if she'd wake up back in 1996.

Mamie tucked and secured the ends of Marin's hair under

all the loops and braids. The hairstyles were probably the hardest thing to adapt to. Marin was accustomed to shoulder-length hair that turned under after a quick blast of the blow dryer. She might have spent a whole ten minutes on it if she was going someplace special. But these days she was forced to sit, for no less than an hour, while someone else tortured her new thick, wavy tresses into a sculpture to match the style of her attire. At least she'd learned not to destroy it by trying to run nervous fingers through it.

"All done. Now ain't you lookin' as pretty as a brand-new day?" Mamie stood back and admired her handiwork.

Marin touched her fingers to her chest in apprehension. The butterflies in her stomach refused to migrate now that her week's worth of planning was about to come to fruition.

Mamie helped her finish dressing—something Marin was finally getting used to—then she checked her appearance in the pier glass.

Never in a million years would she have pictured herself wearing a get-up like this. She scooped up the train of the cream-and-purple-striped muslin gown, tossed it behind her, then headed for the door, the weight of the train dragging behind her still a foreign feeling in this new body.

The dining room was picture-perfect. She stopped long enough to applaud herself for her efforts. Nine place settings glistened on the ecru tablecloth. The chandelier sparkled, and the mirror above the cold fireplace reflected its beauty. Silver candlesticks flanked the low centerpiece of yellow and white roses. Everything in the room, from the floor to the silver, had been polished until it glowed with a life of its own. How strange it was to see the crystal and china with the sparkle of newness, instead of the chipped and dulled beauty of it in the future. And how many times had she caught a glimpse of herself in the pier glass in the parlor, only to be surprised at the flawless silvering on its back?

"It is unheard of to seat an uneven number of people!" Marin only jumped a little. She was getting used to these sneak attacks. "And one can hardly call it a dinner party if seven of the nine are men."

Lucille Pierce raised her chin and surveyed the room down the length of her nose. Her disapproving gaze swept the length of Marin's costume, but Marin was confident her attire was entirely appropriate. While planning this dinner over the last week, she'd spent as much time studying every ladies' magazine for the proper clothing as she had place settings and dinner etiquette. Her smile was serene.

"The guest list was not my doing, Mrs. Pierce. Of course, if you insist on even numbers, I can have Ambrose remove one of the settings. Keep in mind, though, that Hunter insists on my presence."

Lucille's glare was venomous. She puffed out her already considerable chest and seemed to grow three inches in height. Not unlike a cobra getting ready to strike, Marin thought with amusement.

"If anyone's place is removed, it will not be mine. And you will refrain from calling my son by his Christian name. You are an employee in this house, and you will speak of your betters with respect!"

Hunter stepped into the dining room just then, and the room seemed to take on an extra glow. Marin was thoroughly disgusted with herself when she had to fight the urge to moisten her lips and find a mirror to check her appearance. She didn't want to be attracted to the man. She didn't want to ever feel that close to any person again.

Hunter looked magnificent in black trousers and coat,

with a vest of red silk heavily embroidered in black. A black cravat decorated his tanned throat, set off by a stiff, snowy white, winged collar. A pearl tie pin nestled in the cravat. He yanked at his sleeves as if he were in the final stages of dressing, and Marin's stomach flipped at the sight. She did *not* have the urge to go over and straighten his already perfect collar.

"Mother, I believe you should refrain from judging what is respect and who are the betters. Miss Alexander—or Marin—may address me as Hunter if she wishes. After all, this is the 1870's." Hunter's bland expression was unreadable. The slightly raised eyebrow might have been a sign of amusement, or perhaps just long-suffering tolerance.

Lucille opened her mouth to retort, but instead turned about and stormed from the room.

For once Hunter wasn't relieved to see the back side of his mother. Her departure left him alone with Marin, and he didn't feel equal to the task of finding comments about the weather—anything more meaningful could prove fatal to his resolve to stay aloof. She looked disturbingly fetching tonight.

When he'd walked into the room he hadn't been prepared for the jolt of attraction that flashed through him like a bolt of lightning. Up to this point he'd been honest enough with himself to acknowledge the fact that Marin Alexander was an extremely handsome woman. He tried not to use the word "beautiful" because somewhere in his mind he rationalized that "beautiful" elevated the way he looked at her from admiration to interest. But he was not interested. And why had he given the damned woman permission to use his Christian name?

Marin opened her arms in a sweeping gesture and smiled at him. "What do you think?"

"You take my breath away." Damn! He hadn't meant to say it aloud. "That you've accomplished so much in so short a time, that is. Very industrious of you." He tried to scan the room with his eyes, but they barely flickered away from her face.

He was saved from further uncharacteristic babbling by the sound of horses on the drive.

Ambrose appeared from nowhere to open the massive front door as Hunter prepared to greet his guests. It would be interesting to see what Marin's reaction would be to the men who would assemble under this roof tonight.

Lionel Jacobs entered first. His crutch, necessary because of the loss of his left leg, slowed him only a little. Behind him came Eli Beecham, sound of leg but missing his right hand. Neal Harris had survived the war in one piece—his scars were all on the inside.

Hunter greeted the three business partners and turned to introduce Marin.

"Gentlemen, allow me to introduce my social secretary, Miss Marin Alexander." Six eyebrows raised at the mention of a woman as any type of secretary. "She is companion to my mother and will act as hostess for me at social gatherings."

Marin never missed a beat. She surprised Hunter by stepping forward and charming the three skeptics with a dazzling smile and an easy manner. She stepped up to Lionel Jacobs and offered her hand.

"How nice to meet you, Mr. Jacobs." Lionel took her hand and looked as if he would attempt to kiss it, but she pumped his hand once, then turned to Eli Beecham. Without hesitating she offered her left hand. "Mr. Beecham, I'm very pleased to meet you." Eli balked for a moment, then shook her hand. She turned to Neal and gave him the same attention.

"I hope you gentlemen have brought your appetites. Emmaletta has outdone herself in the kitchen."

Hunter was amazed. There hadn't been the slightest clue that Marin had even noticed the two mangled men, let alone seemed the least bit put off by their injuries.

Bill Shriver, Taylor Matthews, and Dale Gibson arrived only minutes later. Taylor and Dale were both missing an arm, and though Bill was still in one piece, an angry, puckered scar covered the right side of his face, the result of a misfired musket at Shiloh.

Marin gave the new arrivals the same warm welcome she'd given the others. There wasn't a hint of revulsion or condescension. Nor was there any sympathy in her voice or actions. She treated them as if they were the whole men they had been before the war.

Hunter felt a hairline crack develop in the armor around his heart. The strange thing was, he wasn't sure he wanted to repair it.

Maybe, his heart said. *Maybe . . .*

"Hunter, I would have a word with you in the study." Lucille stood in the doorway of the dining room.

At the sound of his mother's intruding voice, the tiny opening to his heart closed up and scabbed over. He excused himself and reluctantly left Marin the center of attention while he met with his mother in the other room. She glared at him, her narrowed eyes speaking volumes.

"Why was I not informed these men were cripples? You did this on purpose, Hunter Pierce. How do you expect me to eat while these . . . creatures are at table? You know how I feel about those people. They make me nervous."

Hunter stared at this woman he called Mother until she looked away.

"So nervous you left your crippled husband, your son, and your daughter. No, Mother, you don't have to remind me of your feelings on the subject. I remember every time I walk by Father's grave."

The blue of Lucille's eyes flickered with guilt for just a heartbeat before darkening to stormy gray as she glared at her son. Hell would freeze over, however, before he apologized for his words or made excuses for not telling her about his guests. There were no excuses. He had simply not told her.

He returned her glare, then after a slow, insolent blink he left the room.

Ambrose announced dinner just as Hunter reentered the parlor.

The meal was much more pleasant than he'd expected, considering his mother chose to dine with them. For the most part she picked at her food, every now and then looking up to wrinkle her nose and purse her lips. He ignored her. So did everyone else.

Conversation never ceased throughout the meal, and he found he much preferred the light banter to the funereal clinks and clatter of silver against china.

Izzy sidled into the dining room and filled all the delicate porcelain cups with fresh, steaming-hot coffee. Eli Beecham hooked his finger in the handle of the cup and picked it up, but suddenly the cup slipped. He tried to stop its downward progress with the stub of his hand, but scalding coffee poured over his arm and drenched his shirt with a steaming, brown stain.

Before anyone else had a chance to react, Marin was out of her chair, peeling the hot, sodden fabric away from the now pink skin on Eli's stub.

Hunter paid no attention to the squeak of disgust from across the table. He looked his mother's way only when she pressed her linen napkin to her lips and flung the chair back from the table. It was a blessing to see the train of her skirts disappear from the room.

He watched Marin grab a linen napkin and dunk it in a water goblet. She wrapped the dripping wet cloth around the blistered skin, then soaked another cloth to replace it. Eli was visibly flustered over the whole situation.

"I must apologize for my clumsiness. I seem to have misplaced my good hand during the war, and I still have trouble doing things as a leftie."

Marin knelt beside the man and lifted away the cool napkin.

"That's understandable, Eli. Let's just hope these blisters don't get too bad."

Did the woman have an aversion to using surnames? Hunter's irritation at her familiarity dissolved as he watched her hold and inspect the scarred, puckered skin of Eli's stub. It might have been a child's healthy hand, so casually did she hold it.

For the first time, the angry, hidden scar on his right leg and the crisscrossing ridges on his back felt a healing tingle. It wasn't a physical healing, he knew. That was long over. This was an emotional healing.

Maybe, his heart whispered again. *Maybe . . .*

"I guess a cripple like me has no business being out in public. I'm so danged clumsy I should just stay at home and do my business from there."

The other men around the table looked as if the same thought had crossed their minds about their own presence in public. What a shame. These men were no older than Hunter—thirty-five at the oldest—and they were maimed because they'd fought for something they believed in. Indeed, they had fought for some of the very people who now abhorred them.

"Don't be ridiculous," Marin said with an indulgent smile. "Why, you men aren't crippled! Look at what you do for a living. You're doubly capable, since you do the same job other men do who have no handicap at all. Where I come from we call that physically challenged, not crippled."

It crossed Hunter's mind that if St. Louis was such a free-thinking city, he might be inclined to make a trip there. He said as much and was joined by hearty agreements from most of his fellow diners. Marin's gaze flew to his at the mention of going to St. Louis, then her porcelain complexion paled to a waxy gray. Drat the woman. What was wrong with her now?

"Miss Alexander, are you feeling ill?"

Before Marin could answer, the front door vibrated with a thundering knock. Ambrose passed the dining room at a slightly faster clip than his usual dignified pace. A murmur of voices could be heard before a complete stranger stormed into the dining room and skidded to a halt.

The tall, well-dressed man had obviously traveled some distance. His black trousers and pinstriped shirt were coated with a fine, pale layer of dust. His hat, which was now in his hand, had left a ring around his midnight-black hair. Anxious hazel eyes scanned the shocked faces of the diners and came to rest on a pair of blank amber eyes that stared out at him.

"Mari! Ah, Mari, me love!"

In the space of a heartbeat the stranger scooped Marin up into his arms and proceeded to crush her to his chest. Marin showed no such enthusiasm in return. Her only reactions were a muffled "Oh" and a halfhearted struggle to be released.

"Ah, Mari, I feared I'd never find ye in this godforsaken hamlet! Why did ye not wait for me to return from Ireland? Surely there was money enough after your sainted mother passed to keep ye till I could fetch ye."

Hunter's meal churned in his stomach at the sight before him—Marin Alexander in the arms of a man who was obviously well-acquainted with her. And a seemingly kind, well-appointed specimen of a man at that. Why, then, did she seem to be in shock, and none too happy about being smashed against this man's chest?

"See here, sir! A proper introduction—"

The stranger's right hand shot out from under layers of cream-and-purple-striped muslin, then he appeared to realize his ludicrous position. He lowered Marin's legs to the floor but kept a possessive arm around her waist.

"Beggin' yer pardon, sir. Niles Kilpatrick, at yer service." He pumped Hunter's hand with enthusiasm but gazed at Marin as though afraid she would disappear if he blinked. "I'll be apologizing for interrupting yer gathering here, but I've been away from Mari for six months. Ye must be Colonel Hunter Pierce. She wrote in her letter she'd be coming to work for ye."

"Letter!" Both Hunter and Marin barked the word at the same time. Marin finally showed some animation. The men finally made eye contact.

"Why, yes. I don't know how you folks here in Memphis do it, but in St. Louis a woman keeps in touch with the man she plans to marry."

"Marry!" Again, the two voices joined in jarring unison. Niles finally loosened his hold on Marin and turned to face her.

"Mari, me love. Don't be telling me ye're having second thoughts. I know six months is a long time, but we agreed we'd wait to wed until after my trip."

Marin's only reaction was an infinitesimal shake of her head and a dazed look of confusion. Dale Gibson swung a chair around behind her just in time to catch the bustle that sank with a thud onto the petit point upholstery.

She was engaged! And this man was calling her Mari. How in the world would she ever explain this to Hunter? And how many other people from St. Louis would crop up to haunt her?

Questions and doubts hurtled through Marin's mind while she sat there with eight sets of eyes trained on her. Unfortunately, no answers accompanied those questions. As her thoughts raced for some coherent, plausible remark, Niles knelt beside her and cupped her face with his hands, his knee and boot buried in the depths of her skirts.

"Mari, ye look as though ye've seen a banshee. Ye canna be telling me ye've changed yer mind."

The air in the room smothered her as she tried to force words past the lump in her throat. All she could manage was a tiny shake of her head as she looked back and forth from Hunter's completely emotionless face to that of the total stranger.

A trickle of sweat slid between her breasts; another formed at her temple and zigzagged along her hairline. The room shrank and the men crowded in on her, then the absolute worst thing she could think of happened.

"Hunter, I would like to be introduced to our newest

guest. I understand he is Miss Alexander's betrothed." Lucille gave her a carnivorous smile from the doorway before she turned to Niles. "How strange she never spoke of her intentions to marry."

Marin began to seriously consider whether or not she could faint convincingly. Should she roll her eyes up in their sockets first or just slide out of the chair?

"Perhaps, Mother, it was due to the fact that it is none of our business." Hunter's cold eyes never left Marin as he introduced Niles.

Maybe she wouldn't have to fake a faint. Maybe she would just shrivel up and disappear before their eyes.

"Mr. Kilpatrick," Hunter went on, "I am afraid Miss Alexander suffered an accident upon her arrival here. Head injuries can often be unpredictable in—"

"Who is Miss Alexander?" Niles asked, his brow lowered in confusion.

The only sound in the room was the ticking of the mantel clock, then the rustling thud as Marin slid to the floor.

Chapter 5

IT WASN'T EXACTLY faked, but then again she hadn't exactly fainted, either. Damn near knocked herself out, though, when she went for the realism.

Between all the events of the past week, including the tender stitches still on her forehead and the arrival of an unknown fiancé, Marin *had* felt that light-headed, disconnected warning. But it would take more than a little exertion and a surprise visitor to send her into a swoon. However, not directing her limp slide to the floor a little farther from the edge of the dining room table was a miscalculation her head could have done without.

The hardest part had been remembering to stay limp when Hunter carried her up to bed. And, for Pete's sake, that had only been after Hunter and Niles nearly dismembered her in a tug-of-war over who should do the honors. Hunter won with an explosive, "For God's sake, Kilpatrick, let me get her to her chambers!"

Now she concentrated on not wrapping her arms around Hunter's warm, masculine neck and dragging him down with her as he carefully settled her onto the fluffy feather mattress. No doubt there was a considerable audience to these goings-on. Marin had been keenly aware of the sound of numerous feet storming the stairs behind Hunter, as well as the *thump, thud, thump, thud,* of Lionel Jacobs bringing up the rear on his crutch. There was also the fact that the room now hummed with the uneasiness of a bunch of helpless men confronted with an unconscious female.

One irritated, not-so-helpless voice grated in the silence.

"Send for Dr. Ritter, Ambrose. I vow, at this rate we shall have to put him on retainer."

Damn! The lemon-sucker strikes again.

She hoped she looked convincingly "passed out." It wasn't like she was an expert at simulating a swoon. But of even more concern to her was what to say when she "came to." She needed time to rehearse. While she was draped, rag doll fashion, across the counterpane, her mind tested and tossed out dozens of speeches.

Deep in thought, she didn't anticipate the vile smelling bottle thrust under her nose. The stench of ammonia burned all the way to her lungs and sent her into such a violent fit of coughing she nearly rolled off the bed.

Once the worst was over she fell back, panting. Tears still blurred her eyes when she opened them, then she had to fight the urge to try her hand at simulating a coma.

Dr. Ritter's skeletal hand held the bottle, ready for another dose of toxic fumes. But the coma-inviting sight that met her was Hunter and Niles, side by side, crowded so close to Dr. Ritter they looked like a bizarre set of Siamese triplets.

Niles hovered next to the doctor, his concerned eyes searching her face. It was obvious he held himself in check to keep from touching her.

Hunter stood farthest from her, though still only inches away. His unblinking gaze, indifferent and cold, was like a hammer to the center of Marin's chest. His only movement was the fingers on his right hand squeezing into a tight fist.

What she wouldn't give to have Niles's anxious look flicker for just a second in Hunter's icy blue eyes. Would she ever see those crescent-shaped dimples that could appear with only the barest hint of a smile? She resolved, once this mess was over, to go in search of those irresistible dents in his face and prove to herself, once and for all, that they were not a figment of her imagination.

"Well now, I know symmetry is a must in fashion, my dear, but I don't believe anyone expects you to obtain matching stitches on your forehead."

Dr. Ritter chuckled at his wit while he examined his patient's eyes and checked her pulse. He poked around on the tender bump above her left eyebrow. At least she hadn't hit the same side as the stitches, but that didn't keep her from having a throbbing headache.

"Now I'm certain there is no concussion this time, but I expect you to stay in bed for at least a day."

Marin cringed at the thought.

"But all I did was bump my head!"

"After fainting, which indicates to me that you were in no condition to be conducting a dinner party."

She'd forgotten about the fainting part. And the dinner party. She glanced around, looking for the audience she'd heard earlier. Everyone was gone except Hunter and Niles, and Dr. Ritter, of course—all three still seemingly attached at the hip. Hunter's stare hadn't changed. She started to run her fingers through her hair, but only managed to tangle them in the braids and loops.

"I'm sorry I ruined your business dinner. Perhaps we can reschedule—"

"Nothing has been ruined. In fact, my guests are still here. They all refused to leave until they were assured you were not in danger."

Such total lack of emotion when he spoke. How could this man be her mischievous ghost, who'd shown more emotion in one speechless encounter than the flesh and blood man had in the week she'd spent here?

This was a bad dream. It was the only explanation. She was in the hospital, on some heavy duty drugs, and this was just a result of that. That's it. A bad dream. In fact, if she tried real hard she could probably hear the beep of monitors and smell the disinfectant, maybe even hear some doctor being paged.

"All right, gentlemen. Let's leave the little lady to her rest." Dr. Ritter fastened his satchel, and Mamie walked in as if on cue, bearing a tray with a teapot and cup.

Niles spoke up for the first time, anxiety written all over his face.

"I'll be wantin' a word with me Mari, if you don't mind, Doctor. I've not seen her now for six months—"

"So another few hours won't make much difference." Dr. Ritter clapped Niles on the back and guided him toward the door. "Her rest is of utmost importance, and tomorrow will be soon enough to enjoy a tender reunion. I will be back to check on you then, my dear, and we shall get those blasted stitches out while I'm at it."

Niles left with reluctance, throwing backward glances over his shoulder at Marin.

"I'll be thinkin' of ye, Mari me love," he said as he rounded the door.

Hunter was the last to leave. He stood near the foot of the bed, where he'd been all along, and looked at Marin. Just looked. No emotion whatsoever. No look of accusation, distrust, disgust, or even concern. He might have been staring at a nail in the wall, for all the animation in his face. Before Marin could speak, he turned on his heel and walked to the door. His steps slowed only long enough for him to comment, and even then he spoke with his back to her.

"If Kilpatrick has nowhere else to stay, I will see to it that a room is made ready for him . . . Mari."

The last word held no animosity, but Marin literally felt the thin thread of trust that had formed between them snap and recoil.

There was no chance for her to speak. His stiff back disappeared around the door, and he was gone before she could catch the breath he'd knocked out of her.

What could she have said, anyway. . . .

"I know you won't believe me, but I'm from 1996."

Her eyes never wavered from his. Sitting across from him in her bedroom, she tried to look as sane and sincere as possible.

The sun shone in a cloudless morning sky the color of Hunter's eyes, a breeze from the open window stirred his dark, touchable hair, and they both sat there ignoring the fact that his presence in her bedroom was completely unacceptable. But she'd wanted privacy for this confession, and this was the last place the lemon-sucker would look for him.

His silence was almost palpable following her statement, until he blinked once, inclined his head, and said, "Indeed."

Her heart sank, and she couldn't stop a frustrated sigh. She'd known better. What had she expected him to do—slap her on the back and say, "Well, hey! Why didn't you say so before now?" She closed her eyes, shook her head, and plowed on.

"I don't expect you to believe me. I barely believe it myself. In fact, I don't even know what to believe." She shrugged and waited a moment to see if he had a reaction. He didn't. "All I know is, I was in an accident in 1996, and I woke up in 1876. My name isn't Mari Alexa Sander, but apparently I'm in her body, because I really have light brown hair and gray eyes, and I'm at least three inches taller.

"I've never laid eyes on Niles Kilpatrick before last night, but apparently he and Mari are engaged, but I don't know where Mari is.

"Hey, I'm not even sure where *I* am! I may be in a coma in the hospital and just hallucinating all this. That would make the most sense, wouldn't it?"

Good God, she sounded like a raving lunatic, even to herself. Why hadn't she thought this thing through better before opening her big mouth?

He continued to stare at her, but now the barest glimmer of amusement lit his eyes. She would have questioned if there was even a change in his expression, except that one elusive dimple hinted at its existence. Yes, there was a definite crescent-shaped indentation in his left cheek.

The subtle alteration changed his whole countenance. She could see her mischievous ghost behind the stoic facade, and her heart rate leapt to aerobic level. The already humid air heated up a few more degrees. She forgot about her confession and relived the exchange the two of them had shared on the front lawn.

"Well, Miss . . . I'm sorry. What is your name today?"

Marin came crashing back to reality. She wasn't sure which irritated her more—his interrupting her knee-weakening reverie or his sarcastic question, delivered with such a bland expression.

"Marin. My name is Marin. Always has been, always will be," she said through clenched teeth.

"Ahhh. Marin. Of course. Well, Marin, I can understand changing your mind about marrying someone, but I must tell you that when it comes to devising an excuse, the usual rule of thumb is that less is more." He leaned forward in the chair conspiratorially, a hand planted on each knee. When he spoke again his voice was not much more than a whisper. "In this case you may have gone a tad over the line. Believability should be your watchword. Unless, of course, you want him to think you've gone mad. Would you like for me to help you construct a more convincing story?"

Both dimples were in deep evidence now, flanking the most condescending grin she'd seen since Ryan had laughed at her fear over his last desert mission.

Anger exploded in her mind—at Ryan for dying and at Hunter for his supercilious attitude. She narrowed her eyes and glared at him while her temper settled under control.

"Am I fired?" she asked, her voice dripping icicles.

"Excuse me?"

Ha! She threw him off guard with that one.

"Am I fired? Terminated? Canned? Lost my position?"

He sank back onto the green-and-white-striped satin

chair, obviously perplexed at this sudden change of tone and direction in the conversation.

"Well?"

"Of course not. Your work since your arrival has been exemplary, but I fail to see what—"

"What I told you is the truth. I don't expect you to believe it, but I don't intend to change my story. Bearing that in mind, do you still want to employ me?"

Hunter stared at her, clearly sizing up whether she was indeed insane or just incredibly strange. He shook his head as he rose from the chair and walked to the door.

"I fail to understand what purpose this tale serves, and I have enough trouble with my mother stirring up ill will toward the Pierce name." He grabbed the porcelain doorknob before turning back to her. His face was an unreadable mask. Marin held her breath and thought she might scream before he finally spoke.

"You may retain your position with the stipulation that your . . . story . . . not be repeated."

Marin didn't hesitate. She knew there was nowhere for her to go if he kicked her out. She, or rather Mari, had very little money, and Marin knew no other way to earn an income in the 1800's. At least none she was willing to do.

"Very well," she said. It was hard to keep the relief from her voice, so she raised her chin to a stubborn angle.

Hunter nodded once and yanked open the door.

Lucille Pierce stood on the other side, her mean eyes glittering, her mouth pursed.

"And what story would that be?" she asked.

Hunter balled his fists at the sight of his mother.

"It is a story, Mother, that is not going to be repeated. If you did not hear it while eavesdropping, then you are

doomed to forever wonder what it is you're missing out on."
He shoved past her and flicked the door closed behind him.

These women would have him in an asylum soon. Perhaps he would be in the same one as Marin. She would surely end up in one if she continued to spread that ridiculous fairy tale.

"Hunter Pierce! I have a right to know what is going on in this house! Benjamin Hunter Pierce!"

Her voice faded as his strides ate up the length of the hall. He descended the stairs at a fast clip.

Why had he not dismissed Marin on the spot? He could not credit his behavior. If a friend came to him with the story of employing a woman who wrote under one name, came to work under another, then claimed she was from the future, he would advise that friend to dismiss the lunatic immediately, and without a reference.

Instead, he couldn't even summon up the outrage he knew he should feel. After all, she'd had a head injury. Surely that was the cause of her strange behavior. Surely.

He clumped down the center of the staircase, wanting nothing more than to be left alone. But it was not to be. Ambrose advanced on him, a small silver tray held aloft with a single black-edged calling card in the center. Hunter held in the moan that rose in his throat.

"I am not at home, Ambrose. Whoever it is, send them away."

"I's sorry, Mistah Hunter, but she—"

"Was hoping you wouldn't turn her out."

A chill of dread crawled across his neck at the familiar feminine voice. Even though it had been over five years since he'd heard it, there was no mistaking that voice.

He studied the silver tray and calling card that still hovered in front of him. It couldn't be her. She wouldn't have the nerve to come back here.

His lip curled in disgust before he finally turned his head and met her eyes.

"Delia. How very unpredictable of you." He stepped down to plant both feet on the floor, then shifted his weight to his left foot, his stance deceptively casual. "If I remember correctly, the last time we parted you were retching at the sight of me. Forgive me if I don't anticipate what you have in store for me this time."

She at least had the decency to look uncomfortable.

As she stood there, wringing her hands in the doorway of the parlor, he scanned her body from head to toe.

It was hard to imagine what he had seen in this woman. Yet he had once planned to marry her, until she broke off the engagement. The face whose image had kept him alive during his recovery from his war wounds had contorted with barely disguised revulsion at the sight of the still-livid scars puckering his skin.

Her face—once so precious—now failed to stir any warm feelings at all. Not because the blond of her hair had lost some of its sheen, or because her pale skin looked more gray than porcelain. It was because she had turned her back on him when he needed her most, then returned five years ago to do it again. She'd killed the love in him. She and his mother.

"To what do I owe this questionable pleasure, Delia? Should I go in search of a shield now, to keep your knife from my back, or are you saving that for later?"

Delia started to speak, then glanced up to the landing. Hunter's mother stood under the glistening chandelier, her back ramrod straight as she glared at the two of them.

"Could we possibly speak in the parlor, Hunter?" Delia's voice sounded thready. She muffled a delicate cough as she followed him through the archway. He slid the pocket doors closed with a decisive bang.

He turned an emotionless gaze to her. She settled her black gown around her as she sank onto the deep peach settee. The black of her gown washed her features out to the point of peakedness. With a bit of a jolt he remembered the black-edged calling card. He knew she was a widow. She'd been a widow five years ago. But he was certain this mourning attire was not for that long-dead husband.

"I see you've noticed my widow's weeds." She plucked at the ebony bombazine skirt with a thumb and forefinger. "I remarried after David died. My husband, William, passed away three months ago."

Hunter allowed no look of sympathy to cross his features. "Bad luck with husbands, Delia? Perhaps you did me a favor." He lowered himself to the matching settee and waited for her to get to the point of her visit. He'd be damned if he'd make things easy for her. If she was back to pick up where she'd left off, he was not going to play the fool again.

The silence lasted only seconds before she dropped her hands to her lap and met his gaze.

"I do not have time to mince words, Hunter. I came here because I am sick. Actually, I am dying. The doctors give me only a few weeks." She paused and waited for him to speak, but he could find no words. He was sorry, as he would be for any dying person, but he could not see what it had to do with him.

"I have tuberculosis." She hesitated and picked at her skirts again, her head bowed.

The tuberculosis would explain her pallor and the delicate

coughs she'd been stifling. He still could not see how any of this concerned him.

"The last time we were together, Hunter—"

"You are referring to the second time you gagged at the sight of my body?"

A tide of red swept over her features, all the more noticeable because of her ashen color.

"Yes. I see you remember," she said in a quiet voice.

"Vividly."

"Then you should also remember that during the night we had been . . . intimate."

"Yes. How fortunate for me we failed to light the lamp until it was over. I would imagine it would be somewhat offputting to attempt to make love to a retching woman."

She jumped to her feet and turned her back to him.

"Please, Hunter, let me say what I have come here to say."

She held her peace for a moment, and Hunter kept silent. At his acquiescence she spun around to face him. She gripped the back of the settee until her fingers threatened to puncture the fabric.

"We have a daughter from that night. I want you to take her and raise her."

Chapter 6

NOTHING, ABSOLUTELY NOTHING, could have prepared him for the words she'd just spoken. His first reaction was to feel as if he'd been kicked in the gut. The next was total disbelief.

Women had proved to be fickle creatures since his earliest memory of his mother. Now Delia was telling him that he had procreated one? Preposterous!

"Delia, you have had two husbands, yet you tell me that this child is mine? Let me remind you that the scars I bear are on my body, not on my brain."

Delia circumvented the couch to grab one of Hunter's hands and sink to the Aubusson carpet in front of him.

"It's true, Hunter. Katie is yours." *Katie, is it?* he thought. "Anyone can see that with just one look. William knew she wasn't his, and his family knows. They refuse to take her in once I . . . If you refuse she'll end up in an orphanage. Could you sentence your own daughter to grow up in an orphanage?"

He stared at her, horrified and confused. She returned his stare, and though her illness-ravaged face was drawn, it held no indication that she told anything less than the truth.

Dear Lord, he couldn't have a daughter. What would he do with another female in the house? He was overrun with them as it was.

The stifled cough that escaped Delia's lips became deeper, until she could no longer control it. The cough became so violent she reached into her sleeve and pulled out a rumpled linen hanky. She could barely catch her breath between coughs when Hunter helped her to her feet and backed her onto the settee. When she fell back onto the dark peach brocade, Hunter caught a glimpse of crimson staining the snowy white fabric pressed against her mouth.

He crossed to the crystal decanters sitting on a rosewood table and sloshed a generous amount of brandy into a snifter. When the liqueur spilled onto his hand, he angrily slung the amber droplets from his fingers.

Once Delia managed to catch her breath, Hunter offered her a sip of the pungent liquid. She sipped, muffled a cough, then sipped again. A bit of color returned to her pallid skin, and her coughing seemed to be under control. She crumpled the bloodstained hanky into her fist and patted her hair with a weary hand.

"I assume you now believe me about my illness. That Katie is your daughter is no less the truth. Will you allow me to die secure that my child is with her father?"

Hunter felt sweat dampen the collar of his shirt. Dear God. A father. Everything inside him rebelled at the thought.

"Delia . . ." His mind was unable to produce rational thought. He huffed a frustrated breath and paced the length of the room. "I am not the person to be raising this child."

"You are her father."

"Even if what you say is true, I am still not fit. A quarter of an hour ago I was a childless bachelor. Now I am a father? And to a girl child? I know nothing of children. This house is no place to raise a child. I know. I am a product of its environment."

Hunter stopped his pacing, about to point out that his mother was reason enough to keep a child away.

A sharp rap sounded on the doors.

His hackles rose at the thought of his mother eavesdropping. No doubt she now had an opinion she wanted to voice. Well, he had an opinion or two for her.

"Come!" he roared, his voice nearly rattling the windows.

The doors rolled back to reveal Ambrose, not Lucille, on the other side. Ambrose's long-suffering face betrayed nothing when he spoke; he didn't even look down at the lacy growth attached to his leg.

"You has a visitor, suh."

Just then a strange, portly black woman appeared and tried to detach the child who clung like a leech to Ambrose.

"Chile, you let go of the man. He gots work to do."

The woman tugged at a mass of blue and white ruffled eyelet while Ambrose studied the crown molding along the ceiling. The child's face was buried in the back of the butler's scrawny thigh, her arms wrapped around his knee.

"I's sorry, Miss Delia, but this chile done got it in her head to come in, and she was out the carriage and in the house afore I could catch her." All the while she spoke, the woman tugged at the little girl.

"It is all right, Lucretia. I was just about to send for you."
Delia turned her attention to the bundle of fluff still attached
to Ambrose's leg. "Katie, come here to me, darling."

Hunter watched this scene unfold with a disbelieving
stare. This was the child he was supposed to raise?

At the sound of Delia's voice, Katie stopped struggling
and peeked at them from between Ambrose's lanky thighs.
Hunter's first impression was of a huge pair of sky-blue
eyes, round with curiosity and fringed with black lashes.
The eyes were framed by shiny dark brown curls so wispy
they had to be baby-fine. Her tiny nose and little pink lips
made her look more fragile than a china doll.

She peered from between the safety of the legs, then her
face disappeared. The wide eyes emerged again on the left
side of the butler's legs. She inched her way around Ambrose, then finally let go when Lucretia took her hand and
walked her forward. Her wide eyes never left Hunter's.

She was dressed in a blue ruffled dress with a white ruffled pinafore. On her tiny feet were white button shoes, and
she wore a big blue bow on top of hair that fell in bouncing
ringlets to her shoulders. Hunter had never seen anything so
delicate in his life.

This was the child he was supposed to raise?

He watched her take slow, wary, little-girl steps in her
journey across the room.

"This is your new papa, darling," Delia said in a weak
voice. "The one I told you about after—"

"Delia!" Hunter barked the name and spun to face her. "I
have not—"

Before he could finish, a blue and white blur sped across
the room. He looked behind him in time to see a little face

smash into the back of his right thigh at the same moment her arms went around his knees in a death grip.

He stared at this new appendage with horror. How did one go about removing a child from one's leg? His right foot remained rooted to the floor while his left foot inched around in a circle. He felt like a dog chasing its tail.

"Here now, child. Release my leg. No, no. Don't squeeze there! Damn it, Delia! Have you no control?"

Delia's light laughter sounded like her old self, and there was a familiar twinkle in her eyes when he looked at her.

"Please watch your language, Hunter. She has an abominable habit of repeating the less desirable words she hears uttered. And as for her clinging to you, she has been that way since she was old enough to walk. Whenever she senses she is in trouble, she goes directly to the person she has provoked. It is an effective tactic, is it not?"

The child refused to look at him or lessen her grip on his leg. With an indignant huff, he took several steps, expecting to dislodge the unwelcome visitor, but all he accomplished was to lift her bodily and move her with him.

"Pick her up, Hunter. She is your daughter."

Hunter leaned sideways and grasped the clinging child under the backs of her arms, then transferred his grip once she was at eye level. She dangled at arm's length in front of him like a wiggling sack of snakes. She was all soft and pudgy, yet he could feel her ribs beneath her clothing. As fragile as a bird, he thought, then gentled his grip even more for fear he held her too tightly. He turned to Delia.

"I wish you would not refer to her as my daughter in the child's presence, Delia. We have come to no . . ."

His speech trailed off, forgotten, as the little girl peeped up at him through lowered lashes, then raised her head minutely. Sky-blue eyes peered back at sky-blue eyes. The exact shade of his own dark brown hair framed her cherubic face. Hunter felt the sweat pop out along his neck again. It became a steady trickle between his shoulder blades when the tiniest hint of a smile produced a perfectly round baby dimple in her left cheek.

He was looking at his own face. Any denial of his paternity to this child melted like a snowflake in the sun. A person would have to be blind not to see the resemblance. He glanced at Delia, who smiled up at him with a weak, smug smile.

"One would think I had no part in her creation, so much does she favor her father."

Katie picked that moment, before Hunter had a chance to reply, to propel herself toward his chest and lock her arms around his neck. Her face immediately disappeared into his shirt collar. She snuggled up closer when he drew her near and perched her on his arm.

What an amazing, foreign feeling. All of his senses came alive. Her silky hair brushed him under his chin when she burrowed her face deeper into his neck. She was a healthy, plump little thing, yet she was light as a feather, and her tiny bones could be felt beneath all those ruffles. She smelled of soap and starch and fresh air.

He tucked in his chin and looked down at her, but her face was still hidden. A shiny curl tickled his jaw, and he nuzzled his chin against the ringlets.

An unfamiliar emotion, so fierce it took his breath away, seized his heart and squeezed with a vengeance. He waited for it to subside, but it only mellowed into a steady warmth.

"My daughter." The two words were uttered with wonder; part statement, part question.

Katie raised her head and turned wide blue eyes on him. Her warm little hands rested on his cheeks; the weight of them felt like butterflies. She studied his face a moment with childish coyness, then spoke the one word he thought never to hear himself called.

"Papa?"

His heart thudded in his chest. A desire to protect this little being rose in him, along with panic over whether or not he could learn to be a father.

"Papa, indeed." The hateful voice came from the open doorway.

Hunter didn't have to turn to see his mother's sneer; her prunish face was reflected in the mantel mirror. Her voice quivered with disapproval while his resentment raged inside him. He was not allowed even a few moments of this wondrous feeling of fatherhood.

"Well, well. Delia Cabot. So you have returned to Memphis after all these years." Lucille walked into the room as if queen of the manor.

"Yes, Mrs. Pierce. For a brief stay. I will be leaving in two days."

"Oh, I see. You are just staying long enough to shove your bastard child off on my son."

Delia's gasp lasted longer than the time it took Hunter to deposit Katie in her mother's arms and tower, inches away, over his mother. His voice was not much louder than the rustle of silk skirts, but the words were delivered with all the feeling of a thunderclap.

"You will never refer to this child in such a manner again. If you do, you will be out of this house and on the street before the last syllable is uttered. You will not poison my daughter's childhood with your vitriol as you poisoned mine."

"You cannot seriously contemplate allowing—"

"I am contemplating nothing. Katie will live here." It was surprising how easily the decision came to him. As soon as the words were spoken, he knew there was no other choice he would have made.

A sudden movement caught his attention. He looked up to see Delia staring into the entry hall, her pale skin even more colorless. Marin stood with uncertainty just beyond the doorway. In her arms were the freshly laundered table linens from the night before. Delia misunderstood the domestic picture.

"I did not realize you had married, Hunter. Your wife should be included in this decision. After all, it will affect her life as well."

Marin's eyes darted to Hunter, then back to Delia.

"Me? You think I'm married to . . . Oh, no! Hunter and I aren't married! I'm his social secretary!" She stepped into the room and thrust the linens out, as if making a point. "I was just putting these away for Mamie when I saw everyone in here. I'm sorry I interrupted." She was about to turn and leave when Hunter stopped her.

"Marin. This will concern you in a roundabout way." He looked at Delia, aware that the uses of their first names were the cause of Delia's upraised brows. He did not like that knowing look. Her presumptions were wrong. "Allow me to introduce my social secretary, Miss Marin Alexander. Marin, this is . . . an old friend, Delia Cabot."

Delia nodded to Marin and smiled. "Actually, I am Delia Branson now."

"It's nice to meet you, Mrs. Branson." Marin turned to Katie. "And who is this charming little lady?"

Lucille picked that moment to remind everyone of her presence. "This little lady, it appears, is Delia and Hunter's ba . . . daughter."

Marin's eyes opened wide in question before a noncommittal veil dropped over her features. For reasons he could not begin to fathom, Hunter hoped fervently that she would not think the worst of him.

Marin didn't bother to rationalize why her heart dropped to her stomach at Lucille's words. She had never been one to lie to herself. Try as she might, she hadn't been able to overcome the attraction she felt toward Hunter. It had been this way with Ryan. She'd fought and fought against loving someone, but in the end Ryan's mischievous pursuit and magnetic personality had won out over all her convictions. The difference now was that Hunter wasn't pursuing. And he most definitely wasn't mischievous. But, God help her, he was devastatingly magnetic!

Now, however, there was another woman involved, and a child. It would be a mistake to assume she was a long lost wife, considering Lucille's thin-lipped frown of distaste. Marin didn't think a legitimate union and child would generate that much pulsating disapproval, even from the lemon-sucker.

Uncertain exactly of the protocol called for in this situation—in any century—she decided to simply change the subject.

"Well! I'll just put these linens away and then check your appointment book."

"If you do not mind, Miss Alexander, before you leave I would like to assure the household that I have kept myself isolated from Katie. We even came in separate carriages, so you should have no fear of exposure to my illness."

A gasp of shock erupted from Lucille's vicinity. Marin ignored it and crossed the room to sit beside Delia. She laid her warm hand on the frail alabaster one.

"What kind of illness do you have? Is it serious?"

Delia stifled a cough with a wadded handkerchief. "I have tuberculosis."

Lucille let out an offended squeak and fled the room at a healthy trot. Delia squeezed the hanky into a tighter ball while a pink tinge suffused her chalky features. "I have brought Katie here to live with Hunter."

It didn't take a genius to read between those lines. This beautiful, golden-haired woman was going to die, and soon. She was also embarrassed by the fact that her daughter was not her husband's child. Marin was never good at words in these types of situations, but she could at least make the poor woman comfortable. She turned an accusing eye on the man who had gotten this girl pregnant and hadn't bothered to marry her.

"Would it be asking too much for some tea or coffee for your guest? Lowly employee that I am, I know enough to offer refreshments."

Hunter looked as though he'd been slapped. It was hard to keep the spark of satisfaction from her face at knowing she'd hit a target.

She turned back to Delia, who was gripped in a violent fit of coughing. She fluffed a heavily fringed throw pillow and placed it behind Delia's back, then handed her the abandoned glass of brandy which sat on the table next to her.

"Here now, drink this and we'll have some tea for you in a minute." She leaned close to the sick woman's ear and whispered, "The lemon-sucker is gone. That alone should make you feel better."

Delia's giggle only aggravated her coughing. By the time Mamie arrived with a pot of tea, her face was as scarlet as the splotches on her handkerchief.

"See if you can sip some of this. It should help your cough." Marin held a cup of tea generously laced with honey and lemon to the poor woman's bluish lips.

Hunter had remained uncharacteristically quiet throughout this entire scenario. She darted a dagger-filled glance his way and saw that he sat across from them, staring at her as though she'd sprouted another head. She was formulating a scathing remark when a tiny, warm hand came to rest on her knee.

"Is my mama sick again?"

Thoughts of dressing down Hunter fled when she looked at that worried little face. It never occurred to her to lie.

"Yes, sweetheart, your mama's not feeling very well."

"Is Mama leaving again?"

Marin wasn't sure what plans had been made. When was Delia going to leave Katie here for good?

Delia answered the question herself. "Yes, darling, Mama has to leave, but I will come back and visit tomorrow. Will you show your father what a big girl you are while you stay the night here?"

Katie's eyes, perpetually wide with curiosity, suddenly glistened with unshed tears. She looked sideways at a silent Hunter, then at Marin, before looking back to her mother. Marin's heart tugged when Katie's chin began to quiver.

"Mamie!" Marin called to the retreating back of the servant.

"Yessum?"

"Do I remember seeing a fresh batch of cookies being baked this morning? And don't we have quite a few lemon tarts left over from dinner last night?"

Mamie's white smile lit up her round face. "Why, yessum. We sho do." She allowed her face to take on such an innocence Marin nearly laughed aloud. "Problem is, miss, we cain't find nobody to eat 'em."

"Hmmm." Marin turned to Katie, who was now watching her with a great deal of interest. "Do you happen to know anyone who could eat up some of those extra cookies?"

Katie's quick little nod set ringlets to bouncing. "I could eat up some of those cookies!"

"Wonderful! Do you think you could help us get rid of a few of those tarts, too?"

This affirmative nod jostled the big blue bow into a precarious wobble.

"The only problem is, there are so many, we may have to stay up late eating cookies and tarts. We might even have to eat them for breakfast. Do you suppose you could stay here and help us out?"

Katie turned to her mother, who smiled her approval. Marin rose, shook out her skirts, then took Katie's hand.

"Kiss your mama good-bye, then we'll go see what kind of damage we can do to that pile of cookies."

Delia started to protest. "I might expose . . ." But in the end she pulled her daughter to her and held her hard against her breast. A single tear squeezed through her tightly shut lids, which she dabbed away before setting Katie from her. Marin blinked back some unexpected tears of her own.

"You be a good girl. Mind your father and Miss Alexander . . . and your grandmother." This last seemed to be an afterthought. When Katie turned to go, Delia's voice rang a bit stronger. "I love you, Katie."

"I love you better, Mama."

Marin drew in a sharp, painful breath. I love you better. When Marin thought about her father, she remembered the last words they'd spoken to each other before he got on that transport plane to go to Vietnam and die. Now here was little Katie, about the same age as she when she lost her father, uttering similar words to a mother she was soon to lose. Katie's little fingers wrapped around hers. It was best they find the kitchen before Marin's memories became any more vivid.

Hunter studied the mass of childish blue and white ruffles retreating alongside the sophisticated drapes and swags of a yellow satin bustle. But his mind was not on fashion, nor, for a change, on the woman wearing the yellow satin.

A daughter. Good holy heavens! A daughter. Did one feel so totally unequal to the task of parenthood if one had nine months to contemplate the chore, rather than having it thrust upon him one day between breakfast and lunch?

He swiveled his head back to Delia and stared. He expected her to squirm under his scrutiny, but she returned his level gaze.

"She is a very good girl, Hunter. You should have no trouble with her. I have not allowed us to spend much time together, for fear of infecting her. Because of that . . ." She had to stop for a moment to collect herself. "Because of that, she should not miss me overly much when I . . . leave."

Hunter softened somewhat toward this woman who had once held the power to stir him. "Why did you not tell me of the child, Delia? Were you so repulsed by me that you would not have me as her father?"

"On the contrary, Hunter. I am deeply ashamed of my behavior that night. Since my disease has taken its toll, I have come to understand about physical imperfections." She leaned back, allowing her spine to relax against the cushions. Clearly she was tiring to the point of exhaustion. But she was determined to have her say. "I felt, after the way I comported myself, you would be monumentally disinclined to have me for a wife. I will also admit my pride would not allow me to become your wife if your only motivation was that I was with child. I was a foolish, thoughtless girl who, too late, has grown into a very repentant woman."

Hunter could not argue that she had changed. This forthright woman was a far cry from the overly sensitive girl he'd left heaving into a chamber pot five years earlier.

The memory caused the puckered scars on his back and upper thigh to throb as though not yet healed. To throb as they had when Delia went into a decline at the sight of them. The softening left him as quickly as it had come.

His jaw tightened when he turned a cold stare to her.

"What is my daughter's full name?"

Delia blinked at his sudden change of attitude. It was a moment before she spoke.

"Why, her name is Kathleen Pierce Branson."

He could not say why the second name irritated him so. He would have been even more displeased if his family name had been ignored altogether. But, damn it, Pierce should have been her surname. If he'd known he had a daughter these past years, perhaps his life would not have been so unbearably empty. However, the lack of fulfillment in his life was not a topic he allowed himself to dwell on.

"And her date of birth?"

"She was born so close to midnight I am not sure whether it was the eighth or the ninth of January, 1872. We have always celebrated on the ninth."

This piece of information irritated him as much as the name. His daughter should not have to wonder about her birth date. Someone should have made certain of the time.

"Hunter, I cannot change what I did in the past. I can only apologize profoundly." Delia's voice was thready, almost breathless. "I know my vanity and immaturity caused us both a great deal of suffering. I would undo it all if I had the power."

She struggled to the edge of her seat, then sank once more to the carpet at Hunter's feet.

"I have been a good mother to Katie. She has always been loved, even by William. And, yes, he knew she was not his daughter." She paused, her eyes glistening with unshed tears. "He was a good man. It seems I have been unduly blessed with good men in my life, for all of my fond acquaintances have been such."

Her hand hesitated only a moment before it slowly, deliberately came to rest on his inner thigh. The rigid, gnarled scars beneath the fabric of his trousers were warmed by the heat of her hand. His eyes closed involuntarily as he fought off the sudden, sharp ache her gesture created.

"See, Hunter? You are not repulsive. It is only the small mind of a woman too blind to look beyond the scars that is repulsive. Promise me you will remember that."

Chapter 7

DELIA WAS DEAD.

Marin couldn't believe the lovely woman she'd just met yesterday was now being prepared for burial, and Hunter was asking her to help make arrangements for the funeral.

Lucretia, Delia's servant, had arrived at the crack of dawn with the news. The distraught woman sat across from Hunter and Marin, sniffling into a handkerchief Hunter had produced.

"It like she got her job done here. You say you'll take the little miss in, and Miss Delia knowed you be a good man. That chile just lay her head down last night and finally let herself rest." A fresh spate of keening started up.

Not quite sure of exactly how to react to this magnitude of mourning, and not even convinced that it was entirely sincere, Marin halfheartedly patted Lucretia on the back and made soothing noises.

Hunter cleared his throat. He rubbed his hand across his morning stubble, the rasping sound muted by all the sniffling.

"Do you know anything of children, Miss Alexander?"

So he was back to calling her Miss Alexander. She noticed he only called her that when he was irritated with her or uncomfortable. Right now it was definitely the latter. He sat in the chair, his hair in tousled spikes from a restless night, the belt of his wine-colored brocade dressing gown knotted haphazardly at his waist. A socially unacceptable amount of tanned, muscled chest exposed itself in the deep vee of the lapels. He must really be upset to allow such a breach of etiquette, she thought.

The thought prompted her to check her own appearance, which found the folds of her dressing gown gaping open. Her nightgown provided only a little camouflage to what lay beneath. She jerked the edges of her robe together and held them in a tight grip. She realized she hadn't answered him when he expanded on his first question.

"Have you any experience with delivering bad news to children? How do we go about telling Katie of her mother's death?"

Good question. Marin had no idea.

"I babysat kids when I was a teenager, but I never—"

Hunter scowled at her. "Miss Alexander, would you mind speaking plain English for a change?"

"Babysitting, Hunter, is what we call keeping children where I come from." Her stare challenged him to ask her where that would be.

His scowl only deepened. Lucretia looked at them both as if they'd taken leave of their senses.

Marin realized she was doing what she always did in the

face of death. Ignoring it. She'd had enough experience to recognize the symptoms. She released a frustrated sigh.

"All I know is that Katie is too young to fully understand the meaning of death. The best way, I guess, is to put it as simply as possible in words she can understand."

Hunter considered the advice while Lucretia renewed her howling. Marin decided the best thing to do was to get rid of Lucretia before Katie came downstairs and saw the woman throwing her apron over her head. That wasn't the way she would want to remember hearing about her mother's death.

"You say you have Katie's things out in a wagon?" She leaned forward and put her hand on Lucretia's arm. "Why don't we get one of the men to bring them in?"

Lucretia nodded and stopped her caterwauling. She spoke in between sniffs. "All her things, they's out in the wagon." *Sniff.* "Miss Delia, bless her soul, make me promise to bring them to the chile first thing." *Sniff.*

"Well, let's go see what you have." Marin stood, then helped the portly servant to her feet. The hanky fell to the floor, and Marin scooped it up and handed it back to Lucretia. Apparently this was a cue to begin mourning again, for she let forth a moan that started deep in her chest and echoed through the entry hall. Marin hustled her out the front door before another moan had a chance to erupt.

Hunter was grateful to Marin for dispatching the tedious servant as soon as possible. She'd sent her back to the hotel to collect Delia's effects and bring them to Pierce Hall, before the management found out one of their patrons had died of tuberculosis.

He assumed Marin was dressing now. He heard her in her room when he left his. They had decided to dress and then meet in the parlor. He balked at breaking the news to Katie alone. A woman's presence might soften the blow, and his mother wasn't the woman to soften anything.

Marin entered the parlor just moments after he did. Neither spoke. They just exchanged uneasy glances. The clock on the mantel chimed eight o'clock. They both stared at it as if it tolled their doom.

Marin sank to the deep peach love seat in a rustle of black cotton. He watched her spend several seconds arranging her skirts precisely, then jump and turn in her seat at the sound of someone approaching.

Thankfully it was not his mother. It was much too early for her to be up and about. The footsteps were the quiet *click click* of tiny feet descending stairs one at a time. Along with them was the gentle scuff of Mamie's slippered feet.

The pair came into view on the staircase, then seconds later they appeared at the parlor door. Hunter walked over and scooped Katie into his arms when Mamie relinquished her hold on the child's hand.

The dear old black woman's eyes shone with unshed tears. She stretched out an arthritic hand and patted Hunter on the cheek.

"She a sweet youngun, Mistah Hunter. You break it to her gentle, for ole Mamie."

"I will do my best, Mamie."

He turned his gaze onto his newfound daughter and wondered if he could ever do or say anything that might break her heart.

She smiled up at him, some of her shyness from the day before already gone. The pink of her dress accented the bloom in her chubby little cheeks; the remnant of a milk mustache from breakfast still coated her upper lip. In her fist she held a half-eaten sugar cookie.

He glanced at Mamie. She speared him with a mutinous look before shuffling from the room.

"Is my mama here?"

Reckoning time. He looked to Marin, then carried Katie to the love seat and sat beside the woman who was here for moral support. It was the closest he'd ever allowed himself to get to her.

Katie's little feet dangled between them. When she took a bite of her cookie, sugary crumbs showered down on the back of Hunter's hand. White flecks of cookie disappeared into the black folds of Marin's skirts. Hunter stared at those folds and tried to organize his thoughts. A knot of sympathy formed in his throat.

"Katie, your mama cannot come today."

Katie took another bite of cookie and wiggled her feet.

"Why?"

"Well, because . . . your mama . . ." He looked up at Marin, his eyes beseeching her to help.

Marin took Katie's free hand in both of hers and spoke in her most gentle voice.

"Did your mommy teach you about Jesus, Katie?"

Katie nodded and took another bite of cookie.

"Well, your mommy has gone to live with Jesus so she won't be sick anymore. She wanted to stay here with you, but she was too sick. The only way she could get better was to go and live with Jesus."

Katie thought about this for a moment, then asked, "When will Mama come back?"

Hunter's heart lurched. He answered her in a quiet voice, "She cannot come back, Katie."

Katie's feet stopped wiggling, her cookie fell from her hand. She studied both faces with her big blue eyes. Then she bowed her head and curled into a tight little ball on Hunter's lap. From amidst all the ruffles and flounces of pink dimity, her tiny voice could barely be heard.

"I want my mama."

Marin had never been to a more miserable funeral in all her life. Miserable in every aspect. The only way it could possibly have been worse was if Lucille had seen fit to attend. Thank God she had done her usual overreacting when Delia announced her disease. The morning after Delia's death she had defied nature by getting up before everyone else and being gone before breakfast. Marin didn't envy the "friends" in Natchez who were about to get an extended visit from Lucille "until the poisonous, tainted air dissipates."

Yes, only Lucille's presence could have made things worse.

No more than a handful of people showed up to mourn Delia's passing. Marin had overheard one woman complain that her husband forced her to come because Hunter was a business associate. It seemed—thanks, most probably, to Lucille—the news traveled quickly of Delia's fall from grace by producing an illegitimate child. And in that time-honored fashion, she was ostracized—even in death—while the father of the child suffered nothing.

Marin glared at Hunter from across the carriage seat. His only response was to raise a questioning eyebrow.

The minister had taken it upon himself to save every soul in attendance. He'd droned on for two solid hours while Delia lay in state in front of him. When some of the so-called mourners had the nerve to express their displeasure at the open casket, a stony-faced Hunter put a stop to their grumblings with a terse, "It was at her request." After that, half the assembly sat breathing through hankies pressed to their faces. No doubt the hypocrites were in mortal fear of contracting her disease.

Marin felt that Delia was having the last laugh on these old biddies. The very ones who hadn't allowed their skirts to touch hers were now forced to sit and stare at her dead countenance.

The church had been stifling. Marin's black faille gown had acted like a heat magnet and was covered in no time with sweat stains. And it seemed the majority of the people who had been forced or seen fit to show up for the service were those who still held with the belief that bathing too often was unhealthy. Lord, Marin thought, unhealthy for the people who had to breathe near them.

Thank God, Hunter had listened to her and left Katie home.

The misery of the day lingered even now. They had seen Lucretia onto a riverboat so that she could return to her family in New Orleans, then turned the carriage toward home. The horses kicked up so much dust Marin was sure she would suffocate before they arrived.

Finally they came to a stop in front of the house. A boy ran out from the stables to take the reins. Hunter leapt down, then swung Marin down before she had a chance to think. The heat of his hands burned through all her layers of clothing.

Embarrassment flashed through her. She knew the fabric was as damp as if she'd been caught in a summer shower. He wasted no time in removing his hands. In fact, he let go of her almost before she hit the ground, so that she stumbled and had to grab for the carriage wheel.

She glared up at him and swiped some imaginary dirt from her black skirts.

"Thanks a lot, Hunter. I could have fallen out of the carriage without your help."

"I apologize, Miss Alexander. My hands seem to have slipped."

They continued to trade glares until they got into the house. When they passed the parlor, Marin meant to go her separate way, but they were brought up short by the sight of Katie sitting in the middle of the Aubusson carpet with every toy Lucretia had brought scattered around her. Mamie sat beside her, a huge mountain of coffee-colored flesh, trying to cajole the little girl into taking interest in one of the toys.

"This here baby doll, she be saying, C'mon, Miss Katie. Let's have us a tea party. I'm awantin' some more of them pecan tarts we done had for supper.' " Mamie's waggle-walking of the doll and falsetto voice won a grin from Marin and Hunter, but Katie seemed to not even hear her.

Memories washed over Marin as she watched Katie's chin drop disconsolately to her chest—memories of the confused, deserted little girl she'd been when her father died. It'd taken years before her child's mind accepted that the body in the flag-draped box had been her father.

And her mother's grief had been as bad as her father's death. Not only had it been hard to see her mother in such pain, but with her grandparents on the other end of the country, there had been no one but a younger brother to lift a little girl's spirits or encourage the carefree life she should have been living.

Marin resolved this would not happen to Katie. She snapped into action.

"Hunter, take care of Katie while Mamie helps me out of these clothes."

He looked at her as if she'd told him to cut off his hand.

"I beg your pardon?"

"You heard me." She went over and helped heave Mamie to her feet.

"Miss Alexander, this is not my place! I know nothing of —"

She spun on her heel and glowered at him. She was in no mood to patronize a whining male.

"Do it!"

She left no time for further argument. She was out of the room and halfway up the stairs before the echo of her words died.

Men! she thought. God, they could be irritating! They think they rule the world! They have to drive fast cars and talk loud and shoot big guns and fly fighter jets and wage war, but drop one little child into their hands and they turn into sniveling idiots! God save her from big, strong men!

She punctuated each unspoken thought with a stomp up the steps. Mamie rushed to keep up, keeping a wary eye on her speechless employer as she went.

In no time at all Marin was back downstairs, Mamie still at her heels. When she entered the parlor, Hunter rose from his futile attempt to entertain Katie. The pulsing vein in his temple belied his calm tone of voice.

"Mamie, stay with the child. Miss Alexander, I will see you in the library."

She should have been worried. She should have feared for her job. But, strangely, she felt no emotion at all except an itching to get this argument over with.

He swung around on her before the door finished closing. Veins bulged in his vividly red face.

"How dare you order me to take care of my child in my own house!"

She stared at his righteous-looking face and thought she had everything under control. Until he boomed, "Well?"

Something snapped.

"How dare *you* have to be *told* to take care of your child! The one grieving for her dead mother, with no family to help her through this except a cold, emotionless man who happened to get his kicks one night with her mother?

"Do you know what it's like to lose a parent when you're four years old? Well, I do! You know they're gone, but you don't understand death. All you understand is they left you and you keep hoping they'll come back, but everybody says they won't come back. And you wonder what you did so bad that God would take them away from you! Then the grandparents die, one right after the other. And when they're all dead and you think you're numb, your seventeen-year-old brother dies of a drug overdose. Was it suicide or an accident? What does it matter? Dead is dead. And when you're twenty-two years old and a senior in college, you get a call to come home and identify your mother's body because some drunk plowed into her on her way home from Christmas shopping and put her out of her misery. Do you know how that feels?"

By this time she was almost screaming. But she wasn't through.

"And then you men, you arrogant, self-centered men, have to go off and play G.I. Joe in the Middle East, and the one man I love more than life itself takes his plane out and plows it into some Middle Eastern desert! And the government won't even acknowledge it because it was a top secret mission!"

Her balled fists slammed into his chest and shoulders over and over again. The tears finally came, and when they did, it was like a dam bursting.

"And you have to be told to comfort your four-year-old daughter? Damn you! How dare you even *wait* to be told."

She beat at Hunter's chest with her fists until he grabbed her wrists in an iron grip. The pain welled up from the deepest part of her being, and to her horror, she cried like she had never cried before. When his grip loosened and his arms pulled her in to cradle her to his chest, her uncontrollable sobs wrenched her very soul.

The anger drained from Hunter just seconds after Marin turned on him. Even though part of what she said made no sense, by the time she lit into him with her fists he was feeling about as tall as a snake's belly. He was tempted to let her pound away on him—he deserved it. But if ever a woman needed to be comforted and hugged, it was this one.

He wasn't prepared, though, for the jolting ache that racked his body when she willingly fell against his chest. The warm palm of one hand opened against his torso while her other clenched against her mouth to stifle the sobs. His arms pulled her in and closed around her with a will of their own. Unaccustomed as he was to comforting, or being comforted, he awkwardly patted her back and mumbled, "There, there."

This seemed to be having no positive effect. If anything, she cried all the harder.

Helpless, he stopped thinking and let his instincts take over. With one hand he coaxed her even closer. With the other he tipped her face to his and wiped the trail of tears from one cheek with his thumb. With bowed head, he whispered words of consolation in her ear.

The sobs lessened. When Marin turned her face to his, the velvet touch of her cheek against his stopped his breath. When he remembered to breathe, her perfume invaded his senses and set his pulse pounding. He nuzzled her ear, and she turned to him fully, her sobs turning into whimpers, the whimpers into kisses, until her mouth was on his and she kissed him so deeply it staggered him. She clutched him fiercely as he returned the kiss. Clutched him as though she would die if she loosened her embrace. Both his hands came up to hover at the sides of her head. Finally he allowed himself to gently cradle her face in his palms while the sensation of his tongue meeting hers sent dizzying waves reeling through his body.

The next instant she jerked free of his hold and slapped him so hard he saw stars. The cheek that only moments ago reveled in the feel of her skin now burned with the imprint of her hand.

"Don't ever touch me again!" she hissed, her voice so vehement he half expected her to try to hit him again. As she glared at him through narrowed eyes, the old walls fell back into place around his heart.

"That should not be a difficult request with which to comply. After all, it was not my tongue running rampant."

Her eyes grew wide, and she sucked in her breath.

"Oh! I turned to you for comfort, and what did you do? You took advantage of me in a weak moment, while your daughter is in there aching for her mother!" She stabbed at his chest with a pointed finger. "Well, you coldhearted S.O.B., that won't happen again, because I quit!"

She spun around, and in her haste stumbled over the train of her gown.

"Marin, wait!"

She grabbed up handfuls of train and flung it behind her with a vengeance.

"What?" She speared him with a glare that would have turned a lesser man to stone.

Why did he not want this exasperating woman to leave? By all rights he should have sent her packing when she manufactured that ridiculous story about traveling in time. But in spite of all good reasoning, he didn't want her to go. Hated the thought of her leaving. Not yet. Besides, she was partially right. He had enjoyed the kiss immensely while his little daughter grieved in the other room.

"You speak of my being coldhearted. How do you think Katie will feel when yet another woman disappears from her life?"

Marin stared at Hunter, as if giving the matter credence. She paced a few steps, wringing her hands, her lined forehead revealing portentous concentration. After several seconds she raised beseeching eyes to his.

"Then you must answer me one question, Hunter." Her repentant voice changed in timbre with her next words. "Should I pack my waders for this guilt trip, or is the manure as deep as it's going to get in here?"

She yanked up a fistful of her skirts and stomped toward the door. "Anyone, especially a kid, who's only known me for three days, would not even realize I was gone!"

"I would."

She froze in midstep and slowly looked over her shoulder at him, her skirts still bunched in her hands.

"I beg your pardon?"

"I said I would . . . like to apologize for this unfortunate scene. I should not have chastised you. You were only thinking of my daughter's welfare. Please accept my apologies."

Doubt was evident in her eyes. He expected her to give forth with another speech he would only half understand and then leave. Instead, she turned and faced him. After a moment she released a long sigh.

"Maybe I overreacted, too." She swiped at still damp cheeks with her fingers. "I guess I had more garbage to deal with than I realized." Well, he was right about the speech part. She gave him a sheepish grin when she glanced at his still stinging cheek. "I'm sorry for hitting you. My brother used to tell me I had a mean right hook."

Frustration rose in him. He squeezed his eyes shut and pinched the bridge of his nose. Her letters had not spoken of a brother. Indeed, she had proclaimed to be an only child. Nor had she made sense about the deaths of her parents. Unless, of course, she was sticking to her incredible story about being someone else.

"Miss Alexander," he began, "I feel we really must address this issue of your—"

A decisive knock on the library door echoed in the room. Ambrose stoically opened the door. Mamie's worried countenance peeped over the shoulder of the butler. She looked as if she expected to see mangled bodies on the library floor.

"Supper on the table, suh," Ambrose announced. "Emmaletta done held it so long, she threatenin' to go work for the Hilliards."

Hunter stifled the curse he would dearly love to have uttered. Emmaletta had been using that threat since the war was over. But now was not the time to press Marin on her fabrication. He promised himself he would get to the bottom of this "life" of hers. And soon.

Marin couldn't think of another thing to do to cheer Katie up. Hopscotch, hide-and-seek, and now a pony ride were all met with polite participation, but absolutely no enthusiasm. Since supper she had exhausted every idea she had ever had for entertaining children. All to no avail.

She rested her forearms on the stall door and watched Andre rub down Katie's pony. She was at a loss as to how she might pull the little girl out of her depression.

Thank heavens Hunter's mother wasn't around to contend with and depress the entire household. When Lucille had commandeered the servants to carry a mountain of luggage to the largest carriage Hunter owned and announced she would be visiting friends in Natchez, Marin considered sending her regular reports of new and various illnesses descending upon the household. Glumly watching Andre while she sorted through her mental file of contagious diseases, she became aware of a sound she'd never heard before. The sound of Katie giggling. She spun to see what miracle had generated this mirth and found herself enchanted as well.

A litter of three nearly grown kittens frolicked together in the next stall. They cavorted as three separate entities, then converged as one rolling, multilegged ball of fur. A solid black kitten with enormous feet separated itself from the group, then lay in wait for the other two to stop their tumbling. Crouched like the king of the jungle stalking its prey, the precocious fur ball pounced on its siblings, batting one into a corner and rolling several feet with the other.

Their antics brought peals of laughter from Katie. Marin, struck with inspiration, stooped to try and coax one of the kittens to them.

The roughhousing stopped at Marin's quiet "kitty-kittykitty," but none ventured toward her. Finally, after she picked up a feathery piece of hay and wiggled it enticingly, the black kitten crouched and began stalking this latest adversary.

It crouched, slinking noiselessly toward the wiggling straw, then ruined the threatening effect by rising on its hind legs and swatting at the air.

One huge paw snared the hay. When the half-grown cat attempted to flick away the offending vegetation, it fell backward and wheeled across the stable floor in a series of somersaults.

Katie's laughter was music to Marin's ears. How long had it taken Marin to giggle again after her father died? For the life of her, she couldn't remember a single time she hadn't forced the laughter. Until Ryan came into her life, calling her "Fireball" and teasing her unmercifully.

Fireball. So nicknamed for her fiery temper. But Ryan had said many times that she loved with more passion than she angered.

A furry missile catapulted into her shoulder and knocked her from her reverie right onto her derriere.

The other kittens lost some of their reticence and joined the party. Without quite knowing how it happened, Marin found herself on her back with three cats and a little girl on top of her.

The wad of fabric that was her bustle held her hips aloft and her back so askew she felt like a chiropractor's poster child. Once her hips slid from their perch and she flopped to her side, her four playful tormentors had a field day. She had a cat tangled in her hair and one pouncing on her chest, attacking the lace ruffle at her neck. Katie straddled her waist, screaming with delight at the third kitten, which she'd tucked under her frock. The white muslin midriff of the little drop-waist dress undulated with squirming feline body parts while muffled, indignant meows broadcast a warning.

It was time to garner a little control over the situation. A tender four-year-old tummy was not the place to find out how sharp kittens' claws can be. Marin sat up and intercepted a second kitten on its way to joining its sibling under Katie's dress.

"Katie, I'm afraid the kittens will scratch you if you hide them under your clothes. Let's just play with them on the ground, okay?

"Yes, ma'am." Katie gurgled with merriment as an invisible hump wove its way under her dress until a pink nose peeked from beneath the hem. Two huge green eyes appeared after a tentative sniff, then retreated back out of sight.

Seconds ticked by while the "hump" stayed absolutely motionless. Marin leaned forward, one kitten curled and purring in her lap, and casually walked two fingers across the stable floor in front of Katie.

An enormous black paw darted from its cover to bat once at her fingers, then withdraw just as quickly. Moments later the other paw whipped with lightning speed in a toying arc. Delighted, Katie danced her fingers on the ground, too. The entire cat appeared this time, pouncing playfully for a moment on chubby fingers, then streaking away, circling the stall in a furry blur, chasing an invisible enemy.

A hesitant voice broke into their entertainment.

"Ohhhh, Lordy, Miz Marin."

Marin, still laughing over the kittens' antics, contorted her neck enough to look up and see Andre behind her. Wide eyes rimmed in white, he stood at the gate, shaking his head.

"I ain't had a chance to muck out that there stall yet, ma'am."

Marin didn't miss the irony of the fact that she had just that moment noticed a very identifiable aroma. She continued to smile up at Andre, but breathed with a little less gusto.

"Yeah, I'm beginning to think we may have picked the wrong place to play."

Andre's face was now a blank page. "Yessum. I's thinkin' yo is right." He hustled to help Marin to her feet—no small task with that blasted iron maiden strapped around her waist refusing to bend.

The air was vibrant with the smell of freshly disturbed horse apples. She flicked the worst of the clinging hay from her gown, then turned to Katie.

Several ominous-looking stains covered both their skirts, the fumes rising from them almost visible. Marin chuckled to herself as she brushed golden twigs of hay from Katie's rump, then picked them from mussed, shiny brown curls the texture of corn silk.

So like her father's, Marin thought. Her fingers sifted through a silken strand while she wondered if Hunter's felt as soft.

What was she doing? Speculating about Hunter's hair would not keep Katie's mind off Delia. She gave her skirts a last token shake, then burst into laughter when the black kitten scampered from beneath her hems.

"C'mon, Katiedid," she said as she backed out of the stall,

trying not to step on a cat, "let's go see if we can find a sweeter smelling—OH!"

Hunter's arms wrapped around her when she would have plowed right over him.

"I see you found some manure after all, Miss Alexander. Pity you forgot your waders."

The touch of humor in his voice ignited her damnable mischievous streak.

"Why, Hunter, don't you like my new scent?" She shimmied up and down slowly, thoroughly brushing the back of her malodorous gown against his pristine suit. "It's called *Eau de Fertilizer*."

Suddenly, a disturbing, permeating warmth dawned throughout her body, shocking her to the core. She leaned away from him just as his stance went rigid.

"I believe you have captured the essence well," he choked out, his face an unreadable mask.

Was her stench responsible for his breathing difficulties, or was he suffering the same disquieting symptoms as she? With only inches separating them, Marin wouldn't have been surprised if little horizontal lightning bolts appeared and traveled up the space between them, like the weird, campy machines that brought Frankenstein's monster to life.

"Yes. Well." Damn her mischievous side! She should have known better than to even touch him after that kiss in the library had nearly curled her toes.

"Yes. Well," he echoed uncomfortably. "I was just on my way . . ." he looked around the stable ". . . to a business meeting. Andre, why is my horse not saddled?"

The stable boy poked his head out of the stall he'd been mucking.

"Yo hoss, suh?"

"Yes, my horse." He began to fidget. "Oh, never mind!" He turned on his heel and strode the length of the barn, disappearing into the last stall. A heartbeat later a huge, magnificent horse exploded from the enclosure with Hunter leaning low atop its sleek, bare back. In moments even the distant sound of the horse's thundering hooves dissipated into nothingness.

Marin glanced at Andre, who stood scratching his head.

"He sho 'nuff didn't tell me to saddle his hoss."

Before Marin could reply, she felt a tug on her skirts. Katie stood with the black kitten draped like a limp rag over her shoulder, a tiny fistful of Marin's skirts still in her hand. She knew what was coming.

"Can I keep it?"

Chapter 8

HIS MOTHER WOULD be back as soon as her "friends' " tolerance ran out, he had a brand-new daughter he never knew existed who was grieving her dead mother, and his newest employee caused a glorious ache in the most disconcerting places when she brushed up against him. Even when she smelled of horse dung!

Could his life possibly become more complicated? He was overrun with females in his own home. Perhaps his sister would leave her husband and bring their two daughters to live at Pierce Hall. Dear Lord, no! He dare not even think it.

He gave Mystic free rein and allowed the horse to thunder across a well-established cotton field. He hoped fervently to leave the disquieting feelings Miss Alexander stirred in him behind in the trampled green plants.

Drat the woman! When he'd helped her from the carriage after the funeral, he'd nearly flung her from him, so strong was the shock of her touch. Her kiss in the library had turned his bones to butter until the sting of her slap chased the tenderness away.

And now! Now her frivolous act of leaning against him, even with that reeking gown, had caused every nerve in his body—some in a most unfortunate region—to stand at attention.

Why had he gone to investigate the giggling? Why hadn't he just saddled Mystic, as he'd intended, and gone his merry way? Instead, he had wandered to the open stall and witnessed Marin rolling in horse manure, buried in kittens and little-girl ruffles and making him wish he was welcome in the fray.

Damn.

Well, from now on she would know her place and not leave it. He would speak to her about becoming Katie's governess instead of his mother's so-called companion. That position had been a farce from the first day. She would still perform her secretarial duties, and between that and governing Katie, Miss Alexander would find little time to brush her gardenia-cum-manure scented body against his. Yes, that was the answer.

That problem resolved, Hunter turned his thoughts to Katie. Watching her romp in the stable had inspired him with a plan. With a nudge of his knee he turned Mystic back toward town. Widow Trumbull was the person to see for his needs.

He felt positively brilliant!

And Marin thought he lacked the care to be a father.

The fragrant bathwater had cooled to a refreshing chill before Marin realized how long they'd soaked.

She was curled up in one end of the tub, watching Katie splash at her feet. The little girl had stripped to the buff and scrambled into the water without so much as a by-your-leave. Marin had never known how marvelous and maternal the feel of wet baby skin against her own could be. Katie had cuddled up to her and patiently waited to be soaped down, then executed a mini water ballet while Marin scrubbed the stable smells from herself.

"Are you ready to get out, little Miss Katie?" she asked as she rose from the tub and grabbed a towel.

"No, ma'am." Katie's half-submerged pirouette threw a wave of water dangerously close to the rim.

Marin smiled to herself while she finished toweling her hair dry and slipped on a gauzy nightgown. The little chocolate-haired moppet was so cute. She was blowing bubbles in the water when Mamie bustled in with a pitcher of warm milk.

"My, my. What kinda fish do we got here?" Mamie hovered over Katie and studied her as if she were a candidate for that night's main course.

"Smell me, Mamie! I smell like Mawin!" Katie stood and thrust her dripping little belly out to be sniffed, which Mamie did with exaggerated enthusiasm.

"Mmmm, mmmm. You smells jest like a flower in a garden. But we needs to get you in your nightclothes afore your daddy gets home. He don't want to see no nekkid flowers runnin' round."

Katie giggled and raised her arms to be lifted from the tub. Mamie enveloped her in a huge linen towel, and with a deftness that surprised Marin, had her dried, dressed, and combed in no time at all.

Katie accepted the glass of warm milk Mamie offered with a polite "Thank you." Seconds after Mamie shuffled from the room, Katie smiled up at Marin with a milk mustache clear up to her nose.

"Will you read me a story, Mawin?"

Those huge blue eyes were hard to refuse. Marin slipped a dressing robe over her nightgown and knotted the belt.

"Do you have a favorite story?"

Damp ringlets bobbed in affirmation. "Mama always tells me about the princess and the crow."

Marin's heart sank on two accounts. She'd never even heard about a crow and a princess, and Katie had no sooner mentioned her mother before her eyes puddled up and her lower lip slid out.

"I have an idea!" Marin clasped her hands together enthusiastically, trying to distract Katie from her thoughts. "Why don't we go raid the nursery and see if we can find that book?" She glanced at the basket on the bed. "And, of course, we'll have to take the kitten."

Katie brightened immediately. She ran to the bed and gently lifted the basket. The folded pillowcase Katie had insisted on covering the cat with undulated for a moment, but the buried kitten seemed to settle back into a sound sleep.

Marin mentally patted herself on the back. This kitten had been a stroke of genius.

He could barely wait to see Katie's reaction. Though it had been somewhat embarrassing when Widow Trumbull had sniffed the air and asked him if he had stepped in something, his momentary unease would be worth it. He just hoped Katie was still awake.

Several steps creaked as he crept up the stairs. He would have to get Nathan to fix that. In the meantime, he hugged the edge of the staircase, shifted the heavy box in his hands when he reached the landing, then continued up the stairs.

It was absolutely ridiculous that he was tiptoeing down his own hallway. But oddly enough, he relished the long-forgotten feeling of boyish excitement.

Katie was probably in Marin's room, as she had been the past two nights. He hesitated outside the closed door, uncertain now of how to proceed. Should he wake Katie up if she was already asleep? Did he really want to run into his disconcerting employee again? What if she was all soft and clean and in her nightclothes?

Just then the bedroom door flew open, and the two females in question barreled right into him.

The box he was holding thudded to the floor when Marin bounced off his chest. Katie staggered backward from her collision with his leg, a basket she was carrying swinging like a church bell.

A half-grown cat popped its head above the basket rim just as the startled puppy scrambled from the box.

An indignant yowl rent the air, and a black blur flew from the basket to land, claws bared, directly on the back of the golden-haired puppy. The puppy yelped in pain, and for a moment a huge tornado of gold and black fur swept down the hallway, upsetting everything in its path and leaving tiny yellow puddles in its wake.

The yowling and yelping increased in volume until it rivaled the storm they were so accurately imitating. Finally, the puppy dislodged the outraged cat, then wasted no time in finding the biggest piece of furniture in sight and disappearing into the darkest regions beneath it. Unfortunately it was Marin's bed. The cat, on the other hand, defied gravity by soaring, hackles raised, to first the washstand and then the top of the armoire.

Quiet and sanity settled over the scene like a fluttering blanket. Katie stood stock-still, her mouth open in surprise, her eyes as round as sand dollars. Marin was in better shape, only because her mouth was closed.

"Sweet Jesus in heaven! What you peoples doin' up there? Ambrose, fetch the gun!" Mamie, followed closely by Ambrose, Izzy, and Emmaletta crowded up the stairs at a hesitant pace.

"Everything is fine, Mamie, other than a few . . . er . . . puddles that need mopping up." Hunter waved away her concern. "I believe we just introduced the two newest members of our family to each other, and it appears they took an immediate dislike."

Katie snapped out of her shock with Hunter's words.

"A puppy!" she squealed, then ran back into Marin's room and stuffed her upper body under the bed. "Here puppypuppypuppy," she cooed as her rump disappeared beneath the massive four-poster.

Marin leapt into action and ran to grab a tiny foot before it, too, disappeared, but she was a heartbeat too slow. Hunter stood in the frame of the door and watched Marin's ivory dressing gown pool around her as she sank to her knees. Her still-damp hair cascaded down her back with an occasional wispy curl caressing her cheek.

He was aware of his heartbeat pounding in his ears and the birth of an ache in the pit of his stomach.

"Katie, the puppy's scared. He might bite you if you get too close."

Dear God! He hadn't thought of that! He was on his knees

beside Marin in an instant, the two of them calling out orders for Katie to come out from under the bed.

"But I want to see the puppy! Here puppypuppy!"

She was deep in the nether regions under the bed. Too far to reach without going in after her. He was just about to slide himself under when Katie started giggling hysterically and backing out.

When Katie got close to the edge, they could see what all the mirth was about. As she inched her way backward, the puppy inched its way forward, apparently having overcome its fear in pursuit of the delicacy of the dried milk on Katie's upper lip.

Marin broke into musical laughter at the sight. Hunter joined his rumbling chuckle with hers and turned to smile at her.

Her golden eyes sparkled with delight, and her porcelain skin held a rosy glow when she lifted her gaze to meet his. The elusive hint of gardenia swirled through his senses, heating his blood and bringing all those accursed nerves to attention again.

The laughter died on his lips as her eyes deepened to amber. The gaiety there turned serious.

Suddenly he found nothing to laugh about.

He had to get away from this woman. She was making him feel things he'd sworn never to feel again, question his life in areas he didn't care to examine. He picked Katie up and delivered a kiss on her milk-scented cheek. As much as he would have enjoyed staying and watching his tiny daughter get acquainted with her new pets, he knew it would be too dangerous to spend one more minute within breathing distance of Marin Alexander.

"I have several things I need to attend to. Good night, Katie, Miss Alexander."

Her voice drifted on the breeze as he strode hurriedly to put distance between them.

"Pleasant dreams, Hunter."

The constant rhythmic beep filtered into her dreams as nothing more than a muffled, distant echo. As the sound became clearer and louder, she could no longer ignore it.

It almost sounds electronic, her sleep-fogged mind assessed. She struggled to open her eyes, but fatigue overwhelmed her. What did it matter, anyway? She mentally scrunched deeper into the warmth of her covers and turned her thoughts back to sleep.

"Marin," a quiet, baritone voice spoke. *"Marin, it's time to go."*

Ohhh, just let me sleep, she moaned silently.

"Marin. Open your eyes."

She fought her way through the dark cobwebs of sleep. Why was she so tired? And why was he making her wake up?

Somewhere deep in her subconscious a spark of recognition flared.

RYAN!

It took enormous effort to open her eyes even a slit. *Oh, Ryan, don't leave till I can see you!*

The rhythmic beep increased in speed, then became so rapid it was no longer a beep but an ululating tone.

"Hello, Fireball," his beloved voice broke over her in warm waves.

Marin tried to speak his name, but the sound caught in her . throat. She finally managed to open her eyes enough to focus on the cherished face before her. When she did, the beeping went into erratic fits.

She was in a hospital room—a twentieth century hospital room. And Ryan stood beside her bed, the fluorescent light in the hallway shining through him like candlelight through gauze. He wore his green Air Force flight suit. Under his arm was his flight helmet.

His name came out as a sob this time. He quickly grabbed the hand she tried to reach out, careful of the needle and tube protruding from her wrist. The warmth of his vaporous fingers caused an ache in her too deep to bear.

"Don't try to talk, Fireball. Your jaw is wired shut." He knelt beside the bed, his face so painfully near, yet she couldn't move to touch it. Nothing seemed to work except her left hand, and that not very well.

"You're pretty broken up, Fireball. You can't move because you're in traction." He looked uneasy. His hand passed across her forehead, over what should have been soft curls. But the raspy feel of a bandage blocked the warmth of his touch. *"It's time to go, Marin. I've come to get you. It's easy, sweetheart. All you have to do is let go."*

She tried to convey her panicked questions through her eyes. The beeping turned into fitful spasms. She finally realized the sound was that of a heart monitor. Her heart monitor.

No, Ryan, no! I'm not ready to die! I love you, but I'm not finished living! What about Hunter? What about Katie?

"Just let go, sweetheart, and I'll take you home."

"Are you doing aerobics in here, or have you just seen Brad Pitt walk down the hall?" A nurse clad in scrubs walked into the room. She smiled at Marin, then flicked the stethoscope from around her neck and listened intently to

Marin's chest. She straightened and placed her hand on Marin's finger.

"If you're in pain, tap your fingers once. If you're really hurting, tap twice."

Marin, paying no attention to the nurse, heard only to tap her fingers. She tapped agitatedly until the nurse's hand stopped her. Compassionate eyes searched Marin's. There was pain there, Marin knew, but not the kind the nurse was looking for.

"Let me give you something for that. Your heart rate's really picked up, and this will help the pain." She produced a syringe from her pocket and slid it into the I.V. tube.

Ryan remained by the bed, only inches from the nurse, yet unseen. She continued to check Marin carefully, all the while Ryan coaxing, *"Let go. Come with me, Marin. All you have to do is want it."*

Tears filled her eyes as she was torn between worlds. Ryan was dead. Hunter and Katie, in her other life, were alive. Could she get back to them?

The nurse saw the tears spill from the corners of her eyes to soak the bandage covering her temples.

"You'll feel better soon. I guarantee it," she said with compassion, misreading the tears.

Marin tried to thank her with her eyes, but Ryan held her gaze.

His face was the picture of peace. Oh, how she was tempted to go with him.

I'm sorry, Ryan. I'm not finished yet.

The nurse turned to leave, gasping and nearly staggering as her body passed right through Ryan's. Though she must have felt some sensation, it was obvious the woman still saw nothing. She glanced around the room, checking her own pulse as she backed out the door.

When Marin looked back, Ryan was fading from her vision, his hand stretched out to her, beseeching her to come with him. As he disappeared, she feared he took a large part of her soul with him.

The painkiller sent waves of lethargy crashing over her. The thought of Ryan became harder and harder to focus on. She closed her eyes as more tears soaked her bandages.

Maybe she *should* let go.

"Marin."

Oh, God. She couldn't take much more of this.

She turned her head toward the sound of the now familiar voice.

Hunter sat on the edge of her bed. Her ghost in black trousers and waistcoat. Her mischievous ghost with the impossible dimples, which now wavered in all their glory through her drug-blurred vision. His eyes grew serious and the dimples disappeared when he leaned close.

"Come back to me, Marin." The yearning in his steady blue gaze was so different from the peaceful green of Ryan's eyes. An almost tangible pain leapt from him and entered her soul. The wounded spirit of a little boy, then a young soldier, and finally an embittered man, spiraled through her.

"Can you not feel my need for you?"

She could barely nod, so strong was her drug-induced weariness. She lacked the strength to move, but her thoughts reached out to him. As her eyes fluttered closed, though her jaw was wired, she knew the taste of his kiss on her tongue before the blackness swallowed her completely.

Chapter 9

THE INSISTENT METALLIC clank of the brass door knocker continued to resound through the house, even after the acceptable number of knocks. Continued, in fact, until Ambrose, who was serving Hunter's morning coffee in the dining room, made his way to the front door in his usual unhurried fashion and opened that portal, removing the knocker from Niles Kilpatrick's reach.

The dining room was not so far removed that Hunter couldn't hear their conversation.

"I'm here to see Mari, and I'll not be leavin' until I do."

"Miz Marin still be abed, suh."

"I'll not be put off! I'll see her in her bed, if need be. After all, I'm to be her husband. And her name is *Mari!*"

Hunter whisked the napkin from his lap and flung it onto the table beside his coffee cup. The man was making a pest of himself. Hunter refused to analyze the insidious emotion he was experiencing over Kilpatrick's pursuit of Marin.

"Pierce!" Niles called upon seeing Hunter enter the foyer. "I'll not be put off another minute. I demand to see me Mari, and see her I will. Your people will be giving me no more excuses, nor turning me away at the door." Niles elbowed his way past Ambrose and stood nose to nose with Hunter. "What have ye done with me Mari?"

Hunter resisted the urge to use his fist to put distance between himself and Kilpatrick. Instead, he remained motionless save for the flexing of the fingers on his right hand.

"Don't be ridiculous, Kilpatrick. I've done nothing to Miss Alexander."

"Her name is *Sander! Mari Alexa Sander!*"

Hunter felt the hair lying across his forehead lift with the *S*'s Kilpatrick blasted across his face.

"Call her whatever you like, but it is barely dawn. Miss *Alexander,*" he stressed the last name, "is still asleep!" He blasted a few of his own *S*'s back at Kilpatrick and was rewarded with a darkening of his early morning visitor's ruddy skin.

Kilpatrick took a step back and drew himself up to his full height, which was almost that of Hunter's. His voice was calm and quiet, and his eyes were absolutely serious.

"I demand to see Mari. I'll not be leavin' till I do."

Hunter sighed disgustedly, staring Kilpatrick down.

"Ambrose, go and have Mamie wake Miss Alexander. Tell her that her . . . betrothed . . . is here to see her." He continued to glare at Kilpatrick, and vice versa. Several minutes passed with nothing more than the tick of the clock to break the silence until Mamie called down from the landing.

"Mistah Hunter, Miss Marin ain't in her bed."

He broke his stare only long enough to glance over his shoulder and give Mamie a long-suffering look.

"Then please go and fetch her from wherever she is."

"She ain't in the house. And she ain't in the privy."

A lump suddenly formed in the pit of Hunter's stomach.

"Are you saying you do not know her whereabouts?"

"Yessir, I's sayin' that."

"Pierce!" Hunter barely heard Kilpatrick's rantings as he took the steps two at a time. "If you've harmed a hair on her head, Pierce, you'll have me to answer to!"

Marin's bed was, indeed, empty. But it had been slept in. He threw open the doors to her armoire. A bit of relief rushed through him when he saw her clothing still there.

"Mamie, check and see if one of her gowns is missing."

Mamie riffled through the clothing, shaking her head and muttering to herself, while Hunter checked the upper veranda. Niles had seen fit to follow them to Marin's room, and he wasted no time in poking his nose into every corner. When he moved to open Marin's whatnot box, Hunter decided he'd had enough.

"Do you not think, sir, that the lady is entitled to some privacy?"

Hunter reached over and closed the lid as Niles attempted to open it. The other man's hazel eyes narrowed, but his hand stayed on the box.

"I seek only to be finding if me Mari left of her own accord, or if there is reason to be suspecting foul play."

This man was begging to be introduced to Hunter's fist.

"Do you insinuate I would play foul with the employees in my home?"

"I don't remember bein' specific, Pierce. Do ye hold a guilty conscience?"

*   *   *

Marin stood on the bluffs and watched the river run black.
The white gauzy fabric of her dress fluttered and billowed
around her with the dancing breeze. The moon, full and
white, hung low over the Arkansas horizon. A million stars
winked at her from the black velvet sky. A river of moonlight cut across the dark waters, ending at the shore below
her.

A moon river, she thought sadly.

She drew in a deep, cleansing breath of the sharp-scented
air and sank to the grass as she exhaled.

She had come here to think, but her mind refused to do anything but wander. She imagined that was a sanity-retaining
mechanism. If she thought too much about this night's
events . . .

If she could even be sure of exactly *what* she had experienced. Had it been a dream? If it was, it was the most real-
istic, yet at the same time surreal, dream she'd ever had.
There was a time when she would have rolled her eyes with
a muttered "Yeah, sure," at the slightest suggestion that she
may have, indeed, experienced the whole thing.

She shivered and rubbed her arms fiercely. It had to have
been a dream. If it wasn't, that meant she—or her body—
was alive in 1996. Had she lost complete control of her life?
Did she have a choice of staying with Hunter, going back to
her time, or . . . being with Ryan?

There. She'd finally let herself think about them. The ache
in her chest was worse than she'd expected.

Oh, Ryan. Her fantastic, perfect, funny, warm Ryan. How
wonderful it had been to see his face again. How tempting it
was to go with him.

And Hunter. Why had his ghost shown more life than the

flesh-and-blood man? Why did she feel that he'd called her to him across time?

Was it a dream, or did she hover somewhere between past and present, life and death?

She skimmed her hands across the grass beside her, collecting the droplets of dew on her fingers. She rubbed her hands together to warm them, then flinched as a pain shot up her wrist.

The moonlight shone on the back of her hand, and Marin heard the blood roaring in her head. As she brought her hand slowly to her face to inspect it, every nerve in her body came alive.

On the back of her left hand, the pale, porcelain skin—so different from her skin in 1996—was bruised a deep purple. The kind of bruise made by an I.V.

Every window in the house was alight, and the activity from afar looked like ants preparing for the winter.

As she walked up the drive to the front of the house, Marin wondered if the place was always this active before daybreak. She couldn't remember any special plans for this morning.

Suddenly her stomach rolled. She prayed that Lucille hadn't returned.

Stopping with her hand on the doorknob, she debated whether to barge right in or sneak around back and avoid the witch for as long as possible.

The knob flew from her grasp as the door was yanked open, and Hunter charged through at a run.

"Ambrose, have Andre saddle my—OOPH!"

Marin bounced off Hunter's chest and would have fallen if his steely grip had not grasped her arms.

"Marin!"

He pulled her to him, but stopped just short of enveloping her in his arms. Instead he released her so quickly they both staggered backward.

"Where have you been? I was preparing to send out a search party! Have you any idea how dangerous it is for a woman to be out alone in the middle of the night?"

Marin brushed past him, trying not to let her shoulders slump. Her heart had taken flight for that brief moment when he'd pulled her to him. Now she would do well to get to her room without her disappointment showing.

"Try walking around in 1996 if you think this is bad," she muttered, then stepped into the foyer, only to groan at who met her there.

"Mari, me love! Where had ye gotten yourself off to? Why, I was worried sick, I was. Ye should be knowin' better—"

Marin threw her head back, giving in to the sigh threatening to escape her lungs.

"Mr. Kilpatrick, why are you here at the crack of dawn?"

Niles stopped dead in his tracks on his way to what Marin expected was a bear hug. He tilted his head in question, then his eyes narrowed and his gaze slid to Hunter, who was leaning against the doorframe, a casual observer.

"And since when am I Mr. Kilpatrick to ye, love? Is that how ye intend to address me after we're wed?"

Oh, God, give me strength, Marin thought when she looked into Niles's hurt hazel eyes.

"Niles." He brightened. She sighed. "Let's go into the parlor. We need to talk."

She didn't miss the glare he shot Hunter, nor the one Hunter returned as she and Niles disappeared into the parlor.

Marin motioned for Niles to precede her. When she turned to pull the doors together, Hunter still stood at the front door. His back was to her as he stared into the pearly gray dawn. He stood for a moment, then his chin dropped to his chest and he slammed the door shut with a flick of his wrist.

She turned to Niles, who scooped her into his arms before she could speak.

"Ah, me little Mari. It's been so long, darlin'. Say ye'll wed me this very day."

Marin started to struggle but found she lacked the will to bother.

"Put me down, Niles."

"Not until ye say ye'll marry me today."

"Niles, we need to talk about that—"

"And talk we shall. Can ye have your bags packed by noon? Ye cannot imagine how frustrating it was, to come callin' on ye only to have these darkies tellin' me such nonsense about a death in the family, or that ye be busy with 'Mistah Hunter's chile.' " He drew out Hunter's name with an overdone Southern accent. "Ye'll not be a nanny to any man's bastard as long as I—"

"Don't you dare call Katie a bastard! Put me down! NOW!"

Niles stared at her with a look of disbelief, then slowly, almost challengingly, lowered her feet to the floor. He left his arm around her. She shrugged off his hold and walked away. Turning, she said, "Niles, I can't marry you."

Niles looked hard at her first, then stared at the wall, as if he could see through it to where Hunter had last stood.

"It's him, then. He's courtin' ye. He's only lookin' for a mother—"

"How flattering that you think he'd only want me as a mother to his child, but no, Hunter is not courting me." He could barely stand to touch her. She stifled a sigh before continuing. "You have to understand. I've had . . . something . . . happen to me. The accident . . . well, I'm not the same person you knew in St. Louis."

Niles crossed to her in two strides and placed his hands gently on her arms.

"Why do ye say that, darlin'? You're the selfsame Mari I fell in love with."

Marin closed her eyes and shook her head. It would serve no purpose to tell this man her name was not Mari. He seemed to be a very nice person, and she hated to hurt him, but there was no way she was going to marry him.

She met his gaze, her eyes deadly serious, as his hands rubbed up and down her arms. There was no magic in his touch, as there would be if it were Hunter's hands on her.

"Niles, whatever we had before, I don't remember. I don't remember you, or us, or St. Louis. I'm not going to marry you. I'm going to stay right here in this house for as long as—"

"Ye say ye don't remember the night I asked ye to be my wife? After ye said yes I slipped that ring on your finger, then carried ye to—"

"I don't remember." She backed away until he released his hold on her arms. He stood there with his palms up, as if asking for answers. "Please don't make this any harder than it is." She pulled the ruby ring from her left hand and gently placed it in his palm. Dear Lord, she hadn't even known it was an engagement ring.

His fingers curled over the ring, and he dropped his hand to his side in defeat.

"Very well. I'll not be forcing the issue. But I'll not accept this and walk away. I'll be stayin' with the Richardsons at least a fortnight. If ye change your mind, ye can find me there." Marin didn't bother to tell him she had no idea who the Richardsons were or where they lived. "And I'll be seein' ye again before I return to St. Louis."

He snatched a black derby from a chair and threw the doors open, obviously expecting to catch Hunter lurking on the other side. Fortunately, both foyer and staircase were empty.

He swung back to face her. "This is not over, Mari."

When she didn't answer, he turned on his heel and stalked out of the house.

So, she was going to hold to her ridiculous story of being from the future.

"Try walking around in 1996, indeed," Hunter muttered to himself as his horse galloped down the road to Mississippi.

Not for the first time, he wondered about his own sanity in allowing this very odd woman to remain under his roof. Now that he had a daughter to consider, perhaps he should retain a governess who didn't believe she was inhabiting someone else's body.

Dear God. When he allowed himself to think about it in those terms, the whole story sounded even more preposterous.

He spent the two-hour ride into Mississippi trying to convince himself to rid his home of Miss Marin Alexander, or Mari Sander, or whoever the hell she was. He could come up with dozens of reasons to dismiss her and not one reason to allow her to stay. Except that he didn't want her to go. Simple as that. He just didn't want her to go.

He felt sorry for her. That was it! She'd lost her mother and had nowhere to go. He felt partially responsible for her present mental condition, considering she was on her way to his employ, and in his carriage with his driver, no less, when the accident happened. Why, he owed it to her to keep her on.

Unless Kilpatrick convinces her to marry him and leave.

Just the thought of the man caused Hunter's lip to curl into a snarl. He shoved all thoughts of the troublesome pair from his mind as he turned his horse up the pebble drive to Tranquille. He had more things to worry about than a crazy employee and her future husband.

Hunter studied the beautiful old home through the trees, and his heart warmed as he approached.

Tranquille. The childhood home of his grandmother Pierce. The home was as peaceful as its name. He had come here at the age of ten to regain his strength after nearly dying with yellow fever, and it had been dear to his heart ever since.

Grandfather and Grandmother Pierce had been in residence at the time, having given Pierce Hall to his father. His grandmother had seen to it that he had daily exercise, fresh air, and plenty of hearty food.

Hunter could almost hear her voice now, with the slight accent of her French-born father. "My little one," she would croon while running her fingers through his hair, "you will be better soon. You will grow to be a fine man."

Hunter could barely remember his arrival at Tranquille as that young boy. Even though he was ten years of age, he'd come through his illness remembering nothing, not even his parents or grandparents. His grandmother had spent hours at a time reminding him of childhood memories until the memories became familiar to him.

Perhaps that was the reason he felt as he did toward

Marin. She had no one to hold her close and tell her she would be fine. No one except him, for Kilpatrick would surely have no patience with her story.

As he led Mystic to the front of the house, the massive front door creaked open and William limped to the steps. His weathered black face split into a huge white grin when he recognized Hunter.

Hunter leapt from his horse directly onto the porch and slapped the smiling old servant on the back with enthusiasm.

"Mistah Hunter, you devil. We didn't get no message sayin' you was comin'. But, dang, it good to see you. I'll get Maggie to make up a room for you."

Hunter shook his head, touched by the old man's affection. "I didn't send a message, William. And I won't be staying overnight. I found myself on the road to Mississippi, so I decided to ride down and check the crops."

"They's disappointin', suh. Between the boll weevils and that there fungus, we done lost a third of the plantin'. I's figurin' we'll harvest about half when it's all said and done."

That was disconcerting news. He'd been counting on that crop. Hunter craned his neck and inspected the exterior of the house. All seemed to be in good repair, thanks to William and Maggie. After the war they had stayed on at Tranquille, closing up all but two rooms of the house. They used those two rooms to live in, and they'd made repairs and maintained the home with the money Hunter sent them every month. Money that would come less often if the crops failed.

William must have sensed Hunter's concern. "The house in good shape, Mistah Hunter. Me and Maggie checked all the rooms just last week, and all she needed was a shingle or two fixed and a new pane of glass in your old bedroom. The rooms can wait for a new coat of paint until we has us a good harvest."

Hunter patted William's shoulder and steered him into the house. He didn't want the old servant standing on his feet too long.

"I've been craving a cup of Maggie's coffee and a thick slice of her nut bread. Do I stand a chance of getting either?"

William's grin spread from ear to ear. "Whooee, Mistah Hunter. Maggie done baked some bread this mornin'. She naggin' at me to keep my thievin' fingers off it till it cools. Ha! She ain't gonna keep us from it now!"

When they entered the fragrant kitchen, Maggie, twin sister to Mamie, was stirring a pot on the stove and holding the small of her back. When she looked up she let out a whoop that could peel wallpaper. Hunter opened his arms to her, bestowing his most devilish smile, at the same time planting his feet, bracing himself.

"There's my baby! You give your ol' Maggie a hug this here minute!" Maggie lumbered toward Hunter at top speed, not even slowing as she threw her massive arms around him. In spite of the braced legs, he staggered backward from the assault of Maggie's affection.

"I knowed I baked that bread for somebody asides that polecat William. Oh, my baby done come to see me!"

Hunter had been Maggie's "baby" since he'd come there to recover from yellow fever. No amount of persuasion kept her from calling him that in front of anyone and everyone. He still cringed inwardly at the thought of a certain picnic when he was fifteen, when she'd embarrassed him with her endearments.

"You sit yourself down here and let ol' Maggie fix you

some breakfast." She cocked her head and studied him with a practiced eye. "Ain't that Mamie feedin' my baby up there in Memphis? You look scrawny as a scarecrow."

There had always been a gentle rivalry between the sisters. Hunter smiled, basking in Maggie's fussing. "You think anyone you can get your arms around is scrawny," he teased.

"Humph," was Maggie's only response as she busied herself cracking eggs and slicing bacon. Hunter wasn't the least bit hungry, but he knew Maggie would take it personally if he failed to do justice to her cooking.

After polishing off a second breakfast of eggs, grits, bacon, fried tomatoes, and fresh biscuits, Hunter declined the thick slice of nut bread he'd originally craved.

"Well, I's gonna wrap it up for you just the same. You needs somethin' to hold you on your trip back to Memphis."

No use in telling her he'd eaten enough to hold him for two days. She wouldn't believe him. She wrapped an entire loaf of nut bread and shoved it into Hunter's protesting hands as he and William headed for the barn.

In no time at all they rode through the fields, inspecting the cotton plants. His heart sank with each new acre they covered.

"This is not good, William. We shall be lucky to lose only half the crop."

William agreed, which was no consolation for Hunter. William knew cotton, and if his prediction was bleak then Hunter could expect a poor harvest.

The ride back to Memphis was as bleak as his cotton future. A fine mist of moisture turned into a steady drizzle, soaking his lightweight coat and vest and causing his white linen shirt to cling to his chilled skin. By the time he arrived home, rain poured in a stream from the brim of his hat and the crashing thunder had Mystic spooked.

Soft yellow light glowing through the kitchen windows welcomed him, but he rode directly to the stables and waved away a sleepy Andre. His horse needed tending, and he admitted to himself that he'd rather stay in the barn and rub him down himself than go into the house and find Marin gone.

He could not say for sure which had him more upset, the fact that she might be gone, or the fact that he cared.

When he could delay the inevitable no longer he didn't even bother to turn up his collar or duck his head to avoid the rain. He simply waded through the downpour to the back door.

The kitchen, which had been added to the house after the war, was filled with the smells of supper—fresh-baked bread, roasted chicken, apple pie. He groaned at the sight on the table. Emmaletta, bless her soul, had left a linen-covered plate of food for him, since the household had long since gone to bed. Two candles cast their warm glow across the room.

Food, however, was not uppermost in his mind. Nor was his comfort, although the first order of business was to get out of his wet clothing. Then he would find out if his daughter still had a governess and if he still had a secretary.

Water pooled at his boots with every step as he ducked into the pantry. With any luck, he would find some laundry from which to pilfer dry clothes. He peeled off the clinging layers of coat, vest, and shirt, dropping them in a sodden heap. A bathing towel was draped over the washtub, so he snatched that up and scoured his hair dry. His waterlogged boots refused to budge without a fight. Fine. They would wait until he got to the bootjack in his room.

It seemed any articles of clothing he might possibly have use for had been efficiently put away. There was nothing for it but to go bare-chested to his room. Should he go via the back stairs? If so, he would pass Marin's room. Would she be there sleeping? Or would the bed be made up with fresh linens, waiting for its next occupant?

Dear God, he had grown into a maudlin sap! He scrubbed his body down with unnecessary roughness, galled that this woman occupied so much of his thoughts. She was just a woman, after all, like all the rest. Hell, she'd left Kilpatrick by running to Memphis, and now the poor sap was dancing to her tune here. She was obviously a woman who avoided her problems. He didn't need another squeamish female in his life. So what, if she'd left with Kilpatrick? So what, and good riddance. The next woman he employed would be homely enough to stop a clock.

He flung the damp towel to the floor and stormed from the pantry.

Chapter 10

MARIN SCREAMED AND dropped the teakettle, sending water hissing across the still-hot stove.

She hadn't known Hunter was home. The events of the day, her "visit" with Ryan's and Hunter's ghosts and the confrontation with Niles, had left her with a bad case of insomnia. She'd thrown a thin wrapper over her nightgown and crept down the back stairs to make a cup of tea, assuming Hunter was still out because of the food on the table and the candles still burning. The last thing she'd expected was for him to come charging out of the pantry.

"Miss Alexander! What are you doing here?" He very nearly barked the question at her, as if she had no right to step foot into the kitchen.

She was prepared to knock him off his "king of the castle" pedestal with a little acid in her voice, but the sight of candlelight dancing on his well-defined torso lit a warm, mellow fire in her that betrayed her intentions. She took her time and answered him in a low, husky voice.

"Making a cup of tea."

He stared at her. Obviously that was not the answer, or the tone, he'd expected. She smiled sweetly as she righted the tea kettle, all the while taking a long, slow inventory of him, enjoying every inch of exposed flesh.

Her twentieth-century brain took over, and she asked in the same seductive voice, "Would you like some?"

His damp, clinging trousers failed to hide the fact that he took her question the way she meant it. To her surprise, he stiffened his spine and backed up until he leaned against the wall.

"I don't believe I care for any," he answered, and she knew from his level gaze that he was not declining her tea.

He might as well have slapped her in the face, even if she was only teasing him. But she'd choke before she let show the sting she was feeling.

"Suit yourself," she said with a shrug, "but I'm going to have a cup."

He watched her while she refilled the kettle and placed it back on the stove. When she walked into the pantry to unlock the tea caddy, he kept his back to the wall. He remained in that position while she put the leaves in to steep. If his hands had been behind his back instead of crossed at his chest, she would have sworn he was hiding something.

"Can I get you something, Hunter?" she finally asked when he failed to move. "A drink? A bite to eat? Perhaps a shirt?" She threw in the last comment just to prick at the proper side of him.

It worked. He jerked away from the wall and glanced at the door to the back stairs. Why was he acting so strange?

He had to be hiding something behind his back. Instead of moving toward the staircase, though, he nonchalantly backed into the pantry.

"I beg your pardon, Miss Alexander," his disembodied voice drifted in from the dark anteroom. "I attempted to change into dry clothing, but there was none in here." His irritated tone wasn't lost on her.

When he reappeared in the kitchen, he was wearing a dripping shirt and a frown so intense Marin was sure he meant to drive her from the room.

"Satisfied?" he said.

Marin laughed out loud and walked around the table.

"Oh, really, Hunter. I was only teasing about the shirt. Get that thing off before you make yourself sick."

She started to peel the shirt from him, but he shrugged her hands away and stepped back. Had he felt the same jolt as she? The fingers that had brushed his cool, moist skin tingled with heat, like she'd passed them through a flame.

"C'mon, Hunter. Lord, can't you take a joke?" She raised her hands again to pluck at his shirt, but his voice stopped her cold.

"The last time you were this close to me, Miss Alexander, you kissed me and then you slapped me. Do you now intend to disrobe me?"

He was trying to make her mad. He was going for the shock value of his words, Marin knew. A dozen stinging remarks jumped to her tongue, but she bit them all back. When she glanced at his face, his self-satisfied smirk produced the tiniest crease of a dimple in his left cheek.

Without another thought she grabbed two handfuls of the cold, wet cambric of his shirt. With one yank, her lips were on his, her tongue searching, finding his. The warmth of his responding mouth sent streamers of knee-weakening heat curling through her body. She prolonged the kiss until she had to come up for air. When she did, she released his shirt with a little shove.

Marin forced herself to breathe evenly, and to her satisfaction, Hunter struggled with his own breathing.

She dragged her gaze down the length of his rain-drenched body before saying in a husky voice, "Disrobing you isn't necessary, Hunter. It seems you have no secrets from me."

He stood, his chest heaving as he studied her with intensity. That piercing gaze seemed to reach into the depths of her spirit. Before he could speak, before she allowed him to see into her soul, she turned and slowly, deliberately, walked out of the room.

Hunter sat at the dining room table, a cold, congealed breakfast before him, a tepid cup of coffee in his hand, and his chair placed to allow a clear view of any traffic on the stairs.

Where the devil was she? He'd heard Katie galloping about upstairs for a good thirty minutes. Was his daughter to be left swinging from the chandeliers while Miss Alexander languished in bed half the day?

A night of restless tossing in a tangle of damp sheets had left him with the temperament of a rabid dog. But he preferred that over what he'd felt last night when Marin Alexander kissed him and then walked from the room.

A prophetic gesture, no doubt. Especially if she had chanced to see the grotesque scars deforming his back.

Well, he would put a stop to her forward behavior once and for all. As soon as she bothered to stir herself he'd—

Marin walked into the room, a basket of fresh-cut flowers

on her arm. Her hair hung loose, as it had the night before, all soft and curling in the July heat. There was a smudge of dirt on her cheek, and the pale blue cotton gown clung to her with damp sensuality.

Damn the woman!

"Good morning, sleepyhead," she had the audacity to say. "Did you sleep well?" Her cheerful demeanor had the same effect as whiskey poured on an open wound.

She chose a delicate porcelain vase from the sideboard and began filling it with flowers. When he just sat and glared at her, she turned and studied him.

"Did you not sleep well, Hunter?"

The memory of the night he'd spent dragged at him.

"I slept very well, thank you." He stood and threw his napkin on the table. "Miss Alexander, there must not be a repeat of the events of last night."

Marin's back stiffened and a delicate pink rose in her face. Her hands stilled on the arrangement.

"I won't have an employee throwing herself on me. Need I remind you that you've agreed to be Katie's governess as well as my secretary? I realize you took my words last night as a challenge, but I must insist you stifle such urges toward loose conduct in the future."

The moment the words left his lips he knew he should never have uttered them. Marin hid what she was thinking well. Her only reaction was to narrow her eyes slightly, a glimmer of hurt there.

The righteous indignation he'd been cultivating all night evaporated like morning mist against a rising sun. Perhaps he should apologize for being so blunt.

But he was not the apologizing type.

Marin resumed her floral arranging momentarily, then stopped and dusted off her hands.

"I really must thank you, Mr. Pierce. You've just made it easy for me to 'stifle such urges.' In fact, I daresay you've eliminated them altogether."

It was the first time she'd ever called him anything but Hunter. He didn't like the way it sounded on her lips, or the way it made him feel.

He expected her now to tender her resignation and leave in a huff. He almost wanted her to, just so he could congratulate himself on being right. But he knew if she did he would have more sleepless nights looming far into his future.

To his utter relief she placed the vase of flowers back on the sideboard and smiled at him sweetly.

"Well, Mr. Pierce, I guess I'd better go find Katie and govern her. I wouldn't want to be accused of lying down on the job. Or even having the urge to."

Her pointed smile held no warmth. Indeed, the gold of her eyes resembled amber ice.

She swished her skirts away as she passed, making sure not a thread of fabric touched him.

He turned to look back at the vase when she disappeared up the stairs. The multicolored flowers now looked as if a carriage had run over them.

Strange. He felt much the same way.

Marin marched up the steps with as much dignity as she could muster. She had to get away from him before her shaky facade of haughtiness crumbled.

As she stepped onto the landing, a familiar cacophony ruptured the silence of the house.

The huge, golden-haired puppy rounded the corner of the staircase, yelping like the hounds of hell were after him. The half-grown kitten was a black, hissing blur behind him. The two somersaulted down the stairs to the landing, slid to the next set of stairs and somersaulted down those. The puppy ran through the foyer, his toenails scratching at the parquet floor, then slammed into the door when he tried to make the turn into the parlor.

The kitten wasted no time in attacking. In a matter of seconds both cat and dog disappeared into the recesses of the house, their hissing and yelping fading as they found an open back door.

Katie clattered down the steps to Marin, her short little legs only long enough to take one step at a time. Big, glistening tears hovered on her lashes.

"Puffy and Angel don't like each other, Mawin!" she wailed as she buried her face in Marin's skirts.

Marin knelt beside her and dried her tears with a swipe of her thumbs. She almost laughed at the tragic little face, despite the aching in her chest, but she schooled her features into a serious expression.

"Dogs and cats don't usually like each other, but we'll just have to teach them to get along, won't we?"

Katie brightened and nodded enthusiastically. "Can we teach them now?"

Animal training was not on her list of things she'd like to do right now. But maybe the distraction was just what she needed.

"Sure. Let's go see if we can find them. At the rate they were going they could be in Mississippi by now!"

She took Katie's tiny little hand in hers, and together they made their way downstairs.

Marin caught a flicker of movement and looked up to find Hunter standing in the dining room doorway. She allowed herself only the briefest moment of regret, then turned to Katie and squeezed her hand. The pain his rejection caused her would stay buried with all the other pain she'd suffered.

"So, which one is Puffy and which one is Angel? As if I didn't know."

She had a feeling that naming this particular cat Angel was an example of irony at its best.

The dark-haired man with the Irish accent knocked back his third shot of whiskey and signaled for the waiter to bring him another drink. He turned back to the man sitting across from him.

"She turned me down, Richardson. I tell ye, Pierce is holdin' her there with the excuse that his by-blow needs her. She'll not be nanny to another man's whelp if I can help it."

The man across from him showed a bit more interest.

"Pierce has a child born on the wrong side of the blanket? Who is the mother?"

"Was. She's dead. Died a few days ago of consumption. Her name was Delia Cabot Branson. She dropped the child off, announced she was Pierce's, and neatly died during the night. Now Pierce has me Mari playing nursemaid to the chit. Well, I'll sue for breach of promise, I will."

Harold Cabot drew on his cigar and rose from the chair in the exclusive men's club. This might be the opportunity he'd been looking for.

He'd just been sitting there, savoring his last cigar and planning how to duck out of his lodgings without paying the rent he owed. He had to admit, the only reason he'd gotten past the sacred doors of this establishment was thanks to an acquaintance who was too drunk to walk in on his own.

He polished the toes of his shoes on the backs of his trouser legs, smoothed his hair back, and walked up to the two men on whose conversation he'd been eavesdropping.

"Forgive me, gentlemen, for interrupting, but I happened to overhear you mention the name of a cousin of mine whom I've lost contact with, and I thought perhaps you could tell me where to find her. Delia Cabot Branson? My name is Harold Cabot."

The two men glanced uneasily at each other, then stood.

"Niles Kilpatrick, at your service, and this is Bernard Richardson."

Harold shook hands with the men, then took the chair they offered.

"Do you know where I might find my cousin? Has she returned to Memphis?"

Kilpatrick downed another shot of whiskey and cleared his throat.

"Well, Cabot, it's sorry I am to tell ye your cousin passed on several days ago."

Harold forced his face to register shock, then sorrow.

"Oh. How very distressing. Did she leave a husband and family behind? Someone to whom I can offer my condolences?"

The two men exchanged another uncomfortable glance. Kilpatrick spoke again.

"She has a daughter here. She's staying with her . . . Hunter Pierce at Pierce Hall."

"Thank you, gentlemen. I appreciate your help. Terribly sorry to have interrupted you."

Harold was on his feet and out the door before the others had a chance to respond. He had some serious thinking to do. With the right plan, he might never have to work another day in his life.

Chapter 11

IT HAD BEEN two weeks since he'd told Marin to remember her position in this house, and she had done an exemplary job of following his wishes.

He could kick himself.

God, how he missed the sound of her voice calling him Hunter. Just hearing it made him feel as if he'd been caressed. She hadn't addressed him as anything but Mr. Pierce since that day. Even then, there was no emotion. No anger, no hurt . . . no caress.

He tossed his pen aside and scooted the chair backward as he rose from the desk. He'd been working on the books for hours, hoping to find a way to cut expenses in the event the crop yield was as bad as he anticipated.

Perhaps some fresh air would clear his head and get his mind off Marin.

A breeze from the front door carried in the sound of child-

ish giggling and yipping puppy. He followed the noise, mesmerized by sounds that had been so foreign in this house. He
stopped himself in the doorway, not wanting to disturb the
scene. As he watched, the walls around his heart cracked, then
crumbled into dust, and his heart slowly melted and trickled
into every pore of his body.

Marin and Katie sat on the lawn in front of the house, two
colorful splashes on a verdant background. Marin's pale peach
gown billowed in the breeze around her drawn-up knees.
Katie's tiny pink frock was decorated with a number of grass
stains.

Hunter marveled at that. Had his mother been the one with
Katie, the little girl would have never been allowed the chance
to stain her clothes. And if by some misfortune she had, she'd
have been whisked off, with a severe reprimand, to have her
clothing changed.

Katie burst into fresh giggles when the enormous puppy
loped from behind a shrub and fell over its own feet. He tumbled into her lap just as the black cat attacked from behind a
tree.

The animals had become fast friends and any battles now
were strictly spurious. This one had Katie right in the middle.
She squealed and giggled hysterically as the two combatants
circled her in a frenzy.

The cat, ever the troublemaker, deviated from course and
climbed Marin's bodice to yowl at the dog from atop her
shoulders.

The puppy, clown that he was, and larger now than most full
grown dogs, yipped and tumbled into Marin, knocking her
over and sending the cat flying.

The whole scene was so like that in the barn, Hunter could
not resist. He wanted to be part of this. He wanted to sit on the

grass with his daughter and Marin Alexander. He wanted the dog and the cat to pounce on him and knock him backward. He wanted grass stains on his shirt.

He wanted what he had never had.

Oh, God, he wanted her.

Without quite knowing how he got there, he found himself standing over them, the toes of his boots disappearing under the skirts of a giggling Marin. The giggling stopped when he asked, "May I join you?"

Marin sat up with a jerk and dusted off her clothes. Katie grabbed his hand and tugged him toward the ground.

"C'mon, Papa! Come and play!"

He sank to the ground and crossed his legs. The cat immediately jumped onto his right knee and hesitantly sniffed his hands. He held them still, allowing the little black nose to travel along his fingertips. When he tried to pet her, she dodged his hand, but after sufficient sniffing, he must have passed the test, because she daintily tiptoed along his thigh and curled into a ball in the nest of his legs.

Angel. Lord, what a misnomer. The cat was mischief incarnate. In two weeks she had scratched, shredded, or knocked over every item left vulnerable in the house. And what the cat didn't destroy, the dog did. There were now long, permanent scratches in the parquet floor of the foyer from the dog trying to make the turn at a dead run and slamming into the door.

He loved it.

"Here PuffyPuffyPuffy," Katie called. The puppy gamboled to Katie and liberally washed her face with his tongue.

"Say hello to Puffy, Papa."

Hunter reached over and scratched behind the furry ears.

"Say it, Papa!"

He smiled and nodded seriously.

"How do you do, Puffy?" Was there a word in the English language that sounded any less virile than Puffy? It was virtually impossible to utter the word in a masculine manner. He'd rather not say it unless absolutely necessary.

A most unfortunate name to give an animal, but a most accurate moniker in this instance. The dog looked like a huge golden puff of cotton with four legs and enormous feet. If the dog grows into its feet, he thought, it will be the size of a pony.

Katie and the animals finally calmed to a sleepy quiet. Puffy lay stretched out on his back, furiously pumping a hind leg as Katie scratched his pink belly. A veritable roar rose from the black lump of fur in Hunter's lap.

The silence of their surroundings was deafening. It did not escape Hunter that Marin had not said a word since his arrival. He turned his gaze to her and found her looking at him. She did not look away.

If her eyes held any emotion at all it was that of sadness. He felt anew the regret for having reprimanded her. When he was truthful with himself, he admitted that he enjoyed her playful familiarity. Looked forward to it, in fact. And he'd enjoyed the kisses entirely too much. So much so that it scared him right into attempting to enrage her so that she would never make him question his life again.

But his heart, so newly free of the walls around it, had already asked all the questions, and he knew, without a doubt, that he was looking into the amber eyes of his answer. There was one thing he must do.

"Marin, I am very sorry for the way I spoke to you two weeks ago. I was caught unawares, and to be perfectly honest, I enjoyed your kiss too much." He glanced down at the cat and then back at her. "I should not have spoken so harshly, but I fear you . . . spooked me with your openness." He waited for her to respond, but she simply continued to look at him. "I dealt poorly with the situation, but you are a most unusual woman, and I have no experience with a woman of your nature."

She was not making this easy for him. Any moment now he would find himself babbling.

"Do you forgive me for speaking to you as I did?"

Marin watched as Hunter sat cross-legged, gently stroking the cat in his lap and apologizing for jumping down her throat.

If he only knew how much she would forgive. She'd been miserable the last two weeks. At times she physically ached, but she had long ago become a master at masking her emotions. Hunter's rebuke hurt so much, though, it had been a struggle to keep her feelings in check.

She had decided in the last few days, however, that this new relationship with Hunter as her employer was much easier. He'd made his feelings clear, and it was safer for Marin to look at him as an employer. She'd allowed herself to get much too close, to have fleeting thoughts of what might be. But she would never allow herself to care like that again. She couldn't let herself forget that Hunter's ghost looked exactly the age of Hunter now. The thought had scratched at her consciousness until she finally had to acknowledge it. Was he destined to die soon?

She fought down the ache that thought caused and looked back at his beseeching face. A crescent dimpled his left cheek as he clearly tried to look repentant.

Yes. It had been much easier. And now he was threatening to blow her newfound resolve out of the water. But she couldn't allow him to draw her back into his life, back to hoping for something that could only hurt her in the long run.

She smiled at his boyish grin, charmed in spite of her best intentions.

"Of course I forgive you, Mr. Pierce. But you were correct in reprimanding me." Was that a look of disappointment in his eyes? "I've been entirely too familiar, and I needed reminding of my place. I promise you won't have to remind me again."

That *was* disappointment she saw! He looked positively crestfallen. She was tempted to take back her words and start teasing him again, but she bolstered her resolve.

It just didn't pay to get close to people.

He seemed at a loss for words. As he sat and looked at Marin, his hand now quiet on the cat, Katie tiptoed up behind him and slid her chubby little arms around his neck.

Hunter leaned his head back to touch Katie's cheek with his own. His eyes tightly closed, a look of exquisite pain passed across his face.

Marin could only watch with bitter regret. She would give anything to be part of that scene. To be free to slide her arms around Hunter's neck, to pull Katie close and cuddle her next to them. But every person in her life, every single one of them, died if she got too close. She wouldn't allow herself to care. She couldn't bear another death of a loved one. And somewhere in an illogical little corner of her mind, a tiny voice said, "Maybe it's your fault."

"Looks like there may be a storm blowing in." Hunter's emotionless voice cut into her thoughts, and she wondered how long he'd been staring at her.

She glanced at the western sky. Huge dark clouds boiled toward Memphis, bringing with them a fresh wind that smelled of rain. Just then Puffy whimpered and scooted under Hunter's arm until he managed to displace Angel on Hunter's lap.

Angel raised her head only long enough to bestow an indignant glare and halfheartedly bat a paw in protest.

Hunter chuckled sadly at the piles of fur in his lap, scratching both behind pointed ears and murmuring "Coward" to the puppy. A booming clap of thunder sent the animals scrambling to their feet and racing across the lawn, into the open front door. Katie disappeared through it moments later, calling the animals' names and bossily ordering them back outside.

The sound of thunder, the darkening sky, the fresh wind whipping her hair all reminded Marin of her last day in 1996. The tree they sat under now was the very same tree under which Hunter's spirit had merged with hers, sending mindnumbing thrills flashing through her body. She slid her gaze to look at him. The wind ruffled his hair; the soft folds of his shirt billowed invitingly. Unbidden tears burned her eyes, but she fought them back, along with the desire to touch him.

"I don't like the looks of that." Hunter's face was turned to the southwest sky. He was right. A greenish cast lent an eerie glow over the Arkansas landscape south of Memphis. "We had best close up the house and prepare for a bad one."

He rose, dusted off his trousers, then held out his hand to help Marin to her feet.

The instant her skin touched his, a thunderclap vibrated the earth and lightning pierced the sky. Ecstasy raced from his fingertips to penetrate every inch of her body. When the last waves of the memory subsided, she found herself in his arms, her head pressed against his precious chest. He murmured soothing words as he crushed her to him.

Damn! Damn, she couldn't touch him! She couldn't allow herself to touch him again.

This time the tears refused to be stopped. Hot and bitter, they filled her eyes, then spilled onto his snowy white shirt.

Her pain tore at her then. It rose from the pit of her stomach and spiraled outward. She pulled away from him, her face buried in her hands as she forced herself to stand alone. It wasn't fair! The pain she'd suffered, the love that had died. She curled into herself, awash with unbearable memories, then she stomped once on the ground, hard, to force it all to stop.

It wouldn't stop.

"Marin, what—"

She jerked free of the hand Hunter had placed on her arm, grabbed up a handful of skirts, and ran for the comfort of the house.

A howling wind rattled the windows, even though the shutters were closed against it. Rain battered the house so hard it sounded like rocks cascading from the sky.

Hunter was certain he would see hailstones the size of chicken eggs when he opened the front door, and all he could think of was more damage to his crop. Relief washed over him when he stepped onto the veranda and was met with nothing more than a very hard rain.

The energy of the storm was exhilarating. He much preferred it to the atmosphere inside the house. He pulled the door closed behind him and drew his favorite wicker rocker up to the handrail. The cushion felt only a little damp as he leaned back and propped his feet on the rail, one booted foot crossed over the other. The force of the wind blew a fine mist onto the porch. He raised his face to it, breathing in the clean smell of summer storm and wishing he felt free to invite Marin to join him.

He feared that, with his angry words, he had put to death any hopes of becoming close to Marin. Apologies did not come easy to him, but he had sincerely given one in an attempt to rekindle that wonderful, bantering personality so unique to her. He'd been astounded at the degree of his disappointment when she called him Mr. Pierce again and made it clear she would no longer give in to spontaneity.

Spontaneity, hell. He'd been disappointed that he could no longer look forward to the unexpected kiss from a playful Marin.

"Papa?"

He dropped his feet to the floor and turned to see Katie peering out the door at him.

"I'm a-scared of the funder."

He smiled at the huge, round eyes, the color so like his own. They got rounder when a flash of lightning split the sky. He patted his lap.

"Climb up here. I'll protect you from the big, bad thunder."

Katie scampered out the door and scrambled onto his lap just as the expected boom shook the house. She shivered and burrowed her bottom as far back as she could. He wrapped both arms around her and rested his chin lightly on her head.

Lord, she felt good. That tiny, warm body curled so trustingly into his. Her clean, soapy smell mingled with that of fresh grass and puppy. Her dark curls felt like silk against his jaw. He nuzzled her ear as he looked out at the sky.

"I'll tell you a secret," he whispered, "so you never have to be afraid of thunder again."

She sat very still and whispered back, "What?"

"Thunder cannot harm you."

She turned and looked up into his eyes with skepticism.

"It's true," he assured. "Thunder is just clouds bumping together. It is just a noise, like when you bump your hands together. They make a clap. Well, clouds make a thunderclap when they bump together."

She gave this theory some thought, then settled back against his chest, a little more relaxed. He would deal with the lightning side of the coin another time.

As she snuggled against him Hunter rocked gently. He noticed the greenish cast in the sky was gone, and he rested his head back and closed his eyes. He imagined Marin sitting next to him as he rocked Katie. The two women in his life that he never knew he needed, never thought he wanted.

He would never know how the heart of that woman ached with longing when she came looking for her charge and found her quietly watching the rain, wrapped in her sleeping father's arms.

Marin heard the beep and recognized it this time for what it was. A heart monitor.

Momentary panic seized her before a calm settled over her. The beep increased in cadence and then slowed. Would she see Ryan again?

"Yes."

The single word caressed her like a lover's touch. She turned her head to the sound and struggled to open her eyes.

He was beside her bed again, helmet in hand and wearing the green flight suit she'd always loved. He looked so good in it. The monitor beeped faster as she thought of the times she'd toyed with all those zippers, ending the game when she came to the one that zipped open from either direction.

"Thoughts like that'll get you another shot of painkiller, Fireball."

What felt like a laugh came out sounding like a moan.

The warm mist of his hand brushed along her cheek. He smiled that bone-melting smile of his, then whispered in her ear, *"I love you, Marin."*

She tried to smile, but her muscles refused to cooperate. Before she could panic, Ryan's hands cradled her cheeks.

"Don't," he said softly. *"Don't try to move."* He took his helmet from the bed and placed it on the shiny hospital floor. Sinking down to perch on it, his green gaze came level with hers.

"You've fallen into a coma. That's why you can't move." He paused and smiled gently. The serenity he exuded calmed her. *"You can't even open your eyes—"*

But I can see you!

"Your spirit sees me, Fireball. Your spirit can't go into a coma. It can't die. It can only move on."

He was going to ask her to go with him again. She sensed it before he spoke.

"You're right. That's why I'm here." He studied her face, probed into her soul with his gaze. *"It's time to go, Marin. There's nothing left for you here. There's no need to hang on to this life."* The gentleness, the sweetness of his voice brought tears to her eyes. They burned a hot, moist trail across her temples and into her hair.

He stood now and tucked his helmet under his arm. *"Come with me. You just have to want it."* As he backed toward the door with his hand outstretched, his vaporous quality became more and more translucent.

Ryan! Oh, God! Ryan, don't go! She struggled to move but couldn't. The deep sobs that racked her soul were only whimpers to her ears. Finally, as if the bonds that held her snapped, she felt her hand reach for him. Her arm lifted and her head raised. Oh, God, she felt weightless after being trapped for so long in that bed! She hesitantly placed her feet on the cool, smooth floor. It surprised her that it took no effort to rise.

She glanced back at the bed and was staggered by what she saw. She saw herself, pale and broken, with white bandages wrapping most of her body. She looked frantically back at the door.

Ryan was almost gone, and she hurried to be with him. She ran to the door, and though Ryan was still visible on the other side, she couldn't pass through it. She screamed for him to wait.

Pain flared in his eyes, so intense that Marin could feel it herself. She tried to run to him again, but it was as if a thin steel thread held her back.

When he disappeared altogether her mind stopped screaming. She'd tried. She'd tried to let go. It wasn't as easy as he'd said.

A familiar feeling—one she'd lived with most of her life—washed over her. She felt deserted. And alone.

"You are not alone. I won't allow it."

A real sob, not a whimper, broke from her throat as she looked at Hunter. He opened his arms to her as he stood beside her bed.

She wanted to run to him. Wanted him to wrap his arms around her as he had done to Katie. But she couldn't bear it.

His ghost was so young.

Hunter's eyes reflected all the pain she'd ever felt. His arms dropped to his sides in defeat.

"You cannot lose your faith, Marin. If you do, you lose your soul."

She kept herself from going to him, though his words pulled at her. She couldn't give in to him, only to be left staring at his lifeless face framed by the wood of his coffin.

He looked as if she'd slapped him. He started to fade, but his voice still rang strong. "Things are not always as they seem. Have faith in your destiny. You are the only one who can change it."

When the barest outline of him faded from view, Marin's energy faded with it. She was being pulled, inexorably, back into the broken, still body on the bed.

Chapter 12

Hunter woke the next morning with a new determination and a fire in him to put it to action.

And the day was perfect for it.

The storm of the day before ushered in an unseasonably cool day. White clouds marbleized the perfect blue of the sky. The air was light and free of its usual moisture. Everyone, even Ambrose, walked with a new vigor.

Hunter gave one last tug to the burgundy silk tie at his neck and flicked a glance at the mirror. He snatched up his coat, shoving his arms into the sleeves as he trotted down the steps to breakfast.

He could almost laugh out loud. Today was a turning point in his life, and nothing was going to ruin it.

"Mamie!" The wonderful old black servant jumped in alarm, scattering silverware across the tabletop. When she saw Hunter, she held her chest with one hand and fanned herself with her apron.

"Mistah Hunter! Lordy, what you screeching at me for? I ain't doin' nothin' to get screeched at. You don't never go around hollerin' at peoples. What got in your head?"

Hunter grabbed Mamie by the shoulders and planted a loud, affectionate kiss on her massive cheek. He laughed at her saucer-sized eyes.

"Mamie, I have never in my life been accused of screeching until now." He pulled a chair to the table and dropped the napkin in his lap. "But who knows? Perhaps it will become a habit!" He ignored the curious look she gave him. "Have Emmaletta prepare a picnic. I plan to take Marin and Katie to the river for lunch."

As Mamie lumbered past Hunter on the way to the kitchen, he playfully flicked the back of his hand against her enormous rump. She jumped again and rewarded him with the most disbelieving stare he'd ever seen. She reached out and slapped a hand to his forehead, feeling for a fever that didn't exist.

"I feel fine, Mamie, and I'm completely sane. Maybe for the first time in my life!"

When Mamie finally finished eyeing him and disappeared into the kitchen, Hunter plowed into the food before him like he hadn't eaten in weeks.

Marin was quickly developing a whole new respect for mothers, both working and nonworking. Maybe it was easier if a woman started out with a little tiny kid and worked her way up.

At the moment, this kid seemed intent on needing or wanting something every time Marin lowered herself into a chair. The perfect solution proved to be something that entertained this little bundle of energy in a sitting position.

Katie sat on Marin's lap, her hands in Marin's, her chubby index fingers pointed, while Marin helped her play "Chopsticks" for the thousandth time on the grand piano in the music room.

At least this activity kept Marin from thinking too much about her dream last night. Or had it been a dream?

"You play something now, Mawin." Katie looked up at her with big, serious eyes. "It's your turn."

She was such a sweet little thing, even if she was exhausting.

"Okay. Can you sit beside me for a while?"

Katie squirmed off of Marin's lap and settled herself onto a straight-back chair they'd pilfered from the dining room.

Marin hadn't touched a piano since before she started her job as director of Pierce Hall. She adjusted her position a bit, then played a few scales to warm up. Katie clapped as if she'd just rendered a concert performance.

"Moonlight Sonata" flowed from Marin's fingers. She'd played it so many times she didn't even have to think about it. Katie clapped and moved to the edge of the chair as she studiously watched Marin's fingers.

Marin tried her hand at "Memory" and did a pretty decent job of it until she got to the part with all the flats. She gave up on that song.

"Play a happy song. Can you play a happy song?"

A happy song. She couldn't think of one to play without sheet music in front of her. Then she remembered the one song she'd had to play in a high school production. The song all her friends made her play if she got within fifty feet of a piano. She looked down at Katie and smiled.

"You want happy? This is as happy as I get."

Her fingers pounded the ivory keys with a mind of their own as she banged out "Great Balls of Fire," Jerry Lee Lewis style. The good thing about the song was that no one could tell if she hit a few sour notes, which she did. Katie slid from her chair and stood at her elbow in rapt attention. When Marin hit the last note she spun around on the stool to bow to her audience of . . . two!

Hunter stood just inside the door, obviously trying to decide how to react to the unusual music of the impromptu concert.

"What a very interesting piece of music. I don't believe I have ever heard it before." He shoved away from the doorframe and sauntered into the room.

Marin swiveled back and forth on the stool, trying to decide if she should say it.

"Not likely, Mr. Pierce. It won't be written for another eighty years or so."

She couldn't read the hint of his unwavering smile. He raised one dark brow and gazed at her.

"Still suffering from the carriage accident? Perhaps Dr. Ritter should have another look at you."

The statement was rhetorical rather than concerned. Marin simply returned his half smile with one of her own.

"Whatever you say, Mr. Pierce."

He pulled his gaze from hers, reached down and tapped a high C on the piano several times. "Where did you learn to play like that?"

Marin swiveled back to face the keyboard again. The warmth of his nearness and his outdoorsy scent caused fingers of heat to dance across her neck.

"Oh, I . . . just . . . my dad . . . always . . ."

His left hand reached around her and tapped a low C. Both arms now flanked her as he continued to toy with the keyboard. She stared at the ivory and black keys, at the strong, dark hands with such nimble fingers, and every cell in her body ached. She swallowed hard.

"Can you play this one?" His voice sounded uncharacteristically husky.

Her hair rippled with the warm breath of his question, his lips so close to her ear she could almost feel them. He began playing a haunting, sweet melody that encircled her with the heat of his body. The ring of the notes sounded muffled through the roar of her heartbeat racing in her ears. She could feel every inch of his body wrapped around her, as though he held her in an embrace, but nowhere did his body actually touch hers. He just hovered there, pulling her like a magnet, not quite within reach, his warm breath stirring the wisps of hair at her temples.

Every muscle in her body tensed, her breathing slowed to near nothing, and she sat absolutely still while hot chills erupted across her body.

She fought to slow her staccato heart. She fought the urge to lean back against him, so that his hands would lift from the piano and pull her closer. She fought the desire to turn her head the few short inches that would bring her lips to brush against his.

She closed her eyes to block out the sight of his flowing hands. For one brief moment she allowed the flame he'd ignited within her to burn out of control, to consume her from her fingertips to her toes.

And she reveled in it.

Then, in the back of her mind, the image of a youthful

ghost took shape. The image was a cold, drenching shower that reduced that inner fire to smoldering ashes.

The music faltered to a stop in midmeasure. Neither of them moved a muscle. Marin prayed that he would rise and release her from the sweet prison of his arms. Though he had yet to move, she could almost feel him drawing nearer. If he touched her, all was lost. She couldn't fight his touch. The hair at her temples tickled her skin with his erratic breathing.

"Did Mawin teach you how to do that, Papa? She's gonna teach me how." Katie's inquisitive little face ducked under Hunter's right arm and popped into view.

A heartbeat of silence ended as they both released long-pent-up breaths. Marin's nerves twanged like taut piano wires. But bless Katie, for saving her from herself!

Finally, Hunter removed his hands from beside her and rose to scoop Katie into his arms.

"No, my mother saw to it that I learned to play." He narrowed his eyes and exaggerated a glare. "I was taught by a vicious old maid who held a sharp quill under my wrists and a ruler over my fingers." Katie's eyes widened and she twisted in his arms to look at Marin. "Don't worry, Katiedid." Hunter changed the glare to a grin. "There's not a sharp quill in the house."

Katie giggled with delight. "Mawin calls me Katiedid, too, Papa!"

He flicked a glance in Marin's direction with a smile that said, *So we have something in common,* then slapped his hands together and rubbed them with enthusiasm.

"How would you two ladies like to go on a picnic this afternoon?"

Katie clapped her hands and cried, "Oh, yes, Papa. Yes!"

All Marin could think of was an afternoon of torment, to be so close to Hunter, to see him happy and relaxed. It was difficult enough to keep her distance when he was overbearing and disagreeable. No, a picnic would not be a smart thing to do.

"And how about Marin? Will she do us the honor of accompanying us?"

She glanced up at Hunter, and he held her gaze. Lord, he could look like an innocent little boy when he wanted to. Both dimples were out in full force, cracking her resolve. Though her brain said *No,* the word that came out was, "Sure."

"Wonderful! I shall have Nathan hitch up the buggy while you ladies freshen up!" He spun Katie around as he lowered her to the floor. She squealed and giggled, then staggered when he let her go. "The buggy will be out front in five minutes." He bestowed one last, long smile on Marin, a smile that was anything but innocent. Then he strode from the room.

She was in trouble.

Hunter sat with his back against a tree and stared at Marin, trying to will her to turn around and look at him.

She busied herself with laying out the food, positioning herself as far away from him as she could on the old quilt.

He was sure she'd felt . . . something . . . as much as he had, when he'd trapped her at the piano. The world had ceased to exist for a few brief moments. He couldn't even recall when he'd stopped playing. There had just been him, and her, and that soft, flowery scent she wore that impaired his mind far more quickly and effectively than whiskey.

He tired of watching her drag out the process of emptying

the basket, so he hooked the handle with one booted foot and pulled it to him. She didn't quite look up, even though he knew she was watching. The woman was clearly uncomfortable.

He rummaged through the remnants of the hamper, blessing Emmaletta as he pulled out a vintage bottle of wine and two stemmed goblets.

Marin still wasn't openly watching him, but he was sure she knew every move he made. He found the corkscrew and opened the wine, then poured them each a healthy measure. For Katie he unearthed a small crock of milk.

"Wine?" he asked as he extended one golden-filled goblet in her direction.

"No, thanks. Wine goes straight to my head." She still refused to look up, giving an inordinate amount of attention to placing each container of food just so.

He made a great show of inspecting the remnants in the hamper, then offered the glass again with a helpless grin.

"It seems there's nothing else to drink."

This time she looked straight at him.

"Oh, give it to me then," she said as she snatched the stemware from his fingers, sloshing wine over his hand. She took a sip, and then another, then met his eyes with a level gaze, as if to say, *Satisfied?*

Hunter couldn't suppress the tiniest grin as he flicked away the wine. He quite enjoyed the defiant side of Miss Alexander.

"Katie, come and eat," Marin called after breaking her gaze from his.

Katie continued to stalk a colorful butterfly until it fluttered out of reach. Dejected, she returned to the quilt and knuckled her eyes with tiny fists. A huge yawn followed, but she perked up a bit when Marin handed out plates of fried chicken and mashed potato salad.

Hunter refilled both wineglasses while Marin busied herself with the food. He raised his glass in salute.

"To cool days in August."

Marin hesitated only a second before touching her goblet to his with a *ching*. Katie popped up, giggling, joining the toast with her mug of milk. As Marin sipped her wine, Hunter knew she watched him from beneath lowered lashes.

"Papa, why couldn't Puffy and Angel come? They would like a picnic, too."

"Because, Katiedid, Angel and the puppy would like the picnic too well. I daresay they would both be in the middle of all this food, and we would be left with nothing." Hunter reached over and topped off Marin's wine. "I believe I am safe in saying that we do not have the most well behaved pets in Memphis."

Katie yawned again and nodded. "Uh-huh. Puffy was naughty on the rug in the parlor yesterday."

Hunter decided that lunch was not the time to find out the details of that particular event.

Katie's eyelids drooped lower and lower, as did the half-eaten plateful of food. Marin intercepted the toppling china before it landed on the quilt. Gently, she lowered Katie to her side, where the little moppet curled into a ball, her thumb disappearing between her lips.

They both watched Katie sleep for a few moments before resuming their meal in uncomfortable silence.

He couldn't help but notice that Marin ate very little. She picked at her food a while longer, then set her plate to the side and stared out at the river and the Arkansas landscape, her knees drawn up in front of her. Her wineglass dangled from slender fingers. Every now and then she took a sip.

"It's amazing how it hasn't changed much," she said as she continued to study the Arkansas horizon.

"What hasn't changed much?"

The hum of insects, Katie's quiet breathing, and the gentle lapping of water on the bank were the only sounds to be heard.

Marin drew in a deep breath and turned to face him. She held out her glass to be refilled. He filled first hers and then his own. She seemed disinclined to answer his question, content with just looking at him.

As she held his gaze she sipped from the crystal goblet. When she lowered the glass to once more dangle from her fingers, her lips were moist with the sweet white wine. One pale gold bead hovered on her lower lip before her tongue slowly appeared to lick it away.

His entire body flared with aching longing. It took a supreme act of will to suppress the moan rising in his throat, to keep from pinning her to the lush grass with his lips on hers.

Instead, he just drained his wineglass. She did the same, then extended the empty glass to be filled again.

"I thought you said wine goes straight to your head." He hesitated before pouring.

"I did. It has. Now I might as well enjoy it."

She leaned back on her elbows, her head thrown back to gaze at the sky through leafy branches. After several moments she closed her eyes and eased farther down to recline on the quilt, her head just inches from Hunter's thigh.

He stared at her face, so flawless with that porcelain skin, a hint of healthy pink dusted across her cheeks. It would take such little effort to lean over and claim those lips with his.

His glance shifted to a sleeping Katie. He quietly thumped his head against the tree, reminding himself of where he was and who he was with. Katie could wake at any moment.

To take his mind from the woman who lay so achingly near to him, he snatched up a bunch of grapes from a bowl of fruit and began popping them, one by one, into his mouth.

"Can I have one?" Marin looked up at him from her vantage point on the quilt.

That seemed a safe enough request. He plucked a grape from its stem and held it out to her. She made no move to take it from him. She simply opened her mouth and tilted her head farther back. His heart thudded faster at this intimate gesture, and when he attempted to drop the grape into her waiting mouth, it bounced off her lower lip, rolled across her pleated bodice and plopped into the grass. She smiled up at him, patiently waiting while he tried not to fumble plucking another.

This time he lowered the morsel of fruit to her lips. She captured it between even, white teeth and held it there for a moment before slowly taking it into her mouth and chewing it as if it were the rarest of delicacies.

"Mmmmmm. That was good." She peered up at him again, a sultry smile sending waves of heat across his neck. The heat intensified when she slowly raised her fingers to her lips and, with painstaking care, removed the seed from the tip of her tongue. "Can I have another?"

He wanted to bang his head against the tree again, to pound some sense into his besotted brain, but instead he picked the most perfect grape and lowered it to her lips.

Along with the grape, her lips closed around his finger,

the hot amber of her gaze telling him it was no accident. Liquid fire shot to the very core of him, then erupted again when her warm tongue traced a lazy path along his fingertip. The gentle suction of her mouth jolted him with more force than a shot of bad whiskey, but he was helpless to remove his finger from between her lips.

His skin tasted of white wine and fresh grapes and that special taste belonging just to men.

Somewhere in her wine-clouded mind Marin knew she was asking for trouble, but at the moment she didn't care. She'd been on her guard almost constantly since the moment she'd arrived, and it seemed every time she let her guard slip a notch she would have that dream again. If it was a dream. She pushed the thought from her mind and basked in the lazy heat that snaked through her body, reveling in the purely sensual sensations of her tongue on Hunter's skin.

Hunter's finger jerked from between her lips at the sound of an approaching horse. For the briefest of moments he reminded her of a schoolboy caught doing something he shouldn't, then the man was back, all serious business.

He rose, rather stiffly she noted with amusement, then helped her to her feet. She tried her best not to weave back and forth, to have a sober expression on her face. Really, it was too ridiculous that she couldn't drink a glass of wine without feeling like it'd been poured directly onto her brain.

Nathan dismounted and brought a piece of paper to Hunter.

"This just come for you, suh. William done sent you somethin' on the wireless."

Marin watched as Hunter ripped open the envelope and read the message within. His face became a stony blank as he crumpled the paper in his fist. He looked out over the river, ignoring everyone. Marin reached over and touched his arm.

"Is it your mother? Is she ill?"

Hunter continued to stare across the water for several moments, seeing something that only he could see. He blinked once, as if blinking away the vision, while the paper crackled in his fist.

"A tornado hit the crop yesterday during the storm. The crop is lost."

Marin didn't know what to say to comfort him. It was obvious the loss of the crop was not just a minor setback.

Before she had a chance to think of any sympathetic words, she heard the sound of another horse approaching. A man she'd never seen reined in his horse and dismounted. For reasons she couldn't name, she disliked the man on sight. He seemed to be in his mid-thirties and was dressed in expensive clothes that did little to hide the ample spare tire at his waistline. The color of his hair was impossible to distinguish from all the pomade he'd used to slick it back. At least she *thought* it was pomade. She would guess his hair to be a dirty blond. His face was so pasty white it looked as though it had never seen the light of day, and a huge brown mole grew right in the middle of his left eyebrow. She stifled a shiver as he swaggered toward them as if he owned the place.

"Hunter Pierce? Sorry to disturb your little picnic here, but your darkies told me where to find you."

He sounded about as sorry as if he'd just won the lottery. Hunter looked over at Nathan before acknowledging the man.

"Thank you, Nathan. You can go on back home." He

turned back to the newcomer. "I am sorry, sir. This is not a good time—"

"My name is Harold Cabot," he interrupted. "Delia Cabot was my cousin. And this little lady," he nodded to the sleeping Katie, "must be her daughter."

"Yes, she is," Hunter answered. "But now is not a good time for a social call, Mr. Cabot. I—"

"Oh, this is not a social call, Pierce. As the child's only living relative, I've come to take her off your hands."

The way the man looked at Katie gave Marin a sick feeling in the pit of her stomach. His oily smile only added to the sensation.

"You have been misinformed, Cabot. You are not her only relative. I am her father. And no one is going to 'take her off my hands.' "

Cabot puffed himself up with a condescending look.

"Well, now. Do you have any proof that you are her father? I cannot allow just anyone to take the child in."

Hunter narrowed his eyes. Even in her slightly drunk state Marin knew enough not to cross him when he looked that way. Apparently, Cabot did not.

"You have only to look at her to know Katie is mine," Hunter said in a low, menacing voice. "Do you have proof, Cabot, that you are Delia's cousin?"

"I can name three people off the top of my head who can attest to the fact that our grandfathers were brothers. I shall present sufficient documents if need be. Can you say the same?"

Marin knew the first words out of Cabot's mouth had placed him on Hunter's bad side. She found herself hoping Hunter would wipe the smug smile from Cabot's face.

"You have chosen a most inopportune time to address this situation, Cabot. If you—"

For the third time the man interrupted Hunter as if he weren't speaking. Veins bulged in Hunter's temples.

"They tell me in town that you have no wife, Pierce. Hard to believe the courts would award custody of a little girl to a bachelor with dubious claims of parentage when a proven relative and his wife are willing to take the child in and raise her as their own."

She would never know exactly how the words happened out of her mouth. She could only attribute them to the wine she'd consumed on an empty stomach and her concern to keep Katie away from this snake of a man.

"You were misinformed again, Mr. Cabot." She stepped up beside Hunter and took his arm in a caressing embrace. "Of course, since we wed only yesterday, I must assume that the news hasn't had a chance to spread."

Cabot's mouth fell open momentarily as every muscle in Hunter's arm went rigid under her fingers. She cast an adoring look upward to her spurious husband's face. A slight queasiness flipped in her stomach at the sight of his clenched jaw and the almost imperceptible flexing of the muscle above it.

A sense of apprehension crawled up her spine as Hunter slowly slid his gaze around to study her with those searing eyes the color of a summer sky. At first his face was totally devoid of emotion. Then the tiniest hint of a dimple appeared. The heat of his hands burned a trail through layers of muslin gown and corset as he slipped his arms possessively about her waist and pulled her intimately to him.

"Yes, Cabot. My bride is correct. You were misinformed."

He bestowed a melting gaze on Marin that turned her knees to spaghetti.

Something told her that she'd just set herself up for a situation she wouldn't be able to back out of. She'd expected to tell this man they were married, then Cabot would go away and leave them alone to get on with their separate lives. But Hunter was being terribly believable. His hands moved slowly, caressingly, up and down her rib cage. His head dipped to what seemed to be an innocent peck on the lips. But a shock of heat flared throughout her body when the tip of his tongue darted out unexpectedly.

A split second later he was again speaking to the man, while Marin fought to still her trembling knees and drumroll heartbeat.

"So you see, Cabot, our little picnic here is part of the celebration of our nuptials. It was good of you to be concerned for Katie's welfare, but as you can see, she is in the best possible hands. Her father's." Hunter stepped forward to shake Cabot's hand in dismissal, but Cabot ignored the extended hand, his face such a deep red he looked like a thermometer ready to burst its top.

"It seems we got off on the wrong foot here, Pierce. My only concern is for my dear cousin's daughter." Cabot fidgeted as the color in his face returned to its sickly hue. "My wife, bless her soul, has given me eleven children. Another child amongst that brood would hardly be noticed." He flicked another glance at the sleeping Katie, a look that made Marin's skin crawl and gave lie to his words. He cleared his throat and hesitated before continuing. "As you can imagine, feeding and clothing a family that size can be a great financial hardship."

Hunter's face hardened at the man's words. He slowly

raked his gaze down Cabot's overfed, expensively clad frame.

"I must commend you, then. If the children's comforts come before your own, then they must be very well cared for indeed."

Cabot's face again turned the color of ripe strawberries, but he did not challenge Hunter's statement.

"I had imagined that my cousin left the child an inheritance that I would use to keep her in the lifestyle to which she is accustomed."

"And elevate your own at the same time, no doubt."

"Now, see here, Pierce! I would be the rightful guardian to the child and her inheritance—"

"If," Hunter interrupted, "she did not have a father, which she does. An inheritance she does not have, but that is of no concern to you. Now, Cabot, if you are here looking for money, you've come to the wrong place." Marin watched as Hunter grabbed their slimy visitor's upper arm and propelled him toward his horse. "I suggest you leave us to our wedding celebration. As far as I'm concerned this conversation is over."

As Marin had found with most cowards, Cabot waited until he was safely on his horse and ready to bolt before he spoke again.

"Well, I don't consider it over. I'm sure Delia left the child well-heeled. I intend to seek custody of her, regardless of your"—he eyed Marin slowly—"fortuitously timed marriage. You've not heard the last from me, Pierce!" With that he gave his horse a vicious kick and disappeared toward town.

The hollow sound of the hoofbeats faded and the hum of insects grew unnaturally loud in the silence that stretched between them. Finally Hunter sucked a deep breath into his lungs and released it slowly.

"I imagine if I fetch Reverend Mesker now, he can have us married before supper." Hunter spoke to the empty landscape in front of him. "He's so old and absentminded I doubt if there will be a problem convincing him this is the tenth of August rather than the eleventh, since according to you we were wed last evening."

Marin's thought processes stopped with Hunter's first words while alarm bells went off in her head like tornado sirens on a stormy night. He couldn't be serious! Yet when he turned to face her there was no hint of humor in his features.

"You know, I didn't actually mean for us to get married!" She scrambled to stop this insanity before she found herself married. "I only said that so the creep would—"

"I know why you said it, Marin," Hunter said with what seemed like resignation. "But surely you knew that publicly announcing that we are married would ultimately lead to that very thing. I assure you, by the end of the day Cabot will have spread the story, or at least asked questions about the marriage. If it's known that we both stood here and declared we had married, and then later deny that we'd wed, the entire city of Memphis would think the worst and ostracize the two of us, as well as Katie. We wouldn't be received in a drawing room in Shelby County."

As Hunter spoke, a sense of dread enveloped Marin like that dark fog she'd walked through before. She couldn't get married. She couldn't marry this man, become close to him, make love to him, and then bury him. She wouldn't.

"And don't forget about Katie. Recanting our story now would surely give Cabot an advantage in a custody battle."

Chapter 13

". . . WITH THE POWER vested in me . . ."

It was later than Hunter had planned. Katie was long abed, and after Mamie's ecstatic histrionics over the woman "her baby" had chosen to marry, she and the other servants had gone off to celebrate even before the deed was done.

Now Reverend Mesker's reedy voice concluded the ceremony that only days earlier Hunter would have sworn he would never participate in.

He held Marin's hands in his. Her fingers felt like slivers of ice, which confirmed the anxiety mirrored in her face. He squeezed her fingers gently in an attempt to reassure her, but she merely cast him a distracted, worried half smile.

"I now pronounce you man and wife."

The reverend cleared his throat in his most pompous manner and smiled benignly at the newlyweds.

"You may osculate," he suggested.

Hunter smiled and stifled a chuckle at the old man's formality, then turned his attention to his new bride. Gently cradling her precious face in his palms, he slowly dipped his head. She seemed terrified, reluctant. Was this the same woman who'd had the audacity to yank him to her by his shirtfront and kiss him soundly on that stormy night last month?

He brushed his lips across hers in a whisper of a kiss once, twice, then threw propriety to the wind, melding his lips to hers, searching for her tongue, trying to convey to her his love and the joy he felt at making her his wife. Marin's body melted against him, molding all her stirring peaks and valleys to his. But to his surprise he felt the passion die in her kiss, and she almost imperceptibly moved away from him.

He raised his head and questioned her with his eyes. After an uncomfortable glance at Reverend Mesker and his wife, she smiled a very unconvincing smile.

Ahhh! So that was it! The minister's presence was inhibiting his fiery little bride. Well, he could resolve that problem easily enough.

Turning to the minister, he shook the old man's hand with enthusiasm.

"I cannot thank you and Mrs. Mesker enough, Reverend, for coming this evening on such short notice. August tenth is a special day for us, and we wanted it to be our wedding day. Will you join us in a glass of champagne? Of course you'll stay for supper."

Neither he nor his wife seemed to notice Hunter's error in the date. Plus, Joseph Mesker did not disappoint Hunter. The man of God had officiated enough weddings to know when to take his leave.

"Appreciate the offer, Hunter, but it's past this old man's bedtime. If you won't be offended, I believe the wife and I shall head on back home."

"Well, if you insist." Hunter tried to sound like he meant it, but was certain he fell short of his goal.

In no time Joseph and Lyda Mesker had been waved down the drive, and the couple found themselves alone in the parlor, their only company their reflections in the gilt-framed pier glass.

Marin had barely uttered a word all evening except to repeat her vows. Hunter had never expected this subdued side of his new bride and was at a bit of a loss. He had to admit that he preferred the outspoken, passionate temptress to this quiet, preoccupied young woman, and he could not help being just the slightest bit disappointed.

Perhaps it was just wedding night nerves.

Of course! What a dolt he had been not to expect it!

Tenderness flooded his heart as he watched his nervous bride pace the length of the carpet. Without another thought he retrieved the bottle of champagne, which had been resting in a silver bucket of ice, and popped the cork with practiced ease.

Marin jumped as if she'd been shot.

Ah, yes. Wedding night nerves. Well, he would be the soul of gentleness. He would introduce her to the joys of the marriage bed with such patience, such gentle tenderness, that he would conquer any fears she had. He would restrain his passion with every ounce of self-control he possessed.

With a teasing flourish he filled two crystal goblets to overflowing. Handing a still-dripping glass to Marin, he twined his arm with hers and held her amber gaze.

"My cup runneth over," he whispered, his lips against the

rim of the crystal. As they sipped and then untwined their arms, he marveled at the aching intensity of the love he felt for this woman. She was everything the other women in his life had never been.

He raised his glass in toast.

"To us," he said with a smile, "and the night to come."

He lowered his glass to clink against Marin's. She hesitated before taking a tiny sip. She seemed to be having trouble making eye contact with him. Finally she clasped the glass with both hands and resumed pacing.

"Hunter," she said as she paced away from him. "I've been thinking. Perhaps it's best if we are married in name only. After all, this marriage was to avoid a scandal and save Katie from a custody battle."

Hunter set his glass on the table and closed the gap between them. He stopped her pacing and turned her to face him.

"Marin, look at me." He guided her chin with the tip of his finger until she finally looked up at him, worry evident in her eyes.

"Sweetheart, there is no scandal threatening enough to induce me to marry a woman I do not wish to marry. My sainted mother has made our family grist for the gossip mills enough times that I am immune to any censure I might encounter. As for custody of Katie, that will be an added bonus to the pleasure of having you for my wife." He smiled and kissed the tip of her nose. "Had you been any other woman, I would have preferred to remain a bachelor and fight for Katie's custody all the way to the highest court in the land. I did *not* marry you out of convenience."

Instead of the expected relief, Marin seemed more disturbed than ever. He could tell that her mind was racing with his words. Her eyes cast about the room, landing on nothing, focusing on some internal fear. He slid his hands to her shoulders and gave her a reassuring squeeze.

"Don't worry, sweetheart. I'll be gentle. We shall take our time. We will take things as slowly as we need to."

Dear God, he thought she was a virgin!

No sooner had she completed the thought than another occurred that sent shock waves exploding through her, nearly jolting the glass of champagne from her hands. There was a very good chance that she *was* a virgin. Mari Sander had never been married.

Marin shivered as realization struck her. Would she be the only woman in history to lose her virginity twice?

She would have found the whole thing hilarious if she hadn't been so worried about falling head over heels in love. A condition, she feared, that she was already doomed to experience.

". . . nothing to be nervous about. Every young bride goes through this." She snapped her attention back to Hunter. He pulled her to him until her thighs pressed against his. She could feel the effect his conversation was having on him even through all the layers of clothing that separated them. "I promise you will not regret it."

That's the one thing she worried about. Living to regret it while she watched one more coffin lowered into the ground.

But, oh, his touch tempted her so. The very scent of him intoxicated her, stirred the long-buried tingles that a man's smell could conjure. It had been over three years since she'd allowed a man to touch her with passion. Ryan had been the last. And now the simple act of Hunter sliding his hands down her bare arms made her skin feel like a match being dragged across its cover, ready to ignite.

As she looked up at her new husband, he seared her with a melting gaze. The crescent-shaped dimples caused butterflies in her stomach. She wondered if he could feel her heartbeat through her skin. He looked exactly as he had when his spirit so exquisitely melted into hers that last night in her own time.

She jumped away from him, away from the heady touch that clouded her judgment.

"Hunter, I'm not a vi . . . afraid of the wedding night. I'm not afraid of making love. That isn't why I think we should be married in name only."

"Then what has you so concerned?"

He held out his arms and took a step toward her, but she backed away several feet. He could not have looked more stricken if she had balled up her fist and slammed it into his jaw.

"Marin—"

"Please, Hunter. I have my reasons. Don't ask me to make love to you. I don't think I could bear it."

The gentle confusion in his eyes turned to hard, icy shards. His hands fell to his sides, his back stiffened ramrod straight.

"So, I've repulsed yet another woman, and you haven't even seen the scars yet. Delia must have painted a very ugly picture indeed to sicken you so."

Marin shook her head to clear it.

"Delia? What are you talking about? Delia didn't tell me anything about you."

Hunter started to take a step toward her, then stopped himself.

"My mother then," he sneered. "It would have pleased her immensely to describe my scars in vivid detail."

Marin shook her head again and started to deny his words. Before she could speak he was on his way out the front door.

It was clear she had somehow hurt him terribly, had touched a nerve that was a source of great pain. By the time she ran to the door, he was halfway to the bluffs, his long strides putting more and more distance between them.

"Hunter, wait!" She ran after him, wanting only to heal his pain, her only concern the tormented hurt in his eyes.

He continued toward the bluffs, hands jammed in his pockets, his hair rippling in the cool breeze from the river.

"Hunter!" Marin followed him, working hard to catch up. "What scars? No one told me about any scars!" Her damned lacy skirts dragged in the grass and caught on prickly weeds. When they tangled in her legs she stopped only long enough to hike them to her knees and wad the excess in her hands. She continued to run after him, closing the space now that her legs were unencumbered.

"Hunter, you don't repulse me! Damn it, I love you! And it scares the daylights out of me! I want you to make love to me so bad I *ache* with it!"

He spun and closed the distance between them in two strides, his lips meeting hers, his hands at first gripping her arms, then sliding around her in an embrace that melded their bodies from head to toe.

Marin's body exploded with the force of his passion. Mindless desire blossomed in her like a flower in time-lapse photography, bursting open into a beautiful, glorious creation.

A whimper caught in her throat—a trait of her lovemaking that had driven Ryan wild. It had much the same effect on Hunter. He answered her whimper with a groan, pulling them down to their knees and then laying her back onto the velvety grass of the fertile bluffs.

"Do you want me to stop?" his husky voice whispered against her lips, his hands burning fiery trails across her bodice. "I'll stop if you want me to."

Another whimper escaped into the night air as she shook her head with a miniscule movement. She knew he wouldn't stop. They were both well beyond that choice. They stood a better chance of pulling the moon from its orbit.

The dew on the grass seeped through the lacy pink gown that was her wedding dress. The moisture did nothing to cool the heat Hunter's mind-drugging hands and lips created. The night air caressed newly bared skin as her skirts crept up her legs and her bodice miraculously fell away.

It had been so long. So long since she had allowed herself to even think of these feelings. And now the power of them nearly paralyzed her. She lay back in the fragrant summer grass, the moon twinkling on the water of the river below, and let Hunter work his magic.

Sensations swirled through her like fine flakes of snow spinning in the wind. The exquisite feeling of bare skin against bare skin nearly brought tears to her eyes.

Hunter stopped weaving his spell long enough to raise up on one elbow and gaze at her with wrenching heat.

"What do you want, Mr. Pierce?" Marin whispered, her voice husky with passion.

"Everything I want, Mrs. Pierce, is right there in your eyes." His own voice rasped with the strain of his restraint. "And what do you want?"

Ribbons of fire unfurled through her at the very thought.

"I want you naked and in my arms."

"Oh, God."

The moon and the stars outlined his black silhouette as Hunter rose above her. With infinite tenderness he made her his wife in every way . . . in many ways.

And as brilliant fireworks shimmered through her being, she was only partially aware that yes, she'd been a virgin.

The gray light of dawn was only an hour away when Hunter swept his new bride into his arms and carried her back to their home. His knees, he noted with exhausted pleasure, were weak from the evening's activities. His heart, however, was so light, his mood so euphoric, he felt that he could have flown home had he set his mind to it.

He still carried her when he kicked open the front door. She "ooohed" dramatically, declaring him her hero. As he took the stairs with her in his arms, his imp of a wife left a trail of their garments behind them. She plucked them from her lap where she'd piled them, tossing his cravat over her shoulder. A petticoat was draped over the bannister, others were left to flutter to the floor, and one stocking covered the head of the small Cupid on the newel post.

He pushed the bedroom door closed behind them with his foot while Marin tormented him, tracing her fingers across his bare chest, around to his back, and down beneath the waistband of his trousers. When he reached the massive bed, he stopped only long enough to cast her a devilish grin before hurling her through the air to land in the center of it.

She squealed with the same delight that Katie might have shown. Her arms and legs flailed through the air as her unfastened dress—the only article of clothing she'd bothered to even partially don—billowed around her. But instead of continuing the rowdy game he'd started, Marin changed the rules.

Silky auburn curls fanned across the pillows as her head sank to the counterpane, the mahogany strands glossy even in the dim light of the single guttering candle. The pale, whisper-pink lace of the loosely worn dress settled around her, the skirts riding high on her thighs and the shoulders of her bodice dipping enticingly low on her arms. She gazed at him through a black fringe of lashes as she slid her arms above her head to tangle her fingers in her hair. As he stood transfixed, his mouth going dry at the sight of her, she smiled the sensual smile of a siren and writhed into an even more seductive position. She never took her gaze from his as she raised her hand and crooked her index finger at him.

That simple little gesture was his undoing. His shoes clattered to the floor; his trousers followed seconds later. He hovered over her momentarily, his body spanning the length of hers, then he rolled to his back and pulled her atop him.

She giggled as she finished dragging off her single piece of wedding attire. The view from his vantage point demanded his utmost attention. He folded his hands behind his head and decided he'd married a goddess as she pulled the mass of pink lace over her head with excruciating slowness.

"So," she whispered, tossing the gown on top of his wadded trousers, "what more could I ask for? I have you naked and in my arms . . . and in my bed."

There was no need to respond. His body did that for him—immediately and violently. He reached for her, but she backed away.

"Oh, no. It's my turn now. You just lie there while I have my way with you."

He squeezed his eyes shut and shook his head.

"I'll not make any promises," he growled. "I'm not the passive type." He doubted very seriously if he had the willpower to restrain himself now.

His stomach muscles jerked involuntarily as her index finger scorched a fiery downward path. He anticipated the direction of her hand, and a groan rumbled in his throat. The minx surprised him, though, when her finger detoured down his leg.

"Oh, my!" she cried, her voice exaggerated with mock alarm. "Is this the big, bad scar we were so worried about?"

Damn! He hadn't realized the light was bright enough for her to see it. He tossed the sheet over his leg.

"Leave it alone, Marin. You don't want to see it."

"Oh, yes, you're right." She flicked the sheet away. "I don't want to see the big, bad scar. It's so unsightly"—her hand explored the length of it—"it might scare me." She leaned forward and massaged the deformed skin, her fingers burning him with her touch. "I wouldn't want to be repulsed. . . ." She lowered her head, her hair tickling his thigh. "Oh, yes . . ." Her lips replaced her hands. She murmured with her mouth against the scar, "I'm so repulsed."

Her hot breath fanned across his leg, banishing forever the insecurity he'd suffered since the war.

Her tongue slid along his thigh while his mind screamed incoherent thoughts of passion. He reached down and dragged her upward until her lips came to rest on his.

"If your back repulses me as much as your leg," she breathed into his mouth, "then the only scars you will have to worry about are the ones my fingernails are going to leave before I'm through with you this night."

The love, the passion her words inspired, could not be

contained. He found her hands and brought them to his lips, kissing each and every fingertip.

"In that case," he murmured, "let's get on with the maiming."

The exhausted couple lay in a tangle of arms and legs, Marin's sleeping head resting on Hunter's chest. He stroked the silky fringe at her temple and marveled that he had the energy to do even that.

As warm tendrils of relaxation began to creep over him, he was vaguely aware of a distant noise. He ignored it and gave himself up to well-deserved sleep. Only seconds later, though, the noise became the unmistakable sound of horses' hooves and carriage wheels crunching on the gravel drive.

If this was Cabot, back to lay claim to Katie again, he would call the man out.

He tried to slip from Marin's embrace, but she rallied at his movement and raised a tousled head.

"What is it?" she asked softly in the fuzzy light of dawn.

"It's nothing, sweetheart. Go back to sleep." He donned a dressing gown and knotted the belt at his waist. "I think it's Cabot coming back to harass us again."

"I'm coming with you."

Marin slipped from the bed and rummaged for something to put on. Since her clothing had not yet been brought to his room, Hunter tossed her one of his robes from the armoire. The burgundy silk fluttered over her bare skin, and he swore to himself that he would beat Cabot to a pulp for disturbing them.

The carriage had come to a noisy stop at the front of the house. Sounds of activity could be heard from the foyer. He waited for Marin to adequately wrap herself in his robe, then he draped his arm over her shoulder and they left the room together to do battle with Delia's cousin.

As the two of them made their way to the landing, they shared a mischievous smile at the sight of the hallway and stairs littered with bits of intimate apparel.

A nightshirt-clad Ambrose was just unlocking the door when they appeared at the top of the stairs. Hunter busied his mind formulating a scathing speech to deliver to this parasite of a man. But before he could finish his thought and take another step, the door was flung open and Lucille Pierce marched into the foyer, yanking off her gloves and talking to herself.

". . . forced to ride all night because that cretin of an innkeeper refused me lodgings. He'll rue the day—"

The tirade stopped abruptly, followed by absolute, deafening silence as Lucille's widened eyes scanned each and every piece of scattered clothing that littered the house so profusely. Her contemptuous gaze came to rest on the couple on the landing as Ambrose shuffled from the room in all possible haste. Her eyes raked the length of each of them, returning to stare pointedly at Marin in Hunter's haphazardly arranged dressing gown.

"So! When the cat's away . . ." she spat with a bitterness excessive even for her.

Hunter found himself wishing now, with every fiber of his being, that the early morning intruder had been Cabot. His first instinct was to immediately tell her they were married. But her judgmental stare, her pursed, wrinkled lips, changed his mind.

"The mice will play!" he declared with enthusiasm, then dipped his head to plant a kiss on Marin's lips. Lucille jerked her head back as if she'd been slapped.

Marin's lips twitched with merriment as she slanted a devilish, golden glance in his direction. She slid her hand into his and started down the steps.

"Really, Hunter! It looks like a chifforobe exploded," she said as she plucked his linen smallclothes from their resting place on the banister.

"You know, that is a very accurate description," he agreed, then bent to scoop her corset from the bottom step. He allowed it to dangle from his fingers while he studied it as if it were a laboratory specimen.

Marin reached for the silken stocking and was dragging it from the Cupid's head when suddenly Lucille stepped up to her and slapped her soundly across the cheek.

"Slut!" she hissed with tangible hatred.

Before Hunter could recover from his shock, Marin pulled back her hand and delivered a stinging slap in return.

"Bitch!"

Lucille staggered back from the force of the blow, her palm covering the vivid red handprint already visible on her cheek.

"Mother! How dare you—" His voice roared, but no one heard. Marin had stepped up to his mother, her face so close their noses nearly touched. She spoke in a voice so calm it was barely audible.

"If you ever so much as lay a finger on me in anger again, Lucille, I will take that finger and break it in a dozen places. And smile while I'm doing it." Her voice rose slightly in volume. "I am not your average Southern belle who can be cowed with a hateful glare. And furthermore . . ." She turned to Hunter and raised an eyebrow. "May I have the honor?"

God, this woman was amazing! He inclined his head and stifled a grin.

"By all means."

"And furthermore," she turned back to Lucille, "your son and I are married."

Lucille's gasp echoed through the foyer. "You're lying! He would never lower his standards—"

With absolute perfect timing the newest members of the household made their usual entrance, bursting through the open door in a whirl of hurtling, furry bodies, yowling and yipping with playful abandon.

"Dear God!" Lucille croaked as the animals discovered this new person to play with and began circling her with frenzied curiosity.

Puffy, the friendlier of the two, had apparently found the only mud puddle in the city of Memphis. Lucille screeched and backed away as the enormous, happy puppy raised up on hind legs to slurp a dripping kiss on this new potential friend.

Lucille staggered backward as Puffy continued to hop toward her, undeterred in his affection. When her back encountered the wall, the golden fur ball planted his monstrous, muddy paws in the center of Lucille's pristine lap, refusing to remove himself until he had properly welcomed her.

Marin was screaming with laughter, hanging on to the newel post for support and holding her side. Hunter fought hard to stifle his own mirth, rubbing his hand across his eyes and biting the inside of his cheek.

Not until he began to fear for the puppy's safety did he bother to intervene on this touching welcome home.

"Puffy!" Lord, how he hated that name. Why could he not have a proper name, like Killer? "Puffy, down! Come here, you hairy clown."

Puffy immediately left Lucille screeching against the

wall. He trotted over to Hunter and sat in front of him, gazing up with expectant, adoring eyes, dusting the floor with his wagging, bushy tail. Hunter's hand automatically reached out and scratched him behind his ears.

"Dear Lord!" Lucille panted with outrage while she made a futile attempt to knock the mud from her skirts. "How dare you pet that monster? It should be taken out and shot!"

Before the last word died on her lips, a black, yowling projectile launched itself from the top of the hall clock.

It had become a happy game with Angel to ambush unsuspecting victims from her hiding place atop the clock. Hunter could only watch as she soared through the air with feline grace to land heavily on his mother's shoulders.

If only Lucille had not reacted as she had. But when his mother went into hysterics, it was not surprising that Angel held on for dear life, ultimately moving to higher ground, dislodging the hat and tangling her claws in her victim's hair.

After one final yowl, Angel gave up her position atop Lucille's head. The cat leapt to the floor with obvious disgust for this woman who knew not how to play the game. Her tail pointed stiffly toward the ceiling in her most haughty manner as she strolled away with unconcerned dignity. Only then did Lucille stopped screaming.

While Hunter and Marin both watched Angel vacate the room as only a cat can, no one noticed Lucille slide to the floor in an undignified heap.

Chapter 14

THE HAPPY, IDYLLIC days of Pierce Hall seemed like a distant memory. The only sounds echoing through the house now were Lucille's screeches whenever someone did something to displease her—which averaged about every thirty seconds.

It didn't take long for the servants to find pressing chores to do at distant points on the property. After only two days, even Emmaletta suddenly insisted that the flavor of her cooking was enhanced if she did most of the preparations locked in the farthest regions of the wine cellar.

Marin tried to stay out of the fray, making sure she crossed paths with her mother-in-law as little as humanly possibly. Hunter made a halfhearted attempt to placate the woman, but the encounter ended with several pieces of expensive china shattered into smithereens. It wasn't until Katie became the target of Lucille's vitriol that Marin decided to step in.

She might have talked things over with Hunter, but he had ridden into town to meet with his banker. So when Katie came to Marin in tears because "Wucille" had screamed at her over some minor offense, Marin had dried Katie's tears, sent her out with Mamie to play, and prepared to do battle with the lemon-sucker.

It wasn't hard to find her. She had only to follow the shrill, intermittent calls for Mamie, who, of course, was nowhere within earshot.

Marin strolled into the spotless sitting room that adjoined Lucille's bedroom and sat down in the brocade chair opposite her mother-in-law. The woman looked up from her needlepoint, then went back to viciously stabbing the fabric with her needle.

"Get out of my sight."

Marin leaned back in the chair and got more comfortable.

"I don't believe I will."

Lucille jerked her head up at Marin's audacity. Her eyes blazed with bitter hatred.

"I did not invite you in here. Get out."

"Lucille, you and I are going to have a little talk. No, no. Don't speak. Actually, I am going to talk, and you are going to listen."

Lucille jumped to her feet and threw her needlepoint to the floor.

"If you won't leave, then I will."

"If you walk out of this room, then keep walking right on out the front door, and don't bother coming back. Now sit down and shut up."

Marin would be lying if she said she wasn't disappointed when Lucille—after the barest flicker of uncertainty—chose to perch defiantly on the edge of her chair.

"That's better. Now . . ." Marin picked up a book that lay next to the chair and nonchalantly read the title. She replaced it with studied attention, then turned her gaze back to her simmering adversary. "I want to remind you, Lucille, that you are no longer mistress of this house. I am. And I am no longer willing to tolerate your abrasive personality, especially when you begin to target my loved ones."

Lucille's only reaction was to glare at her with even more hatred.

"I don't know what terrible thing occurred in your life to make you so bitter. But it's made you a small woman, Lucille. Not in stature, but in spirit. And every time you open your mouth to inflict a hurt on someone, you become even smaller.

"Until now, Hunter has put up with you because of a misguided promise to his father. I, on the other hand, made no such promise to anyone. With my persuasion—and if you had even an hour of marital bliss, you will know how men can be persuaded—I can and will see to it that you are removed from this house. One can only be a bitch so long, Lucille, before people cease to put up with it. And when you hurt little children, even a deathbed promise can be revoked."

Marin kept her tone of voice conversational. She'd always found the quieter one spoke, the more threatening the words.

"So, in case I haven't managed to get my point across, I'll recap our conversation in simple English. Stop being a bitch. If you can't say something nice, don't say anything at all. Commit random acts of kindness. Do unto others as you would have them do unto you—and any other clichés that happen to come to mind that your mother probably told you. If you find it impossible to be civil, then remove yourself from the family. But under no circumstances are you to utter one more deliberately hurtful word to anyone in this household. If you do, you'll be out on your heavily bustled butt. If you don't believe that I mean what I say, then I invite you to utter one of those words. Just to see if I'm serious."

Marin's level gaze met venomous blue eyes. If the act of casting hateful glares could be elevated to a fine art, Lucille was the woman who had done it. But it would take more than a mean-spirited look to sway Marin's stand.

She rose and walked to the door, not so much as turning her head when she spoke.

"If you will only try to be pleasant I will treat you with equal consideration, as will everyone else in the house. But from the moment I walk out of this room, the servants, and even Katie, will be instructed to treat you with the same degree of respect with which you treat them." Marin turned and threw one last look at the glowering woman. "An eye for an eye, so to speak. It's your decision."

The crashing piece of china shattering against the oak floor as Marin closed the door was probably the teapot. Pity. It had been such a lovely, delicate thing. Two more crashes in quick succession had to be the teacups. Within a quarter hour, Marin suspected that not one breakable object remained intact in Lucille's rooms. After the final, enormous crash—probably the cheval mirror—an ominous quiet descended.

The servants were still in hiding and Katie was still outside with Mamie when Lucille emerged from her room an hour later and returned with a broom and dustpan.

*   *   *

Hunter supervised the loading of their bags into the carriage for their trip to Mississippi.

Thank heavens his mother had declined the obligatory invitation to go with them to Tranquille. Surveying the damage to see if any of the crop was salvageable would be unpleasant enough.

His bride was just descending the stairs when he entered the front door. A warm wave of love washed over him at the sight of her.

"Ready?" he asked.

She stopped and glanced in the mirror, spent several seconds rearranging her jaunty little feathered hat, then plucked it from her head and tossed it on a table.

"Now I am. Just let me find Katie."

Katie rounded the staircase from the back of the house just as Marin spoke. She carried a half-eaten biscuit in one hand and Angel tucked under her arm. The cat dangled limply from its precarious perch. A white, frilly doll's bonnet adorned its head. Hunter couldn't stop the smile from curving his lips at the sight of that ridiculous, misnamed cat.

"I can't find Puffy."

"That's all right. Puffy and Angel have to stay here," Marin told her.

An obstinate lower lip slid out slightly, and Katie surprised Hunter by stomping her tiny foot on the floor.

"I want to take Puffy and Angel!"

Katie looked at Hunter with a four-year-old's truculence. When she got no reaction from either adult she began bouncing up and down. The cat's hind legs bounced with her.

"I want to take Puffy and Angel," she whined. "Why can't I take Puffy and Angel?"

Hunter was at a loss as to what to do. This was the first time his sweet, angelic little daughter had ever shown the slightest sign of a temper. How did a father handle little-girl tantrums? Dear Lord, she was turning into his mother!

While he contemplated the best course of action, Marin, with hands on hips, stepped up to Katie and studied her as she continued to bounce and whine.

"You're doing it all wrong," Marin instructed as she shook her head.

Katie bounced to a stop and cocked a defiant glare at the woman who towered over her.

"Yeah. That's all wrong." Marin studied Katie with deep concentration, the tip of her thumbnail wedged between her teeth. "You need to lie down and roll around. Then scream real loud and bang your head on the floor. And you need to kick your legs, too. Yeah. Hold your breath. That might help."

Katie had clearly not expected this type of reaction, and quite truthfully, neither had Hunter. But it was proving to be quite effective. Katie's look of defiance had turned to one of uncertainty.

He was impressed.

"Now," Marin continued, "if you want to leave Angel and Puffy here, you may go with us. If not, you are welcome to stay here with Mamie."

Within minutes the carriage rolled down the drive, carrying the three of them to Mississippi. Katie's sweet nature had returned when her little tantrum had failed to create the desired effect. The last thing she'd expected, Hunter was sure, was to be instructed in how to throw a fit.

The carriage had not gone far before trickles of perspiration slid down his back. The heat of the day was stifling, even at such an early hour, but Hunter would have been hard-pressed to tell if the heat came from the weather or from Marin's hand, which not so innocently jostled against his thigh. If Katie had chosen to stay at Pierce Hall, he and Marin might have set a record for taking the longest time in history to travel between Memphis and Tranquille.

As it was, the trip seemed interminable, but in an exquisitely torturous way. While he had expected to occupy his mind with thoughts of the ruined crop, instead he found himself immersed in daydreams about making love to his wife in every conceivable place on the plantation. And some not so conceivable. The higher Marin's hand slid on his thigh, the more chaotic his thoughts became. He shot a glance at Katie, who had snuggled down in the seat, her head on Marin's lap, her eyes drooping.

He loved his daughter dearly, but he was not accustomed to planning his rendezvous around the sleeping patterns of a four-year-old moppet.

Marin's hand moved another half inch. Hunter closed his eyes and fought the reaction. When he cast a sidelong look at his mischievous wife, she returned the look with one of feigned innocence.

"What?" she asked.

"You know what," he answered, unable to stop the smile that curved his lips. "And if you continue," he looked down at his sleeping daughter, "Katie may wake to a lesson in how babies are made."

Marin's eyes widened.

"Oh, Mr. Pierce! Do you mean you want me to stop doing this?" Her hand snaked up his thigh several inches.

He stopped its progress with an ironclad grip and placed it back on her lap.

"No." He cursed the raspiness of his voice. "But under the circumstances, I think you'd better. As it is, my heart's racing faster than a thoroughbred's."

Marin's right hand rested lightly on his chest. With her other hand she opened his palm and slowly placed it over her heart.

"Is it beating as fast as mine?"

All traces of amusement vanished as they stared at each other, her unspoken desire clear in her eyes.

With blessed timing the gates to Tranquille came into view. If they had had any further to travel, Hunter would have found the nearest secluded spot and taken the chance that Katie would sleep for a good hour or two.

The horses automatically turned up the drive while he dragged his gaze from Marin's. He was in no condition to climb out of this carriage and greet Maggie and William.

"Hunter, this place is absolutely breathtaking! I expected a little house surrounded by cotton fields. How in the world did it survive the war?" Marin felt like a scuba diver who had found sunken treasure.

"Some of President Grant's senior officers commandeered the house for their use. Grant and his men seldom destroyed a home they had taken over."

Marin walked through the music room, bewitched by the gleaming wood of the piano, a violin on the table, a harp in front of a chair covered in red velvet. Dark red draperies pooled on the floor. A huge mirror hung above the marble mantel and reflected not only the red fluted candle chimneys on the chandelier of the music room, but the crystal chandelier in the adjacent parlor.

She couldn't have said what impressed her more. Her first view of Tranquille had been one of sprawling wings of golden beige brick. Four rectangular brick columns topped by Ionic friezes flanked the front door, and a huge, circular window graced the center of the third-floor gable. Stepping through the front door, she met with an entrance hall so large it had its own fireplace. A massive central staircase, also flanked by Ionic columns, led up to a landing backlit by a wall of windows overlooking a pecan orchard and an overgrown garden. From there the stairs split to lead upward from both sides of the landing.

While William entertained Katie, Maggie and Hunter had proudly walked Marin through the entire house. She had been rendered speechless and was sure her chin had dropped to her chest. Maggie nervously dusted where there was no dust, and Hunter simply looked on with mild amusement at her awe.

What a gem! Either this house was privately owned in 1996, or else it had fallen into decay and no longer existed in that time. She'd have to check when she got back.

Sudden icy tendrils of premonition crawled over her like an army of spiders. Where had that thought come from? Did her subconscious know something she didn't? The euphoria she'd felt since her wedding night on the bluffs burst, shattering into millions of pieces, like a balloon blown too full.

She glanced over at Hunter, whose tender smile was a blow to her heart. Was she going to return to her time? Would Hunter's death be what caused it? Would her return cause Hunter's death?

Defeat such as she had never known settled over her in a heavy, suffocating fog. Why had she let her guard down? Why did she let herself fall in love again? She should have known better. She was never meant to have anyone in her life.

She fumbled behind her for a chair. As she sank to the cushion she vaguely heard Hunter call her name with alarm. In a heartbeat he was down on one knee, his precious face only inches from hers.

"Marin! Sweetheart, what's wrong?" He cradled her face in his palms and studied her. His forehead creased in worry. There was no trace of those beloved dimples. "Are you ill? Maggie, would you fetch a glass of water, please?"

Marin was aware of Maggie bustling from the room, then Hunter's fingers rapidly undoing her bodice. His light, caring touch on her skin kindled a passion in her that rose through the fog of defeat.

She met his worried blue gaze with tears burning behind her eyes. She took his hands in hers.

"I'm all right. I just felt light-headed for a second."

Hunter breathed a sigh of relief, then jerked his gaze back to her, raking the length of her body. He looked at her with hope-filled eyes.

"Is it possible you could already be . . ."

Dear Lord! One more thing to worry about that hadn't even occurred to her! What if she got pregnant? Would she carry a baby to the future?

"No." She looked into his hopeful eyes. "At least, I'm pretty sure I'm not."

"Well." He shrugged and stood, though he didn't manage to hide the flicker of disappointment in his eyes. "That will come soon enough"—he cast her a grinning leer—"considering how our first two nights have gone."

Her entire body screamed for her to drag him back onto his knees and fall with him to the carpet. To make love to this man in every room of this house, every building, every secluded spot in the woods, until they both died of exhaustion or, through sheer force of will, she clung to him and carried him with her to her own time.

But she couldn't take a chance on getting pregnant. What she wouldn't give for a year's supply of birth control pills, or even a box of condoms.

What did people use in this time for birth control? She vaguely remembered something about small pieces of sponge soaked in vinegar, but that had rendered some women sterile. At the very least, vinegar fumes rising from her body would make her about as sexy as an unwashed dock worker.

"Here the water, Mistah Hunter." Maggie shuffled in, her shoes slapping against her heels. She handed the glass to Marin. "How you feelin', sugar? You gettin' your color back. That a good sign."

"I'm fine," Marin lied. "Thanks for the water." She took a sip and tried to gather control of her rampaging emotions.

Maggie fussed over her for a while, fluffing pillows with her meaty fist, tucking them around Marin as if she were a china doll, and grumbling something about skinny people and a good gust of wind blowing them away.

Marin knew Maggie meant well, but she wished she'd just leave her alone to dwell in her misery. Her mind was so paralyzed she could barely form a coherent thought.

Hunter's shadow fell over her and he brushed a curly tendril from her cheek. She looked up at him, her heart seizing in her chest while he smiled down at her, a sweet, tender smile that created crescent shadows in both his cheeks and a storm of butterflies under her ribs.

Dear God, how she loved this man.

She loved him as much as she had loved Ryan. And the thought of losing him, too, of either burying him or returning to her own time without him, was like a dull knife slowly piercing her heart.

But she couldn't let herself dwell on that. She stiffened her spine and made a decision. Hunter was still alive, and she would make sure they lived every moment they had together to the fullest. And if he gave her a child, no matter what century she ended up in she would have a piece of him with her forever.

Every nerve in her body ignited at the thought. She blinked at him slowly, seductively, hiding the desperation she felt.

"Thank you, Maggie. Perhaps I should lie down and rest before lunch," she said, without ever removing her gaze from Hunter's. When he raised a hopeful eyebrow at her words, she answered by moistening her lips.

"Yes! Let me see you to our room!" Hunter replied with amusing speed as he took the glass from her fingers and shoved it at Maggie.

Maggie, who Marin already knew was nobody's fool, wheezed a quiet chuckle.

"Yessir, Mistah Hunter. You gets this little gal up to your room and let her rest." Another wheeze. "Mebbe you oughtta rest, too. Me and that shiftless William'll keep your sweet baby girl happy whilst you all rest."

Hunter obviously didn't need to be told twice. He wasted no time in pulling Marin to her feet, then he scooped her into his arms and took the stairs two at a time. Maggie's wheezing faded from earshot, then was cut off completely when Hunter kicked the bedroom door shut behind them.

No sooner was the door closed than Marin had her lips on his. He released her legs and slowly slid her body down the length of his until she stood on tiptoe, the heat of their kiss never cooling. This was what she ached for, longed for. But it was altogether too civilized.

While her tongue played hide-and-seek with his, her hands found the lapels of his coat. It took no effort at all to pull the well-tailored garment over his shoulders and off his arms. After dropping it to the floor, she returned to concentrate on his tie. With that strip of silk also discarded she shoved him back against the door and murmured against his lips, "Are you particularly fond of this shirt?" When he breathlessly groaned, "No," she yanked apart the plackets, ignoring the clatter of buttons as they fell to the polished oak floor. An animalistic growl escaped his throat, then the thirty-odd covered buttons from the back of her bodice created the sound of rain on a windowpane as they scattered about the room. She frantically pulled his shirttail from his trousers, then, with a fistful of snowy white cambric in each hand, her lips still on his, she guided him to the plush carpet behind them, sinking to her knees, pulling him down with her.

They knelt there briefly, wrapped in each other's arms, drinking deeply of the storming passion that buffeted them both. Finally, she lowered herself to the carpet, staying him with her hand when he would have followed. He hovered there on his knees, rising above her, just the sight of him searing her soul. She raked the length of him with her gaze—his heated eyes and sculptured jaw; the open shirt revealing a bronze chest that begged to be caressed; his trousers so snug they strained across his hips. He rose above her like a god, and she burned the sight of him into her memory, to be taken out and enjoyed, or savored, later. After she looked her fill, she slid her hands up his chest and twined both sides of his shirtfront around her fists, pulling him down to her as she rose up to meet him, intent on burning a memory into his own soul that would live throughout eternity.

Hunter fell back, both exhausted and exhilarated, to the quilt covering the mountain of freshly ginned cotton. Somehow he found the strength to roll his head to the right so that he might enjoy the view of the best thing that ever happened to him.

Marin lay beside him, her face already turned to his, a languid, dreamy smile curving her lips. Her body glistened with a fine sheen from their exertions. Her porcelain skin and mahogany hair held errant clumps of snowy cotton that had risen into the air—caused by their earlier vigorous activities—then drifted slowly earthward to settle and stick to her moist flesh. Without bothering to look, he knew his own body suffered the same fuzzy malady. In fact, at that very moment she reached to caress his cheek, then brought her fingers to her lips and blew a tiny blizzard of cotton from her fingertips.

Looking to the ceiling of the cotton barn, she slid her arms above her head, stretching with all the feline grace of a lazy cat in the sun. As she stretched, she sighed a musical, satisfied sigh.

"Penny for your thoughts." Hunter rolled to his side and dragged her even closer.

She smiled and looked at him from the corners of her eyes.

"I'm wondering what Lucille would say if she saw us here, like this. Or in the gazebo by the pond; or the pond itself, for that matter; or in your old treehouse at the back of the orchard." She giggled. "And I haven't figured out yet how we ended up under the dining room table last night. One minute we were in the parlor and the next we were—"

"Momentum." Hunter's body tingled at the word and the image it evoked. "Shall I demonstrate?"

Marin rolled toward him, her voice like the purr of a cat. "Please do."

A playful growl rose in his throat while he hooked a leg around her firm, milky thighs. He ached to sear a trail of kisses along her sweat-dampened skin, but the very first attempt gained him a mouthful of fuzz. They both laughed like children, then she helped him remove the offending cotton from his lips . . . and other places.

Could he ever get enough of this woman?

"I don't know where yo mama and papa is, Miss Katie. We done looked everwhere they is to look. Ain't no reason I can figure for thems to be in the cotton gin shed."

Marin's hand flew to her mouth to muffle first a gasp and then a giggle. Hunter stifled a curse that begged to be voiced. Instead, he grabbed the edges of the quilt and wrapped himself and Marin into a giant, lumpy cocoon. They both fought to remain absolutely motionless as William and Katie moved deeper into the barn.

"But Papa promised to take me for a ride on my pony if I took a nap! He didn't forget, did he?"

Their voices came closer.

"No, Miss Katie. I's sure yo papa didn't forget. Mebbe him and yo mama—"

William stopped talking abruptly and completely. Several seconds of uncertain silence ticked by while Marin's eyes widened above the hand she had clamped over her mouth and nose. Hunter had the terrible feeling she was about to erupt in a fit of giggles . . . or sneezes.

"Why, Miss Katie," William veritably shouted, "I believe I sees yo mama and papa at the edge of them woods. Mebbe if we hurries we can catch 'em.'"

The sound of tiny feet running across a dirt floor faded in the air. The slower clomp of William's followed moments later.

Funny, Hunter had never before noticed that William, too, wheezed when he laughed.

"Hunter, I've been thinking about the cotton crop and our financial situation." Marin paused and assessed her husband's reaction from across the parlor the next morning. Though he had proven to be amazingly ahead of his time in many areas, she was not quite sure how he would accept business advice from a woman. Nineteenth-century men—even the good ones—were woefully obtuse.

He lowered the newspaper he'd been perusing and gave her his attention.

"What are your thoughts on the matter, sweetheart?"

That was promising. She pressed on.

"Have you ever thought we might be sitting on a gold mine here?"

He quirked an eyebrow at her.

"What I mean is, look around you! You have an honest to goodness Southern plantation, a little worse for wear, but just a little. It's very nearly the same as it was before the war. You still grow cotton; you still have most of your grandparents' furnishings and heirlooms; the house is breathtaking and in good repair." Here was where it could get tricky. "Don't you suppose people would pay to come and see a

real working Southern plantation? To catch a glimpse of
what life was like before the war?"

"You mean open Tranquille to the public? Charge admis-
sion? As if it were a circus?" He dropped the paper to his
lap, and her heart dropped with it. "I do not believe I would
care to have the populace roaming through my home. Besides, I could not gamble what funds we have on making the
necessary repairs—"

"But you wouldn't have to!" Marin slid to the edge of the
seat beside Hunter and clasped her hands. "Leave Tranquille
as it is. Let the Northerners, the ones who would be most curious, see it in its postwar state. We could even take them to
the ruins of some homes that fell during the war, to show
how fortunate we are to have the ones still remaining. The
devastation of the war has made Tranquille and all the rest
of the surviving plantations a valuable asset to this part of
the country. With these homes as a living legacy, the gener-
ations to come will be able to see firsthand what life was like
for the people of the genteel South."

If only he believed her about being from the future. She
could describe to him the looks of awe on faces that had
never seen the grandeur of such a lifestyle. There'd been
times when she'd watched tourists transport themselves to
the days of their ancestors, that faraway look in their eyes as
they imagined glittering ladies and dashing gentlemen sitting through an evening's musicale or playing croquet in the
sun at an elegant lawn party. She'd seen visitors wipe away
tears at the sight of slaves' quarters, seen their watery smiles
at heartwarming stories of loyalty between master and servant. These homes were priceless museums. And with her
twentieth-century experience in managing antebellum es-

tates, Tranquille could be the source of income that would relieve the burden caused by the crop failure.

Hunter, however, seemed more interested in his newspaper than in her brilliant plans. He rattled the paper, murmured, "I'll give it some thought," then buried his nose in the financial section.

A man hiding behind his paper had always irritated her. She'd shredded her weight in newspapers when Ryan was alive.

But Hunter wasn't Ryan, and she had to handle her new husband with the mentality of a nineteenth-century woman.

Hunter glanced at her over the top of the newspaper, a distracted grin creasing his left cheek with that devilish dimple. Her heart fluttered at the sight.

What an idiot! She knew exactly how to get his attention.

She reached over and gently crumpled the center of the paper to half-mast. When Hunter slowly lifted his gaze she closed her fist on the paper, pulled it inexorably out of his grasp, then tossed the thing over her shoulder. Sliding onto his lap, she ran her fingers through his hair, twirled a lock around one, then left the hair to concentrate on tracing the outline of his ear. Squirming once under the ruse of getting more comfortable, she determined—even through all those layers of clothing—that she very much had his complete and undivided attention.

"Hunter, could we finish talking about this open-house idea?"

Hunter's eyes had closed and it was clear he was in no mood to talk business. He opened his eyes to sensual slits while his hands began burning trails across her bodice.

"Must we?" He groaned when she captured both his roaming hands in hers. "Oh, very well. I see the validity of your idea, sweetheart, but I have to say I am not at all comfortable with people traipsing through our home day in and day out." He lowered his eyebrows and nailed her with a torrid gaze. "When would we ever have a moment's privacy?"

It was getting harder and harder to think clearly, sitting on Hunter's lap, stilling his busy hands.

"We wouldn't have to open up year-round." Her breathing became a bit erratic as his hands found their freedom. "I mean, we could open, say . . . four times . . . ummmm . . . a year. For a week or two. We could decorate the house for holidays. Maybe open up the first weeks"—she gasped when his hands hit pay dirt—"of December to show off the decorations and how you prepare for the spring planting." She fought to keep her mind on track when it was telling her to shut up and lock the parlor doors. "Then . . . ooohhhh . . . we could ummmm . . . we could open in the spring for the planting. Then during the summer and again at harvest." It was nearly impossible to keep her voice even while his lips rained kisses under her ear. "Eight weeks a year. That's all it would be. And no overnight guests. Just day trips. With the river in the backyard we could . . . ummmm . . . get all the riverboats to stop. Maybe serve them . . . oooohhhhh."

His warm breath ghosted across her neck as he worked his way to her lips. His mouth on hers, he murmured quietly, "Whatever you say. It's a wonderful idea. Now shut up and kiss me."

Chapter 15

THE BUNDLE OF energy that was his daughter jumped from the carriage in a flurry of yellow ruffles, almost before they rolled to a stop. As if on cue, Puffy and Angel rounded the corner of Pierce Hall at a tilt, two furry missiles that came together to form a slobbering, mewing welcoming committee for the delighted, squealing child. The three of them frolicked on the lawn with undiluted joy.

Hunter bounded from the carriage with some excessive energy of his own, then turned and looked up into the treasured face of his bride as he waited to hand her down. She shivered when his hands encircled her waist in a slow caress. With teasing, exaggerated ardor she melted against him. Her arms cradled his head while he nuzzled her stiff, boned midriff with his cheek. If only the layers of bone and cotton and silk would fall away . . . but they would soon enough. He lost himself in the feel of her fingers running through the back of his hair and the scent of her that would forever be her own. With a sigh born of contentment, he wondered if life could possibly get any better.

"Ahem."

Well, hell. That would teach him to ever get too happy. The fact that he had not heard her approach irritated him. He held Marin a moment longer, took one more deep breath of her intoxicating scent, then braced himself and turned to Lucille.

"Good afternoon, Mother." A biting retort formed in his mind for her inevitable, venomous greeting.

"Good afternoon, Hunter. Marin."

A summer breeze could have blown him over. Where was the expected tirade over their unseemly behavior in broad daylight? Her sneer at the very sight of his wife? Why, she had greeted them in a manner surprisingly close to pleasant!

An awkward silence fell and several seconds passed while Hunter tried to overcome his shock. Finally Lucille shot an uncomfortable glance back at the house.

"I will see to it that Mamie knows you are here for dinner." Before he could reply, she vanished through the front door.

Hunter stared at the closed dark oak panel, expecting her to reemerge and vent her rage at him for not following immediately on her heels. When the door remained closed, he turned to Marin and shrugged, completely at a loss to explain this unusual behavior.

His unpredictable wife smiled sweetly with an air of unconcern.

"Lucille and I had a little talk before we left for Tranquille," she said in answer to his bewilderment.

"A little talk?" he echoed. "What, pray tell, did you say in this 'little talk'?" He lifted her down from the carriage while waiting for an answer.

"Oh," she began as she peeled off her gloves, "just how life will be more simple if everyone is pleasant to everyone else."

"Pleasant?" He was beginning to sound like a parrot. For the life of him, he could not imagine his mother pleasant.

"Uh-huh. Just a little food for thought while we were away. Come along, Katie, and wash up for dinner." She reached up on tiptoe and planted a kiss on his jaw. "I'm starving."

Marin waited while Katie separated herself from the tumbling animals. Puffy gamboled along while Angel dangled limply from Katie's tiny forearm. Angel's feline eyes closed to green slits, her ears flattened in long-suffering boredom, but she made no attempt to dislodge herself.

Hunter could only stare, dumbfounded, as his wife and his daughter swished into the cool interior of the house.

"She told her to be pleasant?" he asked himself. He would like to imagine that was all that had transpired. But knowing his fiery wife and his sainted mother, not a force on earth could convince him that the conversation was as innocent as portrayed.

"Mistah Hunter, you gonna stand out there all day catchin' flies? Dinner done been on the table till it's cold."

Yet another female caught him unawares as Mamie attacked from the rear. Could he be losing his hearing? He turned and nodded to the stable boy as the horses were led away, then grinned at Mamie.

"I'm coming, you tyrant."

Mamie snorted her opinion of his sass, then waddled back from whence she had come, muttering.

"Disrespectful young pup. Emmaletta gonna go to work for the Hilliards, then who be doin' the cookin'? Well, it ain't gonna be me. I's got enough to do around here without . . ."

No. He definitely was not losing his hearing.

Marin sat at Hunter's desk, working on the figures for opening Tranquille. Just as she thought, the initial cost would be minimal. They could make this work!

Massaging her lower back and popping the kinks out of her neck, she rose to go find Hunter and tell him the good news. As she passed a gilt-framed mirror on the staircase, she paused to check her finger-ravaged hair.

"So there you are." He came up behind her and slid his arms around her waist. "I've missed you." His lips nibbled the length of her neck, turning her blood to warm, thick honey. She leaned against his chest, his clean scent engulfing them both and stirring the flutter in her breast that his nearness always caused. "I thought we were going to work on the plans to open Tranquille. Where did you disappear to after dinner?"

His mouth hummed against her skin when he spoke. She rolled her head to the side to make more room for the delicious things he was doing.

"Ummmm." She lost herself for a moment in a swirl of heated sensations before bothering to answer his question. "You looked so tired, I decided to work on them and surprise you."

Hunter's only response was to dip his head and trail kisses along her bare shoulder, smothering all thoughts of Tranquille and open houses.

"I'm not as tired as I look," he growled against her neck.

"Does Mawin have a boo-boo, Papa?"

Hunter's lips stopped in their exquisite journey, stilled by the most effective birth control known to man.

" 'Cause Mawin kisses my boo-boo when I hurt myself."

Katie stood at the bottom of the stairs, fresh from her bath and ready for bed. Her little pink toes peeked from beneath the soft cotton nightie, and the doll tucked under her arm wore matching attire. She stood, her head tilted back, looking up at the two of them, waiting for an answer.

Hunter kneaded Marin's shoulders while he asked in a most serious voice, "Just what exactly is a 'boo-boo'? Good lord, that word is as disgusting as 'Puffy'! I shall endeavor never to repeat it."

Katie giggled. Marin turned a smile on him. Poor baby. Obviously Lucille had never seen fit to deal with a little boy's mishaps in the time-honored manner.

"A boo-boo, Mr. Too-manly-to-say-certain-words, is something that hurts. And a kiss always makes it feel better."

With male predictability, Hunter's eyes lit up at her words, just before he leered at her in his best lascivious manner. He said in a voice only Marin could hear, "Well, then, I believe I have a boo-boo that requires quite a bit of attention later." He turned to Katie and swung her into his arms. "Now tell me, where are all these boo-boos? On your nose?" He kissed her nose. "Behind your ear?" He growled a kiss on her ear. "The tip of your little finger? I know! On your foot!" He held one leg by the ankle and closely inspected the pudgy little foot. He shook his head. "Nothing there. Must be the other foot." He performed the same ritual. "Nothing. Oh! I forgot to look at the bottom!"

He dropped the arm Katie perched on and she swung upside down in screaming delight as Hunter studied the pink, baby-soft bottoms of her feet. He raised his arms aloft until Katie's face dangled in front of his.

"I cannot find a boo-boo. Are you certain you have one?" Katie's arms hung trustingly limp as she giggled, wild in the ecstasy of her father's attention. "What? Was that a yes or a no? You really must speak more clearly if I am to kiss these boo-boos. Ah, well, I shall do my best."

He lowered his arms and planted a loud, squeaky kiss on the bottom of each chubby foot, then tucked her under his arm like a football player going for the goal.

"Lordy, lordy, Mistah Hunter!" Mamie lumbered down the stairs as fast as her girth would allow. "You's gonna fluster that youngun till she won't never go to sleep!"

Marin wished Mamie had timed her arrival a little later. The playful scene between father and daughter was so heart-warming she hated to see it end. What a good father he was. With a touch of melancholy she wondered if he would ever see a child born from their own union.

"Here now! What's you doin', holdin' Miss Katie like a sack o' meal? If'n you don't watch out, you gonna make her lose her supper."

Hunter did nothing but grin a huge, little-boy grin that creased his cheeks until his dimples had shadows.

"Now, Mamie, I was performing a very important service. Apparently unkissed boo-boos are nothing to sneeze at."

Mamie panted down the remaining stairs, then planted her feet wide and stood with fists where a waist should have been.

"Don't you give me no sweet-talkin' sass. Now you tells that child good night so's I can calm her down and tuck her into bed."

Hunter lowered his eyes with an exaggerated look of re-pentance. Then a mischievous smile broke across his face as he grabbed the tiny flailing ankles in front of him and dangled Katie at eye level once more.

"Good night, Katiedid," he said with a deadpan face. The hysterical child slid her arms around her father's neck and squeezed, stopping her giggling only long enough to smack a kiss on his cheek. Hunter swung her around, her body arcing out like an amusement park ride, until she faced Marin.

"Give your mother a hug and kiss before this old tyrant ruins all of our fun."

Hunter's words echoed in Marin's brain, and she repeated them to herself, hugging the words to her heart. Mother! As much as she loved this curly-haired cherub, she had never expected to be considered her mother. A heartstring tugged as her newly acquired daughter delivered an energetic, inverted hug and a kiss the consistency of wet liver onto Marin's cheek.

"Good night, Mama."

Marin never dreamed the first time she heard those three simple words directed at her would cause such an ache in her chest. She wanted to grab Katie and hold her and Hunter in a tight circle and never let go. But Katie was already climbing the stairs, one step at a time, her tiny alabaster hand in Mamie's strong brown fingers.

Marin watched until they disappeared around the corner, then Hunter resumed his position with his arms about her waist and pulled her back against his rock-hard chest.

"Now, where were we?"

They were interrupted yet again before she could answer.

"Hunter, I would have a word with you."

Hunter's frustrated breath blew across Marin's neck, then he kissed the hollow beneath her ear. He continued to kiss as he spoke.

"Terribly sorry, Mother. I am busy at the moment." His murmur raced across her skin in hot little waves. "I can see you first thing in the morning. Check with my secretary about the time."

It would be interesting to see how the lemon-sucker reacted to this. She had been almost congenial when they arrived from Tranquille. But though dinner had buzzed with lively conversation, Lucille had maintained her usual tight-lipped dinner table silence. Marin wasn't sure if her mother-in-law's air of disapproval was from the talking itself, the topic of opening Tranquille to the public, or from Katie's presence at the table. And to be honest, she didn't care.

As it turned out, the lemon-sucker's response was to move around in front of them with a defiant stare, obviously determined to throw the proverbial cold water on their amorous activities.

"Oh, bloody hell," Hunter swore as his ardor nose-dived under Lucille's incessant gaze. "What is so important, Mother, that you feel the need to abort my attempt to woo my wife?"

Lucille flicked the briefest of glances at Marin.

"I feel certain that wooing this wife is a needless exercise." She paused long enough to allow the intended insult to sink in.

"Oh, yes! How scandalous that I have a willing bride!" He turned to Marin and said with mock severity, "Stifle your improper urges, wife, and go in search of a much needed dose of virtue!"

Marin bit the inside of her cheek to keep from smiling. Instead she blinked a slow, seductive blink and moistened her lips.

"Once before you told me not to throw myself at you. To stifle my urges. I guess I'll never—"

Hunter grabbed Marin's wrist and hauled her behind him into the parlor before she could finish her sentence.

"Come and sit down, Mother, and tell us what is bothering you so." Under his breath he said to Marin, "Stifle even the smallest urge, and I shall throttle my mother for the nuisance she is!"

Now *there* was a temptation.

Lucille was visibly displeased that Marin was to be included in the conversation. Nevertheless she followed them into the parlor, then sank with stiff-backed haughtiness onto the peach brocade of the chair.

"What is this utter nonsense about opening Tranquille?" She spoke to Hunter but glared all the while at Marin, as if to say, *This was your idea!*

Hunter leaned back against the settee, one booted ankle propped on his knee as he toyed with the ribbons decorating Marin's sleeve.

"It is not nonsense. This could be a very lucrative business venture. And considering the lost crop, and previous disappointing years, if you wish to continue to swath yourself in silks and satins," he scanned the length of his mother's expensively clad body, "it is a necessity."

Lucille harangued Hunter for a good quarter hour before he lost all patience and told her that the matter was not open to discussion. Marin had to admit that though Lucille wouldn't have won a congeniality award, the acid in her voice was more or less absent.

"Well, then, shall we move on to another matter? One that has tongues wagging throughout the city."

Hunter pulled a deep, long breath into his lungs, and Marin could almost hear him count to ten as he let it out.

"What is it?"

"I would like for you to have a proper wedding."

The blank look on Hunter's face as he stared at his mother was priceless. Where was a camera when you needed one? He blinked a couple of times but continued to stare at her, as if waiting for the punch line.

The silk of Lucille's gown rustled as she rose from the chair in a huff. Marin noted that Hunter didn't bother to stand in his mother's presence.

"Really, Hunter. You cannot be so thimble-witted. You have had a ba . . . child born out of wedlock delivered to your door. The mother drops dead within hours. And then you hastily wed the woman you hired as my companion, who quickly turned into your secretary and governess to your child. Did you think eyebrows would not raise and tongues would not wag?"

He resumed toying with the ribbons on Marin's sleeve, staring into the distance at nothing before looking at his mother with total boredom.

"Forgive me, Mother. For a moment I was struck with the notion that you desired a proper wedding for the memories it might make. Not to hold down the local gossipmongers. That *was* thimble-witted of me." The tug on the ribbons stopped. "As for the wagging tongues, why do you not wag your own a bit and tell the town harpies that Marin was hired as your companion as well as my secretary, that you chose not to have a companion, and that Katie loves her like a mother?" He uncrossed his legs and leaned forward. "And *I* love her, by God, and I do not need an elaborate wedding with a group of two-faced spectators to make it any more legal than it is!"

Marin didn't know what Lucille's reaction was to Hunter's words. She didn't notice anything after Hunter said, "And *I* love her." Though he'd shown her in countless ways, she'd never heard him say the words.

Her heart sang. It soared. It felt like it had sprouted wings and now held her on a cushion of air. She stared at his fierce face as he watched his mother disappear from view. When she was gone he turned to look at Marin.

His expression gentled when he whispered, "Dear God, I love you."

"Fireball."

The now-familiar beep gradually became louder, and though her eyes never opened, Ryan and the hospital room appeared to her as if out of a black fog. He leaned over her, running the warm mist of his hand across her forehead. The love in his touch was almost a living, breathing entity.

"Your condition's getting worse, Marin. You can't continue to hover here. You're afraid to let go. That's why you couldn't follow me. Trust me, sweetheart. Just trust me. I promise you'll be happy."

Marin looked at his precious face, unshed tears stinging her eyes. She tried to speak, to move, but couldn't. But through her spirit she would say what needed to be said. She had to take this opportunity now to apologize for their last day together.

I'm sorry about the fight. She had to swallow a sob before going on. *The day you left on your mission. I was afraid you wouldn't come back. I was so afraid.* She stopped once more to quell the aching sob welling in her chest. *I've never for-*

given myself for my last words to you being in anger. You died and my last words to you were "Who cares."

Ryan sat on the edge of the hard hospital bed. He placed his hands above her shoulders and leaned down, his beloved face only inches from hers.

"Your last words to me were, 'I'm so sorry, honey. I love you more than life itself. Come back to me.' "

A wave of relief swept over Marin, tears of joy slid from her eyes to zigzag across her temples.

You got my letter.

"Yes, Fireball. I had it in this pocket," he glanced down to the zippered pocket over his heart, *"when my plane went down."*

The vivid orange ball of fire she had imagined her husband dying in, the technicolor nightmares she had worked to smother in her conscious mind, all came back with crushing force.

Oh, Ryan.

"Don't you see, sweetheart? Our life together isn't over. That's why I'm here."

The temptation to go with him was so great. But when she'd tried the last time he'd come to her, she had been unable to cross through the door. Would the same thing happen again? Was it her love for Hunter that held her? But Hunter was going to die soon, too.

"Marin, sweetheart, just trust me. I can only come to you once more." He stood and held out his hand. It faded to a thin vapor. Ryan's gaze jerked upward and he yelled, *"No! Wait! It's too soon!"*

Marin reached for his hand, but there was nothing to grasp.

"Ryan!" she screamed. "Oh, Ryan! Come back! Oh, God! I love you!"

The sob finally tore from her chest, the pain so intense her heart might have been torn with it.

A warm, solid hand grasped her upper arm as the black fog returned to engulf her.

"Marin. Marin, wake up."

She turned her head in the direction of Hunter's voice and slowly opened her burning eyes. Instead of encountering his translucent ghost in her hospital room, she stared at the flesh-and-blood face of her new husband as they lay in their bed.

He turned to the nightstand and lit the lamp, adjusting the flame with studious care before turning back to her.

Her heartbeat had just started to slow when he fixed her with his soul-searching gaze.

"Who . . . is Ryan?"

Chapter 16

THUNDER RUMBLED IN the distance as Marin stared at him, the tears from her dream still glistening in her eyes. Hunter prayed that Ryan was a brother, an uncle, a friend. But in his heart he knew better. He had not forgotten the night right after she arrived when he'd taken her the letters she'd written him. He'd found her asleep, and after leaving the letters, he'd taken a moment to admire the view. That's when she'd sighed a sensual, unsisterly sigh and whispered, "I love you, Ryan." Surely she never called Niles Kilpatrick "Ryan." Could it possibly be his middle name?

Hunter's heart banged against the wall of his chest while she just stared at him with a haunted look in her eyes. All the old feelings of betrayal began to creep back into his mind.

"Who is Ryan?" he repeated with a little less patience.

Marin sat up slowly, her movements slow and stiff, like that of a very old woman. She leaned against the headboard, drew her knees up to her chest, then rubbed her eyes with the heels of her hands. He waited for her next words with dread.

"Ryan was my husband."

Shock and disbelief jolted him. That was the one answer he had not anticipated. But that was the one answer he could not believe. The scars on his back and thigh began to ache at the thought of another betrayal. He searched her face for some clue as to her feelings. The dim golden light of the lamp on her features revealed nothing.

"Your husband," he said, the only reply his brain could manage.

"Yes." She blinked, and the tears on her lashes fell to her cheeks. "He died."

"He died. I see." He didn't see at all, but he decided to play along with this game. He tried to keep his voice gentle. To keep the anger out of it. "And how long were you married?"

Marin drew in a deep breath and tilted her head back until it thudded on the headboard. A tear traced below her temple and into her hairline as she swallowed.

"A year."

Hunter squeezed his eyes closed and rubbed the middle of his forehead with his fingertips. Did she honestly think he would believe this? He had to force himself to ask the next question.

"And did you love him?"

He watched as she brought her gaze level with his, praying that her answer would be no. She stared at him, as if willing him to believe her next words.

"I loved him very much. I loved him as much as I love you."

Heat surged across his neck and over his scalp, but he didn't know if it came from hope—or regret.

"Did he love you?"

Marin bowed her head and swallowed again. Her only answer was a nod.

"Dear God in heaven!" He lunged to his feet and buried his fingers in his hair. This conversation was preposterous. He dropped his hands and turned back to her, spearing her with his gaze. "For God's sake, Marin! You were a virgin on our wedding night! How do you explain *that* if the two of you were so much in love?"

He didn't know what he expected, but it wasn't the reaction he got. Marin narrowed her eyes in anger and jumped from the bed, flinging her pillow behind her.

"Mari Sander was a virgin! Not me! I told you when I got here, this is not my body! I'm five seven, gray eyes, light brown hair. I've never kept my origins a secret from you!" She turned away, only to whirl back around and poke him in the chest with her finger. "I'm from 1996. I was curator of this house! Pierce Hall! It was open to the public, just like what I want to do at Tranquille. I told you the gist of my life the day we buried Delia and you were being pigheaded. Did all my information match Mari Sander's? Did you bother to ask any questions then? I gave you the perfect opportunity, but no. You didn't even bother to ask. Hell, if it wasn't for you I wouldn't even be here!" She turned her back to him and walked away. "Life was easier when you were a ghost."

She caught her breath in a horrified gasp after her last statement and darted a look over her shoulder at him. Then she buried her face in her hands and curled into herself, as if in unbearable pain, a heart-wrenching sob like none he had ever heard in his life rising from her. She stomped her foot on the floor, as she had done that day on the front lawn before the storm. As though if she stomped hard enough, whatever was causing her to cry would go away.

Hunter was at a complete and total loss. He was angry and jealous over this Ryan person, but everything in him that loved her told him to comfort her. His love for her won out, and he found himself gently turning her around by her shoulders. She buried her face against his bare chest and clung to him with desperation.

His anger cooled somewhat in the face of her despondency. She had made no sense at all with this talk about not being here if it wasn't for him. Of course she wouldn't. He had paid her way and employed her. But what in heaven's name did she mean about life being easier when he was a ghost?

He tangled his fingers in the mass of auburn curls and tried to imagine the rich color a light brown instead. What would it feel like if her head rested three or four inches higher on his chest? It wouldn't feel like Marin.

He cupped the back of her head in his palm and patted with what he hoped was comforting gentleness.

"Marin. Can you tell me what's wrong?"

Her breath shuddered in her chest before she sobbed, "No."

Another unexpected answer.

Now what? He was not at all good at this sort of thing. Maybe if he kept her talking.

"What did you mean when you said life was easier when I was a ghost?"

Obviously that was the wrong question to ask. The weeping that had begun to taper off came back full force. But Marin cried like no other woman he'd ever seen. Hers was almost a silent cry, as if she fought to hold all the pain in so no one could see how she was hurting.

She backed away from him as lightning illuminated the room and thunder crashed overhead.

"Just forget what I said, Hunter. I don't know what I meant. I was just babbling."

Hunter sat on the edge of the bed and pulled her down beside him. Tomorrow he was going to fetch Dr. Ritter and make sure Marin had recovered from that head wound. In the meantime, he would try to put aside the thought of her calling out another man's name in her sleep.

He pulled her to him and tucked her under his arm. With one finger he pushed several damp tendrils of silky mahogany from her tear-stained cheeks. He slowly lay back, pulling her with him, until they were cuddled together, their legs tangled over the side of the bed.

Another crash of thunder was rivaled seconds later by the crash of the bedroom door hitting the wall. The sound of bare feet running across the floor could be heard right before Katie catapulted between the two of them. Seconds later two furry grenades joined the trio. Katie curled into a little ball, her face replacing Marin's on his chest, as she repeated over and over to herself, "Funder can't hurt you. Funder can't hurt you."

Marin sat through the examination with defiant boredom. Before Dr. Ritter had arrived, she'd objected to his visit.

"I'm fine. And even if I wasn't, it wouldn't change my past." But her arguments had fallen on deaf ears.

And now this morning the air was decidedly chilly between the newlyweds. If Hunter had been able to make love to her last night after their confrontation, she might have been able to reassure him about Ryan. Katie and the animals had picked an inopportune time to get scared. All Marin knew was that she wasn't going to be the first one to make a move. She'd told him the truth. She had nothing to apologize for.

"Say 'Ahhhh,' " Dr. Ritter ordered.

"Ahhhh."

He checked her eyes, listened to her heart with that antique stethoscope of his, and asked her several silly questions that Marin had to bite her tongue to keep from laughing over. He dropped all his medical paraphernalia into his bag and snapped it shut.

"You are as fit as a fiddle, little lady."

Hunter jumped from the chair in protest.

"Are you certain? There is nothing wrong? No lingering problems from the head injury?"

Marin just raised an I-told-you-so eyebrow.

"What are you getting at, Hunter?"

Hunter flicked a glance at Marin, but she scooted back into her chair in declaration that she wanted to hear what he had to say.

"Well, she still holds to that story about being in someone else's body . . . among other things."

"What other things?"

Hunter was clearly disgusted to be having this conversation. The muscle in his jaw flexed a few times, then he stared at her while he spoke to the doctor.

"She thinks she was married before. For a year. She thinks she's a widow."

The doctor's sunken eyes widened, then turned to Marin in query, but she refused to deny Hunter's words. Indeed, she gave a little shrug to the doctor that said, "He's right."

The doctor cleared his throat and dragged his gaze back to Hunter.

"Er, ah, was there any . . . indication that she was previously married?"

"None whatsoever. In fact, quite the contrary!"

"Well. Ahem." Dr. Ritter cast an uncomfortable glance at Marin, who continued to remain silent, then he turned back to Hunter. "You have to understand, son, that the mind is a complex organ that is still more mystery to my profession than medical fact. There is no way of knowing if this . . . condition . . . will be permanent or if it will correct itself tomorrow. I surely wish I could tell you. But," he lifted his bag with peppy optimism and walked to the foyer, "I would venture to say that as long as she is in such robust health, then thank the good Lord and ignore this little notion of hers. It's harmless enough, after all."

Marin rose and followed Hunter and Dr. Ritter to the door, smug at her obvious health, yet disappointed that Hunter continued to think she was either lying or crazy.

But she couldn't blame him. She'd tried to put herself in his place, and even in 1996, if a guy showed up on her doorstep and claimed to be from the year 2116, she'd fix him with a glassy-eyed stare and reach for her tear gas.

"Well, I suppose the wife and I shall see you at the reception Saturday next." The doctor turned at the door and extended his hand to Hunter. Hunter shook it but cocked his head in question.

"Reception?"

"Yes. The reception your Northern business associates are holding for you in celebration of your nuptials." At Hunter's blank stare, the doctor grimaced and shook his head. "Oh, my. I hope I have not spoken out of turn. There was no indication that the party was to be a surprise."

Hunter slapped him on the shoulder and walked him to his carriage.

"No harm done, I'm sure. Marin and I were at Tranquille until yesterday."

"Ah. I see." The doctor folded his skeletal body into the small carriage. "As for this other problem, son . . . just give it time." He winked at Hunter. Marin thought it such an incongruous gesture from such a cadaverous face. He turned and tipped his hat to Marin. She waved from the doorway and watched as the carriage left a cloud of dust hanging in the muggy air over the drive.

When the carriage turned onto the road, Hunter spun on his heel and stormed past Marin into the house. At first she thought his anger was at her, until he stopped in the middle of the foyer and roared, "Mother!" When there was no answer to his shout, he bellowed again. "Now, Mother!"

Absolute silence reigned for several seconds, then the familiar click of Lucille's shoes could be heard in the upstairs hall. From the casual, slow pace it was clear she was taking her good old time answering the summons of her irate son. Finally she appeared on the second-floor landing. She just stood there, apparently waiting for him to state the reason for his unseemly behavior.

"Where is it?" he demanded with barely controlled ire.

Lucille's expression was just a trifle too innocent to be believed.

"Where is what?"

"The invitation!"

"I know nothing of—"

"Get it! Or get out!"

"Hunter!" Marin gasped.

Lucille jerked as if she'd been slapped. Marin was nearly as shocked as Lucille. Never had she heard Hunter speak to his mother so. And never had he even intimated that he would throw her out, except the time she'd called Katie a bastard. Marin's gaze flew from Hunter to Lucille. Her mother-in-law stared back with all her legendary venom. After a moment's hesitation, she walked across the landing and descended the steps. Hunter and Marin both followed her into the parlor, where she snatched up her embroidery basket and produced a creamy vellum envelope. She shoved it into Hunter's hands.

"Enjoy your afternoon with those Yankee heathens," she hissed, then marched past him to the foyer.

"I will, Mother. As I am sure you will, also."

She stopped dead in her tracks and whirled to meet his gaze.

"You cannot be serious!"

"On the contrary. I am deadly serious. If these people have been kind enough to arrange a reception in our honor, you will be there to stop all those wagging tongues you so detest by giving us your public blessing."

If Lucille had been a dog, the hackles on her spine would have stood straight up.

"You expect me to go to the home of one of those Yankees and act as if I am enjoying myself? I will not do it!"

Hunter's voice lowered to a threatening level.

"You will do it, or you will pack your bags and leave."

It was time to put a stop to this.

"Hunter. Lucille. Listen to yourselves." Marin stepped between her husband and his mother. "Lucille, the war is over. It's been over for a decade now. Surely if Hunter bears no animosity toward the North, you have no reason to. If he can forgive them for his scars, surely you can find it in your heart to be civil to his business associates."

Lucille stared at her as if she were crazy. Hunter blew out a frustrated breath and dropped onto a brocade-covered chair.

"I bear Northerners no ill will, Marin. They fought for their country and a cause they believed in just as I did. And no matter how I incurred my injuries, I would feel the same. But the North did not inflict the wounds that caused my scars. A Confederate cannon blew up while being fired. The scars on my leg are from the shrapnel. The scars on my back are from the burns." He looked at her and said, "I thought the scars meant nothing to you."

"They don't. Why would you think . . . Oh, for Pete's sake. I give up." She threw up her hands and turned toward the foyer. Since last night he had found fault with everything she'd said. "You two go at it, for all I care. I can't stand to be around either one of you."

With that parting remark she turned and left the parlor, wanting nothing more than to put distance between herself and their poisonous animosity.

"What do you mean, the brat has no inheritance?" Harold Cabot could barely control his rage at the confirmation of Pierce's words. The shyster lawyer teetering on the stool across from him lowered his glass. He swayed to and fro while focusing his bleary gaze on his client.

"S'what I said. Mother used what was lef' lookin' for a cure."

"Are you absolutely certain of the facts? There is no money if I gain custody of the brat?"

One drunken nod of the lawyer's head was his only answer. Cabot looked at the man named Smithfield with disgust. This was the best he could afford, but he had to believe him. The man had nothing to gain by lying. Indeed, Cabot was probably his first client in months.

Smithfield tapped a grimy fingernail on the bar next to his empty glass, indicating a refill. Cabot stayed the bartender's hand when he would have replenished the drink.

"I have bought my last drink for this sot," he said as he stood.

The bartender shrugged and turned away. Smithfield yelled "Hey!" and lunged for the bottle. Cabot grabbed a fistful of dingy, stained cravat and shirtfront. He pulled the man so close, the familiar smells of sour whiskey and unwashed body assailed him.

"If there is no inheritance, there is no need for your services," he breathed into the man's face. He shoved him away, then turned to leave. Some of his hostility was momentarily assuaged at the sound of Smithfield's body crashing into the bar. He almost smiled to himself when shouts of outrage were followed by the sounds of breaking glass and splintering wood.

Outside the sleazy bar he found his whore of a wife plying her trade to some whey-faced young dandy who probably couldn't do the deed without a picture drawn for him. Cabot grabbed her by the wrist and yanked her down the street.

"Ow! Harry, you idiot! I had that sap ready to pay up front!"

"Leave it," he bellowed over his shoulder. "We have more plans to make."

Shirley tugged to free her arm, but he held on that much tighter and gave another hard yank to boot.

"The brat hasn't a red cent. Damn, this ruins all my plans."

Shirley dug in her heels. Cabot let go of her arm so quickly she almost fell on her ass. Too bad she didn't. It might have brightened his mood.

"You sorry excuse for a man! How the hell am I to put food on the table if you just take a notion to haul me away and leave the johns standin' there droolin'? Ain't you concerned that the wallet on that pimple-faced twit was bigger than his—"

Cabot rounded on her and screamed in her face. "Do not say 'ain't,' you ignorant slut! If I ever have the misfortune to introduce you in a court of law as my wife, you had damned well better speak as someone who can put two thoughts together to make a complete sentence. Do you think for even a moment that custody of the chit would be given to me if my wife appears as the uneducated, backwoods trollop that she is?"

It never failed to amaze him how immune his wife could be to the most heinous slanderings. She simply shrugged and continued walking to their meager rooms.

"It don't—"

"Doesn't!" he shouted. "It doesn't!"

She rolled her eyes and his hand itched to slap her, but a constable strolled by, studying them with more than a passing interest.

"It *doesn't,*" she continued with a flip of her head, "make no never mind, since you just said she ain't got no money."

He gave up. The bitch was hopeless. He should have never married her. That would teach him never to smoke opium with a whore again.

They arrived at their building, then had to pick their way down a nasty alley rife with rotting food to get to the door of their rooms. He stepped in a pungent pile of horse dung and took it out on Shirley by shoving her through the door.

"Jesus, Harry!" she cried as she stumbled into the room. "Break my leg and won't neither of us eat for a month." She fell onto a stained, lumpy mattress that had seen its share of her customers.

"Shut up. I have to think." He lit the one lantern and turned to pull out a chair. An enormous cockroach scuttled from the depths beneath the table. "Hell!" Cabot squashed the huge insect with a boot still coated with manure. "God, how I hate this place. I was never meant to live like this. If those damned Yankees hadn't burned my home and stolen—"

"Ain't you got another song to sing besides that tired old ballad?" Shirley interrupted his soliloquy, because he certainly was not talking to her. "You've whined about the damn Yankees since we woke up married a year ago. I guess you don't remember that time when you got a couple of drinks in you and told how you deserted in '61, then spent the war livin' off the fear of Confederate women, stealin' their last bit of food and threatenin' to rape them. Why, you ain't no better'n me."

Cabot picked up a filthy tin cup and hurled it at her head. She dodged it with practiced ease so that it bounced off the wall behind her. The rim left another half-moon dent to match all the others that had come before.

"If you hate this place so bad, why don't you spend a little of that money you been hoardin' and get better rooms?"

Cabot looked heavenward before tuning his bored gaze to his idiot of a wife.

"Because, you ignorant wretch, I am saving that money to

institute my plan. Somehow there is a way to turn this brat into surefire profit. Now shut up and let me think."

He discarded several ideas as his mind spun out one plan after another. Within a quarter of an hour he had his answer. A no-fail plan that would pay off no matter which way his luck blew. He glanced at Shirley, who had nodded off to sleep, her head against the wall, her mouth hanging open. He could not suppress a grimace of utter loathing every time his eyes fell upon this woman. But she'd kept him fed this past year while he'd been down on his luck, and he might need to use her yet. But, he promised himself, as soon as the money was in his hands, Shirley would be just an irritating memory. He jumped up and shook her awake.

"Wake up, you lazy slut."

She blinked, batted his hands away, then wiped her mouth with the back of her hand.

"What do you want, you son of a bitch?"

"I want some information."

Marin struggled to keep a smile on her face as she watched her husband from across the front lawn.

"I could not take my eyes from my husband, either, when we were first married." Leah Jacobs leaned close and whispered conspiratorially. "Of course, Lionel was the most handsome boy in our little hometown."

Marin pulled her eyes from Hunter and smiled at her hostess.

"It was so kind of you and your husband to offer your home for this party. It has meant a lot to Hunter that the men he does business with would go to this much trouble."

Leah tapped her fan on Marin's knee.

"Mr. Pierce is not the only one the boys think highly of.

Why, Eli Beecham came back from your husband's dinner party convinced that you are a saint. And the others feel the same. They even stopped by to make certain you were well the day after the dinner, but Mrs. Pierce told them you shouldn't be disturbed." Leah darted a glance in Lucille's direction. From Leah's expression, Marin was sure there was more to the story than what was being told. But at the moment she had no fire left to be angry at Lucille.

She simply murmured to her hostess, "Yes, my mother-in-law is a hard person to warm up to."

Marin sat and tried to look interested as the ladies around her flitted from one topic to another in their conversation. But her mind continually turned back to her husband. For the last week he'd kept an emotional and physical distance from her. Of course he'd been polite, even solicitous, whenever they were together—which wasn't often. But the thing that most worried her was the fact that Hunter had found some pressing work to do every night that kept him up until well after Marin had fallen asleep. He must be very upset indeed to make them both suffer this way.

His laugh caught her attention, and she searched the group of croquet players until she found him. Jealousy spiked through her at the sight of Hunter smiling down at a simpering airheaded girl clad in a ton of ruffles and drapes. His glance scanned the crowd until it met Marin's, but she forced herself to blink slowly and look away with unconcern. She refused to play this game, but tonight he would have a surprise waiting up for him. It was time she put a stop to this nonsense.

Her gaze fell on Katie, who had also been invited to the outdoor reception. Several of the little daughters of the families had immediately swept her away upon arrival to endless tea parties with a multitude of dolls. But at the moment she was alone. Marin watched her little daughter walk across the lawn, a plate of cookies and a glass of lemonade in her hand. She walked very slowly, placing one foot carefully in front of the other, watching the lemonade so as not to spill a drop. Marin wondered at her destination, since there were no other children in sight. If she didn't know better, it would seem as though Katie were walking toward . . . She was! Katie made her slow, deliberate way to stand in front of Lucille, who'd been sitting alone on a bench for the biggest part of the afternoon. The sour expression permanently etched in Lucille's face was enough to dampen all but the most stalwart social butterfly's intentions. But Marin was certain that the lemon-sucker's reputation had preceded her to the point that no one cared to investigate the truthfulness of the rumors. And obviously no one took pity on the bitter woman who'd been left to sit alone, like a one-woman leper colony, in the midst of the party.

No one except Katie. Marin watched in fascination as Katie stood quietly, waiting to be acknowledged. Lucille finally looked down her nose at Katie, who promptly extended the plate of cookies and glass of lemonade. Her little arms hovered in the air, bearing her gift, for a good five seconds. Just as Marin prepared to go to Katie's rescue, Lucille took the offering. Katie smiled the heart-melting smile of a happy child. Without bothering to be invited, Katie clambered up onto the bench beside her grandmother. An immediate conversation was struck on the part of Katie, then Marin was absolutely flabbergasted to see Lucille straighten Katie's frock and offer her a cookie.

Would wonders never cease? If someone had told her they'd been witness to this scene, she would have asked them what they'd been smoking. This was too good to ignore. She excused herself and wandered over to the bench the odd pair occupied.

"Mind if I join you?" She snagged a glass of lemonade off the tray of a passing waiter and sat down opposite them without waiting for permission. Lucille refused to look at her. "Katie, how thoughtful of you to bring your grandmother these goodies. Did you think of that all by yourself?"

Katie's little feet stuck straight out in front of her, her black patent leather shoes bobbling in the air at the edge of the bench.

"Yes, ma'am," Katie said through a mouthful of cookie. She took another bite. Crumbs skittered down her pleated front to hide in the folds of the pinafore. "Do . . . do . . . do you know Gwandma couldn't go to parties when she was little?" Katie looked at Marin with that wide-eyed look that said: Now that I have your attention. "Her mama and papa drank stuff that made them mean and people didn't like them." Lucille's gaze flew to Katie, but the older woman remained silent. "And one time Gwandma's papa got his arm caught in a re . . . a re . . . a reaper. And he was drinking the mean stuff and Gwandma had to cut it off."

Was Katie trying to say that Lucille had been forced to cut off her drunken father's arm in order to save his life? What a terrible thing for a child to be forced to do.

"And Gwandma had to take care of him 'cause her mama left."

"Kathleen, I believe you have said enough." Lucille turned to Katie and forced another cookie into her hand, but not before Marin was left speechless at the sight of excess moisture glittering in Lucille's eyes.

"But I want your party to be happy, Gwandma."

"It is, Kathleen. Thank you for the cookies and lemonade."

This could explain so much, Marin thought. Raised by alcoholics, probably abused in some way—she shuddered to think of how. Forced to amputate her father's arm and then to care for him when her mother ran off. Or did she die? Either way, that would explain Lucille's aversion to handicapped people. They were vivid reminders of what was probably an abusive father and what she'd suffered. No doubt her venomous nature came from adopting the policy to wound first before anyone could wound her.

The dinner bell rang on the back porch of the Jacobs's home, calling everyone to the linen-covered tables groaning with food on the front lawn.

"I'm starving!" Marin declared. "Shall we go get something to eat?"

Katie scrambled off the bench, a shower of cookie crumbs sprinkling the lawn.

"C'mon, Gwandma."

Lucille sat, stiff-backed, her lips pursed in their usual way. It had not escaped Marin that Katie was altogether too well informed to have learned all that information during her and Lucille's brief conversation. And when had Lucille become "Gwandma" to Katie? And Katie was now Kathleen to Lucille.

Yes, the tiny moppet had struck again. She'd wrapped her little fist around one more adult's heart—an incredible feat, considering who the adult was.

Marin looked at her mother-in-law differently now.

"Will you join us, Lucille?"

Chapter 17

HUNTER'S EYES WERE gritty with fatigue. He rubbed them with the heels of his hands, stretched until his limbs shook, then pulled out his pocket watch and flicked it open. Two a.m. She had to be asleep by now. He closed the ledger he'd been killing time with and scraped the chair back to rise. The softness of their bed beckoned his weary body. He tried not to think of how Marin's arms beckoned his weary soul.

Things could not go on this way. Sooner or later he would have to deal with all his emotions concerning Marin's abstract view of her past and his jealousy over the man she cried out for in her sleep. But not until he'd had a good night's rest.

He slipped noiselessly into the darkened bedroom and peeled off his waistcoat and shirt. His boot made a gentle thud on the floor and he froze, listening for sounds of Marin stirring. When no rustling sounds rose from the bed, he pulled off the other boot, then finished undressing, careful to leave on his smallclothes to help avoid any temptation. He slipped between the cool sheets and sank thankfully into the bed.

Something was wrong. The bed didn't feel quite right. He lay quietly for a moment until he realized he was alone. He slid his hand over to Marin's side and encountered nothing but cold, empty sheet. His heart went suddenly as cold and empty as her side of the bed. A clammy sweat formed on the back of his neck. Bile rose in his throat. Had she left him? Had the bride he'd neglected for over a week left him for the man in her dreams? It was his own fault if she had; he would never forgive himself. But, damnation, the sound of her tortured voice calling "Ryan" stirred too many memories.

Dead husband, indeed.

A muffled noise sent a shock of hope rippling through him. He swung his feet to the floor and followed the sound. It seemed to be coming from the dressing room. With hope and dread he soundlessly eased the door open and peered inside.

He didn't know what he'd expected, but it definitely was not the scene he encountered. The small room was lit with a dozen scattered candles. A soft breeze from the stained glass window stirred the flames with an elusive hint of gardenia in the warm, humid air. But the focal point of the room—dear Lord, the focal point lit a fire in his blood and stole his breath. He swallowed hard past the sudden lump in his throat.

Marin soaked in scented water in the huge, enameled bathing tub in the center of the room. Her hair, normally styled in flawless, intricate braids and loops and twists, was piled loosely atop her head. Huge, silky tendrils cascaded haphazardly to frame her face. Some were damp and stuck to her cheeks. Some had fallen to float in the water which rose only high enough to barely cover . . . he swallowed hard again. Oh, Lord.

Marin's head rested against the high back of the tub. Eyes closed, dark lashes fanned across her cheeks, she exuded an air of serenity. Her elbows rested on the edge of the tub while she dangled her fingers in the water, making languid ripples every now and then.

Hunter could hear his heart beating in his ears. The lump in his throat grew as his breathing became shallow and the room suddenly became very hot. Marin presented a picture that would make a priest give up his vows.

And he was no priest.

"Would you hand me a towel?" Marin asked in a low, husky voice, without opening her eyes. From her tone, Hunter knew she hadn't mistaken him for Mamie. How had she known he was there? She opened her eyes and rose from the tub without waiting for an answer. He watched, mesmerized, as the sheet of water turned to rivulets, then trickles, then dewy droplets shimmering on alabaster skin in the candlelight. The droplets slid, one by one, to join another, hover for a moment, then continue the downward journey. How he wished his hands were those droplets of water.

He dragged his gaze back to her face. She watched him through smoky, half-closed eyes. Just watched him. He waited for her to say something, anything, but she just stood there. Finally her gaze traveled slowly downward, burning him as if she were physically touching him. Her eyes lingered for a moment, then returned to his face, a knowing smile barely curving her lips. He knew what she was thinking. He could neither deny nor hide his feelings. Nor did he want to.

He picked up a towel from the chest by the door, held the ends and opened it as he walked to the tub. Instead of stepping into the towel, however, Marin pulled it from his grasp and dropped it. The towel slipped into the water with barely a noise. Her eyes never left his as she slid her finger into the band at his waist, pulling him nearer as well as loosening the thin garment. Her free arm wrapped around his neck as her lips brushed a feathery kiss against his.

The feel of her welcoming him into her arms lifted a weight that had pressed on him all week. He was no longer tired. His eyes no longer burned. Other parts of him burned now, but he would quench them soon enough. He stepped into the tub as she continued to pull him to her. The lukewarm water did nothing to cool the fires she stoked in him as she reached behind him and untied the drawstring at his waist.

Hunter was helplessly weak, euphorically drained from the strenuous night Marin had put him through. If he hadn't felt the evidence for himself on their wedding night, he might be persuaded to believe she really hadn't been a virgin after all, so inventive was his bride.

But in the midst of his mellow afterglow, he couldn't help but wonder if his virgin bride had acquired her knowledge of men from the elusive Ryan.

At some point during the night the lovers had given up the bathing tub and then the deep carpet in front of the cold fireplace for the comfort of their bed. And now here he lay, his wife curled against him, her head nestled on his shoulder, her arm draped possessively across his chest. Her love wrapped around him like a warm, soft blanket. But a man named Ryan was an arctic wind in his soul.

"Hunter?" Her breath fanned across his collarbone.

"Hmmm?"

"I love you."

Amazing, how one minute those three simple words could cause such elation and the next raise such terrible doubt.

She raised up on one elbow and stared down at him when he failed to respond. She continued to look at him solemnly. "I don't ever want you to forget that I love you. Only you. No matter what."

His jealousy had caused her to feel the need for that declaration. But he was not the type of man to shrug off hearing his wife call out for another.

"I don't want things to ever be between us again like they were this past week," Marin said. "I don't think I could bear it. Just believe me when I tell you that I honestly mean what I've told you about myself." She touched his cheek with her fingertips, then traced the outline of his stubbled jaw. "But that's over now, and Ryan is dead. You're the most important thing in the world to me, and I don't want anything to come between us again." She hesitated for a moment. "Do you think it will?"

Hunter took a deep breath. What he said now, how he reacted, could ensure or destroy their future together, but no matter what, he had to be truthful.

"Marin, when you first came here I heard you call out that same name in your sleep. You said, 'I love you, Ryan.' I have heard this man's name more than once. The last time, you said it with such tortured pain, there could be no denying that you love him." He stared at the circle of mosquito netting above the bed and wondered if he would ever completely trust her again. She drew in her breath as if to speak, but he stopped her. "Put yourself in my place. What if I told you I was from the 1700's? That I had a dead wife whom I mourned for in my sleep. Yet on our wedding night you knew beyond a shadow of a doubt that I had never been with another woman. None of this makes sense, Marin. I tried convincing myself this was all a result of your accident, but I cannot make myself believe that. We corresponded two months before you arrived here. Your handwriting is the same. For God's sake, you had a fiancé show up on my doorstep!"

He finally turned his head on the pillow and looked at his wife. He expected her to reiterate her story. Instead, she searched his eyes with a sad, defeated look. For a moment he thought she would confess to loving another.

"How can I win back your trust? Just tell me and I'll do it," she said after several long, heart-stopping seconds.

Win back his trust. What would it take from her to make the ache in his scars, as well as in his heart, go away for good? He went back to staring at the mosquito netting.

"I am not certain there is anything you can do, Marin. This is something I must work through on my own. You have said your piece, and I have said mine. Now I have to deal with it in my own way, in my own time."

Marin was quiet for several minutes, the only sounds in the room that of their gentle breathing and the high-pitched chirp of dozens of crickets outside the open window. He felt her warm palm slide onto the center of his chest, but he didn't allow himself to move.

"Could I ask one thing?" she said, her sweet breath caressing his ear.

He turned his head just far enough to look at her.

"While you're working this out, will you try to act like nothing's wrong? Don't ignore me or avoid me?"

He let the question hang in the air. The silence stretched like a long, empty road as he considered her request. If he didn't avoid her, he wasn't sure he could think clearly enough to get through this. Even now it was all he could do not to pull her atop him and try to absorb her through his skin. Earlier in the day, even the gardenias by the veranda muddled his thinking and warmed his blood simply because they wore the same scent as she. He wanted so badly to trust her.

"I shall try," he finally said. "But I cannot promise things will be as they were. Not until I resolve this in my mind."

Marin nodded, then cuddled up closer.

"Did you see your mother and Katie at the reception this afternoon?" she asked in a blatant attempt to change the subject. Here was his chance to try acting normal.

"Do you know," he said, "she actually seemed to be tolerating Katie's presence? And what is even more odd is for one moment I could have sworn I heard my mother laugh! I cannot remember the last time I witnessed my mother laughing. I am sure it was well before the war—and not often, even then."

Marin's head nodded against his shoulder.

"Apparently those two have been spending more time together than we thought. Do you know that they are now 'Kathleen' and 'Gwandma' to each other?"

"No!" Hunter could not believe his ears. Thoughts of their earlier conversation faded momentarily at this news. Marin related the story of Katie bringing his mother lemonade and cookies, and how the three of them had had a pleasant lunch together.

"Of course, Lucille didn't say much, but Katie jabbered enough for the three of us." Marin fell silent for a moment. "Did you know your grandparents were alcoholics?"

"Alcoholics?" Hunter wasn't sure he knew what she meant. He'd never heard the word used in that way before.

"You know. Drunkards?"

"Oh. Yes, I suppose I had heard it mentioned that my grandparents liked their liquor. I don't remember them, though. They both died before I contracted the fever."

"Did you know that your mother had to amputate her father's arm from a reaping machine because there was no one else there to do it? And that your grandmother packed her bags and left? Lucille took over your grandmother's duties when she was ten."

Hunter didn't know what to say. He'd never heard even a hint of this story.

"Did Mother tell you this?"

"Part of it. Katie started the story. While we had lunch I asked Lucille a few things. She answered my questions but didn't offer any other information."

Hunter tried to assimilate this news. Why was he never told? Did his sister, Blake, know? Was it possible his mother's hatred was directed at someone other than him?

How very interesting. And how very sad.

Niles stood in the center of the room, running the brim of his derby through his hands, when Marin stepped into the parlor.

"Hello, Niles."

"Mari, me—" Niles broke off the endearment. "Mari. Ye look well."

"Thank you. You're looking prosperous yourself." Marin

sat and motioned for Niles to do the same. She waited a moment for him to state his business, but he just looked at her and nodded. Did he mean to take up where he and Mari had left off? "You know Hunter and I are married now, don't you?"

"Ah, yes." He nodded. "I heard the news right enough. I'm supposin' I should extend my best wishes."

Marin nodded her thanks, then the two sat there in silence for a moment longer.

"I've come to tell ye good-bye, Mari. I'll be leaving for St. Louis at first light."

"Oh?"

"I told ye I'd be seein' ye again before I left." Niles, every bit as uncomfortable as Marin, mangled his hat some more. "Are ye happy with him, Mari?"

So this wasn't to be a simple good-bye. But Marin knew instinctively that Niles was a good man, and she didn't want to hurt him any more than she already had.

"Yes. I'm very happy with Hunter. Niles," she leaned forward in her chair and took his hand, "don't you think it's best that this happened before we got married? We might have lived to regret our choice of partners."

Niles placed his other hand on hers and brought his face to within inches of Marin's.

"And then again, we might not have," he answered quietly. "We might never have had reason to question our choices."

Marin could think of no answer to his statement. She leaned away from his pleading face and searched her mind for something to say to ease his pain, or at least fill the awkward silence.

"Shall I have Mamie bring us some tea?"

"No," Niles breathed with a frustrated sigh. He stood and placed his hat just so on his head. "No, I'll be leavin' now. I just wanted to say good-bye." He pulled Marin from her seat and slid his hands around her waist. "If ye ever regret your decision, if he ever makes ye unhappy, ye know where to find me."

"Awfully accommodating of you, Kilpatrick, but I have no plans to make her sorry she married me."

Hunter stepped into the parlor, wearing a forced smile if ever there was one. Niles took his time removing his hands from her waist, so Marin moved backward enough to break his hold. Hunter slid his arm about her shoulders as Niles dropped his hands to his side.

"I loved her before you did, Pierce. And I love her still. I won't be leavin' without her knowin' she has someone to turn to."

Hunter's dimples were both in evidence, a very misleading sign as to his humor. The flexing muscle at his jaw showed his true feelings.

"She has someone to turn to. Her husband. But we appreciate the gesture. Don't we, sweetheart?" Marin found herself tucked possessively under Hunter's arm as she and her husband walked Mari Sander's former betrothed to the door.

Once on the veranda, Niles turned and glared at Hunter, obviously wanting a moment with Marin. Hunter simply deepened his dimples with his smile and stood his ground. Niles chose to ignore him.

"Mari," Niles began, then searched her eyes with determination. His mood changed to one of acceptance. "I hope ye have every happiness, Mari." Before she could reply, he bounded down the steps to his horse and swung into the saddle.

"Kilpatrick!"

Hunter stepped down onto the first step when Niles turned an irritated gaze on him. Hunter bowed his head for a moment and studied the gravel drive. Lines creased his forehead when he raised his eyes to look at Niles.

"What's your middle name?"

A knife plunged through her heart as surely as if Hunter had buried a dagger to the hilt in her chest. He still didn't trust her. He was going to be civil, but all the while he would be looking for a Ryan that she might call out for in her sleep. God, how his distrust hurt her! She looked at Niles and prayed his middle name was not Ryan.

Niles glared at Hunter with one raised eyebrow. He glared so long Marin thought he would refuse to answer. Reining the horse around until it turned full circle, he stared at Marin, then back at Hunter, a look on his face that said he knew all was not well between them.

"Robert," he finally said, then kicked his horse into a dead run without so much as a backward glance.

Marin closed her eyes with a mixture of relief and pain. When she opened them, Hunter stood before her, still on the top step, unrepentant in his stance. She narrowed her eyes and tried to convey to him with that single look how he had made her feel. When his expression failed to change, she looked back at Niles's retreating figure, silently apologizing to him for ruining his life with Mari.

She watched him gallop down the length of the shady drive. Marin couldn't help experiencing a sadness for him. If not for her, Niles and Mari may well have found happiness together. She felt personally responsible for two lives being torn apart. But what choice had she had? The events of her life were not of her choosing. And now her husband in this alien time didn't trust her, was jealous of a man who hadn't yet been born, but who'd been dead to her for years. She felt as if she had lost all control over her destiny.

She wouldn't allow herself to dwell on those thoughts. She would lose her mind if she did.

"Marin," Hunter interrupted her depressing thoughts with only civility in his voice, "William sent a message from Tranquille. He needs some advice on how to proceed with preparations to open. Can you be ready to leave by this afternoon?"

So, he wasn't going to apologize. There was not even a hint of remorse in his face for his flagrant show of distrust. Part of her wanted to lash out at him, but she quelled the urge and refused to show any more pain. Instead she concentrated on the prospect of returning to Tranquille. At least doing something she knew how to do well might give her back a sense of control.

"I can be ready if I start right now." She stood on tiptoe and defiantly pecked a kiss on his cheek. "I'll have Mamie pack Katie's things." She turned to step into the house, but Hunter's words stopped her.

"No need."

"Excuse me?"

"Katie wants to stay home and keep Puffy and Angel company. Seems she's invited to a tea party at the Galways'."

In spite of her anger at him, a delicious shiver skipped up her spine at Hunter's words.

Alone with Hunter for days! They had never been alone, just the two of them, with no worries about a mother or a daughter or someone else happening upon them. Maggie and William were certain to leave them to themselves.

Maybe this was the chance to wipe all the doubts from Hunter's mind, once and for all!

"The only thing that will cost much money initially is to build the dock so that all the riverboats on the Mississippi have access to us." Marin slipped her hand into Hunter's as they walked along the riverbank. She refused to acknowledge the little pang in her chest when he failed to deliver the usual gentle squeeze to her fingers. Give it time, she told herself.

The setting sun painted the landscape shades of muted orange, its dying rays glistening on the water that gently lapped against the dock. Hunter led her over to a large wooden bench that faced the river. He sat sideways on the bench, one foot propped on the seat, and Marin nestled between his legs, her back resting against his chest.

She could sit here like this forever, looking out over the water and listening to the occasional bird chirping. The frogs had begun to croak and a lone cricket tuned up somewhere in the tall weeds. The scent of freshly cut grass mingled with the river smells of muddy water and fish. As the sun set, the heat of the day gave way to something that resembled coolness.

"Why so quiet?" Hunter asked. She wished he would nuzzle his cheek against the top of her head, as he had done so many times before.

"Oh," she relaxed further into his chest, inviting the coveted nuzzle, "I was just thinking how I could stay here forever. It's so serene and beautiful." She cocked her head and looked up at him. "Why do you live in Memphis? Tranquille is larger, and you'd be better able to see to the crops."

He studied the rippling water for a moment.

"I never really thought about moving here. I grew up at Pierce Hall. This was my grandparents' home, my father's parents. They died before the war was over, and when I returned home, Maggie and William had already closed Tranquille and everything was under control. Would you like to live here?"

Marin wasn't used to living the lifestyle at Pierce Hall. Now Hunter was offering her an even more grandiose home.

"Oh, I don't know. I wonder if it would be so special if we lived here every day." She looked up at him again and he grinned, his dimple deeply shadowed by the dying sun. She savored the little flip in her stomach. "Besides, we'll probably spend half our time here getting the house ready to open every season. That should keep it special for us."

"Tranquille will always be special, no matter how much time we spend here. There are so many happy memories here. So many stories."

"Oh, really? Tell me some."

Hunter leaned forward and helped Marin to her feet, then he stood and pulled her along the riverbank.

"I have something to show you. We should have time before the light is gone."

They walked to a slight bend in the river, then Hunter stopped. He shielded his eyes against the orange glow of the sun, then pointed Marin toward a dark spot on the river.

"Do you see that tiny little island out there?"

"Uh huh."

"When I was a boy, after I recovered from the fever, my sister, Blake, and I would row out there and fight the 'hostile pirates' that threatened to capture our home. But that's not what I want to show you. Halfway between the island

and the bank is a sandbar that's usually twenty feet or so under water."

"Yeah." He wanted to show her a sandbar?

"During the war my grandparents had about eight hours' notice that a Yankee battalion was on its way. Grandfather took as much silver, china, crystal, coins—whatever was small enough to pack, and he and Grandmother, along with William and Maggie, packed as much as they could in rolls of beeswax, then sealed that into huge barrels. They took those barrels out to the sandbar, tied them together, then sank them with a pallet of bricks to keep them from drifting or rising to the surface. They left them there until after the war was over. Maggie and William's sons salvaged them. The plates we use at dinner are from that china. The candelabra on the table, as well as most of the crystal, are survivors as well."

What a wonderful story! She'd heard of war-ravaged Southerners burying their valuables, hiding them in wells, even loading them on boxcars and following them around the Confederacy, but this was a new one.

"Hunter, that will be a great story to tell the visitors that come through! We can display the items that were hidden in the Mississippi. Do you have any other stories?"

"Of course. And we should ask Maggie about any she might recollect from before my fever." He took her hand again and steered her back toward the house. "Would you be interested in a secret passage or a hidden room?"

"You're not serious!" Marin exclaimed. That would be too good to be true.

"On the contrary, do you see the column on the far left?" he asked as the front of the house came into view. "It's hollow."

"No! You're teasing!"

Hunter slapped his palm against his heart and struck a dramatic pose.

"You doubt the word of your husband?" he asked in a wounded tone.

It'd been so long since she'd seen this playful side of him that she loved so much.

"Yeah! Prove it!" She shoved him toward the house, anxious to see this hollow column and secret room, and to prolong this moment when he seemed so like his old self.

Hunter told his story as they made their way through the house.

"Tranquille was built between 1833 and 1836. There was still a large population of Indians in the area at that time. Grandfather had the column built out of wood, then a brick facade built around it, so that if they ever had to escape the Indians, the family could run to the attic and descend through the column into the room below the porch. At one time there was a tunnel that came up inside the old barn, with the entrance hidden in a stall, but it collapsed not long after the war was over."

Marin cursed the damned corset that kept her from breathing while she climbed the stairs to the attic. But the idea of hidden rooms and passages was too intriguing to put off seeing until she was more comfortable.

When Hunter threw the door open to the attic, a blast of heat engulfed them.

"Still want to see the hidden entrance to the column?" he asked as he wiped a bead of sweat from her temple. The finger that slid along her skin dipped down along her jawline, then trailed a lazy path downward to trace the high neckline of her gown. As she looked into his eyes, his gaze changed from playful, to heated, to one of regret. She didn't want to lose the moment! Didn't want the teasing Hunter to turn back into the jealous husband.

"Yeah." She shivered even in the heat of the attic. "But then I think I'm going to need to take a dip in the pond before supper. And I'll need a big, strong man to go with me. Know anybody who would care to wash my back?"

He didn't answer. He just continued to look at her, his eyes sad, his dimples nowhere in sight. Finally he let out a short breath he'd been holding, lowered his head, and ducked into the blasting heat of the attic.

Harold Cabot had been watching the house for days. Money was running out, and if he didn't get a break soon he might have to do something drastic.

Pierce and that meddlesome wife of his had left the house yesterday afternoon, leaving the brat and a sour-looking old woman behind. It looked to him as if they had taken enough luggage for several days, but it was hard to tell. Since he couldn't be sure when they would be back, the sooner he made his move, the better. Patience was all he needed now.

The inside of the closed carriage turned into an oven as the heat of the day increased. And as the temperature rose, so did Cabot's foul temper.

Damn the chit! Every day he'd watched she'd been outside nearly from dawn to dusk, but always with Pierce and his wife or a servant. And never without that infernal dog. Well, he was prepared for the dog if he could just catch the brat alone.

Perspiration ran in rivulets from his armpits, down his temples, even from his knees, drenching his clothing with huge dark stains. The feel of the sweat snaking along his skin was reminiscent of the cooties that had been his constant companion during the war years while he'd dodged both Yankee and Confederate soldiers and terrorized their women. Just the thought of the war and the injustices he'd suffered started his blood boiling.

Damn, he was hungry! He'd eaten only a stale biscuit since that slut of a wife hadn't bothered to come home. The customer she'd been servicing had damned well better make it worth her while or she'd be wearing matching shiners.

"Rube!" he yelled and banged on the side of the carriage with his walking stick. The small window behind the driver slid open and a face the color of wet coal appeared with crossed eyes and a blank expression.

"Suh?"

"Do you have any food up there, you idiot?"

The expression never changed as Rube stared for a moment, then mumbled, "No, suh."

Damn! He reached for his pocket watch, then remembered he'd pawned it. He dared to pull back the curtain on the window far enough to check the sun. It must be five o'clock! No wonder the sides of his belly were rubbing together.

Just as he was about to order Rube to go steal some food nearby, the front door of Pierce Hall swung open. That enormous dog and equally huge cat pitched through the door to circle the yard in predictable fashion. The brat skipped out behind them in all her innocence. Cabot watched intently to see if anyone would exit the house.

Damn! The sour-faced woman, who must be Pierce's mother, followed the brat out, carrying an embroidery hoop and small basket. She marched down the steps and crossed the manicured lawn to sit, stiff-backed, on a bench under a linden tree. Cabot sat back and watched from the depths of the carriage. There must be a way to separate the brat from her grandmother.

To his utter astonishment and wonderful good fortune, he watched the woman rummage for a moment in the basket, pull out several skeins of thread, then say something to the child and return to the house. The dog, which had been sniffing the shrubbery beside the veranda, suddenly unearthed a ground squirrel and disappeared in a yelping blur behind the house.

Without wasting another moment he banged on the carriage.

"Pull to the front of the house immediately."

The carriage jerked as the horses trotted around the slight curve of the road to stop at the bottom of the drive. Cabot slicked back his hair with the palms of his hands and struggled back into his damp coat. A pat on the pocket ensured that the parcels were still there.

He walked up the drive with all haste, then wheezed as he knelt beside the child, who was busy mixing dirt in a cooking pan.

"Hello, there." He tried out his most congenial tone.

"Hello," she returned, continuing to stir her dirt. "Do you want some stew? Me and Gwandma are going to have stew for supper."

He ignored this apparent non sequitur. There was no time for idle chitchat with the little twit.

"You must be Katie."

"Uh-huh."

"How delightful! My name is Harold. Your mother was my cousin and we were very close. Do you know I have a little girl just your age?" he lied. "Would you like to go with me and play with her?" He started to rise, but the brat continued to stir her dirt.

"No, thank you. I have to fix the stew for Gwandma. Can you bring your little girl here?"

"No. No, that won't be possible. But look what I have for you."

He reached into his pocket and rummaged for the bag. Surely the candy would lure her away. A long licorice whip dangled enticingly from his fingers. Her eyes brightened at the sight, but she didn't take the candy.

"Mama says I mustn't eat sweets before supper."

Just as he was about to foist the candy into her hand that blasted dog streaked from behind the house, leapt wildly beside the child for a moment, then snatched the licorice from Cabot's hand. Huge, sharp, glistening teeth chomped three times and the candy was gone.

"Puffy!" The child rose and stood with her hands on her chubby waist. "Naughty doggie. No no no!"

The dog's tail wagged so hard its entire body wiggled. Cabot glanced around to the house, then pulled the other parcel from his pocket. The moment the package left his coat the dog's ears perked. Cabot found himself with the front paws of the dog in the middle of his chest, its nose frantically poking at the oiled paper. The child stomped her foot and bossily ordered, "Puffy, get down!" The dog ignored the command, slobbering all over Cabot's good suit as it hopped toward the package on its hind legs. The monstrous black cat appeared out of nowhere, arched its back, raised its hackles, and hissed menacingly.

"What the devil you doin' to them animals, Miz Katie?"

Cabot jerked his gaze to the side veranda where a mountain of a woman came waddling out of a pair of French doors, wiping her hands on her apron. At the same moment, the front door opened and Pierce's mother stepped outside.

Time to get the hell out of there. He ripped the paper off the large beefsteak and hurled the piece of meat with all his might in the opposite direction. The dog immediately left him to chase the meat. Cabot snatched the brat around the waist and ran down the drive.

"Here, now! What are you doing?"

"Oh, Lordy, Miz Lucille! He takin' our baby!"

"Stop! Help! Nathan, help!"

Cabot was halfway down the drive when he heard a yowl that was almost human, then a heavy thud hit the center of his back, immediately followed by countless claws piercing his skin. Before he could react, the tearing claws climbed his coat. Darting black paws came from behind his head to rip at his cheeks and eyes. With one hand he held the screaming brat. With the other he fought to knock the hissing cat from his shoulders.

"Stop! Help!"

The crunch of running feet on the drive behind him spurred him toward the carriage. The door stood open. Rube waited with reins in hands. Only a few more feet. With one mighty effort he grabbed a handful of fur and tore the cat from him. Claws sliced deep into his cheeks before he flung the cat to the ground. Just a few more steps.

A hand snatched at his coat, catching a fistful of coattails. He stumbled and fell back a step. The dog, who should have been dead from the poisoned meat, charged at him from the side. The damned dog must not have eaten the meat.

He grabbed the carriage frame and dragged himself in. The hands still held his coat and he kicked viciously behind him, satisfied when his foot connected and he heard a muffled "Ooph," then a body hit the ground. He swung the door shut just as the snarling dog leapt at him. The horses bolted sideways, and as the carriage careened recklessly out of control the rear wheel jolted over something in the road. As they sped away he turned and looked to see if they were being followed. He smiled at the sight that met him.

The huge servant woman waddled down the drive, waving her apron and screaming for help. The cat lay motionless at the foot of the drive. The dog stood in the path the carriage had taken, whining and licking the face of the now unconscious body he'd kicked . . . the body of Pierce's mother. And not another soul was in sight.

Chapter 18

THE DISTANT, NONSTOP sound of someone banging on the front door woke Marin out of a deep sleep. Hunter was already scrambling for his trousers in the dark when she realized what the noise was. She quickly lit the lamp, then rammed her arms into the sleeves of a dressing gown as she ran behind Hunter down the stairs. When they reached the front door Hunter threw it open.

Nathan stood on the other side, a fine film of dust coating his sweat-covered face. His chest heaved as he tried to catch his breath.

"Miss Katie," he managed to rasp out, "she done been kidnapped!"

Nauseating alarm weakened Marin's knees. Hunter grabbed Nathan by the shoulders and shook him.

"What do you mean, Katie's been kidnapped? When? Who? Dear God! William!" He swung around just as Maggie and William shuffled into the entrance hall. "Saddle two horses! We leave in five minutes." He turned back to Nathan. "Go to the kitchen. Maggie will get you what you need to refresh yourself. You can tell me what happened on the way."

Marin was already running back to their room when Hunter passed her. Two handguns and a rifle lay on the bed by the time she got to the door. Hunter grabbed his discarded shirt and shoved his arms in as Marin snatched a pair of his trousers and yanked them on.

"What are you doing?" he asked as he pulled on his boots.

"I can ride easier in slacks," she said, rolling up the legs.

"Marin, it's too dangerous for you to ride at that speed. You can't keep up."

She snatched up her boot and stopped only long enough to glare at him.

"Have you ever seen me ride?"

"No, but—"

"Then shut up! I can keep up and I'm going!"

He didn't take time to argue. It would have been a waste of breath, anyway. She put on her other boot, buttoned three buttons of the shirt she'd pilfered from him and tied the lower half in a knot at her waist.

"I'm going to saddle my horse. I'll see you at the barn."

She took the stairs two at a time, then ran to the barn just as William finished saddling three horses.

"Ol' William ain't nobody's fool," he said at her surprise. "I knowed you weren't no way gonna stay behind."

"William, you're a sweetheart!" She kissed his leathery old cheek, then they led the horses to the front of the house. Nathan and Hunter burst through the front door just as Marin swung into her saddle. Without a word the two men jumped astride the horses and the three of them thundered down the drive toward Memphis.

"Mistah Hunter, they's something else you need to know," Nathan shouted above the pounding hooves. "Yo mama hurt real bad. She try to stop the man and a carriage wheel runned over her."

"Dear Lord," Hunter moaned. "How bad is she?"

Marin saw the look Nathan cast Hunter. The news couldn't be good.

"The doctor just come when I left. But she ain't good, Mistah Hunter. She ain't good at all."

"Who did this, Nathan? Who took Katie?"

The trio slowed as they entered a heavily wooded area where the moonlight failed to penetrate the foliage.

"Mamie be the only one what saw him besides Miz Lucille. She say he look like the man what Izzy sent out to see you that day you got the message about the tornado. She say he real greasy lookin' with a big ol' mole growin' out'n his eyebrow."

"Cabot!" The nausea increased and her skin crawled as Marin recalled the scumbag of a man and the way he'd looked at Katie that day. Hunter spurred his horse faster at the mention of the man's name, heedless of the pitch black road they traveled.

"Mistah Hunter," Nathan called again. "They's more," he said as he and Marin caught up with Hunter. "They was a letter on the ground where the carriage was parked. It said if you want yo baby back, you gots to pay fifty thousand dollars."

Hunter lowered his head and shook it.

"Dear God. The blackguard thinks I have fifty thousand dollars," he said, just loud enough to be heard. He leaned low over his horse's neck and charged ahead. Marin and Nathan followed suit.

The ride seemed interminable after Nathan gave the few sketchy details he knew. When at last the lights in the windows of Pierce Hall appeared, the horses were lathered and Marin ached in every muscle of her body.

Hunter leapt from his horse before they completely stopped. Ambrose threw open the door as Hunter charged up the porch steps with Marin right behind him.

"Ambrose! Any word?"

"Oh, no, suh, Mistah Hunter. We's got the sheriff lookin', but we ain't heard nothin'. That poor chile. That poor, poor chile."

"Did you see anything?"

"No, suh. I were down in the cellar when it happen."

"Where's Mamie?"

"She up with Miz Lucille and the doctor."

Hunter ran past Ambrose. Marin followed him up the stairs to Lucille's room. Dr. Ritter stepped out and closed the door just as they arrived.

"How is she?" Hunter asked as he glanced worriedly at the closed door.

"She is in bad shape, son. Apparently the scoundrel kicked her in the chest, then the carriage swerved when she was down and glanced over her lower abdomen. She has several broken ribs. She was bleeding internally, Hunter. I had to go in and find the source to repair it."

"Will she be all right?" Marin asked, shuddering at the thought of nineteenth-century surgery.

Dr. Ritter shook his head. "I have done all I can. If she survives her injuries, we still have an abdominal infection to worry about." He looked Hunter in the eye. "Better make your peace with her before you go after that scoundrel."

Hunter clenched his hands into fists. "It's that bad, then?"

"Yes, son. It is."

Hunter opened the door to his mother's bedroom, hesitated a moment, then stepped inside.

Mamie patted Hunter on the shoulder as she passed him on her way out, then pulled the door shut behind her as she wiped her tears with her apron.

No one spoke in the hallway. The only sounds were those of Mamie's quiet crying and Marin's pacing.

She wanted to be in there with him, to give him support and ease his pain. A few more endless minutes passed, then she made up her mind. Quietly, she opened the door and slipped inside.

Hunter knelt on one knee beside his mother's bed, her frail, bruised hand in his strong one. He held the back of her hand to his cheek as he stared, unblinking, at her ashen face. After a moment he bowed his head. A solitary, choking sob escaped him.

Finally he gently placed her hand at her side and pulled the coverlet to her chin. He stood, raked the heels of his hands across his eyes, then leaned over and kissed his mother's pale forehead.

"I . . . I love you, Mother," he whispered, stroking her hair with his fingertips. He turned to Marin and took a deep breath. "If she lives, we'll have that proper wedding she so greatly wanted." Marin nodded, blinking back tears. His expression hardened as he turned to leave. "Now it's time to find our daughter."

Dr. Ritter and Mamie resumed their positions in the sickroom while Marin followed Hunter to their bedroom. He went directly to his armoire and pulled out a bedroll and a couple changes of clothing. Next he opened the chest at the foot of the bed, rummaged deep, then pulled out a knife in a leather sheath. Alarm shot through Marin as he slid the wicked looking blade from its cover and examined it, testing its sharpness with the pad of his thumb.

"Hunter, what are you planning on doing?"

He slid the harness of the knife over his shoulder.

"I plan to do whatever it takes to bring Katie home safely." The carved bone handle of the knife rested behind his right shoulder, in perfect position to be drawn at a moment's notice. He whipped it from its sheath in practice, tested its weight, then flicked his wrist and caught the knife by the tip of the shiny blade.

"I never thought to use this again," he said, more to himself than to Marin. Then he looked up at her. "This saved my life more than once during the war."

Marin grabbed his arm and pleaded, "Hunter, don't do something that will land you in jail! You won't do Katie, or me, any favors by ending up behind bars!"

He looked at her as if he didn't understand her words.

"I plan to do whatever it takes to bring our daughter home and keep my family safe. It is the criminal that goes to jail, Marin. Not the victim."

She was so accustomed to a lawsuit-happy, criminals' rights society, she'd forgotten that there was a time when things were not so skewed.

"I'm going with you."

"No! You are not going. I have no idea where I will have to go to find them, and if I am worrying about you I cannot concentrate on Katie."

She knew he was right. She could keep up with the best

of them on a horse, but tracking criminals was something different.

"Alright. I'll do what I can to help Lucille. But *please* be careful. Don't do anything crazy."

He smiled at her with a questioning look and tipped her chin with his index finger.

"What have I ever done to make you think I would?"

She looked at those meltingly blue eyes, those irresistible dimples, and saw the ghost of Hunter Pierce smiling at her from the upper veranda. Tears burned her eyes and nausea rocked her stomach, but she fought it off and slid into his embrace. A fist closed around her heart when his arms wrapped securely around her, protectively, lovingly, for the first time in weeks. She looked up at him. He lowered his head to brush her lips with his, once, twice, then settle for a tender kiss meant to sustain her through the coming ordeal.

Would this be the last hug, the last kiss he ever gave her?

Would this be when he becomes a ghost? Her pain at the thought was more than she could deal with.

Finally, he set her away from him, picked up his bedroll, and stopped at the door. He took one long, last look at her, then turned and left.

It had been many years since Hunter had seen the inside of a saloon.

He hadn't missed them.

For two days the smell of stale liquor, smoke, and un-washed bodies conjured visions of youthful misadventures as well as wartime nightmares. He never wanted to breathe these odors again.

"Well?" he asked the greasy, balding bartender.

"Never seen the man. Don't mean he ain't been in here, though."

Hunter flicked a coin into the air. The dirt-encrusted fingers of the bartender caught the coin before it started to fall.

Hunter had heard the same story in every barroom he'd been in. Cabot wasn't hard to describe. Either the man steered clear of these establishments or Hunter just hadn't found the right person for information. Hopefully Nathan would have better luck scouring the streets and talking to the Negroes who saw and heard everything that happened in this section of town. More than one deviant mind had erred by forgetting the fact that their servants were not deaf, dumb, and blind.

He strode through the doors of the saloon, swung up onto his horse, then headed north to meet Nathan at their designated spot. A particularly seedy section along the way boasted several more saloons, most with accommodations upstairs for the ladies who plied their trade in the bar and on the streets. Hunter reined in at the first one he came to and decided to make a quick check of the area.

He was about to leave the third bartender behind when a hand darted out and clutched at his arm. He instinctively went for his gun as he shrugged the hand away.

The drunkard behind him staggered backward, patting the air with his palms and shaking his head.

"No harm, mishter! Didn' mean no harm!"

Hunter relaxed his grip on the pistol a bit.

"What do you want?"

The filthy, odorous man weaving on his feet before Hunter slid a glance in both directions, then whispered loud enough for the entire room to hear.

"You lookin' for Cabot?"

Hunter studied the repulsive figure. The man sported a black eye that was on the mend and several old cuts on his face. One front tooth was missing its lower half. Perhaps the sot might know something worthwhile.

"Do you know where I can find him?"

The drunkard hesitated for a moment, eyed Hunter's clothing, then licked his lips.

"A man gets awful thirsty when he talks," he said, one eye squinted smaller than the other as he leered hopefully at Hunter.

Hunter kicked the seat of the nearest chair with his boot, sending it sliding backward. He motioned for the man to sit down as he dropped into the chair farthest away from his informant. The bartender appeared with a bottle of whiskey and two glasses.

"You payin'?" he asked Hunter before setting the liquor in front of them. Hunter tossed yet another coin in his direction. The bartender slammed the bottle and glasses on the table and left them to their conversation. The drunk sloshed a glass full of whiskey then knocked it back in one swallow. He performed the same movement two more times before he stopped and blearily stared at Hunter from across the table.

"Where can I find Cabot?"

The drunk leaned back in his chair with a thud.

"Well, now, I dunno."

Rage and frustration overtook Hunter. He shot his hand across the table and yanked the blackguard up by a fistful of shirtfront. Terror filled the bleary eyes of the drunk as Hunter brought his face to within inches of the other, the sickening fumes from his breath turning Hunter's already knotted stomach.

"Do not let my clothes fool you," Hunter warned in a low voice. "I would as soon slit your throat as look at you. Now," he shoved the man back into his chair, "tell me I misunderstood your answer."

"Yeah! Yeah! You mis . . . misunderstood. I know where he li . . . lives. But he ain't allus there." He peered up at Hunter through half-closed eyes, recognition dawning on his face. "Hey! Your name's Pierce. I seen you around. You used to—"

Hunter just stared at him. "Where does he live?"

"You're the one he wanted to take the kid away from." The drunk suddenly puffed up with righteous indignation. "Tried to retain me as his attorney! But I tur' him down. Got this for my troubles." He waved vaguely at his face, no doubt looking for a pat on the back for his noble deed. If Hunter patted him on the back it would be to knock him to the ground.

Hunter stood, then yanked the drunk up by the coat collar and shoved him forward.

"You are going to show me where Cabot lives, or I am going to add to your injuries. Anyone standing in my way of finding this man will wish himself six feet under."

As the drunk stumbled out of the saloon, Hunter wiped the hand that had touched the drunk on his trouser leg. It still felt dirty.

The drunk quickly staggered several blocks, darting anxious glances over his shoulder the whole way. He stopped at the entrance of an alley and pointed into the depths.

"Behind this building. S'room opens onto the alley."

"Fine," Hunter said as he shoved the drunk into the dark between the buildings. "Show me."

Hunter paid no heed to what he walked through or the

noisome odors rising from all around him. His eyes stayed fixed on the darker shape of the man in front of him. The muted, dull yellow glow of a lamp filtered through a small, filthy window. The drunk stopped in the middle of the alley and pointed to a door.

"S'there. Tha's Cabot's room."

Hunter slowly took the man's filthy tie in his hand and pulled until it was taut. The drunk raised up on tiptoe.

"If you are lying to me," Hunter said quietly, "I will kill you. Slowly."

"Ain't lying," the drunk rasped, then coughed and grabbed his throat when Hunter let go. The man scuttled into the darkness when Hunter turned his attention away.

He watched the window for a moment. A distorted shadow moved occasionally in front of the thin, ragged curtain. The person appeared to be moving normally, as if unaware of the threat on the other side of the glass. He heard no sounds except those made by the rats in the nearby garbage.

He stepped to the door. One mighty kick sent the wood splintering against the wall. When he rushed inside with his gun drawn, all he found was a whore servicing her customer. Hunter knew at first glance the pockmarked youth was not Cabot. The boy leapt from atop the woman, grabbed his scattered clothing, and ran from the room stark-naked. Hunter looked back at the trollop.

"Who are you?" he asked without preamble.

"Well, now, darlin', who do you want me to be?"

In two steps Hunter was beside her, a fistful of hair in his hand. He stopped himself from yanking it.

"I will ask only once more. Who are you?"

The bravado left her when she looked into his eyes.

"Shirley Cabot."

At last, he was closing in.

"Where is Harold Cabot? Where's the child?"

Fear, real fear, flickered in her eyes at his words. She refused to meet his gaze as she said, "I don't know where he is. He ain't been home today." She flicked a glance at him, then looked away. "And we ain't got no child. I'd get rid of it before I'd drop one of his whelps."

Hunter released her hair. She immediately pulled it back out of his reach.

"You know exactly what child I am talking about, do you not?" Her eyes answered his question. "He has my daughter. He's kidnapped her for ransom, and I mean to get her back. Now," he sat on the edge of a rickety chair and tried to stay calm, "I want to know where he has her."

The woman searched Hunter's face, wrestling with something inside herself. As she looked at him her eyes became clear and lucid.

"He's got her in a cabin somewheres north of the city. If I knowed exactly where, I'd tell you. All's I know is it's close to the river, and there's a ferry nearby."

He believed her. He stood, pulled a twenty-dollar gold piece from his pocket, and tossed it on the grimy table.

"I am grateful," he said, then turned to leave.

"Mister," she called from the bed. He turned and looked at her. "He's got other plans for your little girl." Hunter stepped back into the room, a sense of dread coiling in his stomach. "He made me give him the name of a customer that likes little girls. You know . . ."

He spun and charged through the broken doorway. Terror, sheer terror as he had never known it, filled every recess of his body. His mind screamed for the innocence of his daughter. His feet slid in nameless pools of filth as he raced down the alley. His pace never slowed until he reached his horse, and then only long enough to untie the reins and jump astride. He thundered down the street, riding like a cyclone until he met up with Nathan on his way to their meeting place.

Nathan, recognizing Hunter, wheeled around and spurred his horse to match Hunter's speed.

"The bastard's going to sell her," Hunter yelled over the pounding hooves, "like a whore in a brothel!" His stomach lurched with the words.

"Oh, sweet Jesus," Nathan cried.

Hunter leaned low over Mystic's neck. Nathan did the same as they rode north out of town.

He knew where the ferry was that Shirley Cabot mentioned. He guided them toward the river, planning to search every inch of territory around the ferry until he found the shack where Cabot held Katie.

The pair combed the woods for several hours. When Nathan's horse stumbled and nearly threw him, Nathan said, "Mistah Hunter, it be easier in the daylight. We mayhap miss somethin' in the dark."

Hunter knew Nathan's words were true, but a gut reaction told him to keep searching. He wouldn't be able to lay his head down and rest until he had Katie safely in his arms.

Another hour passed and all they'd found were farmhouses with reputable families and a shack or two that had fallen into heaps of rubble. Despair grew with every inch they covered. Would he be too late? If they touched his precious daughter he would kill them with slow, deliberate torture.

The moon was low in the sky when Hunter motioned for Nathan to stop.

"Listen."

The muffled sound of a lone horse moving slowly up ahead drifted through dense foliage. Nathan nodded that he heard. Hunter silently motioned to follow at a distance. Anyone out at this hour, in these woods, was up to no good. He allowed the horseman to put more distance between them, then Hunter fell in behind, staying far enough away to keep from being heard. They traveled for perhaps half a mile before the horseman slowed even more. Hunter guessed the man was near his destination, one which he was unfamiliar enough with to have to pick his way through the woods.

Hunter dismounted, leaving Mystic with Nathan. He then followed on foot, gaining ground on their prey. The man found an overgrown trail and took it. Before long he swung from his horse and tied it to a low-hanging branch. The horse whinnied softly as the man walked deeper into the tangled foliage.

Hunter would have never found the shack at night. Even in the light of day, the tiny, bramble-covered hut would have been difficult to find, or even see, unless a person was standing right in front of it.

The man walked up to the shack and knocked twice. A yellow light flared, then receded to a dim gray within the only window Hunter could see. The door opened and the man slipped inside.

Before the door closed completely Hunter charged the house. He threw his weight against the door, enjoying the feel of it falling back to hit something large and soft. Before the inhabitants could move, Hunter had both pistols drawn and aimed at the heads of Harold Cabot and Hezekiah Pickering.

The latter was well known to Hunter. Pickering owned one of the banks in Memphis and was a very prominent citizen.

Hunter quickly scanned the room. A tiny mound under a ragged quilt lay on the floor by an ash-filled fireplace. A lump rose in his throat, then relief swept over him when he saw the rise and fall of Katie's breathing under the quilt.

Nathan stepped through the door after warning Hunter of his entrance. Hunter handed the guns to him.

"Keep them covered. If one moves, kill him."

"Yessuh!" Nathan said with enthusiasm.

Hunter walked over the dirt floor and knelt beside his daughter. He lifted the filthy cover from her, then gently scooped her sleeping body into his arms.

"She alright?" Nathan asked as he kept an eye and a gun on the two men.

"She seems to be." He looked up at Cabot, intense hate twisting his gut.

Neither Cabot nor Pickering had uttered a word nor moved a muscle other than to raise their hands. Hunter walked over and stood in front of Pickering. He looked the quaking man up and down. Revulsion at the thought of those lily-white hands touching the precious sleeping bundle in his arms roiled in his stomach.

"The only form of life lower than you, Pickering, are the Cabots who procure your victims." Pickering tried to speak, but the words came out as a whimper. Hunter shot his hand out and grabbed the man's throat. "If you say a word I will snap your windpipe. Now," he went on conversationally, "for the rest of your life I will have someone watching you. If you so much as pat a child on the head, I will personally see to it that your . . . tastes . . . are made known to every-one. That will be, of course, after I have seen to it that you have been rendered a eunuch. Or perhaps *less* than a eunuch."

The man's eyes widened with terror. He blubbered incoherently, his legs squeezed together protectively at Hunter's words.

"And by five o'clock today I want . . . oh . . ." Hunter searched for a number, ". . . fifty thousand dollars to be donated to the home for orphaned children. Now, I suggest you remove yourself and your perversion from my sight before I change my mind and perform the surgery now."

Pickering scrambled sideways to the door, anxiously glancing first at Hunter, then at Nathan, who had lowered his aim to correspond with Hunter's threat. As he ran from the shack he pulled the door shut behind him, slamming it with a bang.

Katie jerked awake. She immediately began to cry for her mama and papa and fight her way out of Hunter's arms. Hunter held her gently and tried to calm her.

"Shhh. Shhhh, baby. Papa's here, baby. It's alright. Papa's here."

He nuzzled the silky hair over her ear as he whispered the soothing words. But he stared at Cabot, conveying with his eyes that the bastard would not get off as easily as Pickering.

He dragged his gaze from Cabot, then held Katie so she could see who he was. She continued to cry, her eyes squeezed shut, until he jostled her and called her name.

"Katie. Katiedid. Shhhh. Open your eyes. Papa's here."

When his voice reached through Katie's fear she suddenly stopped struggling and opened her eyes. The next moment she had a death grip around his neck.

"Papa papa papa papa papa!"

Hunter returned his glare to Cabot's pasty white face while

he continued to comfort Katie. His heart warmed at the feel of those tiny arms back around his neck, but deep inside his warming heart lay a chunk of ice that refused to melt.

He patted Katie on the back and kissed her silky curls. Finally he pulled her away and looked at her face. Her tear-streaked, chubby cheeks held the dimples of her smile.

"Did this man hurt you, Katie?" he asked quietly.

She twisted in his arms to look at Cabot. The moment she saw him she buried her face in Hunter's shoulder and held him tight.

"He's a mean man." The words came muffled from his shoulder. "Make him go 'way."

"I will. I will." He cupped the back of her head in the palm of his hand and let the rage at her reaction to Cabot build. "But tell Papa. Did he hurt you?" Katie made no comment, squirming deeper into his arms. "He cannot hurt you if you tell me. He will never hurt you again."

Another few seconds passed, then her muffled voice rose. "He hit me right here." Her tiny finger poked her cheek.

He lifted his gaze to Cabot and asked, "Did he hurt you . . . or touch you . . . anywhere else?" Cabot frantically shook his head back and forth in denial. Sweat streamed from the man's face. Huge wet rings grew on his grimy jacket.

"No." She raised her head, her finger still on her cheek, and glared at the man, now that she was safe in her father's arms. "But he hit me two times right here."

He studied her skin beneath her finger. The rosy glow held a tint of violet smudge.

The bastard!

"Here," he moved her finger, "let Papa kiss the boo-boo." His guts wrenched as he brushed several kisses across her velvety skin. "There now. All better." Hunter shot a glance at Cabot, then turned back to Katie. "Would you go help Nathan find the horses while I talk to this man? Then we shall go see Mama. She's missed you."

Katie leaned toward Nathan, her arms sliding trustingly around his leathery neck. Thankfully, she didn't seem to avoid the old servant. Perhaps they'd found her before any terrible damage was done.

Nathan transferred the guns to Hunter, then turned to leave.

"Nathan, where is the rifle?" Nathan stepped outside the door and picked up the firearm from where it had been propped against the shack. "How far away are the horses?"

Nathan slid his gaze to Cabot and let it linger before asking, "A quarter mile be far 'nough?"

"Better make it a little farther."

Nathan nodded. He and Katie disappeared through the door. Hunter held both guns on Cabot, then backed to the window and cast an occasional glance at the retreating pair. As the distance grew between them, he turned to the lowlife who had dared kidnap his child.

Up until then Cabot had failed to say a word. His silence broke when Hunter aimed both guns at his head.

"I didn't hurt her, Pierce! You saw for yourself! Just a tap on the cheek to get her attention! I wasn't going to sell her. Just use her to con some money from—"

His speech broke off when Hunter placed the barrel of the pistol in the center of Cabot's forehead.

"Your wife and I had quite a conversation before she told me where to look for you." A flash of rage flared in Cabot's eyes. "Let's see. How many times have you done this before? Sold children like my daughter to perverted scum." Fear replaced the rage, and Cabot nearly fell to his knees in denial.

"That whore hates me! She'd tell you anything to make things worse for me. I never—"

Hunter calmly cocked the gun against Cabot's forehead. The man began to quiver like pudding in an earthquake.

"How many times? You see, I left in such a hurry—"

"She's lying! The youngest I ever sold was ten! And, hell, most of them were niggers! Just a couple of white girls, and they were trash! I wasn't going to sell your daughter!"

Hunter uncocked the gun and walked away from Cabot. Bile rose in his throat at the thought of what those children had suffered and what Katie might have gone through. He laid the pistols on the table that now separated him from Cabot. The man looked at him, a flicker of hope in his eyes. Hunter enjoyed killing that hope with his next words.

"You're a dead man."

New beads of sweat erupted on Cabot's temples and upper lip. He dragged his sleeve across his face as the moisture trickled into his eyes from his receding hairline. A little red circle still marked the skin of his forehead from the barrel of Hunter's pistol.

"Is that a threat?" he sneered, puffing himself up with false bravado. Hunter snorted and shook his head.

"No. That's a death sentence." He paused to let his words sink in. "Pick up the gun."

Cabot began to tremble again. A dark spot spread across the front of his trousers.

"You can't do this, Pierce! I didn't hurt her! You saw for yourself!"

"Pick up the gun."

Cabot licked his lips and looked at the two pistols on the tabletop. The bastard was so transparent. Hunter knew exactly what he was planning.

The only sound in the room was that of Cabot's erratic breathing. He flicked a glance at Hunter, then lunged for both guns. Hunter shot his left hand out and slammed it on the nearest gun as Cabot tried to grab it. The blackguard backed off, his moment of bravado gone, but his hand remained on the other gun. Though Cabot didn't release the weapon, he refused to lift it off the table. Hunter's hand stayed on his gun as well.

"This is the 1870's, Pierce. You can't just kill me!"

Hunter ignored the other man's words.

"Did you know that you kicked my mother in the chest, then ran over her with your carriage? She might be dead as we speak, thanks to you. And then you took my four-year-old daughter to sell to a deviant. Oh, by the way," he quirked an apologetic eyebrow and allowed just a hint of a smile, "your wife never mentioned the others to me."

Cabot's breath wheezed in his throat. His limbs shook so violently the gun rattled against the wood of the table. The bastard who stole little girls looked ready to cry.

"You'll never get away with this, Pierce!"

Hunter's smile faded from his lips.

"Famous last words, Cabot." He stared hard at his adversary, then cocked his head as if a thought had just occurred to him. "You know, that is usually just a figure of speech," his smile returned, "but in your case, it's true."

The rattle of metal against wood stopped as Cabot lifted the gun. A hint of a smirk grew in his sweating face. The barrel shook as it rose to point at Hunter. Hunter's left hand never moved as he held his gun on the table. But his right hand shot to the back of his neck. In one movement he slid the knife from its sheath and hurled it through the air.

A dull thud was followed by a muffled "Ooph." Cabot's

victorious smirk changed to a wide-eyed look of surprise. His gaze dropped to the bone handle protruding from the left side of his chest, then rose to stare at Hunter with the look of a man who had just seen his own ghost. Even as his eyes glassed over, his body hovered upright for a moment. Then he toppled backward, a cloud of dust rising as his body fell to the floor.

Hunter stared at the dead man, then moved around the table, stepping over the filthy, thin quilt that had covered Katie. He reached down and yanked the knife from Cabot's chest, wiped it across the already bloody shirtfront, then slid it back into its sheath. He pulled the gun from Cabot's hand, picked up the other one from the table, and, without a backward glance, walked through the door of the shack.

Chapter 19

THE FAMILIAR CACOPHONY of barking dog and yowling cat brought Marin out of a fitful sleep. Those stupid animals hadn't made a noise in days, and now they wait until she'd finally fallen asleep to—

She sat straight up, then flew from the bed, leaving the bed linens to flutter to the floor. As she ran down the hall in the early morning light, she heard the skittering of Puffy's toenails on the parquet floor as he slid into the front door.

And then she heard that munchkin voice so dear to her heart greet the animals with joy.

Oh, thank God!

She raced to the landing and there they were, trying to fight their way up the stairs through leaping dog and meowing cat and Ambrose and Mamie, Izzy and Emmaletta. They seemed to sense her presence. Everyone stopped and looked up.

"Mama!" Katie squealed when she saw Marin. Hunter put her down on the steps and she ran, meeting Marin halfway as they rushed to each other.

She swung Katie up and around, the chubby little arms encircling Marin's neck. Relief calmed all her knotted muscles at the sight of both of her loved ones safe and sound and all in one piece.

She slid into Hunter's embrace. He wore two days' growth of beard and smelled of horses and smoke and woods. It was wonderful!

"How is Mother?" he asked, his grin turning to a look that expected the worst.

"She seems to be recovering from her injuries. We still have to worry about infection from the surgery, though. That can be as deadly as the bleeding." She looked toward Lucille's room. "She's probably awake, if you want to go see her."

Hunter laid his guns on the table and slipped off the holster for his knife.

"Come with me," he invited, then hesitated after a couple of steps. He glanced at Katie before asking, "Should we take K-A-T-I-E?" Marin smiled at this age-old form of parental communication.

"Lucille looks fine, and I think it would do her a world of good." As they made their way to Lucille's room, Marin could wait no longer to ask. "What happened out there? Was it Cabot?"

Hunter slowed his pace.

"Yes. He's dead." He turned and studied her face, waiting for her reaction, and she knew Hunter had killed him.

"Good."

The door to Lucille's bedroom stood half-open, so they dropped the topic for the time being. Hunter peered into the darkened room, then looked back at Marin, clearly uncomfortable.

"Is Gwandma awake?" Katie's high-pitched voice pierced the silence. She scrambled from Marin's arms and ran into the room the minute her feet hit the floor. Marin and Hunter followed her in. Marin caught up with Katie just as she was about to hurl herself up onto the bed.

"No, no, Katie. Grandmother is sick. We have to be very gentle with her."

"Stop coddling me. Kathleen, climb up here immediately." The thin, reedy voice rising from within the dark bed hangings held all the vinegar that made it Lucille's.

Hunter gently placed Katie on the bed while Marin parted the draperies to the early morning sun. When she turned back around, it was to find Katie and Lucille in a tight embrace. Katie's dirt-stained bottom swayed in the air; her grimy cheek rested against Lucille's pale one. A warm feeling tugged at Marin's heart at the sight of Lucille's tightly closed eyes, the silvery trail of a tear sliding from the corner.

"Well, now," Lucille muttered with a weak voice when the hugging was over, "as you can see, I survived. Now, when is the wedding?"

Marin tried to stand absolutely still as Madame Lefarge pinned and tucked the ivory silk wedding gown for its final fitting.

"Oh, *ma chérie,* if you would only allow the strings of the corset to be tightened, your waist would be tiny as the wasp's."

"She ain't gonna let nobody tighten them corset strings. I done told her it ain't fittin' to be wearing that corset so loose." Mamie put in her two cents' worth.

"But it is unheard of. You have a figure the ladies would . . ."

"She ain't gonna do it. You can talk till you's hoarse, but she ain't gonna tighten them strings. We been round and round . . ."

Marin allowed Mamie and the dressmaker to hash over her waistline. She wasn't in the mood to talk today.

Something was wrong. Very wrong. And it had her scared to death. In the last few weeks, since Katie's kidnapping, she'd had some very disturbing experiences, and they were becoming more frequent.

The first thing she'd noticed was the bruise on the back of her hand. It looked like the one she'd found after Ryan had come to her in the hospital the first time. Then, every now and then she would hear a beep . . . just like the beep of the heart monitor. But this was during the day! And Ryan hadn't come to her in weeks! She'd even willed him to come. Prayed for him to come. But her nights were haunted with nightmares, not ghosts of dead husbands. Nearly every night she woke in a sweat after dreaming that Hunter had died some horrible death. Each time the dream was different. And each time Marin could only stand and watch while her screams came out as hisses and her muscles refused to move.

And then there was what happened this morning.

As she'd strolled the gardens with Katie, collecting a bouquet of roses for Lucille, she suddenly became very lightheaded. Then a voice, as clear and real as Katie's, had said, "Dr. Gayford, line three. Dr. Gayford, line three." It was a voice from a hospital PA system.

If only she had someone to talk to. Hunter was out of the question. When he'd woken her from one of her nightmares, she'd told him how he'd died in it. He had just held her tight for a while, then when she'd calmed down he rolled over with his back to her. It seemed nothing she did could break through that wall he'd built around himself. It would only alienate him more to tell him about hearing sounds from 1996.

Something was wrong. Something was going to happen. Could she control it when it did?

"Marin, the musicians are here for us to go over the . . ." Hunter's speech faltered when he stopped in the middle of the door and raked her from head to toe with his gaze.

"Hunter! Get out!" she screeched and jumped from the footstool she'd been standing on. "It's bad luck! Get out!" She shoved her bewildered husband through the door, screaming, "Get out! Get out!"

Dear Lord, she was going crazy! She was pushing her husband out of the room over some stupid old wives' tale. But all she could think of was that she was tempting fate. Her nerves stretched to the snapping point. Finally she just sank into a puddle of ivory silk in the middle of the floor and let the dam burst.

"Marin!"

"Ma chérie!"

"Miz Marin!"

She covered her face with her hands and ignored the frantic voices. All the pressures were getting to her. Every time she looked at Hunter she wondered if it would be the last time. Every time she put her head on her pillow, she wondered if Ryan would come. Now she felt as though she were being pulled back to 1996. She didn't know where she belonged. She couldn't stay here and lose another loved one. Yet she couldn't bear the thought of leaving her husband.

Hunter lifted her to her feet while Mamie and Madame Lefarge fussed over her. She brushed all their hands away, then ran a knuckle under her eyes to wipe away the tears.

"I'm alright," she said, forcing herself to sound upbeat. "I don't know why I got so upset." Three pairs of eyes slid to her abdomen. "Oh, for Pete's sake! No! I'm not pregnant!"

Bright spots of pink glowed in Madame Lefarge's cheeks. Marin cringed at her nineteenth-century faux pas. No doubt if she said the word pregnant again in mixed company the poor dressmaker would have a fit of the vapors.

"I guess with the wedding tomorrow, and everything that's happened lately, I'm just a little edgy." She looked up at Hunter with a shaky grin. But worry still darkened his eyes. She tried changing the subject. "Madame Lefarge is almost done with the fitting. Will you talk to the musicians until I get there?"

"Are you certain you feel up to it?" he asked, while studying her face. He'd given her that same look more than once in the last few weeks. At first she'd thought she'd covered her concern over the nightmares and the brief flashes from her time, but Hunter was too sensitive to her moods to be fooled. Too bad he wasn't sensitive to when she was telling the truth.

"I'm fine. Really. Just a case of prewedding jitters."

He gave her one long, all-encompassing look before he turned slowly, clearly unconvinced, then disappeared down the hall.

"So, *chérie*, I must now alter the gown, just a little, since your handsome husband has seen you in it, *oui?*"

It was tempting to have the gown changed, sort of like knocking on wood, but Marin refused.

"No. I don't think so. After all," she smiled at the dressmaker with false confidence, "we're already married. What could go wrong?"

She shimmied from the yards of ivory silk and lace, then gave distracted answers to the dressmaker's questions while Mamie laced and buttoned her into her day gown.

When Marin arrived in the parlor, she found her husband entertaining not the musicians, but Katie and his mother. Katie immediately scampered across the room and climbed onto Marin's lap as soon as Marin settled into her favorite chair.

Lucille still looked terribly pale from her surgery, but was in remarkable shape considering her ordeal. Hopefully some of her health could be credited to Marin, who'd made sure sterile bandages had been applied every day to a thoroughly cleansed incision. She'd also forced the stubborn woman to get up and walk every day, even if it was just a step or two. That process had become easier when Marin finally wised up and enlisted Katie to ask in her most angelic voice for "Gwandma to get better." Dr. Ritter had been horrified when he'd found that his patient wasn't getting absolute bed rest; then his horror turned to astonishment at the progress she made.

Marin had a feeling Lucille would have survived no matter how serious her injuries had been, just to hold Hunter to his promise of a proper wedding. She apparently had been conscious when he'd visited her room before going after Cabot. And though she never mentioned the tender scene, she was a changed woman. Not all soft and cuddly. Nothing so different as that. Marin wasn't even sure if she would like her mother-in-law if the woman had done a complete about-face. But the bitterness and hate were gone. Lucille helped with the planning of the wedding with gruff enthusiasm, unable to hide the change in her no matter how hard she tried.

"Hunter said you were not feeling well, so I instructed the musicians as to the music. I was sure you would not mind."

"No, I don't. Thank you." She really didn't mind. That was one less thing for her to think about. Besides, this was really Lucille's wedding. A promised reward for her recovery. Let her have it the way she wanted.

Puffy and Angel rocketed into the room from the nether regions of the house. No doubt they'd been camping out in the kitchen, begging shamelessly for tidbits of food. They'd discovered early on what a soft touch Emmaletta could be.

Puffy halted in the middle of the plush carpet and hesitantly sniffed each occupant of the room, just in case any of them happened to possess something edible. When his efforts failed to produce a treat, he circled once, then fell heavily onto Hunter's booted feet and instantly fell asleep.

Angel leapt soundlessly to the arm of the love seat Lucille occupied, then strolled along the back, holding her tail absolutely perpendicular. This was another change in Lucille Marin could not believe, as she watched the enormous black cat daintily pick her way to Lucille's lap, then curl into a loose ball that left paws and tail hanging limply. A loud purr reverberated from the black lump. When Lucille's hand unconsciously stroked the shiny fur, Marin could only blink and shake her head.

Marin's gaze fell on Hunter, who had picked up a newspaper and buried his nose in it. She wasn't surprised. He'd been using every technique available to avoid close contact. Even though he was polite, complimentary, and sometimes even warm, there was an underlying distance between them that broke her heart. Would he ever believe her about Ryan?

Would he ever again treat her with the teasing warmth she'd grown to love about him? Would he die before he realized the truth? Would he die thinking she'd betrayed him?

Her mood reflected the gloomy day. She rose to light a lamp against the gray afternoon. She nearly dropped the burning match when Ambrose burst into the room.

"Mistah Hunter, the sky don't look good. It got that same green look like when the twister hit Tranquille. I thinks we's in for a bad 'un."

At that moment a shower of hail clattered against the house. Everyone, including Lucille, jumped to look out the window. Hail the size of marbles fell from the sky and ricocheted off the house and grounds.

"Ambrose, have Nathan come help us close up the shutters, then we'll secure the outbuildings." Hunter opened the window to yank the outer shutters closed as he spoke.

Marin ran for the stairway.

"I'll fetch Mamie and we'll get the upstairs. Lucille, keep Katie in here." Mamie lumbered onto the upstairs landing as Marin grabbed a handful of skirts and took the stairs two at a time. "Help me close up, Mamie!"

The sounds of shutters banging closed warred with the clatter of hail against the house. Marin had never realized there were so many windows in the home until she ran from room to room, closing first the outside shutters and then the ones inside. She ran into the last bedroom, cursing her corset and bemoaning how out of shape she'd gotten. The sight that met her turned her blood to ice water.

Slumped in the rocker, a young man in buff trousers, white shirt and riding boots sat with his head leaning crookedly against the seat back. The snowy perfection of the shirt was marred by a huge, vivid red stain over his chest.

Marin's feet rooted to the floor just inside the doorway. Her heart bounced around in her rib cage as she stared at the apparition. He lifted his head to gaze at her with pain-filled eyes. Her feet refused to carry her backward out the door, refused to move at all. A scream formed in her throat but came out as nothing more than a terrified squeak.

This felt nothing like her first encounter with Hunter. She had been intrigued, warmed, and uncharacteristically calm when she'd first seen Hunter's ghost. What she felt now was pure, icy terror. Her eyes stayed riveted to the bloody wound as she tried to force her body backward.

"I's through with them windows up here. We best be . . ."

Mamie's words drifted off when she rounded the doorway behind Marin. Thank God. Surely Mamie would be able to scream. Surely she saw the ghost, too. Any second now she would—

"Mistah Nate! You devil! You ain't got no business showin' up here, scarin' the daylights out'n Mistah Hunter's wife!" Mamie's mountainous form waddled into the room and headed straight for the apparition. "Now you just get on out of here. Go on! Shoo!" She flapped her massive arms in front of her as if she were simply shooing Puffy away from her prized vegetable garden. To Marin's astonishment, the young spirit grinned a devilish, dimpled grin, then vanished into a mist.

Dear Lord! When he'd smiled, he'd looked enough like Hunter to be his brother! His younger brother!

"Is you alright, chile? They ain't nothin' to be afeared of. Mastah Nate has a way of showin' up when ain't nobody expectin' it." Mamie bustled to the nearest window and closed the shutters as she spoke. "I guess there ain't no time a body be expectin' to see somethin' like that, though. But he harmless." Mamie finished closing the shutters, then came to stand in front of Marin. Gentle chocolate-brown eyes studied her, then Marin felt herself being guided to the rocking chair. That was enough to put life back into her limbs. She shied away from the recently occupied seat and sank to the edge of the bed instead. She sat for a moment, trying to jump-start her heart and form a coherent thought.

"Who was that, Mamie? Did Hunter have a younger brother die in the war?" Her hand still covered her chest, and she could feel the thrumming of her heart beneath it.

Mamie's wheezing chuckle rose from the bottom of her lungs.

"Lordy, no! Why, chile, that were Mastah Nate! He be Mistah Hunter's pappy! That rascal been showin' up in this room about five years now. Strange, he ain't never showed hisself to white folk afore. First time I seed him I 'bout laid down and died myself. But ain't nobody got the best of ol' Mamie yet, and I weren't gonna let some mischief-makin' haunt be the first. So now we just plays us a game. He shows up ever now and again and I talks to him like he ain't dead and then—"

"His father? That was the ghost of Hunter's father?" Marin couldn't believe her ears. "He couldn't be! That man was barely in his twenties! Hunter's father died eight years ago! He had to be at least in his fifties!"

The mattress sank when Mamie eased herself down beside Marin. She took Marin's icy hand in her massive fist and patted reassuringly.

"The age of a body when it dies ain't got nothin' to do with the age of its spirit. Some people just born old. And some people don't never grow up. Mastah Nate, he young at heart. And he a devil, too. Why, he fought that duel he's all bloodied up over afore he met Miz Lucille. Some polecat accused him of welchin' on a bet. But he didn't die then. He just a rascal what thinks he's bein' romantic, showin' up like the young pup he were then."

Marin's thoughts swam with the implications. Hunter's father had died an older man, yet Mamie claimed the young spirit was his.

"How do you know he's Master Nate?"

"Why, chile, I was borned at Tranquille. I growed up with that boy. I helped in the sickroom the day they brung him in from the duel. He had on them same clothes. The doc said the bullet didn't hit nothin' to kill him, but the fever danged near did."

Could all of her worrying have been for nothing? Was it possible she and Hunter could live a long, happy life together? Her spirits rose as her worry lifted from her. As if nature itself mirrored her mood, the sun broke through the scudding gray clouds and flooded the shuttered room with elongated bars of warm gold. Her soul felt flooded, too, with a soft glow. Even colors seemed brighter to her now, with this newfound knowledge, as if everything that had come before had been viewed through a dark veil that had suddenly been lifted from her eyes.

Mamie waddled to the nearest window and threw open the shutters.

"Well, now, ain't that just the way it always is? No sooner get the house closed up than the storm passes over. And it's just too blamed hot to leave closed." She busied herself with reopening the windows in the room, shuffling from one to the other and muttering to herself while she worked.

"Ain't done nothin' but steam up the place. Least it coulda done was blow in a cool wind. Chile!"

Marin jumped. Mamie shuffled over to her and slapped a hand on Marin's forehead.

"You's as white as Mastah Nate's ghost!" She let her hand drop to her side. "Now don't you go worryin' 'bout that blasted, no-good haunt. He don't never bother nobody. He just a skunk that shows up in this room to get my dander up. You ain't afeared of him, is ya?"

Marin dragged her euphoric thoughts from the possibility of growing old with Hunter and focused her attention on Mamie.

"No. He startled me at first. But I'm not afraid now. Not if you're sure he was Hunter's father."

"Sure as I was borned."

Marin slid from where she'd perched on the edge of the high bed.

"Then I'm fine. In fact, I feel great! Let's finish opening up."

Marin crossed the center hall into her room to the sounds of shutters downstairs clacking open against the house. The front door banged shut, and when she opened her window, which overlooked the front lawn, she saw Katie skip across the jeweled, velvet grass. Marin's fingers slid along the brocade draperies as she leaned her forehead against the glass and watched.

Katie's little orchid frock ballooned every time she stooped to pick up a large, glistening piece of hail that had not yet melted. Puffy scampered circles around a haughtily strolling Angel; the court jester ignored by the queen of the castle. Puffy stopped in midscamper. His ears perked and his pink, wet tongue lolled from the side of his mouth, giving him a goofy look of expectancy as he trotted toward the house. The reason for the look appeared from beneath the veranda.

Hunter knelt and rubbed the pointed ears of the pony-sized
puppy, then had to give equal time to the jealous feline rubbing against his calves. The baritone words "spoiled" and
"troublemakers" drifted up to Marin on a steamy breeze.
The words were affectionate, with the teasing tone Hunter
often used with the ones he loved. She hadn't heard that particular tone directed at her since the night she'd called
Ryan's name in her sleep. She ached to hear it now. Ached
for the easy comfort they'd shared: his whisper-light kisses
on her neck below her ear; the way his eyes would search
her out when he walked into a room; the way he would press
himself against her back and ask her what she was thinking.
She wanted things to be good between them again, but all
she got was a husband polite to a fault, solicitous of her
well-being, and absolutely devoid of any hint of passion.

She watched him make his way to Katie, his long, relaxed
strides hindered by animals cavorting at his feet. Katie ran
to meet him, pulling him down onto the grassy carpet as
soon as her hands met his. He sank to the ground, heedless
of the damp grass that darkened his gray trousers and waistcoat with instant wet patches. He stretched out on his side,
propped up on one elbow while Katie and the animals
clowned around for him on the lawn.

His masculine laughter lifted on the breeze and caressed
her senses. She wanted so badly to join them on the front
lawn. But she knew what would happen. Everything would
look the same and sound the same, but beneath his cordial
smile there would be an invisible wall as impenetrable as
two feet of stone.

She wondered if he had considered calling off this farce of
a wedding tomorrow. Surely, if he didn't trust her about who
Ryan was, he must not be anxious to stand before a roomful

of curious onlookers and pledge his undying love. But she was at a loss as to what to do. Should she make up some story he might believe about Ryan and her past? No, damn it. Ryan had been her husband, and a brief part of her life that had been the sweetest. She wouldn't lie about who he was. Hunter would have to accept her as she was, no matter how far-fetched her story sounded to a nineteenth-century man.

While she watched the two people who meant more to her than anything else in the world, while she thought about the chance of Hunter ever believing her story, she felt like an island. A lonely deserted island surrounded by a deep blue ocean, without another living thing in sight. Even as she watched, there seemed to be an ever-increasing distance between them.

"Dr. Rashad, line three. Dr. Rashad, line three."

Marin went absolutely still at the sound of the disembodied voice. Hot chills lifted the hair on the back of her neck when the translucent images of her hospital room superimposed themselves over her view of Hunter and Katie. She whirled around, her back to the window, and still the hazy images were there, every detail just as it had been when she was visited by Ryan.

She spun again, searching the misty setting for the beloved face of her husband. Her mind called to him in a chant that was half prayer. He had to come to her. He'd said he would come one more time. She needed to see him, needed the comfort of his presence. Yet she was afraid. Could she say good-bye to him forever? Could she stay here with Hunter when he distrusted her so? She felt as if she were being ripped in two—pulled between two worlds that refused to let her go.

Ryan! Where are you?

But Ryan never came. After the longest ten seconds of her life, the hazy image of her hospital room slowly faded away, leaving her staring at the empty bed she and Hunter only used for sleeping now.

As she stared at the flawlessly smooth satin coverlet, her eyes burned. A knot of misery formed in her throat at the playful sound of Hunter's voice beneath her window.

"Katiedid, would you like to take a ride with Papa before supper?"

"Oh, yes, Papa! Let's get Mama, too! And Gwandma!"

Quiet filled the air for a moment.

"Mama's busy. But run and see if Grandma wants to go."

Marin squeezed her burning eyes shut against this latest rejection.

He was withholding himself from her when she needed him most. Dear God, she'd just seen into the twentieth century! She knew her spirit somehow hovered between two times. She needed him to want her, to pull her into this time and never let go.

She stiffened her spine and narrowed her eyes. A new resolve banished the last tremblings from her twentieth-century encounter. If he planned to ignore her, she wouldn't make it easy for him.

Chapter 20

LUCILLE HAD DECIDED not to go for a ride with Hunter and Katie, so Hunter had saddled Mystic and ridden a euphoric Katie in front of him. They stopped to visit with several of the neighbors and arrived home from their outing just in time for Mamie to relay Emmaletta's latest threat to go to work for the Hilliards.

"You peoples is gonna fool around and Emmaletta's gonna leave and then we's all be starvin' to death 'cause I sure ain't plannin' to do no cookin'." Mamie met them at the front door and followed them into the house, yapping the whole way. "Miz Lucille the only one what's at the table. Even Miz Marin ain't nowhere to be found."

"Here I am, Mamie. I'm sorry I'm late."

Hunter's foot hesitated on the bottom step at the sight of the woman coming down the stairs.

The yellow glow from the chandelier haloed her loose

mahogany curls and washed her porcelain skin with gold. The deep green silk of her gown dipped low off her shoulders and even lower at her breasts. Hunter distractedly wondered what would happen if she took a deep breath, then prayed that she would. Marin ignored him as she descended the stairs in a whispering rustle of silk skirts and an elusive trace of gardenia.

"Katie, sweetheart, go with Mamie and get ready for bed. She has your supper in your room."

Katie's little eyelids were already at half-mast and falling fast. Mamie scooped her into her massive arms and puffed up the stairs, leaving Hunter alone with his breathtaking wife.

He took his foot off the bottom step to relieve the painful stance Marin's stunning presence had created. Dear God, she was beautiful. He ached to hold her, to feel her arms welcoming him to her. How long had it been? It seemed like years. How much longer would it be before he would stop hearing her call out another man's name?

Too long.

She gave him a lazy, heated stare before she swept past him on her way to the dining room. He watched her skirts swish behind her, then she turned and looked at him with eyes the color of dark honey.

"Should we wait for you, Hunter?" Her voice was low and slightly breathless. A bolt of heat shot to the center of his being and tightened his groin. She had to know what she was doing to him.

"Yes." He fought the raspiness in his voice. "I won't be much longer."

She continued to stare at him, hot and unblinking, as her breasts rose and fell slowly.

"I hope not. I'm . . ." she slid her glance to the evidence of the effect she was having on him ". . . very hungry."

She turned and opened the pocket doors to the dining room, stepped through, and slid them shut behind her.

Hunter stood at the foot of the stairs and scrubbed a hand across his face. She wasn't playing fair.

He tried to block her image from his mind while he dragged himself to their room, and while he baptized his head and shoulders with an entire pitcher of cold water. Her scented bath still filled the tub in the dressing room, and an occasional whiff of gardenia heated his blood and intensified his ache. When he caught himself breathing deeply, in search of her scent, he stormed across the room and slammed the dressing room door.

Enough was enough. He shoved his arms into a clean white shirt and refused to think about how soft and fragile his wife had looked on the stairs. He buttoned on a collar and tied a royal blue tie and refused to think about how good she smelled. He slid into a blue waistcoat and yanked on his gray jacket and refused to think of that hot, promising look she'd given him before entering the dining room. When he stomped down the stairs, he decided he would not even look at her during dinner.

She was the first thing he saw when he slammed the pocket doors back into the wall.

The soft glow of the candles lent her creamy skin a delicate peach hue. Her rich dark curls hung free, save for the sides, which were caught up loosely at her temples. Gleaming curls caressed her silky shoulders, and one long, wispy tendril was draped enticingly across her breast. Though her gown was formal, her hair was so casual as to be socially unacceptable.

Hunter found the combination to be almost too erotic to
bear.

He realized he'd been standing in the doorway for several
seconds, staring at his wife and creating a most embarrassing position for himself. Lucille watched him with pursed
lips but remained silent. Marin raised long black lashes and
gazed at him with exaggerated innocence. He strode to the
end of the table and dropped into his chair, threw his napkin
in his lap, picked up the nearest bowl, and began filling his
plate with whatever substance was in the bowl.

He kept his eyes on his plate, his mother, Izzy. He forced
polite responses to any conversation directed to him and felt
he did an admirable job of creating an air of insouciance. He
consumed every bite of his meal, though he couldn't have
named a single item he'd eaten. Quite possibly it had been
chicken, but it had all tasted like sawdust.

He was aware of Lucille eyeing him with speculation. She
gave Marin her fair share of attention, too, yet she amazed
him by not commenting. After dabbing his lips with his napkin, he threw the linen square onto his plate and was about
to make his escape when Izzy reentered the dining room
with dessert.

His first instinct was to decline, but he made the mistake
of looking at Marin. She still exuded that controlled, exaggerated innocence as Izzy placed before them huge crystal
goblets filled with some frothy pink concoction topped with
stemmed cherries. Marin seemed so smugly confident that
she was besting him, he decided to stay and prove her
wrong.

He popped the first pitted cherry into his mouth and
pulled off the stem. The creamy mousse coating the fruit
tasted cool and delicious. The simple fact that the dessert did

not have the consistency of sawdust made him the tiniest bit cocky. He cast a glance at Marin.

She concentrated on lifting one pink-coated cherry by its stem and drawing it lazily into her mouth. Her lips parted slightly as she captured it between white, even teeth. He watched as her lips closed when she pulled off the stem, then chewed the tiny fruit as if it were the rarest of delicacies.

She lifted the second cherry and lowered it onto her tongue. Her eyes and lips closed at the same time. As she withdrew the stem he could almost feel her roll the cherry across her tongue, feel her savor the taste and the shape and the texture.

When she picked up the last of the fruit, she raised her amber eyes to his for the first time. With deliberate slowness she dipped the garnish into the frothy mousse. Without taking her gaze from his, she pulled the cherry between her lips and gently licked away the pink foam.

He watched her, unblinking, never realizing how long he'd stared until his eyes began to burn. When he finally blinked, he realized how easily she'd pulled him into her seductive little scene. Anger quickened his already racing heart. He shifted his gaze to Lucille, who'd watched the entire episode with her spoon hovering halfway to her mouth. When he realized that he, too, sat with a spoon forgotten in midair, he placed it with studied care back on a plate, then rose from his chair.

"You'll excuse me," he said to no one in particular. He refused to look at Marin again. His gaze passed over his mother, who had not moved a muscle except for her eyes.

With as much dignity as he could muster after having nearly salivated over his wife's little display, he clenched his jaw and walked from the room.

*   *   *

He walked the bluffs, a restlessness in him churning up the fires of passion he had fought to stamp out. He would not give in to her, by God. He would prove to her that he was immune to her games.

As he paced he kept one eye on the distant dim glow from their bedroom window. He lifted the nearly empty bottle of Kentucky whiskey to his lips and enjoyed the smooth burn in his throat and the liquor curling warmly through his veins.

He wished now he'd stopped long enough to grab a full bottle instead of one that was already half gone. He wouldn't mind loosing a few sheets to the wind on this night. He could count on one hand the number of times he'd been drunk, but tonight he would gladly add another.

An image of her dusky tongue licking the foam from those cherries sent him spinning on his heel and pacing north along the river. She had gently sucked that cherry into her soft, moist mouth and . . .

He pulled another long draft of whiskey down his throat and waited for it to reach his brain. His blood flow was in dire need of redirecting. If he could numb his thoughts . . .

The dim rectangle of light in his bedroom faded to black. So, she'd already given up waiting for him to come to bed. He'd been determined she would wait all night. Somehow the ease with which she had given up gnawed at him. Had she lost interest in the game? Wasn't he worth waiting for?

He lifted the bottle to his lips but stopped before his first sip. In one flashing movement he hurled the bottle skyward. Its dark shape spun end over end across a silver-and-black sky. He was on his way back to the house before the splash of water reached his ears.

All the windows were black rectangles against a pearly

gray house when he crossed the west lawn. A cloud passed over the moon and darkened the landscape. He tripped over a large, jutting rock and cursed it soundly for being in his path. He cursed the cloud that covered the moon and cursed the woman in whose bed he should be. When the silvery moonlight returned, he looked back at his home glowing black and gray and cursed it, too.

A movement upstairs caught his attention. His gaze shifted to find the source, then his breath faltered and desire lodged in his chest.

Marin stood on the upper veranda, the darkened window framing her like a black canvas. The wind molded her robe to her body and lifted yards of pale, gossamer silk to billow around her like a mist off the river. Her waist-length curls tangled wildly with the flowing silk as the moon washed her skin with its colorless light.

He didn't want to breathe. He didn't want to blink. He didn't want to miss one glorious second of her beauty.

Did she know he was there, below her, watching?

He got his answer when she lowered her gaze and looked straight at him. No emotion showed in her eyes. Just long, heated promises.

He stared up at her, willing his blood to cool and failing with each passing second. His throat ached to swallow, his eyes burned to close, until her fingers slowly unbuttoned the edges of her robe and pulled them wide to catch the breeze.

What breath he'd been holding rushed from his lungs. She offered up her magnificent body like a goddess to the wind. The silk billowed around her, caressing her as he'd burned to for weeks.

His dry throat worked as he fought to swallow. It seemed all the whiskey he'd consumed slammed at once into his brain and all the blood left his extremities save one, which now swelled in painful reminder. The breeze died and the yards of silk rippled down to settle in draping folds around Marin's body. She continued to gaze at him a moment longer, then turned and stepped into their bedroom.

His first deep breath in what felt like hours brought a dizziness that fanned the flame of his anger. Without benefit of thought he stormed through the front door, the heels of his boots pounding up the stairs to their room.

The door bounced off the wall when he threw it open. She stood beside the window, moonlight glinting off her hair and the yards of silk that only partially covered her.

She watched him, her body motionless but for the uneven rise and fall of her breasts. The silk of her robe quivered against her ivory skin, then fell open even more to tease his senses.

And suddenly, it was more than he could bear.

Rational thought evaporated as he strode across the room. His lips fell on hers, his fingers plunged into her hair with all the anger he'd been stoking for weeks. He took the kiss from her, drew it from her with no thought to her wishes or her will. His tongue sought hers, again and again, with every upthrust of his body. His hands wadded the silky fabric, tangled in her hair as his mouth twisted on hers, taking what he'd wanted for so long and what she'd dangled before him. Somehow his clothes fell away and he pressed against her, wanting to pull her soul right into his. When he couldn't get close enough he lifted her angrily and wrapped her legs around his waist. He did it all with anger. In his anger he was safe.

And then they were one, and he drove himself on as he

held her, taking desperately what he feared would never again be his. He drew from her recompense for calling another man's name, for giving him reason to doubt her.

For making him wish he were Ryan.

Then in one long, blinding shudder he gave back to her all that he had taken, and more.

His ragged breathing slowed as he held her thus, his feet planted firmly to keep his knees from buckling with the release. He opened his eyes and looked at his wife, knowing he would see only hurt and accusation.

Her eyes were closed, her lips slightly parted, her head thrown back so that the long satin of her curls brushed the tops of his thighs. As if she sensed he watched, she lifted her head and looked at him through half-closed eyes . . . the look of a woman who had just been thoroughly satisfied.

He hadn't meant to satisfy her. He hadn't meant to give her anything. He'd taken her, viciously and with no regard to her needs.

No doubt, just as she'd planned.

No words passed between them. Just the ageless communication of two lovers who had drained each other dry.

He slid her slowly down the length of his body until her feet touched the floor. With a yank, he pulled together the edges of the robe she still wore, then bent and scooped up his clothes. He walked to the door, put his hand on the knob, then turned.

Damn the whiskey. And damn himself for drinking it. It had dulled his judgment and fired his passion. It had dented his will until it brought him to her. And he'd known from his first drink that it would.

"You won," he said, his voice devoid of emotion.

*   *   *

Marin watched the door close behind Hunter. It was all she could do not to run after him to apologize for baiting him so.

But she'd wanted what he'd done to her tonight. They'd both needed to purge the ghosts. He'd come to her in anger, fed his passion with his anger, and no doubt believed he'd made love to her with it and because of it. But she'd felt the love, the desperation with which he'd claimed her, and she'd found that to be the most powerful emotion. She'd returned his love with the same desperate hunger, had taken as much as he, but he had not allowed himself to notice. The exquisite release, when it had come, had nearly left her shattered.

But she had never expected him to cover her body, then walk away from her with disgust in his eyes. "You won," he had said. Did he really believe she looked at him as a prize to win or lose? Could he not see that this was her pitiful attempt to set their lives right?

If she thought he would listen she would go after him, make him see how their lives could be again. But she realized now what she should have seen before. He would have to work this trust thing out alone, in his own good time. And she would have to pray with all her heart that he would someday believe her. In fact, as she stood in the middle of the room, she bowed her head and did just that.

When she raised her head, she gasped and closed her eyes again.

It couldn't be!

She opened her eyes to slits, then widened them slowly.

The hospital room surrounded her, not with a hazy, dreamlike quality, but with the solidness of reality. But she was awake! Wasn't she?

Oh, dear God, I'm going crazy!

"No you're not."

Ryan! Oh, thank you, God! Thank you! Her thoughts flew to him. She didn't even try to speak anymore.

He stood beside her bed, the sleeves of his flight suit rolled above his wrists, the small, red silk scarf knotted loosely at his throat.

"Our time is up, Fireball. I can't come back like this again. And you have to make a decision."

I can't do this!

"You have to do it. Your body is weakening every day. The spirit lives on forever, Marin, but the body can't live without the soul. You've been gone from yours too long. Gone even before the accident."

Marin knew he spoke the truth. A part of her had died the day he died.

"Only my body died that day." He'd intercepted her thought. *"And the only thing that died in you was trusting in love to bring you happiness."* His warm, solid hand slid over hers. *"You trusted your parents, your grandparents, your brother. You trusted me with your love, and I left you, too."*

Tears sprang to her eyes and burned as they hovered there.

"But we've been given a second chance to be together. All you have to do is trust."

Marin felt all of her losses—all the deaths, all the unbearable pain—well up and slam into her chest like a booted foot. The tears ran off her face to seep into the thin hospital pillow.

Ryan! Ryan! I don't know what to do! I don't know how to do it!

"If you can't trust me, Fireball, can you trust Hunter?"

Her gaze flew to Ryan's. She'd never brought Hunter into this. She'd never mentioned him.

"If you can trust him, sweetheart, if you can find happiness with him, then choose him. Love him with all the passion that you loved me."

He stared at her, his eyes filled with peaceful serenity. She could only stare back, the tears a steady stream now through her hair and onto the pillow.

Ryan bent low and his warm lips feathered across hers; then she tasted the sweetness of his tongue as he kissed her. His kiss quickened her heart. Her thoughts became a confused jumble. How could she choose between the two men she loved?

"You don't have to choose, sweetheart," he whispered. *"Your spirit has already decided."*

The room began to darken and Ryan's image began to fade. Panic jolted Marin to the core, but a draining lethargy held her immobile. As the engulfing darkness settled over her she heard the rhythmic beep of the heart monitor falter, then change to one long, steady tone.

Chapter 21

SHE OPENED HER eyes to darkness. With a choked whimper, she searched her neck for signs of a pulse. Only after her fingertips found the regular, rapid throb did she allow herself to relax.

When her eyes adjusted to the darkness, the black of her surroundings faded to dark gray. She rolled to her side and felt blindly for a match. In the flare of the flame she reached for a candle.

"Are you feeling better?"

She nearly dropped the burning candle at the sound of Hunter's voice.

He rose stiffly from the shadows, looking like hell with dark circles under his eyes and black stubble on his jaw. He was the most beautiful thing she had ever seen!

"I came back last night to apologize and found you kneeling in the—"

She kicked the covers from her legs and catapulted into his chest. She slid her arms around his neck in a Katie-style death grip and cut off his words with a kiss that rivaled the one he'd given her last night.

He hesitated only moments before his hands encircled her waist, then moved up and down her body as if verifying she was real. The result was like two sticks rubbing together—with every stroke their heat increased.

He held her in the air, almost exactly as he had a few hours earlier, but this time his kisses gentled. He gave as well as took each time their tongues met.

When her feet touched the floor she leaned back, sinking into the inviting mattress and pulling him down with her. He didn't try to speak, didn't ask her any questions, and she offered none of her own.

What she offered was enough love for two men—for one flesh and blood man who could love her back, and one beautiful spirit who had loved her enough to let her go.

Her eyes stung at the memory of Ryan's face, but she blinked away the pain.

With a mixture of joy and sadness, she turned her attention to the soft whispers and gentle caresses of her beloved husband.

The morning of the wedding dawned with a flawless robin's egg-blue sky and crystal-clear air that held not a trace of Memphis humidity.

Flowers were freshly picked and arranged, hams were baked beside breads and pies, wedding attire was given a final smoothing with the iron. Ambrose supervised the setting up of chairs and tables outside with his usual long-suffering stoicism. Emmaletta shooed everyone out of her kitchen and threatened to quit if Miz Lucille came back in. Lucille turned her attention to Katie and tried to keep her occupied while a hired girl came and tortured Katie's silky hair into dozens of corkscrew curls. Puffy and Angel were locked in the barn so as not to add to the general confusion. Everything went as expected until Katie looked up at Lucille and asked, "Where's Mama and Papa?"

Mamie was summoned to go in search of the errant bride and groom and to bully them into readiness if they were dillydallying the morning away. What she found, when she finally thought to see if they possibly had overslept, was a scene that brought a rosy hue to the coffee-colored cheeks of even that seasoned servant.

She found an exhausted couple, their bare bodies wrapped in a tangle of arms and legs and mahogany hair, atop a mound of bedding that looked as if it had exploded off the bed. The pair slept like the dead. She tried slamming the door to wake them, but when she peeped back into the room, all they'd done was unconsciously shift their hands around so that she was darn sure she wasn't steppin' foot back in that room until they were good and awake.

Only one thing left to do.

Puffy and Angel were released from the barn and rocketed into the room with all the calm of a raging typhoon. In a blur of black and gold bodies and clicking toenails, they circled the room once before leaping dead center into the bed with the sleeping couple.

Marin woke to the dubious pleasure of having her face alternately washed by a lolling wet tongue and dried by the blast of dog breath. Hunter seemed to emerge from his coma with the black fur of Angel scraping along the stubble of his chin just moments before she dropped her considerable weight to his chest and curled into a roaring ball.

Marin cringed at the sight of the open door. She let out her breath when she saw no sign of Katie or Mamie, or worse, Lucille. She just hoped fervently that the door had not stood open all night.

Hunter obviously read her thoughts and smiled with unconcerned lust. She shoved Puffy off her legs, dragged a corner of the sheet over their bodies, then snuggled against her husband. A switching black tail made contact with her nose. The next instant an indignant Angel joined Puffy at their feet.

The four of them lay quietly for several minutes, then Hunter rubbed his prickly jaw against the top of Marin's head.

"Are you feeling better?"

She snuggled closer and nodded against his shoulder.

"I came back to apologize for . . . I'd had too much whiskey. When I came in you were kneeling in the middle of the floor, sobbing, and I couldn't get you to stop. You weren't even aware I was there, Marin. I put you in bed and tried to calm you, but at first I couldn't get through to you."

Marin was glad he couldn't see her eyes as she relived her last moments with Ryan. When she spoke, her voice was so raspy it sounded like a whisper.

"I don't remember you being here."

Neither spoke for several seconds. When she felt the pain in her eyes was gone, Marin raised her head and looked at Hunter. Neither spoke as he apologized with his eyes for the weeks he'd shunned her. She accepted with feathery kisses along his jaw, praying he would ask no more questions about Ryan. She would never betray Ryan's memory.

"Lordy, lordy! Don't you rabbits ever stop? You chilluns gots a weddin' to go to!" Mamie puffed her way into the room, ignoring the flashes of bare skin, the soles of her slippers slapping against her heels. She threw back the heavy curtains to the brilliance of a midmorning sun.

Marin and Hunter both groaned, squeezing their eyes shut and fending off the light with protective forearms.

"There you are!" Lucille rounded the door to the bedchamber. "There are guests coming up the drive and you haven't even—" She stopped short at the sight of the two bodies tangled with the covers. Unruffled, her gaze swept Marin's length, taking in bare shoulders and feet that peeped from beneath the blanket. Her lips pursed.

"Do you need some help getting dressed, Marin?" she asked in her best steamroller voice. "Because the guests are beginning to arrive." Lucille acted as if she might haul Marin from the bed and dress her herself. "Hunter, leave your bride alone for once and get yourself dressed." Her gaze slid to the pair of shiny Hessians toppled beside the bed. "And you are *not* wearing those boots to get married in."

Lucille left the room like a drill sergeant who had no doubt her orders would be followed, while Mamie bustled about, chuckling softly.

Hunter kissed the tip of Marin's nose, rolled from the bed wrapped in the blanket like Julius Caesar, then scooped his boots off the floor.

"See you at the altar," he said in a voice husky with promise. He left the room grinning from ear to ear.

Excitement exploded like fireworks in Marin. Hunter's ghost didn't have to be old! She was getting married— again!

She bathed quickly and was toweling dry in less than a minute. Layers of cotton and silk and lace slipped over her perfumed skin, and then the task of dressing her hair was begun. Mamie sculpted the shiny auburn tresses with practiced deftness and was putting the finishing touches on her creation when Hunter stepped back into the room.

"Is it bad luck?" he asked as he slipped inside and leaned against the door in his wedding attire, his booted feet crossed at the ankles and a seductive smile on his lips.

"Mistah Hunter! You polecat! You knows it's bad luck! Now you gets on out'n here!"

"I don't believe I will, Mamie." He shoved himself away from the door and propelled the hefty maid out of it. "I believe I am already wed, so therefore this doesn't count. And I believe I am going to help my bride finish dressing."

Mamie squawked when he closed the door in her face and turned the key.

"I lied about seeing you at the altar," he confessed with a bone-melting grin. His twin dimples caused Marin's stomach to take a Ferris wheel ride.

She turned her back to him and looked at his reflection in the mirror.

"I have to warn you, Hunter, if you come any closer we might be late for our own wedding."

He walked across the room toward her, scooping up the ivory silk wedding dress on the way.

"What if I promise to behave myself?"

Marin turned and looked up at him through her lashes.

"Can you promise to make *me* behave?"

Hunter's only reaction was to bend and capture her lips with his. He kissed her lazily, as if they had all the time in the world. "Never," he murmured against her mouth. "I'd be a fool to try."

A knock sounded on the door.

"Hunter? Marin? We are nearly ready for you." Lucille's muffled voice brooked no nonsense.

Hunter blew out a frustrated sigh. "Let us do this thing. The sooner we get it over with, the sooner we can be alone."

He slid the cloud of silk over her head with finesse. When she settled the bodice into place, he went to work on the dozens of tiny buttons.

His fingers slowed, then stopped working their way up the back of her gown. He pulled her against his chest and nuzzled her neck. His breath ghosted across her ear as he rained kisses along her jaw.

Marin sighed and tilted her head back against his solid, warm chest. Life would be perfect now if he would only believe her about being from the future. Would he ever believe her? Could she blame him if he didn't?

Another rap on the door preceded the no-nonsense voice again.

"You two stop what you're doing right now! You'll have time for that later. Benjamin Hunter Pierce, I want you downstairs this instant. And you'd better not be wearing those boots."

Hunter nearly choked on his laughter. He buttoned the last two buttons and dropped a kiss on the back of Marin's neck.

"She'll give us no peace until this is done. God save us from her next idea."

He turned her by her shoulders and smiled as he took in the sight of her.

"Lord, but you are lovely."

*   *   *

The "proper" wedding Lucille had so desired backfired like an antique jalopy.

When Marin appeared at the top of the stairs, Katie wasn't there to do her designated job, that of scattering the rose petals daintily in Marin's path. The pianist took Marin's appearance as her cue and began playing too soon. Everyone turned their gazes to the stairway just as Katie appeared with muddy cat tracks and a big brown smear on the front of her pale pink dimity. Lucille, trying to brush the dirt away with as much dignity as possible, hit the basket of rose petals and sent it bouncing down the stairs, the petals exploding from the basket on the first bounce. The minister developed a sneezing fit—he insisted it was from cat dander—and Marin was wed to Hunter between bouts of clerical sneezes. Katie fidgeted through the closing prayer, then announced to no one in particular that she had to go to the outhouse.

Lucille had done an admirable job of remaining calm throughout the destruction of her plans, but when the wedding party emerged onto the front lawn to the sight of Puffy happily devouring the wedding cake, she lost it. Personally, Marin thought the sight of Lucille chasing Puffy across the lawn with a silver serving spoon was much more entertaining than watching her and Hunter feed cake to each other.

In the end Lucille had actually been seen smiling grudgingly over the whole ridiculous fiasco. The general consensus was that the guests enjoyed the impromptu entertainment much more than the normally solemn ceremony.

Hunter and Marin waved off their last guests in the orange glow of a dying sun. Every member of the household had melted away to parts unknown, leaving Marin and Hunter blessedly alone.

Marin took the deepest breath she could manage in the confines of her corset and turned back to the house with Hunter by her side.

She couldn't help but feel a touch of sadness. She couldn't help but remember her first wedding day, with Ryan. Their lives together had been much too brief, cut short before their love had fully blossomed. But now she had Hunter, and she'd made a promise she would love him with as much passion as she'd loved Ryan.

"There is a gift in the parlor for us," Hunter said upon stepping into the entry hall. "Shall we open it now?"

Marin was exhausted from their long night of lovemaking and her last encounter with Ryan. All she really wanted to do was get out of her corset and take some deep breaths. But she'd get this last task behind her before calling it a day.

She walked ahead of Hunter into the parlor, scanning the tables for the gift.

"Where is . . ."

Suddenly her heart skipped a beat and she forgot to breathe. She stood absolutely still, afraid to move or blink.

"Oh, my God, Hunter! Do you see? Tell me you can see!"

Hunter could only nod, his "Yes" barely audible.

Reflected in the massive silvered pier glass was not the image of his tiny, auburn-haired bride, breathtaking in her ivory wedding finery. Instead, there stood a tall, gray-eyed beauty with sun-streaked hair, wearing a filmy, flowered, calf-length skirt and a clingy yellow top.

Marin turned to Hunter and held out her trembling hand. He took it, hypnotically twining his fingers in hers and stepping to her side. He stared at the mirror in awe. Without breaking his gaze, he whispered, "I believe you."

Dawning acknowledgment swirled into his mind as layers

of truth opened up to him. He remembered the little boy of ten who had become so ill he was given up for dead. He remembered the confusion and the blank spaces where there should have been memories when he came out of his coma.

Marin looked into his face and then into the mirror. Her gasp of shock was followed by an *"Ohhhh"* of absolute exaltation.

Beside his bride, beside the woman with huge gray eyes and twentieth-century clothes, stood her groom. But this groom wore the green zippered flight suit of a fighter pilot, and a white visored helmet replaced the top hat in his hands. His grin spanned one hundred and twenty years when he spoke.

"I believe you now, Fireball."

Originally from West Virginia, Jenny Lykins has lived everywhere from Clark Air Base in the Philippines to Little Rock, Arkansas. She now makes her home in west Tennessee with her husband, son and daughter, and a very spoiled dog. When she's not writing, she spends her time traveling, researching, taking fencing lessons, and riding her motorcycle. Her next conquest is scuba diving.

As well as *Lost Yesterday*, Jenny is also the author of *Echoes of Tomorrow*, (due out from Jove in June 1997), a third book, *Waiting for Yesterday*, (in August 1997) and a Christmas novella.

You can write her at P.O. Box 382132, Germantown, Tennessee 38183-2132.